He
Gathers
the Lambs

He
Gathers
the Lambs

Cornelius Lambregtse

PAIDEIA PRESS
St. Catharines, Ontario, Canada

First published in Dutch as *In zijn arm de lammeren*, © Uitgeverij T. Wever of Franeker.
Translated by Harry der Nederlanden.

Copyright 1979 by J.H. Enterprises Ltd. © All rights reserved. Published by Paideia/Premier, P.O. Box 1450, St. Catharines, Ontario, Canada L2R 7J8. No part of this publication may be reproduced, stored in a retrieval system, or transmitted in any form without the written permission of the publisher.

ISBN 0-88815-903-X
Printed in the United States of America.

In precious memory
of my only son
CALVIN JOHN
who at the age
of three years and seven months
had finished his earthly sojourn
and on the day of his departure said:
"I am going home to Jesus.
Don't cry, Daddy."

1

When Fransje woke up, it was still dark in the attic. He found himself in a dark cave and tried to recapture the fading images of his dreams, but in vain. He sat up and groped about, and when his hands touched the high sides of his little bed, he suddenly remembered that he had been sleeping in the attic. That pleased him; at once he leaned forward from underneath the canopy to orient himself. He turned his head right and left until at last his eyes, still swollen with sleep, discovered the pale patch of light of the little attic window. He could not see anything else, however, and he was overcome by a feeling of uneasiness. But now he heard the snoring of his brothers, though he could not see their beds. The knowledge that they, too, were in the attic made him feel a little better. What he would have liked best of all would be to climb out of his crib and feel his way into the warm little hollow beside Mother. But that was impossible. Mother was sleeping downstairs in the built-in bed, and his crib was no longer there. He had helped take it apart with his own hands yesterday, when Father came home from town with the beautiful little bed.

For a moment he thought about climbing out of bed and going downstairs anyway, but the dark cave of the attic frightened him. What's more, the trapdoor was shut and he couldn't lift it. He did not want to call for Mother, because showing his fear like that would be humiliating. Now that he could sleep in the attic he was a big boy, and big boys had a status to uphold. One way to do this was to sleep dry. Quickly he checked the diaper that Mother put on him last night. Good! It was dry! Mother had said that if he slept dry for a whole week he would no longer have to wear a diaper. This meant a lot to him, for it would bring him a big step closer to the fulfillment of his greatest wish—to grow up fast.

The thought of wetting the bed suddenly awoke in him a strong urge to pee. He could use the small chamber pot under his bed, but then he would have to step into the dark cave of the attic. He decided to wait until it was a little lighter. He crossed his legs underneath the blankets, but the more he thought about it, the greater the urge became. Since big boys don't do it in bed, he decided to go on the pot. With his eyes tightly shut he clambered down and groped under the bed with both hands. Then, shivering, he yielded to the glorious sense of relief that expanded through his body. Quickly he dived back into bed and snuggled down under the warm blankets. He wished for daylight so that he could go downstairs.

Now he heard stumbling noises down below. Father's voice said something to Mother. The door to the back room scraped open, and a shaft of yellow light crept through the crack of the trapdoor and up the whitewashed wall, a slanting line that stopped just above the small attic window. The faucet started running, and a moment later Fransje heard snorting and puffing. Father was washing his face. Fransje could have walked over to the trapdoor and asked Father to open it for him, but Father might not approve of that. He had better wait a while.

The bolt of the back door was slid back, and wooden shoes clattered as they were shoved aside. Then the door squeaked open and Father went clomping outside. Going to feed the rabbits, Fransje supposed. If only the trapdoor were open, then he could slip downstairs while Father was gone. He imagined the warm comfort of lying snugly beside Mother.

There was movement in the dark corner of the attic where the big boys were sleeping. Bram yawned and then began to cough. Now Fransje dared to venture out into the attic. He clambered out of bed once more and carefully made his way toward his big brothers' bed.

"Bram, will you open the trapdoor for me?"

"Pretty soon, Fransje. Why don't you come in bed with us for a while?"

Fransje bumped into a chair and stumbled over a pile of clothes on the floor. Shutting his eyes tightly, he stretched his arms in front of him and groped his way to the corner where Bram's voice came from. He touched a hump covered by a blanket, and slid his hands over it until he felt a head. It was Eine's, who was still snoring. He climbed over the hump and rolled into Bram's arms. Quickly he slipped down between the two boys and nestled cozily against Bram's warm body. Then he began to talk. He told Bram that he had slept dry again, so soon he would get to wear pants.

"Wow!" Bram said admiringly. "You sure are getting to be a big boy! How old are you now, Fransje?"

To answer this question properly, Fransje had to put one hand above the blankets and hold up three fingers in the dark. "Three years," he said. "How many nights must I sleep until I'm four, Bram?"

"Oh, lots more," answered Bram.

Now Eine was awakened by the voices beside him. He turned over and, groaning, stretched his arms. As he did, his hand touched one of Fransje's feet, which he started to tickle. Fransje jerked and rolled over, laughing convulsively. Grabbing Bram for support he kicked wildly. But Eine kept tickling him with both hands all over his little body—in his belly, under his arms, and, as the diaper came off in the skirmish, between his bare legs. Suddenly Fransje's body went limp against Bram's. He had been laughing too hard and now couldn't catch his breath. Bram jerked the limp little body straight up in the air by the arms. Fortunately Fransje's breath returned. He vented his frustrated helplessness and vexation in a screaming fit of rage.

"Stupid old Eine!" he howled. "You're always hurting me!"

Bram tried to calm him. Eine, afraid that Father would interfere, tried to soothe him too. But Fransje spat at him.

Then the back door opened again and Father's voice called out. "Hurry up, boys! Get up! It's time, you hear!"

"Okay!" they chorused back.

Meanwhile, the sky outside had brightened a bit. The vague outlines of the attic furniture were becoming visible in the gray December light that hung hesitantly at the little window.

Eine got up first. He quickly put on his clothes, pulled open the trapdoor, and stepped down the ladder. He liked to play the foreman, and his constant regret was that not he, but Bram, was the oldest of the boys.

Fransje got out of the big bed too and headed for the open trapdoor. But Bram stopped him, saying, "Fransje, did you see what's on the hood of your bed? Last night I met Saint Nicholas, and he gave me something to take home for you."

Fransje wheeled and peered toward his bed, but he couldn't make out anything from where he was standing. A lot of boy's clothes were hanging from the center beam between him and the bed. He trotted over to his bed, but then he couldn't see the top of the canopy. So he climbed into bed and sat on his knees, facing the flat top of the canopy. There was silence for a moment, but then suddenly a high-pitched voice cried out, "Ooooooh!"

Then silence again.

His eyes dwelt tenderly on the little scene spread out in the semi-darkness. It was a collection of little candy figures—a pink rooster, two brown and two white chickens, with eight yellow chicks scattered among them. Though it was only a meager handful of coarse sugar candy, Fransje thought it was the greatest treasure he had ever possessed. Hesitantly he touched the big rooster with one finger, and then one of the chicks. He was enormously fascinated by the bright colors and the natural grouping of the chicken family.

Meanwhile, Bram was dressing. Smiling, he looked at the little scene in the half-dark attic corner. He picked up Fransje's diaper and walked over to him.

"What do you think of it, Fransje?"

"Bootiful!" he answered wholeheartedly, using a word that had entered his vocabulary only yesterday. He had learned it from Wantje, who had used it to express her admiration for the little bed Father had brought home.

Fransje wanted to know where Bram had met Saint Nicholas, and what he had said, and why Saint Nicholas hadn't brought these chickens himself, and how he knew there was a Fransje. Bram gave satisfactory answers to all those questions, but Fransje was disappointed that he hadn't seen Saint Nicholas himself. He supposed that he had been asleep in his new bed when he came.

Arjaan and Kees, who had been roughhousing since Father called, came and took a look too. But when they wanted to touch the sugar figures, Fransje cried out in alarm: "No, don't touch!"

Mother's voice called from the foot of the ladder: "Come on, boys, hurry up! We're ready to eat!"

Fransje ran to the open trapdoor and shouted, "Mommy, come

and look! I have a whole bunch of chickens—a rooster, and chickens, and little chickies!" But Mother had returned to the living room. Fransje quickly scampered back to get his treasure. But he couldn't hold them all in his hands.

Bram came to his aid. "Here," he said, "just put them in your diaper—it's dry anyway." Together they descended the ladder, Bram carrying Fransje in his arms, and Fransje carrying the chicken family in his arms.

In the living room he ran from one to the other, letting Father, Mother, Maria, and Wantje take turns admiring his treasure. In his excitement he completely forgot to tell them he had slept dry. But when Mother suspiciously fingered the diaper, he cried, "No! It's dry!"

That made Father laugh. He chuckled, "If I were you, I would put him in pants pretty soon. He's getting much too big to be running around in skirts."

When all had finished washing up—except for Fransje, whose turn came after breakfast—they took their places around the long extension table. Fransje sat between Arjaan and Kees on the bench in front of the window. Bram and Eine sat at the end near the linen closet. Maria, Wantje, and Mother sat opposite Fransje and Father sat alone at the other end near the pot-bellied stove. The cat had left her warm spot under the stove and crouched on the bench between Kees and Fransje. Placidly she watched Fransje displaying the sugar pieces on the table in front of him.

"Fold your hands and pray," Father commanded, looking especially at Fransje. He removed his hat and held it under his chin. When he finished reciting the Lord's Prayer, he said, "Fransje!" and Fransje piped, "Lord, bless this food and drink, for Jesus' sake, amen."

Father put on his hat again. Mother had cut a slice of bread into cubes for Fransje. Because he was the youngest, he had sugar on his bread. She told him, "First eat your bread, Fransje. Then you may play with your sugar pieces." But excitement had dulled Fransje's appetite. He balanced a sugar chicken on each cube of bread. The rooster had to eat too. Fransje pressed its blunt beak on the piece of bread so that some lard and sugar stuck to it. "Look, he's eating!" he chortled. Then he licked the beak clean and repeated the game until the rooster's head softened and remained in Fransje's mouth along with the "chicken feed."

"Fransje, first eat your bread, and then you can have a piece of candy. Candy's bad for you on an empty stomach," Mother repeated.

"Fransje, can I have one of those little chicks?" Wantje begged. After casting numerous covetous looks at all those goodies, she could no longer contain herself. But Fransje vehemently shook his head and held both hands protectively around the entire flock, looking at Bram. This refusal was not the result of stinginess, even though that was Wantje's first and final conclusion, as her looks and gestures made plain. But Fransje simply could do nothing but refuse. Neither his sense of happiness nor his joy of ownership had yet been consummated. But the real motive for his refusal lay in his greatly developed sense of togetherness, which he applied to inanimate as well as animate objects, since as yet everything was alive to him. When one of the big boys or Maria went away at night, he experienced their absence as a painful void and a disruption of the peace and security of the family circle. To him this break seemed in some mysterious way to be connected with the unknown, unsafe world outside his own.

His sense of togetherness now forbade him to disturb this interdependent family of chickens. It was impossible for him to give up a single member—and certainly none of the innocent chicks, to which he felt the greatest affinity. That is why his busy hands began to rearrange the pieces still closer to the decapitated rooster. He didn't know that there were thirteen members in this family, for numbers meant little to him. The rooster, of course, was the father. It did not seem strange to him that this family had four mothers. That's the way it's supposed to be with chickens, he thought. But together they were one family, and if even one were missing, the family would be mutilated.

But now Father interfered. He slapped Fransje across the hands with his hat and barked, "Now eat your bread! And don't you dare touch them again!" Fransje's hands flinched back like a snail's tentacles that had been touched.

All the others had finished breakfast. Kees was told to get the Bible from the mantel. On weekdays Father usually let one of the big boys or Maria read, but on Sundays he assumed his full priesthood himself. First he read where he left off the night before, and then the Law. The latter was read every Sunday. Now the closing prayer. It seemed very long to Fransje. On Sundays Father did not recite a form prayer after meals as during the week, but he interceded for all the material and spiritual needs of his family in his own words and intonation. Nor were country and people, church and society, the queen and her subjects forgotten. Fransje couldn't possibly sit still all that time with his eyes closed and hands folded. He understood as little of all those reverent words as he did of the Bible reading. To say grace only meant the last stage—albeit a very long one—of the meal, during which he had very little freedom of movement. He confined himself to taking the cat's forepaws and pressing them together. The cat had to pray too. Every now and then he blew gently in her eyes: then she shut them automatically. This, of course, absolved him of the duty to close his own.

When the prayer was finished, everybody started moving. Father again donned his hat and lit his pipe. Fransje was allowed to blow out the match, so he must be back in Father's good graces. Bram rolled a cigaret for himself. Maria was clearing the table and washing the dishes, and Wantje had to dry. The sugar chickens had to be moved to the windowsill for now. Fransje was told to go with Mommy to the back room to get washed up. When she gave the inside of his ears their infamous cleaning, Fransje did not stifle his loud displeasure. But when he returned to the living room, his cheeks shone like apples, and his dark forelock stood up like a little brush. Next Mother put on his skirts, and although they were a familiar part of him, he nevertheless brought up the subject of pants. Mother promised him that perhaps this coming week he might wear them.

"That is, if you don't—"

"—pee in them," Fransje finished glibly.

"Come on, kids, get dressed for church! It's high time," Mother warned. She opened the doors of the linen closet and took out the coin box. She counted out six little piles of pennies—three of three pennies and three of two. She also put something into Father's hand, but none of the children could see how much.

"Mother, may I stay home?" Wantje begged, her eye on the sugar animals. "Then I can help you a little; otherwise you'll be so busy all by yourself," she added cajolingly.

Mother smiled. She could read Wantje's mind. Yet after a moment she said, "All right then." It was not the sugar candy that swayed her, however, but Wantje's shoes. Though they desperately needed new soles, Mother had not yet been able to afford the repairs. She was apprehensive enough as it was at the thought of the shoemaker's bill soon due.

Maria returned from the attic, where she had stripped the beds, and started dressing for church. Fransje loved to watch Maria making herself pretty. She put the golden headpieces in place and the big, white, lace Sunday hat. Lying ready on the table were her beads with the golden clasp, deep red coral beads, six strings of them. Fransje playfully pulled the necklace across the oil cloth like a harrow. The round little red balls felt nice and smooth and cool. But Father said, "Hands off!" and even without the swat of his hat the snail pulled in its tentacles.

Mother had to help Maria pin the big hat to the under-hat. With several pins between her lips, she stood on tiptoe to reach Maria's head; Maria was a head taller than she. "Bend down a little, will you!" she said, but her words were garbled by the pins in her mouth. Now Mother pinned down the big hat to the smaller one. Fransje watched carefully as she pushed all those pins, one after another, smack into Maria's head. But Maria did not seem hurt, for she kept right on talking. Instinctively Fransje raised his hands to protect his own head.

"It's almost time to leave," Father warned.

Wantje dutifully placed four chairs in a row in the middle of the living room. They all knelt around them, their hands folded on the arm rests or seats. Fransje knelt between his parents. Father prayed again. Fransje was used to this on Sunday; this time he would not have to say, "Lord bless this food" after Father finished, because they were not going to eat.

When everyone had left, Fransje went back to playing with his chicken family. Wantje was on her knees sweeping the floor, but every now and then her head bobbed up above the edge of the table to check the status of the little flock of chickens. Mother was preparing the noon meal. When she sat down at the table, Fransje asked, "Mommy, when is Daddy coming home again?"

"At noon."

"Is he going to work on the farm this afternoon?"

"No, today people don't work. It's Sunday today."

"Why don't people work on Sunday?"

"Because the Lord doesn't want them to."

"Why doesn't He want them to?" He gazed at his mother searchingly, leaving even the sugar pieces alone for a minute.

"The Lord gets angry when people work on Sunday. If you work on Sunday, you can't go to heaven to live with Him afterward."

"Where is heaven?"

"Oh, far, far away. High up in the sky. Heaven is just like a big house. The Lord lives there. And living with Him are many, many angels. And so are all the good people and the good children who loved Him very much and who have died. All good people and good children on earth who love Him very much will go and live with Him too when they die. If you are good and love Him very much, you, too, will live with Him one day. But bad people and bad children who do not love Him may not go and live with Him. The Lord is angry with them."

Fransje pondered this for a while and then asked, "How do you get there—to heaven? Is there a ladder to the sky?"

"No, there's no ladder. First you must die and be buried in the cemetery. And then the angels come down and carry you up to heaven. Then the Lord says, 'Hello, is that you? Come on in! I sure am happy to see you!' And then you'll stay with Him forever. Then you'll never again get sick or die. And it's very beautiful in that big house with the Lord, far, far more beautiful than in the Queen's house. You'll get lovely white clothes to wear. All those angels can sing so beautifully. And you'll always be able to listen to them and even sing along with them."

Fransje sat behind the table solemn and still, suddenly transported into an unfamiliar world. He looked around, estranged, feeling small and helpless, and inwardly he stretched out his hands for support. He imagined the angels coming down and digging up the grave to take the dead with them to heaven. But how could they get back to heaven without a ladder? And how did they jump down exactly on the right grave? Following his own train of thought, he asked, "Don't those angels ever jump into the sea and drown? Or on a house? And how do they get back if there isn't any ladder?"

Mother explained that angels have wings and can fly, just like big birds, and that they know exactly where they are going.

Again he was very quiet. Unconsciously his one hand fingered the beheaded rooster. Then he asked, "And where do the bad people and bad kids go? Do they stay buried in the grave?"

"No, they go to hell. That's a deep, dark pit full of fire. They are thrown into it, and they can never get out again."

"Is that high up in the sky too?"

"What?"

"The pit! Hell!"

"No. Hell is . . . far, far away."

Mother sighed. This questioning wearied her, and secretly she hoped he would stop now. For she felt distress at how difficult, how nearly impossible, it was to explain the purpose of his birth and the meaning of life to a three-year-old.

But Fransje had not yet extricated himself from this world of new images that had so unexpectedly captured his interest. After a long pause he asked one more question: "Mommy, when you go to heaven, will you take me with you in your arms? And will you hold me tight, so that I won't fall?"

Mother looked at him in amazement. She could not have said what went through her mind. She noticed how intensely those big blue eyes stared at her. She saw one of his small hands unconsciously picking at one of the sugar candies. Suddenly tears welled up in her eyes; a tear rolled down her face from one eye, and then from the other. She walked over to Fransje and lifted him from behind the table. Pressing him to her chest, she gently kissed him on both cheeks. Her tears were wet and warm, tickling his face. He looked at his mother in quiet puzzlement.

These two worlds, one of them owing its origin to the other, were separated now by time and space. Could they still touch? They would never again be the unity they were when she carried him under her heart. That oneness was broken when he was born: now each world revolved on a separate axis. Or was it possible that after many years and many, many revolutions both would have the same Axis once more?

Jesus! a voice whispered inside her. She was amazed at its suddenness, so much like an audible voice. Only that word had entered her consciousness from her unformulated thoughts. Would she one day be able to stand before Him with uplifted head and say, "Behold, Lord, I and the children Thou hast given me"? She thought of her seven. Never before had she been so deeply aware of the great responsibility and dependency of her motherhood.

When Father and the children came home from church, the sugar pieces were spread around the table. Near Father's place a brown chicken waited. There was another one near Eine's place. Maria and Bram each got a white one, and Arjaan and Kees a yellow chick. Mother and Wantje also had chicks, though they had each had one earlier. Fransje himself had already eaten the pink rooster. Now there were only two chicks left.

Someone had come home with Father. Since he often stopped in after church Fransje knew him. His name was Verplanke, and Fransje rather liked him.

"Can you shake hands with me?" Verplanke asked. Fransje offered him the hand that was holding both of the chicks. Verplanke pretended that Fransje was offering the candies to him and exclaimed, "Why, are these for me? Well, thank you very much, Fransje!" But Fransje cried shrilly, "Give me back my chickies!"

They all laughed at this honest response, Verplanke most of all. He gave the sugar chicks back and added four small cat-shaped pieces of licorice, which he had fished up from one of the pockets of his waistcoat. Fransje accepted them only out of politeness, for they really repelled him, coming as they did from Verplanke's warm vest pocket. He knew he would not eat them. At once he put them on the table and moved the chicks a safe distance away from them.

Fransje dropped from the bench, crawled under the table to Arjaan, and asked him to play horsey. Having mounted his horse, he steered it by the ears down the short hallway to the back room. But it was too cold there, so he guided his horse back to the living room with loud commands. Father, however, didn't like such a racket in the house, and ordered them both to their places at the table. Fransje decided to play with his blocks. Kees helped him build a big barn.

Maria and Bram were reading together from the same book. Sometimes they burst out laughing at a funny passage. Maria was no longer wearing her big hat; it had been put away in the linen closet. Wantje was paging through an old psalter, and Father and Verplanke were talking together, while Mother quietly listened to their conversation. Every now and then she got up for a moment to stir the steaming pots and pans on the stove. Eine was also listening piously, his chair right next to Father's.

Once in a while Fransje caught the word "Lord" in the conversation, and he thought of what Mother had told him that morning. He turned his head to look through the window at the gray sky. But the house of the Lord was nowhere to be seen. Nor did he see any angels on their way to the cemetery. All he saw were sparrows alighting near a pile of trampled horse droppings on the road. But he decided to keep an eye open and look every now and then. Who knows, maybe someday he'd be lucky enough to catch them by surprise. But if he did, he'd be very careful; otherwise they might take him along too. He wanted someday to go to heaven too, of course, but not just yet. First he wanted to grow up, and wear pants, and go to school, and later work in the field with horses, just like Father sometimes did.

Verplanke got up from his chair saying, "Well, I had better be going."

"Why, what's the hurry?" Mother asked. "Won't you stay and have a bit to eat with us? You have such a long way to walk. Then you can go right to church from here this afternoon."

"No, I better not. My family doesn't know I stopped here and they would be worried."

"Oh, goody!" a voice suddenly cried from behind the table. It was Fransje, who had followed the last conversation in great suspense.

None of them could keep from bursting into laughter—which made Fransje blush. Mother's face turned bright red too, and she scolded him severely: "Why, shame on you, you bad boy! How dare you say a thing like that!" But Verplanke didn't take it badly at all. He was laughing so hard that his eyes disappeared in the webs of little wrinkles on his friendly face.

Father said, "Do as you please. But don't leave without having a word of prayer with us."

Verplanke sat down again, and Mother alerted the children by saying, "Kids! Fransje! We're going to pray!"

Puzzled, Fransje looked from one to the other. There wasn't any food on the table yet, and the family had just come back from church. He cried in protest, "Daddy already prayed a great big heap this morning!"

The boys were bursting with suppressed laughter, struggling to keep their composure. Father, too, clenched his jaws to keep from laughing. But Verplanke laughed out loud, which was a good thing, because now the boys could let loose too.

But Fransje didn't laugh at all. He wasn't even proud that they were laughing at his remark. He just couldn't see why they had to pray again, for then he had to sit still so long that he felt prickly all over his body.

After the noon meal came the usual preparations for going to the second church service. This time Mother was getting ready too. Maria would stay home with Fransje this afternoon. He thought he'd like to go to church too sometime, but he knew this wasn't the time. It was much too cold out and too far for him to walk. But the greatest obstacle, certainly in his own eyes, was the fact that he was still not out of skirts.

This time Wantje had to go too. She'd just have to wear her best wooden shoes, painted black for just such occasions. After all, she wouldn't be the only one to enter the courts of the Lord in that kind of footwear.

To Fransje's great joy, it was decided that Kees would stay home too. Among other things, this meant that once Father had left the house they could play horsey without being disturbed. Fransje started to pull the chairs in a row, and he knelt down at his. He wished the others would hurry. "Are we going to pray now?" he urged.

When the prayer was done, Mother put on her black woolen wrap, kissed Fransje and made him promise to be a good boy. To Maria she said, "Don't let the stove go out." And then they left, first Father and Mother with Wantje, and a little later, Bram and Eine. Arjaan waited a few minutes at the window for his friend. When he saw him coming, he left too.

Now the game could start. Kees was no dull, plodding farm horse; he was a spirited stallion. He pawed at the floor mat with his forefeet, snorting and blowing, impatient for his rider to get into the saddle. "Giddap!" Fransje urged, quite superfluously. And off they went, racing wildly about the room. The horse was more than wild, he was ungovernable, always wanting to go a different way than his rider. Fransje had to steer him firmly by the ears and cry, "Right!" and, "Left!" Sometimes the horse was scared by one of the small, wooden boxes called footstoves, or by a chair, and then he reared up, pawing the air with his forelegs. Then Fransje screamed in fearful delight, clutching Kees's neck with both arms to keep from crashing to the floor.

Maria sat at the table, memorizing her questions and answers for catechism class. She propped her head in her hands, her elbows on the table, pressing her fingers against her bonnet where her ears were. Over and over she recited long rows of words under her breath. But Fransje had no time to listen.

At last he tired of the game. He guided his horse to the stable under the table and said, "Now I'm a horse, too, a little horsey, you know, a colt. You're the big horse and I'm the colt." On his hands and knees, he neighed in a high-pitched voice like a real colt. One of the footstoves was the manger, from which the horses ate. They weren't really eating of course, just pretending. Hanging his head above the perforated box, Fransje smacked and swallowed and snorted to show how much the colt was enjoying his feed.

But of course this game could not last the whole afternoon. Fransje took out his junk box. It didn't contain much of value—a string of empty wooden spools tied together with a dirty piece of string, all kinds of plain wooden blocks, several big glass marbles,—Arjaan's, but Fransje's to play with until marble season—and for the rest a lot of nameless and worthless objects like all children of farmhands with big families played with.

There was also a rag doll in the box. Fransje had a weakness for dolls, because Wantje, the next youngest, often played with them. But they also expressed Fransje's unconscious need to have someone below him too—someone who looked up to him as he did to his big brothers and sisters. For even Wantje was four years his senior.

Since the other children teased him about his weakness for dolls, he only played with them when his big brothers were away. He dared to play with them now because only Kees was home, and he wouldn't say anything. Besides, Kees was drawing on his slate at the moment. Soon Fransje would take a look at it, because Kees could draw such beautiful pictures. But for now, he knew a much nicer game. He picked out all the long blocks and set them on end in a row on the linoleum square in front of the stove. Then he sat down a short distance away and tried to bowl them over with the glass marbles.

Finally he had enough of that too, and he began feeling bored. By this time, however, Maria knew her lesson by heart, so Fransje could come and sit on her lap for a while. She sang all kinds of songs for him, one of Fransje's greatest joys. Maria had a lovely, clear voice, and although Fransje couldn't judge it, he could feel its charm. He leaned back quietly, his head against her *doek* and *beuk*, and dreamily let the beautiful melodies cascade over his head.

Maria sang of the great valley, the beautiful valley, in which little flowers are bloo-oom-ing. Fransje didn't know what a valley was, and yet he could see thousands of little flowers, little white daisies and yellow buttercups, sparkling brightly in a green meadow of young grass. And even if the words did not penetrate, the pure voice and the somewhat melancholy tune certainly did. Fransje preferred tunes that were somewhat sad.

With her voice Maria led him through violent snowstorms and blustery winds. He saw the poor little beggar girl pacing the cold, wet streets all alone, begging for a handout; but not a soul would give her anything, and in the end she perished in a snowbank from hunger and misery.

She also sang of a young soldier summoned to war by the drums. He came, together with other young soldiers, and they marched off side by side. Maria let him die too, and Fransje had great difficulty swallowing back his tears. And she let him hear the bugle call, re-echoing from mountain and valley with its full, pure tone.

Finally she sang "Safe in the arms of Jesus, Safe on His gentle breast." Those were words Fransje could understand: he himself was lying safely in Maria's arms, where he could hear and feel her heart beating through her *doek* and *beuk*. The words and the melancholy tune evoked in him an unspeakable longing for something unknown and unfamiliar. He felt both very happy and very sad at the same time, and again he had to swallow hard to get rid of a lump in his throat.

Fransje was quietly but immensely enjoying himself. Every now and then he heaved a deep sigh as he envisioned the faraway, exotic scenes evoked by Maria's voice. No doubt his images were unlike Maria's, but no less beautiful and enchanting for that.

Before he realized it, the long afternoon had passed; he was amazed to hear the door open and see the boys enter. Maria let him slide from her lap and made tea for supper, which was much earlier on Sunday than during the week because of the evening service. A little later, the others, too, arrived home, and Fransje greeted Mother with exuberant joy. When she asked if he had been a good boy, he could truthfully say yes.

Mother took off only her woolen shawl and put it behind the doors of the built-in bed for the time being. She tied an everyday *beuk* over her *doek*, and started slicing a loaf of bread. Then Fransje knew what was up—in a little while Mother would go to church again. Not liking that one bit, he whined for her to stay home with him. But Mother said that Bram would sit with him tonight; Arjaan, too, might stay home. That was all very nice, but no one could take Mother's place. So he kept whining for a while, until Mother said, "You know what? When you get tired, you may crawl into Mommy's bed for a while, until we come home again." Mother and Father's bed was built into the wall of the living room and was concealed during the day behind closet-like doors. "Then Bram will light the lamp and you can just lie there and look into the living room. Shall we do that?" Oh, all right. He had become reconciled to the idea.

Sleepily Fransje opened his eyes and looked around. A light shone into his bed and he heard laughter and talking. He was not in his little bed in the attic. He sat up to look into the room. There was Daddy, sitting in his big chair. And there was Mommy, and Maria, and all the others. He blinked into the lamplight, and all at once he knew where he was.

"Mommy!" he called. They all turned their faces toward him as Mother walked to the bed. She lifted him out and carried him to the table. He was allowed to sit in her lap. Protectively she wrapped her apron around him.

"Are you going to church again pretty soon?" he asked, worry in his voice.

"No, my boy. Now we're all staying home with Fransje. In a little while we're all going to bed."

Father looked at the clock. Then he stood up and took the Bible from the mantel. After paging through it for a moment, he shoved it across the tablecloth to Wantje. With his big finger he pointed out a place and said, "Here, start here and read a little ways." But before she could start, Fransje announced that he was thirsty. Mother poured some tea in his mug and added a teaspoon of sugar and some milk. He gulped it down greedily.

"All right, Wantje, you can start," Father said.

Wantje began. She read rather haltingly; every now and then Father had to help her with a difficult word. When she had read long enough, Kees continued to the end of the chapter. Then it was Arjaan's turn. Then Eine's. Then Bram's. Maria read last.

Fransje lay against Mother's breast, musing on matters of his own little world. He hardly heard the word "Lord" that recurred again and again in the reading. Finally the Bible was closed, and Kees put it back in its place on the mantel. Father closed the Sabbath with a final prayer of thanksgiving. Then he got up to go outside for a minute.

Mother put Fransje down to kneel at her feet. He placed his head in her lap and said his evening prayer after her:

O good and beneficent God!
although I have forfeited

this life because of my sins,
in Thy mercy Thou hast again spared
and saved me.
O merciful God,
forgive all the sins
that now stain me.
Cleanse me in Christ's blood and Spirit.
Take me once again tonight
under the shadow of Thy wings,
so that I may not die in my sleep
but wake up in good health
and early seek Thy face
with thanksgiving. Amen.

Fransje's only problem in reciting the prayer was to repeat the words after Mother as correctly as possible. He hated having to say a word over again because he had mispronounced it. Once in a while he ran on a few words ahead of Mother. He didn't consider the words strange. To him it was simply "praying." It meant that the day was ending; that soon he would get a piece of rock candy and go to bed. Even the word "wings" slipped by unnoticed, not even calling to mind the morning's angels.

Mother did not fret over the fitness of the prayer for a young child. All her children had learned that same prayer at her knees. She could not even remember where she had gotten it; maybe she herself had learned it as a child from her own parents. But it was a good and correct prayer she thought, sincerely hoping that her children would continue to use it even after they had grown up, and then no longer by rote, but from the bottom of their hearts.

She handed out clean handkerchiefs and shirts to the boys to take upstairs with them for tomorrow. Monday was just around the corner. The children waited until Father returned to the room, and then they said, "Father, Mother, kids, good night!"

Fransje shook Mother's hand and kissed her, but with Father he only shook hands because of his stubbly beard and the tobacco smell on his breath. Then Arjaan took him upstairs. The little night light was already there. Maria opened the doors of her built-in bed and quickly braided Wantje's hair.

Shivering, Fransje crawled beneath the blankets, and Bram carefully tucked him in. Moments later, when Father came up for the lamp, saying good night as he lowered the trapdoor, he got no answer from Fransje. Fransje had slipped off into a deep, peaceful sleep.

2

At long last the time had come when Fransje could wear pants. True, they were a pair of Kees's hand-me-downs which Mother had dug up out of the linen closet, but Fransje had already become so used to them that he considered them part of himself. The age of diapers and skirts was safely and permanently behind him. Along with the skirts, he seemed to have put away many other childish things. He did still wet his bed occasionally, and even during the day he sometimes wet his pants, but that couldn't be blamed to stubbornness or deliberate wrongdoing on his part. Sometimes the day's menu was partly to blame, and other times his play so engrossed him that he didn't notice he had to go until he was going.

Only once in a while did he say 'Daddy'—and then by accident; otherwise he said 'Father' like the other children. But Mother he still called 'Mommy'. To him this was no common, functional name, not even a proper name, but a name that captured her essence. Mommy was not just *called* Mommy; nor *was* she merely a mommy. No, she was *Mommy*. The word, the gentle sound of it, expressed everything she meant to him.

When he played with his doll, he was never its mother—just its father or older brother. Sometimes he let the doll read out of Wantje's old psalter, saying, "Here, read a little ways." Or: "When are you going to wear pants? You're getting way too old for skirts." He never took it to bed, nor did he ever put a diaper on it. The doll had no name; he always called it by the neutral word "doll." As was evident from his talks with the doll, Fransje identified with it to some extent, but not completely. To give that very primitive object his own name would put too great a strain on his imagination and on his self-respect.

Sometimes Fransje went to the neighbors to play with girls his own age. The boys in the neighborhood were all older than he. He would walk right into the neighbor's house without knocking and would sometimes stay to eat. Since their dolls were much prettier than his, he loved to play with them. They often played house, and then he, of course, was the father.

Because of the cold, he spent most days almost entirely indoors. As a result, he often became terribly bored and was sorely tempted to misbehave. When Mother had to step in and call him back to order, she did so in one of two ways: with just her voice, or with the help of her hands. When things got really bad, she would arm herself with a slipper. That didn't happen very often, but it was no less memorable for that.

Despite these disruptions and remissions in his development, his boyishness showed itself in countless small acts which seemed to be motivated, for the most part, by a strong desire to grow up fast. Therefore came collisions with parental, and even more often with brotherly and sisterly authority. Often life itself had to step in as a corrective. But he usually profited by these lessons, which also showed that his strivings were not without a goal, although he might not be conscious of it.

One morning when Fransje arrived downstairs, Mother told him that it had snowed during the night. As soon as the shutters were opened and the blue light of morning stood at the window, a blurred square, he flattened his nose against the glass to get a good look at the white world. The snow was still falling. He watched the flakes silently sifting down. High in the sky they looked gray and dirty, but when they fell they were suddenly white. The few flakes that fluttered against the window pane hung there for a moment, hesitating; and then they shrank into themselves to slide down the glass as glistening beads of water. Fransje tried to stop them with his finger, but they paid him no mind.

The spartan winter shrubs in the front yard stood up to their armpits in the white fluff, wearing thick white woolen caps. The hawthorn hedge separating the yard from the road was covered with a long, narrow blanket as well. And beyond it, the road and the ditches and the flat fields—all lay hidden under the beautiful whiteness. Fransje stared until his eyes hurt, speechless for a time. More and more snowflakes came tumbling down. If he looked up for long, he grew dizzy.

Mother was busy with her morning housekeeping chores. Hearing her at the table behind him, he asked without turning from the window, "Mommy, is there a lot of snow in heaven?"

Wondering what he meant, she told him, "There is no snow in heaven."

"Then where is all the snow coming from? It's falling from the sky, isn't it? And heaven is up in the sky."

"Oh, but heaven is much, much higher than the sky. First there are the clouds, then the blue sky, and then far above the blue sky is heaven."

Fransje pictured a blue dome that served as ceiling for the earth and at the same time as the floor of heaven. He asked himself how the people in heaven could keep their footing where the arched floor sloped down. His mind quickly grouped everyone safely straight overhead and he banished the unsafe periphery to the back of his consciousness. Besides, at the moment he was more interested in where the snow came from. Strangely enough, he had never stopped to ask these questions when it was raining. But snow was so totally new to him, a phenomenon that he had never before experienced in full awareness, that the questions arose spontaneously.

"Who is throwing all that snow down?"

"Nobody. The Lord makes it snow. He also makes it rain, and He makes the sun shine too. The Lord says to the clouds, Rain! and it rains. Then people and animals have water to drink, and so do the grass and the flowers. The Lord cares for everything. Otherwise we would all die of hunger and thirst."

Now Fransje turned around and asked, "Why does it have to snow?"

"Because the Lord wants it to."

"Yes, but what good is it to people and animals?"

To that Mother had no ready answer—at least, not one that he could understand and that would satisfy him. So she said, "Oh, it's for children to play in. They can go sledding and throw snowballs. And it's to make everything nice and white. The Lord thinks it's pretty, and so do people."

Yes, Fransje also thought it looked pretty. He turned back to the window. The snow had stopped falling. He too would like to go out and play in it.

After breakfast he was allowed to go out with Kees and Arjaan. Mother pulled a woolen cap down over his ears and tied an old shawl around him, criss-crossing it over his chest and back. The boys had dug an old sled out of the shed for Fransje to sit on. They hitched themselves in front of it like two horses and, "Giddyap!" away they flew over the soft, white surface. The sled slid noiselessly over the downy fur, and the boys' footsteps fell almost soundlessly upon the snow. What a great way to play horsey! The trees on either side of the road flitted by. Fransje's cheeks began to glow with excitement and with the brush of cold air against them. When the boys flew past the window, he shouted, "Look, Mommy!" But he couldn't see whether she pushed back the curtain to look. He needed all his concentration to keep from being jolted off the sled. A little later Wantje joined them. The horses stopped and she climbed aboard too; she sat behind Fransje and he sat between her legs. On they went again, passing back and forth in front of the window.

The kids from the Hontenisse Polder came by on their way to school. This meant the end of their fun, for it was time for the boys and Wantje to go to school too. They shouted goodbye to Mother and joined the other school children. They pulled Fransje with them a little ways, but then he had to go back by himself and take back the sled too. But he could handle it: just look—the sled almost went by itself.

But Fransje didn't go straight home. First he had to dig into that mysterious white stuff with his hands. He scooped both hands full and shoved his nose into it. Then he threw it up into the air. Now *he* was making it snow.

As he romped in the new snow, lumps of packed snow formed under his wooden shoes. At first he didn't notice, but soon his ankles began to turn, and then he could hardly walk anymore. The cold was also beginning to bother him, and his fingers hurt as if needles were pricking them. He looked at his hands to see if they were bleeding. No, they were only turning purple and red.

His high spirits were falling fast. "I'm going back to Mommy, by the nice, warm stove," he thought. He stumbled back to the sled and bent to pick up the rope. But because of the large lumps of snow on the bottom of his wooden shoes, he turned his ankle and fell. He hurt his arm so badly that tears sprang to his eyes. But he didn't want to cry. Angry, he stood up with the rope in his hand. Immediately he was wobbling again because his legs were uneven. Instinctively he tried to support himself with the rope, thereby jerking the sled toward him, and its sharp edge came flying hard against his shins. Now he lost his balance completely. Thump! He crashed down on the nose of the sled; the sled tipped forward, and Fransje lay full-length in the snow. Now he had really hurt himself, and he could no longer hold back the tears. Wailing with pain and humiliation he lay prone in the snow, his black shawl completely white.

But Fransje had inherited a good share of his father's temper. Though still, of course, rudimentary, such experiences also helped develop it. He hit on the unfounded idea that some invisible power was playing him for a fool. Violently he scrambled to his feet and, howling with pain and fury, gave the sled a vicious kick. Although everything was alive to Fransje, he knew very well that the sled was not to blame for this outrage. Still, he had to vent his pent up frustration somehow. And it did help. He got rid of his anger, and also of the lump under his shoe. That gave him an idea. He stopped crying and kicked the sled with his other foot. Then, once again standing solidly on both feet, he decided to head straight home.

As he came to the back door—there was no front door—he was once again overcome by grief. His deep need to be comforted triggered a new fit of wailing. And, indeed, he had plenty of justification, with his barked shins and aching fingers. When Mother opened the door, her mere presence was such a comfort that he could at last fully let loose. She took him into the living room, removed his cap, shawl, and coat, and wiped his runny nose and eyes with a corner of her apron, all the while soothing him with her words. With a warm cloth that had been draped over a pan on the stove to hold down the steam, she rubbed his hands. That helped. Then she rubbed a bit of salve on his scraped shins, saying, "You'll make a good farmhand when you grow up. I see you can already drive a team of horses." That fixed everything. Fransje was ready to take whatever came with growing up.

But accidents seemed to come in pairs. Today Fransje's experiences were in shrill contrast to the quiet, peaceful beauty of the white world outdoors. Mother had gone back to work, and Fransje was playing with his junk box. His ragdoll gave him an idea: he would give the doll a sleigh ride too. Fransje set it on the footstove. There was no rope on it, but you could also push a sled. That way he could also hold the doll in place with his thumbs. The footstove slid full speed ahead across the smooth mats. Here and there it didn't slide quite so easily—just like outside. On he went, across the living room, past the pantry, past Maria and Wantje's built-in bed, behind the stove and then, whirling and wheeling, back underneath the table. There he stopped a moment to catch his breath. To the doll he said, "You'll make a good farmhand when you grow up." And then to himself, "Giddyap, horse. Haw!"

Startled, the horse leaped ahead from under the table. But his fierceness cost him heavily; Fransje bashed his head brutally against the bottom of the table. With a loud scream, he flopped down on his knees behind the footstove. Once again he sent up a howl like a stuck pig. This time the doll was to blame. He flung it across the living room in a wide arc. It landed behind the stove, where the cat had just settled down for a nap.

Frightened, she leaped up and dashed for the hall, her tail in the air. There she sat down petulantly washing herself. But Mother was just coming down the hall carrying the coal scuttle before her with both hands. Not seeing the cat, she stepped on her paw. The creature's pitiful, bloodcurdling yowl scared Mother so terribly, she nearly dropped the coal scuttle. "Oh, you stupid cat!" she scolded. "Why don't you stay out from underfoot!"

Then she came into the living room to find Fransje wailing underneath the table and she blurted angrily, "And what are you bawling about this time?"

Fransje howled out an explanation, but Mother couldn't understand a word of it. She put the coal scuttle beside the stove and came to him. When she pulled him from underneath the table, she saw the big bruise on his forehead. This time a cold dishrag provided relief. Mother set him down on the bench by the table and brought the Bible storybook from the linen closet, knowing that he loved to look at the illustrations. Though otherwise he was never allowed to page through the book by himself, this once she made an exception. "Careful you don't tear anything!" she warned him. Eagerly Fransje promised to be careful.

As Mother put it down, the book happened to fall open to the story of Lot in Sodom. The picture showed the angels urging Lot to leave the wicked city of Sodom. Fransje studied it closely for a long time. The angels in the picture were exactly how he had imagined them to be, partly because his imagination had been subtly shaped by these same pictures. The angels wore long, white robes and had huge wings on their backs. Carefully he turned the page, looking for more angels. Yes, he found more, a whole bunch of them, in fact. But what else did he see? A ladder to the sky! At the bottom of the ladder lay a man with his head on a big rock; he looked like he was asleep. The ladder started right beside him and rose high into the sky at a slight angle. It was crowded with angels. No doubt about it, they had wings and beautiful, long white clothes, like night gowns, only even more beautiful than the one Maria had gotten from the lady at the big farm where she sometimes did housework. Mother was hurrying about doing her housework again. When she stepped into the living room, Fransje cried, "Mommy look! There are *so* ladders up to heaven. Just look!"

Mother was very busy and had no time to discuss it. She cast a quick glance at the picture and said, "Oh, that ladder isn't a real ladder. The man was very tired and he lay down to sleep. And then he dreamed about the ladder with all those angels."

"Why didn't he go home and sleep in his bed?"

"Oh, he was bad and ran away from home."

"Why was he bad? What did he do?"

Mother sighed. Another one of Fransje's endless series of questions, and she just didn't have the time. Glancing at the clock, she said, "I'll tell you that story some other time, Fransje. I don't have time now." And she hurried off into the back room.

Fransje sighed too. He sure would have liked to know what those angels on that ladder were doing by that bad man. What could he have done? And why did they bother with him if he was a bad man?

Before Fransje knew it, the morning had flown. The bump on his head had shrunk to a sickly yellow spot. Fransje heard the clatter of leather shoes and wooden shoes on the back stoop and soon Father and the others walked into the house.

After lunch the other children took Fransje out sledding again for a little while. Bram and Eine also joined in. Soon the boys were tossing snowballs. When a few older neighbor boys and girls came outside, a full scale battle developed. Everyone was exuberant, and Fransje would have liked to join in too, but he was afraid that his fingers would start stinging again. He grabbed a few handfuls of snow and tried to hit somebody, but when his fingers began to get numb, he quickly stopped. Bram told him, "Fransje, you go play over there, or else you'll get hit." The words were barely out of his mouth, and, smack! a big snowball hit Fransje squarely in the face. He gasped for air as a searing pain spread like fire over his face. His nose and mouth were clogged with snow. He screamed and coughed and sputtered, and, panic-stricken, he clutched Bram's leg. Bram knelt beside him and cleared the snow from his nose and mouth. Then he wiped Fransje's face with his big red handkerchief and carried him to the back of the house, trying to calm him down.

This time Fransje wasn't angry. It had happened much too suddenly and traumatically for him to experience anything but physical hurt and self-pity. Even while safe and secure in Bram's arms, he could still feel the aftereffects of that sudden, biting pain.

Bram felt sorry for him, but he knew it was really no one's fault, even though Eine had thrown the snowball. It had simply been an accident. He tried to quiet Fransje before they entered the living room. But Father was already taking a hand in the matter. "So!" he said. "Are you proud of yourself? Such big fellows and you still don't know any better!"

Bram looked at his father, feeling that, as the eldest, he was being blamed. And that wasn't fair. He said nothing in reply, however, for that would not have been tolerated. He could not tell from Father's tone that he hadn't meant to sound so sharp and that his unreasonable words were spurred only by his compassion for Fransje.

Bram was, after all, only seventeen himself.

Fransje had forgotten his pain and grief. But he didn't know what to do with himself. Mother was sitting at the sewing machine, and Maria was darning socks. They had no time to pay attention to Fransje. He would have loved to turn the wheel of the sewing machine, but he knew there was no chance of that. Mother's spool of thread ran out, and she readied the machine to wind another spool. Now he was allowed to turn the wheel for a while. That was fun, except that half of the machine was standing still; the little foot on the front wasn't bobbing up and down, and that was just what made it so interesting. Mother started sewing again, and he sat down right next to her on the bench. But then he was blocking the light. Mother said, "Get out of the light, Fransje. I can't see a thing."

So he went around to stand on the other side, close to the wheel, and wheedled: "Mommy, can I turn it? Just once, Mommy? Please, can I?"

Mother let go of the handle to fold a seam into the material with her scissors. Fransje couldn't resist the temptation to give the wheel a couple of quick turns. But something seemed to go wrong under the little foot, for without saying a word, Mother rapped his knuckles with the scissors.

So he turned to the cat for company. The cat was, as usual, sleeping on the pillow of Father's big chair. Behind the cat lay Mother's handkerchief. "Wait a minute," thought Fransje, "I'll cover her." While he gently stroked her head with one hand and murmured, "Nice kitty," with the other hand he carefully pulled the handkerchief from behind her. The cat blinked at him sleepily and pushed her head sideways into his hand, asking for more. Fransje accommodated her, but he didn't stroke all the way down her back, for he had learned from experience that she then stood up with her tail straight up in the air. And he wanted her to stay as she was. Very carefully he now put the handkerchief over her. The cat patiently allowed him his game, purring contentedly. Fransje himself liked to have the blankets tucked tightly under his chin so that there were no cracks where the cold air could seep in. Puss, he was sure, wanted the same thing. Very solicitously he tucked the cloth under her warm body and between her legs. The cat's eyes were now wide open. She moved uneasily. Quickly Fransje stroked and soothed her again. He knelt beside her and explained, "See, Puss, now you and me are going to sleep together."

He put his head near her on the pillow and felt her purring vibrating within his own body. How wonderfully soft and warm the cat's body felt against his cheek! He slid closer and put his head right on top of the cat. He pressed down on her a little—just to show how much he loved her.

But the cat had had enough. She squirmed out from underneath the heavy weight, pushing off with her back legs to make good her quick leap of escape. She was a very gentle creature who would never deliberately scratch anyone, so she was not really to blame when in her fright she pushed off against Fransje's face. He jerked back, but by then he had already picked up four searing clawmarks on his cheek. Howling, he ran to Mother. "If that isn't the last straw!" she exclaimed. "What's with you today? Why don't you leave that poor cat alone!"

That was cold comfort for Fransje. Insulted, he screamed several decibels louder. Though Mother sensed that she hadn't really been fair, she was struggling with cloth too thick for her needle, so she spoke more sharply than she meant to. For the third time that day Fransje's face received first aid. Again a bit of salve was enlisted to soothe the pain.

In this atmosphere of boredom and grief, it had become impossible for Fransje to enjoy himself. After a little while, he asked without really expecting an affirmative answer, "Mommy, can I go play with Neeltje?"

Mother was indeed far from ready to give him leave. But Maria helped him out. "Why don't you let him go. Then at least we're rid of him for a while." Although that didn't sound especially sympathetic, Fransje was happy for any support he could get, even if poorly motivated. He gave Mother a hopeful look. After hesitating a moment, she acquiesced. "Oh, all right, go ahead. When they're tired of you, they can send you home again."

Maria helped him into his clothes, and off went Fransje. A moment later he marched past the window. He was so preoccupied with stamping his feet to keep the snow from building up under his wooden shoes that he forgot to look into the window.

Fransje's house was actually part of a long low building inhabited by six other families. He didn't know all the other people who lived in the building, for, first of all, there were so many of them and, secondly, this past summer he had still been too young to pay attention to such things. In front of the building, was a row of small yards separated from one another and from the tar road by low hawthorn hedges, some of which had small gates in them. Each townhouse had but one window in the front, and all except the end houses had a front door as well. In the back were the vegetable gardens bordered by a common path. Of course each home had a back door which was the one used most often. So the neighbors always passed by Fransje's back door—that is, three of the neighbors, for there was a high fence between the fourth and fifth house (counting from Fransje's side). The neighbors on the other side of the fence walked around the other end when they went to the front. So Fransje knew the neighbors on his side who passed his door every day.

Right next door, all alone, lived Wullemiene. Her husband had been buried in the cemetery for many years. Wullemiene was very old, and her face, full of wrinkles and folds, always seemed to be scowling. She wasn't very friendly, especially when the children walked over her clean stoop just to tease her. If she saw them, her door might suddenly open, and they would be doused by a pail of water. She disliked children—except Fransje, who delighted in being her one love. And he returned her love, even though he was a little afraid of her. She often gave him big pieces of rock candy. He had even been in her living room on occasion, but the house had seemed so quiet and empty. Fransje couldn't understand why she wanted to live in such a big house all by herself. She had two large, built-in beds like his family, and also a back room and a ladder and an attic.

On the other side of Wullemiene lived Ko and Tona. Fransje was a little scared of Ko, although he was friendly and not nearly as tall as Father. But his large red mustache with drooping yellow ends gave him an unsavory look. Tona he didn't like at all. She turned his stomach. She acted very friendly and nice, especially when Mother was around, and she also handed out rock candies to the children sometimes, but only when they were burnt. Then they were so bitter that as soon as she wasn't looking Fransje would spit his out. He didn't trust her friendliness. Tona had a big head with a flabby face, and on each side of her mouth was a big mole with long, bristly hairs growing out of it. She had tried to kiss Fransje once, but he had twisted and turned until, thwarted, she had let him go.

Next came the house of Siene and Marien. That was where the girls lived whom Fransje sometimes played with. They had several older sisters, plus Pier. Pier was Arjaan's age and the two sometimes played together. But Arjaan didn't like Pier, so Fransje didn't either. He was a big jerk, and he swore sometimes. Fransje never went there when Pier was home.

The big fence came next. Fransje did know the neighbors on the other side of the fence, for Neeltje lived there, who was the same age as Fransje and also the youngest in the family. It was his favorite place to play, because Neeltje had such beautiful toys, books and many other lovely things. Her best toy was her tea set. Her mother seldom let her play with it. Usually it sat in a big box on top of the linen closet. It consisted of real china cups and saucers, a real cream pitcher and sugar pot, and best of all, a real teapot. And they were all decorated with pretty red roses and blue forget-me-nots. Although not a girl, Fransje did love to play with the tea set. When Neeltje's mother wasn't in a bad mood—which wasn't very often—she gave Neeltje real tea and milk and sugar to put in the playset. And thereby, according to Fransje, playing house reached perfection.

All this went through Fransje's mind on his way to the house of fulfilled dreams. When he arrived at the back door, Neeltje's mother was just pouring a pail of dirty water into the drain. He examined her face closely to gauge her mood.

"Well, hi there, Fransje!" she cried cheerfully. Great! The signs were favorable. Not only was she in a good mood, she even called him Fransje. When she was in a bad frame of mind, she called him Frans. And to call Fransje Frans was the most insulting thing you could do.

"May I come in and play with Neeltje?" he asked sweetly.

"Well sure, go right in," was the answer. "She's in the living room."

He stepped out of his wooden shoes and into the house, and at once the strange odor struck him again. It didn't really stink as such, but it certainly didn't smell good. But in any case, to him the smell meant that he was at Neeltje's and maybe soon he'd be allowed to play with the tea set.

In the living room he saw the older girls sitting around the table sewing. But Neeltje sat by herself in a corner of the room at her own little table, and, oh joy! before her stood her tea set. All the girls looked up, and one of them laughed, "Well, look who's here: Fransje Weststrate! Come to play with Neeltje, have you? That's the boy! But be careful, or you'll have to marry her."

Then they all snickered loudly. It made Fransje feel a little shy and apprehensive. He didn't understand why it should make them laugh so. Of course he was going to marry Neeltje some day! Or maybe one of the girls of Siene and Marien. He wasn't sure yet. Timidly he walked toward Neeltje and asked her, "Can I play too?" Neeltje nodded and told him, "Yes, you're the father and

I'm the mother, and the doll is our baby. You've just come home from working in the fields, and now it's time to eat."

Fransje immediately stepped into his role. Out of the corner of his eye he checked to see if the older girls were still watching. Assured that they were again immersed in their sewing, he yielded completely to the magic of the moment. He shed his coat, hung it on the doorknob of the built-in bed and put his cap on top of it. "But what do we eat?" he asked. "You don't even have any bread!"

Neeltje stood up from her footstove and stepped into the pantry without even asking her mother. After poking around a bit, she returned with a dry slice of bread and two strips of fried bacon. She broke the bread in half and gave a half with a piece of bacon to Fransje. She herself bit into her share and began to eat.

"Don't you think you'd better pray first?" Fransje admonished his wife.

"Oh, yes, that's right! But you're the father, and fathers always do the praying."

That was true too, and Fransje discharged his duty. He sat down on a footstove, folded his hands and peered through his eyelashes to see if Neeltje was following his example. Then he began: "Our Father who art in heaven . . . ." Too bad he didn't know the rest, but he stretched out the prayer by adding, "Mumble, mumble, mumble . . . , amen!" Neeltje made the baby say "Lord bless," and the meal was now lawfully begun. She put sugar and milk in the little cups and then poured tea out of the pretty little pot with the red roses and blue forget-me-nots. She stirred the tea with her finger, and taking her child on her lap, she sat down again.

Fransje meanwhile talked about work on the big farm, just like Father. He said, "I'm tired of all that heavy work. And the boss was in a bad mood today. We sure got a lot of snow today, didn't we?"

Neeltje played her role no less skillfully. She told him that the baby had been terribly sick with a tummy ache today; she just cried and cried. Then she asked, "Would you like another cup of tea? Then you better pour it yourself, and pour one for me too, 'cause I got the baby on my lap."

This was the pinnacle of Fransje's happiness. But he didn't show it. Calmly he stood up, taking the little teapot in his right hand. He leaned heavily on the table with his left, for he had had a very tiring day at the farm. First he filled his own cup, and then he bent forward over the table to serve Neeltje. But his display of tiredness was too convincing.

The wobbly little table suddenly tipped and threatened to overturn. The cups and saucers all slid toward Fransje, which scared him so he tried to stop them with both hands. In so doing, he momentarily forgot about the teapot in his hand and slammed it against the edge of the table. The lid flew off and the handle slipped from his fingers. He tried to break its fall with his knee, but he only gave it extra momentum, knocking it to the floor with a loud crash.

With a piercing scream, Neeltje jumped up and shouted, "Eeee! And it's all your fault!"

The other girls stood up from the big table and shrieked at Fransje, while Neeltje stood there wailing at the top of her voice.

Fransje stared blankly at the pieces on the floor, his cheeks blood-red, and his heart pounding in his throat.

"You clumsy oaf!" Neeltje's mother bellowed hoarsely.

"You stupid, black-haired monkey!" added one of the girls, tugging viciously at his hair to underline her point.

Tears of misery, regret, and impotent rage burned in his eyes. For a moment he saw the image of Mother before his eyes and an inexpressible longing for home overwhelmed him. But he refused to cry—not here and not now. He bit his lower lip until it almost bled and stood as motionless as if nailed to the spot, staring.

"Get on home to your old lady! And you tell her to get Neeltje a new teapot, you hear! Beat it! Go run to your ugly old lady!" he heard several female voices screeching overtop one another.

That hurt Fransje most of all: that they should call his mother an ugly old lady; it pained him much more than the false accusation that he had broken the pretty little teapot deliberately. Something seemed to snap inside him. He was possessed by a single thought: to get home to Mommy, away from this den of misery and oppression. He snatched his cap and coat from the doorknob and ran from the room without saying a word or looking back, followed by a tirade from the female furies.

They told him he might never come back again. Unless he brought a new teapot with him. But that was impossible. Where would he get a new teapot? He couldn't ask Mother, for then she would learn what had happened, and she would be terribly angry with him. No, he couldn't do that. He couldn't tell her. That mean little . . . ! Confused, his thoughts tumbled over one another in his throbbing brain.

Outside he pulled on his coat as well as he could. He had less trouble with his cap. When he passed Neeltje's front window, he darted a quick glance inside. Just then the curtain was flung to one side, and the angry face of Neeltje's mother appeared at the window. To his horror, Fransje saw that she had a bread knife in her hand, and she made a threatening gesture toward him. He was seized by the mortal fear that suddenly the front door would burst open and she would come running after him. He didn't see the girls standing behind the other curtain laughing at his horror-stricken face. Though he couldn't run because of the snow, he hurried home as if death itself were on his heels.

A quiet, much abashed Fransje came home to Mother. She was finished with her sewing. The machine had been put back in its place on the cabinet to the left of the chimney. Maria was ironing.

"Did you have fun playing with Neeltje?" his sister asked kindly, to show her interest.

"Neeltje is a mean bully, and I'm never going to play with her again!"

Maria didn't inquire further. She ascribed his irritated answer to the bad mood he had been in since morning.

Mother was trying to get her afternoon housework done. Fransje would have given anything to be able to sit with her a little while, his head safely against her *doek* and *beuk*, and to pour out his soul to her. But he couldn't. For then he would also have to tell her about the broken teapot and that he was supposed to replace it. That was out. But what if Neeltje's mother came complaining to Mother? Fransje sighed. His innards were beginning to churn worse and worse.

The other kids came home from school. But Fransje didn't feel like going sledding. He sat quietly on a footstove in front of the glowing stove. Darkness began to settle in the living room. He peered through the oval poker-slot up into the fiery glow of the coals, and he couldn't help thinking about what Mother had said about hell: a huge pit filled with fire! Despite the glow from the nearby stove, a chill went down his back. How awful that must be, to be tossed into a pit full of fire! Mother had said that bad people and bad kids end up there. And he had been bad today. He had kicked the sled and teased the cat and broken Neeltje's pretty teapot. And he had never been to church. Fransje felt that surely he was on his way to hell. He wished the lamp were lit and that the other kids would come into the house.

Mother finished her work and came to sit and relax in the semi-darkness.

"Mommy, are you going to light the lamp?" he asked.

"Don't be silly," said Mother. "Come and sit on my lap for a little bit."

Fransje did, but without finding the comfort he had imagined and which he needed so badly. The awful image of that waiting hell would not leave him. He thought back to this morning and the man sleeping at the foot of the ladder crowded with angels. That man had also been bad. So he had to go to hell too. But then what were the angels doing there? They came only to carry people to heaven, didn't they? Mother wasn't busy anymore, so maybe she could tell him more. And Maria was away, in the back room.

"Mommy, what did that man do who ran away from home and was sleeping outside?"

Mother had to stop and think a moment what he was talking about. Then she remembered. "Oh, he stole something and lied to his father."

"What did he steal? And what did he tell his father?"

"The man was called Jacob, and he had a brother called Esau. His father promised something to Esau and Jacob wanted it. Then he secretly went to his father and said, 'I'm Esau. Can I have it now?' And then his father gave it to him because the old man thought he was Esau. He was so very old and his eyes were so poor, he couldn't see very well anymore. But a little later Esau came home, and when he found out what had happened, he got terribly angry. He got so angry he wanted to kill Jacob. So Jacob ran for his life, and he ran very, very far away from home because he was so afraid. But when he had gone a long way, it started getting dark. And he was awful tired. So he went to sleep, outside on the ground with his head on a rock. And then he dreamed of the ladder with all the angels."

"And then did he have to go to hell?" asked Fransje, keenly interested.

"No. Oh, no! For the Lord loved Jacob very much."

"But I thought he was a bad man? He was bad, wasn't he?"

"Yes, that's right. But the Lord is very kind. And Jacob was sorry for what he did. And he told the Lord. Then the Lord wasn't angry at Jacob anymore, so when he died the Lord let him come into heaven with Him."

Feeling she had to add an application, Mother continued: "All people are bad sometimes, and all children, too. Very bad sometimes. That makes the Lord angry, but He also loves people very much. He says to Himself, 'They should really all go to hell, but I'd like them all to come to heaven with me. But then they must first be sorry for the bad that they do.' He wants them to say, 'Lord, I'm so sorry. Please forgive me, and please help me not to do it again.' And if you really mean it, and if you don't do it anymore, then the Lord is happy, and He'll forget all about it. But then you really have to mean it and not just say that you do. Then the Lord loves you, and then later He'll let you come to heaven with Him. Every day you must ask the Lord to help you love Him very, very much and to help you be His child."

Fransje heaved a deep sigh, a sigh of infinite relief. He felt as if strangling fingers had released their murderous grip on his heart. He didn't fully understand everything Mother told him, to be sure, and such a jumble of questions bubbled up in his mind, that he could not single one out and put it into words. So he didn't ask any. But one thing was clear to him: God punishes people, but not as they deserve. For His own reasons, He restores the broken relationship. And apparently He longs for our pitiful love, even for the love of a sinful man, more than we long for His eternal love. God is merciful and gracious.

Though Fransje could not put this into words, or even grasp it all in his mind, still he sensed it in fluid, unformed intuitions. God loves, and He wants to be loved.

Fransje thought he loved the Lord, although he also feared Him. Involuntarily he compared Him with Father. He would very much like to love the Lord, but he had never met Him. But apparently you couldn't ignore Him. He made you, so He had the say-so over you, and sooner or later you'd have to come to terms with Him. Then you had to be ready to meet Him; your life had to be in order. And this couldn't be done head-over-heels at the last minute; no, you had to work at it every day, bit by bit.

Something like this went through Fransje's mind as, held safe against Mother's breast, he stared at the gray square of the window. No, not in words, and not even in clear thoughts. He didn't yet think in thoughts, but rather in visions that gave form to his feelings, hazy and indistinct forms, like *fata morganas* that kept changing shape until each image became a well-defined spiritual reality which would always remain part of him. This we call, in one word, *faith*, the exemplary faith of a child.

At his own insistence Fransje went straight to bed after supper. He had his own special reason which he told no one. Maria climbed upstairs with him to carry the lamp. She would leave it there until the other boys came to bed, and then Father would come and get it to put in the living room when the big lamp was turned off.

Patiently he allowed himself to be tucked in by Maria. Seeing what a small piece of humanity he still was, and mindful of the rough day he had had, she gave him an extra tender kiss. But as she went down the ladder, his head lifted to listen for the sound of the hall door closing.

Then he carefully slid out of his warm burrow and climbed out of bed. He knelt beside the chair, folded his hands and prayed. Although he had said his usual bedtime prayer downstairs with Mother, he hadn't done what she had told him before supper. He prayed out loud, of course; otherwise the Lord and Fransje couldn't hear it. Yet he didn't pray too loudly, lest it be heard downstairs.

Without hesitating, he said, "Dear Lord, I was bad today. I kicked the sled and teased the cat and busted Neeltje's tea set. And I'm very sorry, because it was such a pretty little teapot. But I couldn't help it. I won't do it again, because I'm not going over there ever again. Those stu . . . those girls were so mad at me. Dear Lord, please love me, will You, so that later I can come to be with You in heaven. I love You lots and lots. Amen. The end."

Shivering, Fransje stood up, and in a flash he was back under the blankets, pulling them snugly up around his neck and shoulders. Downstairs the hall door opened and someone rattled a pail against the tap. Mother's voice called softly from the foot of the ladder, "Fransje, are you sleeping? Are you nice and warm?"

"Yes," he called back. He turned on his side and heaved a deep sigh. And then Fransje was asleep.

3

The snow miracle didn't last long, and it was followed by two days of drizzling rain, which finally changed into a thick mist. The snow on the road turned into brown slush and the tall elms on both sides wept disconsolately at their nakedness. Suddenly, the farmlands, only recently a unified beauty, were empty and uninviting. A few strips of dirty snow in the furrows remained as reminders of the transience of all glory.

Although Fransje's first experience with snow had left him with mixed feelings, its short-livedness grieved him deeply, and the gloomy weather weighed heavily on him. He spent much time kneeling on the bench in front of the window, staring outside; and he took it very ill of the rain for having washed away all that beautiful snow. Of course, now he had to stay indoors all the time, and although he didn't feel the slightest urge to visit Neeltje, his limitations bored him terribly. The cat carefully stayed out of Fransje's reach.

Suddenly the weather changed and the sun appeared. It was so mild that Fransje could play outside without wearing Mother's shawl. Neeltje and the other neighbor girls were out too, and soon the children were caught up in all kinds of adventures. Nothing was said of Neeltje's tea set, but Fransje anxiously kept away from Neeltje's house.

One day Neeltje flew outside with tremendous news: soon they would be getting a Christmas tree! Fransje didn't even know what a Christmas tree was, but Neeltje gave him a detailed description, although she couldn't remember seeing one either. She told him it was a big tree that you set on the table in front of the window, and you put candles and lots of colored things made of glass in it. Fransje looked at the big elms and said, "That's impossible—a big tree in the living room! It would go right through the ceiling and the roof."

"Oh, dummy, not a tree like that. A Christmas tree! A Christmas tree is lots smaller and it's all green," Neeltje informed him.

"Then it isn't a big tree, it's a small one," objected Fransje. But in his mind he had already pictured such a small miracle tree, and he was jealous that Neeltje was to be so favored. So captivated was he by this new concept, Christmas tree, that he couldn't restrain his curiosity and, feigning indifference, he pumped Neeltje for more details. He wanted to know how the tree could stand on the table by itself without being planted in the ground, and how the candles would be fastened to it. Neeltje, who undoubtedly had a clearer image of the tree from conversations at home, acted as if she knew everything. But to many questions she had to give a rather unsatisfactory answer. At last she said, "Just wait till we get it. Then you'll see for yourself."

After school Fransje was allowed to go with Arjaan to the bakery for bread. Before they went into the store, they looked in the window, Arjaan lifting Fransje because he couldn't see over the windowsill. There, among many other things, Fransje saw half-opened boxes of little candles in all the colors of the rainbow. Immediately his heart began to throb intemperately. Although he had never seen them before, he knew they were Christmas tree candles because on each box was a green tree decorated with straight, colored little sticks topped by tiny flames. The little sticks had to be candles, and that had to be a Christmas tree like the one Neeltje was making such a fuss about. They lay there so enticingly, tiny pillars with a velvety sheen. Knowing that they were inaccessible to him gave him a stab in the heart; he only longed for them more earnestly. When he asked Arjaan whether *he* had ever seen a Christmas tree, Arjaan told him that in town he had already seen some in the windows of a few homes.

"Will you take me so I can see them too?" Fransje asked hopefully.

Arjaan told him that first they'd have to ask Mother. Quickly they finished their errand and brought the bread home. Mother gave Arjaan and Fransje permission "to go for a little walk," as Arjaan worded his request. "But be home in an hour," warned Mother.

Arjaan would have to hurry, for it was almost a half hour's walk to town. Lifting Fransje to his shoulders, he told him they were going to play horsey. That made the time go faster. On the way, they stopped in front of the only house between theirs and the village, the home of retired Kees de Visser. Around it lay a large yard with many beautiful trees and shrubs. On one side of the house a stately row of tall fir trees stretched from the front to the back yard. Their green brightened the wintry barrenness surrounding them. Fransje recognized them as relatives of the Christmas trees on the candle boxes in the bakery window.

"Are those Christmas trees, Arjaan?" his voice piped above Arjaan's head.

"Yes, kind of. But they're way too big. You could make one from the top of one of them, though," he added.

Arjaan's shoulders were beginning to ache, and he was almost out of breath from walking so fast. So he made Fransje walk on his own for a while. Finally they reached the first houses of the village. Fransje looked at every window searching for one of those miracle trees. Arjaan, however, strode on without slowing down. Knowing where they could see one, he headed straight for his goal. Again and again he had to admonish Fransje to hurry up. It was only a little farther. At last they came to a house with a tree in the window. The drapes were tied back a little allowing them to see most of it. On its peak was a shiny colored ball with a sharp spike on top. Hanging on the ends of the branches, glistening dimly, were silver balls. And everywhere colored candles had been interspersed among the dark greenery.

Fransje stared, wide-eyed. The candles were not lit, but he could easily imagine what a splendid sight the tree would be then. He pushed his head between the iron bars of the fence trying to get a better look. Too bad there was a large yard in front of the house so he couldn't stand right in front of the window. Fransje still couldn't see how the tree was able to stand on the table without falling over.

"Come on," said Arjaan, "we have to go home. If we go back along that street, we'll see another one."

Fransje could hardly leave; but Arjaan dragged him along.

They had been away from home at least a half hour and they had to be back in time for supper.

A new wonder awaited Fransje at the other house, a very large one where Arjaan said the doctor lived. This house was even farther from the street than the first, but the candles in this Christmas tree were lit! And in the gathering dusk, the flickering lights in the branches were beautiful. How Fransje would have loved to see it from very close! Arjaan literally had to drag him away, and although he was very tired he offered to play horsey again. But from his high perch Fransje kept looking back to that festive window. Oh, how he wished his house, too, had a tree of such magical beauty.

The fir trees in Kees de Visser's yard had become dark specters which threw fear into Fransje's heart. Against the pale evening sky the tops were dark silhouettes. Now they were just big enough for Christmas trees, thought Fransje. Oh, if only he had one of those tops!

Fortunately they got home just in time. Fransje was bubbling over about the Christmas trees he had seen and gave an excited account of their tour. Mother threw a disturbed look at Arjaan, saying, "You mean you went all the way into town with the child?" But Arjaan told her he had carried Fransje on his back most of the way.

Fransje's enthusiasm for the Christmas trees aroused little response, which confirmed his suspicions that they would see no Christmas tree in their living room. So he didn't ask for one either, especially since Father simply ignored his story. But, oh, how he wished they had one—even if it were only a small one!

The mild weather held, and whenever Fransje came outside in the morning and saw Neeltje, the first question he asked was if they had their Christmas tree yet. And every time Neeltje had to admit that it still hadn't arrived. Fransje took a nasty delight in this, and he jumped at the chance to show off his superior knowledge of Christmas trees. He now considered himself the authority on the subject because Neeltje hadn't even seen one thus far. But she finally managed to puncture his inflated ego by remarking that pretty soon she'd have one of her own, and—ha! ha!—Fransje wouldn't. Then he could do nothing more than acknowledge defeat.

But that evening Kees came home with three candle stubs and two metal holders to fasten them to the branches, undoubtedly the product of some transaction with a classmate. Fransje's heart blazed up when Kees spread his treasures on the table.

"Please light one!" begged Fransje. But since matches were forbidden objects in the home, at least for the children, he immediately turned to Mother to plead, "Mommy, Kees has some candles. May he light one of them, Mommy? Just one?"

"Okay, but just for a little while and then blow it out again." Speaking to Kees in particular, she warned, "And remember, don't let me catch you playing with matches!"

Fransje almost singed his nose on the flickering flame. Contentedly he sniffed the fetid, waxy smell, and in his imagination he saw a whole tree full of such flames dancing and glowing softly on the bench in front of the window.

Much too soon Mother said, "That's enough," and told Kees to blow out the candle. With her eyes she ordered him to the mantel to put the matches back in their place. Fransje wheedled one of the candles from Kees just to hold. With his finger he traced the spirals from the top down and then back again. He couldn't get enough of it.

"Mommy, at Neeltje's they're going to get a Christmas tree. Why don't we buy one too?"

"Oh, they cost far too much. We don't have enough money for such things." She felt this the best answer in order to be done with it as quickly as possible without going into a theological explanation that he wouldn't understand anyway. In any case, what she said was part of the truth.

Fransje was deeply saddened by their poverty. But when Kees prepared to go out, Fransje followed close on his heels. He asked if he could have one of the candles and also one of the holders. Kees wasn't at all ready to part with any of his treasures, and in view of what they had cost him, he considered his refusal wholly justified. But Fransje wasn't routed so easily. Although an entire Christmas tree was perhaps beyond his reach, three candles had come into the house, and one way or another these at least had to be within his reach. Grabbing Kees by the sleeve, he followed him to the road like a little puppy, continually whining for one of the candles—just one, the smallest one in Kees's pocket.

Kees had planned to see a friend who lived near the railroad station. He now realized that he'd have to make a choice. If he wanted to get rid of Fransje and keep him from screaming bloody murder, he'd have to make a propitiatory offering. If he didn't he'd be stuck with Fransje, and he wouldn't be able to join in the wild games of his comrades. He proposed to play horsey with Fransje tonight, or to draw him a pretty picture on his slate, or to read to him from the Bible storybook, but to no avail. To Fransje at the moment there was nothing else in the whole world that could compete with owning one of those candles. He stubbornly kept repeating his plea as if he hadn't even heard Kees's other proposals.

Kees heaved a sigh. If he wanted to play for awhile, he'd have to get going. Father and the older boys would be home in another hour. He dug the smallest candle and a holder out of his pocket and handed them to his little brother. "Here, you little pest!" he snapped, and raced off.

Fransje didn't like being called names, but his joy more than made up for his hurt feelings. Proud and happy, he ran back into the living room to show his treasures to Mother. But she wasn't nearly as delighted as he wished, and she adjured him, "Remember, don't let me catch you playing with matches!"

All alone on the road leading to town trudged a spunky little boy. It was Fransje. He kept looking back to see whether he could spot Mother in front of the house, which was dropping farther and farther behind him.

Fransje had a plan which he was in the process of carrying out. When the plan had taken final shape was hard to say. To him it seemed as if it had always been in his mind and that he had lost a lot of valuable time by not acting on it sooner. Where he got the courage he had no idea either. Something inside him was spurring him on toward his goal.

Fransje was on his way to Kees de Visser's house to ask him for a piece of one of his fir trees. His high hopes never wavered until he set foot on the cement bridge between the two iron gates that formed the entrance to the retired man's home.

But to spur his feet onwards—if a bit less boldly than before—Fransje had only to remember the burning desire that had driven him here. Hesitantly stepping up to the back door, he called weakly, "Anybody home?"

With a pounding heart he looked up at the gleaming, big green door, hoping it would be opened quickly. But the door, which was too thick for his small timid voice to penetrate, remained shut. After a few moments, however, the door did open, revealing a man who was apparently on his way out.

"Hello there, my little friend," the man said in a jovial voice. "What's your name?"

"Fransje," he answered bashfully.

"And whose little boy are you?" the man asked further. The wrinkles of laughter around his friendly eyes gave Fransje renewed courage.

"I'm Fransje Weststrate and can I please have a piece of your Christmas tree?"

De Visser looked at him in surprise, wondering what the little fellow meant.

"We don't have a Christmas tree, Fransje. And what would you do with it?"

"You do too have a Christmas tree—lots of them, out in the yard. Just look!" And Fransje swept his arm in the direction of the fir trees. He added, "I have a candle and a little thing to put it on the tree. If I had a piece of your tree, then I'd have a Christmas tree, just like Neeltje."

Kees de Visser asked no more questions. He chuckled conspiratorially and thrust his stocking feet into a pair of wooden shoes standing beside the clean stoop. "Follow me," he said.

Fransje followed him into the yard like a puppy. When they reached the trees, he expected the man to climb one of the stately firs and cut off the top for him. But he did nothing of the kind. De Visser just lifted one of the branches hanging down on the ground and broke off one of its small side-branches. He held it out to Fransje, saying, "There you are, Fransje. You should be able to make a pretty Christmas tree from that."

But Fransje was so terribly disappointed that he didn't even accept the branch and stammered, "But I meant a piece from the top of the tree, just like a real Christmas tree."

Laughing to himself, the man said out loud, "I can't do that, Fransje. The whole tree would be ruined. Then it would look as though the tree had lost his cap, and the top would never grow back. Wouldn't that look ugly? And you wouldn't want an ugly tree like that in your yard either, would you?"

Fransje didn't know what to reply to that, and a flat, green branch was better than nothing. He finally accepted the branch. "Thank you, Kees de Visser," he said politely. Maybe he could set the crooked, flat branch up straight somehow and fasten his candle to it.

Together they walked back toward the house. Fransje immediately started toward the little bridge, but Kees de Visser said, "Would you like to come with me, Fransje? I have something else for you. Come along with me into the house."

In the back room Fransje saw three women—an older one, who must have been the lady of the house, and two younger ones. He was surprised to see that they were all wearing their big lace hats, even though it wasn't Sunday. Rich women must wear them every day, he thought, for he had already concluded that they must be rich. Otherwise they wouldn't be able to have so many big Christmas trees standing around in the yard. And such a huge house! His eyes traveled around the spacious room, taking in the large paintings on the wall and the lovely vases and pottery on the mantel. And one of those beautiful lights with long, sparkling pieces of glass dangling down all over it. Wouldn't they look beautiful on a Christmas tree!

The women were very friendly to Fransje. De Visser told them the reason for Fransje's visit, and they asked him about the Christmas tree he was planning to make. They smiled as he tried to explain his simple plans, but they didn't criticize them.

One of the young women asked him if he would like some chocolate milk, and when he nodded bashfully, she went out to fix him a cup. The other said, "I'll bet you like apples? Right?" She immediately left the room and returned with three large gold rennets.

Fransje was obviously enjoying himself. The peaceful air in the house set him at ease at once. He felt at home, as if he had known these people all his life. Since they didn't quiz him, he didn't have the slightest feeling that he had to be on his guard. All four had his undivided love and trust. But when he had finished his chocolate milk, he suddenly remembered that Mother didn't know where he was. She might be out looking for him. He lowered himself down from his chair and said that he had to go home. One of the girls tucked the apples under his shirt and said, "Boy-oh-boy, do you ever have a fat tummy now!" Then they all shook hands with him and told him to come back again soon. Fransje walked out to the little bridge at a dignified pace. But as soon as he was on the road, he broke into a trot to make up for lost time if possible.

"Mommy, is Father home yet?" was his first question when he saw Mother.

"No, my boy, not for a couple of hours." Then her eyes fell on the fir branch, and she asked in wonder, "Where did you get that, and what are you going to do with it?"

"I'm going to make a Christmas tree with it, and I got it from Kees de Visser."

"From Kees de Visser?" Mother asked, astonished. "You mean you went way over there, and all by yourself? I thought you were playing at Neeltje's house." There was a note of concern in her voice, but Fransje also detected a hint of anger, and as if to exculpate himself he added, "And they let me into the house, and I had a cup of chocolate and three big apples. See, they're under my shirt. And it's real pretty inside and they asked me to come again sometime."

Mother's eyes didn't soften very much and she said in warning, "But you mayn't just go off by yourself like that. What if a wicked man had come along and carried you off? What then? Then we wouldn't have had a Fransje anymore."

"You mean I mayn't go there ever again?" he cried in dismay. "And they were so nice to me!"

Mother knew the people and she knew that they were very friendly. They all belonged to the same church. Deep down she was also somewhat flattered by their interest in her child. Besides, she was willing to overlook this rebellion on his part, and in a more friendly tone, she said, "Yes, you may go there again sometime, but first you must ask me."

Fransje eagerly promised to do so. And that was the end of the conversation. Mother once again bent over her washboard, and Fransje dragged the branch into the living room. He unloaded the apples bulging his shirt and found his little candle and its holder.

He had some trouble fastening it to one of the branch's twigs; the long needles were so slippery, and they kept pricking his hands. But at last he succeeded and he proudly held up the branch. He wanted to admire the effect at his leisure, however, and preferably from some distance. Once more he confronted the puzzle of how a Christmas tree stood by itself without falling down, and he thought it over very deeply for a moment. It brought wrinkles to his forehead. Suddenly he had an idea. He dived under the table and grabbed the footstove. He would poke the end of the branch into the middle hole.

But the stem was too big, so he had to stop and think again. Now he knew what to do. The branch was far too long anyway; he would break a piece off it. The tough wood didn't cooperate, but by exerting all his strength he finally succeeded. His face was flushed with the effort and his hands were sticky and itchy from the resin and the sharp needles. Now the frayed end slipped through the hole.

A new letdown: his tree still wouldn't stand up. However, Fransje seemed to have an advisor within him. He fumbled about in his junk box for a moment and carried an armload of toys to the footstove. First he folded his rag doll around it as the footstove and then he jammed as many other toys around it as the footstove would hold. Mother's gray hanky, which was always tucked under the pillow in Father's easy chair, covered the opening and kept everything in place. At last Fransje could step back to enjoy what he had been looking forward to all this time.

It was but a poor embodiment of the idea, Christmas tree, but Fransje's imagination made up for all its shortcomings. In his mind he could already see his miracle tree aglitter with burning candles; he could already smell that special scent. Involuntarily his eyes turned to the mantel, where he knew the matches were.

Fransje's spiritual concepts were still very misty. He barely knew there was such a thing as a devil, much less that one could escape his seductive voice by commanding: Get behind me, Satan! So Fransje fell under the spell of his own alluring visions. True, his conscience did protest loudly and emphatically, but its voice wasn't nearly as attractive as that other, seductive voice.

Fransje looked up at the mantel again. He could just see the corner of the little box. Then he looked at the door to the kitchen. It was closed, and Fransje conjured up a feeling of security in his throbbing heart. He heard the muffled, rhythmic sound of Mother's hands scrubbing across the washboard, and that too helped put him at ease.

Fransje was already lost. Cautiously he pushed a chair to the mantel, and then to the table. He put his Christmas tree on the table. "Just for a little while," he whispered hurriedly. The sound of the rattling matches was overpowering. The next moment he was holding a burning match between his trembling thumb and forefinger. "Hurry, hurry!" satan urged. Nervously Fransje put the flame to the candle stub. He heard a soft crackle and sputter and then the candle began to burn. The flame was tiny, for apparently the wick had broken off in Fransje's pocket. Then two big tears of wax ran down the candle, and suddenly the flame flared up like a hungry, fiery little tongue. Standing on his chair, Fransje watched in fascination.

Again there was crackling and sputtering, as suddenly a coiling white flame shot up along the green needles. For a second it seemed to die, but then the dreadful tongue flared up with renewed fury. The needles, although green, were old, because the branch had come from the very bottom of the tree. Filthy smoke billowed to the ceiling and particles of burnt fir needles fell on the footstove and the tablecloth.

Fransje was no longer master of the situation. His eyes, huge with fear, nearly bulged from his head. Then he covered his face with both hands, wanting to banish the horrible scene from his life. Overcome by a strong feeling of nausea, he uttered a hoarse cry. Losing his balance, he tipped and crashed to the floor, chair and all.

The door burst open and Mother was standing over him. But Fransje was no longer in any condition to follow the swift course of events. He felt suspended in a vacuum—until a hail of blows descended on him. There was no end to them; Mother was using her slipper, not caring where it landed. His entire body was her target. He felt as if he were being stabbed all over with knives.

Fransje didn't cry—he bellowed. But at last his throat was so swollen the sound could no longer get through. Then Fransje felt himself being lifted up and thumped down in Father's easy chair. He took a quick glance at Mother's face. She, too, had uttered sounds, but Fransje hadn't understood a word. Mother looked terrible. Long strands of hair had fallen from beneath her cap and hung in front of her pale, mottled face.

Then Fransje saw that Mother, too, had been crying, and it broke his heart. Between Mother and himself there yawned a deep chasm which could never again be bridged. And suddenly hatred surged up inside him, blind, searing hatred. He couldn't know that his hatred was irrational, that his tattered emotions were casting about for something by which to pull themselves together. That something became a hatred of the idea, Christmas tree. He cast a quick look at the table. Nothing could be seen but some dirty stripes and smudges. The footstove lay in the middle of the floor, its contents spread all over. But the fire and the hungry tongues of flame were gone. His terror-ravaged heart sobbed with relief.

Mother gave him one last look. Then without saying another word, she walked out to the back room. Fransje was alone again. But then a new fear overcame him. Father would be home soon, and Mother would tell him everything. Another wave of nausea passed over him, and suddenly he was sick. A surge of brown slime gushed over his shirt and onto the floor. He almost choked. When he lifted his head, Mother was standing before him once more. She looked just as pale as Fransje. She carried him into the back room, where she undressed and washed him. Again she gathered him up and climbed the ladder to the attic. Upstairs she put him in his little bed and carefully tucked him in. She stopped and stared at his deathlike face and put a hand on his forehead.

Fransje heaved a terribly deep sigh, broken into pieces by a series of soundless sobs. Mother's hand was like cooling rain that extinguished all those hot flames of hatred, and at once he lapsed into a deep sleep.

A few days later Fransje's disillusioning experience with Christmas trees had faded into a memory he would have liked to forget as quickly as possible. Fortunately no one at home talked about it. He didn't know he owed this to Mother. But he wasn't the only one who had learned a lesson. Not that Mother regretted having punished him so, for it had been necessary. And she was sure that she hadn't hit him too hard and that her blows hadn't caused his vomiting. But she realized that the lesson had been too overpowering for his frail selfhood. So she had kept the whole affair to herself and had managed to clean up all traces of it before Father or the others got home. She was able to truthfully explain his absence from the supper table by saying that he wasn't feeling well and had vomited.

Fransje no longer hated the idea, Christmas tree, as he had at first. For that had issued from his unconscious need to blame someone or something for all the misery into which he had been so suddenly plunged. Yet the mention of a Christmas tree was enough to recall all the horror, so he anxiously avoided it. However, others would remind him of it. A few days before Christmas Neeltje excitedly came to tell him that their Christmas tree had arrived. "It came last night. Come and see! Mother said it was all right if you came into the house."

However, Fransje didn't react at all as Neeltje had hoped and expected. He said, "I don't care about Christmas trees no more. And I bet your mother and sisters want to beat me up for busting your teapot."

"Oh, you silly, they aren't mad at you anymore. I got a new one a long time ago already."

Fransje looked at her suspiciously. He had the feeling that a trap was being laid for him, and he had no intention of walking into it. But then Neeltje began to describe the beauties of the Christmas tree in vivid detail, and against his will Fransje again fell under the old spell. Reluctantly he followed Neeltje to the front window of her house. There he broke loose from her grip, for she had been literally dragging him along.

When he saw the colored glass balls gleaming through the lace flowers of the curtain, his heart again began to throb intemperately. Conflicting emotions fought for supremacy. Why did people want to have such a dangerous thing, one that could so easily catch fire, in the house? And why didn't they all catch fire? He partially expressed his questions by asking Neeltje, "Did you light the candles already?"

"Sure! Last night we had them on for a little while."

Fransje looked at her questioningly, wanting to ask her whether the branches hadn't begun to burn just a little. But Neeltje's front door opened and her mother appeared. Involuntarily Fransje glanced at her hands to see if she was holding a breadknife. His body was already tensed for flight. But the woman disarmed him by saying in a friendly voice, "Ah, here's Fransje! Did you come to see our Christmas tree? Well, come on in, then you can see better."

He eyed her suspiciously, for he still didn't entirely trust her. But then the woman added, "Come on and I'll give you some rock candy. I'm just making some now."

Neeltje helped him over his hesitation by once again taking him by the arm; dragging his feet, he followed her across the front yard into the house. As the woman shut the door behind them, he realized that if they were planning to do him harm, he was like a bird in a trap. He had no choice but to surrender himself to their mercy.

Inhaling the peculiar smell of the house, brought the tea set episode before his eyes. Furtively he looked around to see if the girls were home too. One of them was on her knees sweeping the floor, and the other was just coming in carrying a bowl of potatoes.

"Ah, Fransje Weststrate!" they cried loudly. "Have you come to see our Christmas tree? That's nice!"

Fransje began to feel a little more at ease. Apparently there were no evil plots afoot. Neeltje led him to the table, and there Fransje could at last examine a real Christmas tree closely. At last he discovered how it could stand up all by itself. This tree stood in a large, green flower pot filled to the top with tightly tamped clay soil. But all those candles! They were standing perfectly upright on the ends of the longest branches so that they didn't touch the branches above. The needles on this tree were much shorter than those on the branch he had gotten from Kees de Visser. What a handsome, perfect little tree it was!

He saw his face, hugely distorted, reflected in the colored balls. And he admired the decorative streamers made of silken hair. At the very top perched an angel with wings and everything. Neeltje unnecessarily pointed out all kinds of details. He saw them all and drank in their dangerous beauty without saying a word. At last Neeltje could bear it no longer and she cried triumphantly, "Well, what do you think of it?"

"Bootiful!" Fransje replied in a word that came from the heart.

"Do you have a pretty Christmas tree like that?" one of the girls asked superfluously.

Fransje shook his head.

"What did you think?" gloated the other. "They're much too righteous for that! They're so stinking righteous they almost got halos. They're thricers, you know!" This was an allusion to the church Fransje's parents attended, which had three services on Sunday.

The three women guffawed at the wisecrack, but even more at the puzzled look on Fransje's face, for he could not understand it, much less appreciate it. His uneasiness returned and he proposed to Neeltje, "Let's go play outside again."

"Oh, but you must have a piece of rock candy first!" cried Neeltje's mother, carrying the pan to the table. She poured the gooey, brown mass which had been cooling onto the oilcloth and pinched off two gobs, which she rolled into balls between her dirty hands and gave to the children. Not until the back door slammed safely shut behind them was Fransje able to yield to the sweet pleasure of the warm lump.

His desire to play, however, had vanished. He suspected that Neeltje would keep carrying on, gloating about her Christmas tree, and he was in no mood for that. So he fibbed: "I'm going home. I have to pee." He really didn't have to, but he resolved to try in order to avoid lying. When he succeeded, his conscience was eased.

Mother was sitting at the table drinking coffee. After Fransje had shed his coat and cap, he went and stood quietly beside her. The relationship between them was still somewhat strained, and he didn't quite know how to start the conversation. After some hesitation, he asked, "Mommy, why do people have Christmas trees?"

Mother looked at him searchingly, surprised that he had come back to that subject. She answered evasively, "Because they think they're beautiful."

"Yes, but why do they *have* Christmas trees?" he repeated with more emphasis. Understanding then what he was after, Mother explained, "Because it will be Christmas the day after tomorrow. It's a little bit like Sunday, because everyone goes to church and then they remember that a long time ago the Lord Jesus was born. The Lord Jesus is the Son of God. And He became a little baby just like you were. And on Christmas we celebrate His birthday."

"How old is He on His next birthday?"

Mother saw that she hadn't explained clearly and continued, "The Lord Jesus didn't get very old. When He grew up, some bad men killed Him and He was buried. But three days later He came to life again. And a little while after that He went back to His Father in heaven."

"Where was His mother?"

Mother sighed, knowing that this could go on forever. And she realized that she couldn't make the gospel story intelligible to a child of less than four. Still, she could not just put him off. As well as she could she explained the purpose of Christ's coming. By way of application, she added, "You must love Jesus very much, because He also loved little children very much. When He was still on earth, He took some little children on His knee—that's how much He loved them. And He still does. And if you ask Him to make you His child, and you really mean it with all your heart, then He will. He'll take you for His very own. If the Lord Jesus hadn't come into the world, no one could go to heaven. He took the punishment for the wicked things we do. That's why God is no longer angry with His children."

Fransje was silent for some time, seeming to digest what he had heard. There was a pensive look on his face, and Mother was amazed to see a strange tenderness in his eyes. But then his mind returned to its starting point, and he asked, "Why do people have Christmas trees on His birthday?"

"Oh, that's their way of celebrating."

"Why don't we celebrate?"

"Oh, but we do. Except we don't need a Christmas tree. If you're His child, you're so happy inside, you don't need a Christmas tree."

"Mommy, are you that happy inside?"

Mother looked at him. Slowly she lowered her cup of coffee to the table. She gently pulled him toward her and took him on her lap. The gap between them vanished, and with moist eyes, she said softly, "Yes, my boy. Sometimes Mommy is very happy inside. And I hope you'll be that happy too—so happy, so very happy . . . . Because then when He lets you into heaven someday, you'll sing with happiness."

Christmas day did indeed bring happiness, although it was not exactly the kind Mother had described. Fransje did not experience the lack of a Christmas tree as a deficiency, nor did it bother him in the least that it wasn't a traditional white Christmas. On the contrary, the weather conspired to bring unexpected delight.

It was so unusually mild for that time of year that it felt like an early spring day. Father took the opportunity to finish spading the little vegetable garden behind the house, something he hadn't had time to do earlier. Bram and Eine helped him. Maria helped Mother do the morning housekeeping chores so that they were finished by coffee time. Arjaan and Kees were off visiting friends, and Wantje was avidly paging through Maria's poetry album.

When Father and the boys came in for a cup of coffee, the warm aura of a holiday filled the house. Heightening it was the delicious smell of meat frying on the stove—something they didn't smell very often. Fransje couldn't decide what to do, but he wasn't bored for a moment. Every once in a while he would join Father and the boys in the back yard, and then run back in the house to see what Mother and Maria were doing. Having them all around him and seeing them in such good spirits made him very happy.

Over coffee they talked about the coming afternoon church service. Usually on Christmas the church to which Fransje's parents belonged held a worship service only in the evening. But because of special circumstances, this year it would be held in the afternoon. Since the church was without a minister, one of the elders usually read a sermon, except for the occasional time when a visiting minister or theological student led the service. And today was one of those special occasions, for a minister from another province would preach. Apparently he was married to a Zeeland native who was visiting her ailing mother. Her husband was using the opportunity to make the rounds of vacant congregations in the area. This morning he was preaching in a neighboring congregation, this afternoon here, and tonight in another village. Two children would also be baptized today because the church hadn't had a minister in its midst for several months.

Most of the conversation outstripped Fransje's understanding or didn't interest him. But when Maria asked who was going to stay home with Fransje, he suddenly piped up, "Mommy, when can I come along to church? Can I come along too this afternoon? Please, Mommy?"

Mother looked at Father to see what he thought. Fransje's lack of Sunday clothes wouldn't matter a great deal today. The weather, too, would pose no problem; and then the whole family could take advantage of this opportunity. Father raised no objections. So Mother gave her consent in the form of a warning: "But then will you be a real good boy and sit still in church and not talk?"

Fransje was ready to promise to meet any and all conditions that might be laid upon him and he skipped back and forth through the house, cheering. He asked all kinds of questions concerning the idea, church, and Wantje willingly took it upon herself to fill him in.

Just as they finished eating and Father was getting ready to pray, Maria said, "There comes Kee of Kapelle around the back." Because she was sitting opposite the window, she had the best view of who went by on the road. All heads turned to the window, and Fransje just glimpsed a white cap above a black shawl disappearing around the corner.

Wantje clapped her hands and cried, "Maybe Kee has a bag of peppermints with her!"

And Father commented, "I half expected Kee would stop in."

The latch on the back door was being lifted, so the closing prayer was postponed until the visitor was inside. A voice cried, "Hello-o!" And Mother replied, "Come on in!"

Kee was a thin woman of middle age and height. She was known as Kee of Kapelle, because Kapelle was where she lived, a village about an hour-and-a-half walk away. She often walked over when there was a pastor, because her own congregation was also vacant and she jumped at every opportunity to hear a real preacher. She was widely known as a pious, God-fearing woman, and Father and Mother liked her very much. After shaking hands with everyone, she sat down on a chair Mother offered her. "Did you eat?" Mother asked solicitously. "Otherwise, pull your chair up to the table. There is plenty left." But Kee had already eaten. Both parties inquired after one another's health, and then Father said, "We were just ready to pray. Would you please pray with us?"

Kee folded her thin, bony hands and began to pray. Her soft voice seemed to rise straight to God's throne. In her prayer she remembered the glorious fact that God gave His own Son to save the wretched children of Adam, worthy only of hell and damnation, to reconcile them with God.

It was very quiet in the house during the prayer. Even Fransje listened attentively to the reverent words, and an echo of the same happiness that he had felt two days earlier reverberated within his soul. He could follow her prayer easily, because Kee spoke the Zeeland dialect even in her prayer, even though he understood very little of the words themselves. He simply sensed the spirit that emanated from this simple soul, without knowing that this was the sweetness of the communion of the saints.

Nor was the prayer too long. A moment of silence followed the amen. Mother quietly blew her nose in her gray hanky.

Maria rose to clear the table, and conversation resumed. After a while, Kee said, "Fransje, come and sit with me a minute." He went to her, and she hoisted him onto her lap. Her right hand slid under her black apron and took something from her pocket. She handed him a little bag, saying, "Here are some peppermints for you for Christmas. But you must share them with Wantje and the other children like a good boy."

Fransje accepted the gift with great joy, and like an adult Wantje instructed him, "What do you say to Kee, Fransje?" Dutifully he said, "Thank you, Kee." But he made no move to get down from her lap. He looked up into her face, vaguely aware that, unlike Mother, she was not very handsome. She had rather irregular features and high cheek bones. The small roll of hair coming onto her forehead from under her cap was coal black, and she wore black beads and a black *doek* and *beuk*. Fransje discovered that she had downy white hairs around her small, wrinkled mouth, and that most of her teeth were missing.

Kee in turn looked down into his upturned face. Their eyes met, and Fransje did not know that his eyes had the same soft radiance that made Kee so well loved. Whenever she spoke, her head shook slightly, and this, too, Fransje accepted unquestioningly as part of this kind woman.

"I'm going to church too," he told her proudly.

"Well, that's wonderful, my boy. Listen closely to the preacher, because he's going to tell you about the Lord Jesus. The Lord likes it when little children come to church and love Him. You be sure and ask Him every day to make you His child."

Though these words had a familiar ring, they seemed more spacious, broader, richer than before. Again Kee looked into his face and said, "The Lord loves children very much. He loves you."

Fransje did not reply, but if he had dared, he would have rested his head against her *doek* and *beuk*. Just as this passed through his mind, Kee put her thin hand against his head and gently pressed it to her flat breast.

On the way to church Fransje walked between Mother and Kee, his hands safely tucked under the woolen shawls of the two women. He took long steps in order to keep up with them. He was wearing Wantje's button shoes and Wantje was again wearing her black wooden shoes. At first he hadn't been very happy about having to wear girl's shoes, but it hadn't spoiled his joy for long, because after all the shoes were his passport to church. Wantje was strolling between Father and Mother, but she wasn't holding Mother's arm. Maria and the boys were either ahead of them somewhere or were trailing behind with their friends. Various groups of churchgoers were scattered along the long road.

As they passed the house of Kees de Visser, he and his wife and two daughters were crossing the little bridge to join the other churchgoers. They gave Fransje's group a friendly nod and Kees jovially called out to him, "Do you still have your Christmas tree, Fransje?"

Fransje blushed deeply and cast a furtive glance at Mother. Fortunately Father was deep in conversation with Kee and he didn't appear to have heard the question. Fransje's happy mood, however, had been dealt a severe jolt, and the fact that De Visser and the three women were walking right behind made him very uncomfortable.

As they walked through the village, he couldn't resist looking at the windows trying to spot any Christmas trees. When he did see one, he looked at it out of the corner of his eyes without turning his head or saying anything about it.

At the church Mother asked Father where Fransje should sit, and Father felt that Fransje had better come along with him. Men and women sat apart in their church. The church was divided by two aisles, the women sitting in the middle and the men sitting on the shorter benches on each side. Mother, Kee, and Wantje disappeared somewhere in the middle of the church among the other women, and Fransje followed Father all the way to the front of the church. In his pew Father stood up for a while with his hat in front of his face, while Fransje, somewhat abashed, sat peering about. A little later the boys joined them, shuffling past Father and Fransje. Bram sat next to the wall. Beside him sat Eine. Then Arjaan. Kees sat between him and Fransje. Now the pew was completely full.

There was a constant shuffle of feet in the aisles, but because they were sitting so far to the front, Fransje couldn't see very much. He glanced over his shoulder, but quickly turned around again at the sight of all the faces behind him that seemed to be staring at him.

At last the church became quiet. A door opened in the unadorned wall in front of Fransje and a row of men walked into church with a dignified stride. One of them drew Fransje's attention because of his unusual build and dress. He was a huge, heavy man with a long black coat and a small white bowtie on his white shirt. He separated from the others, and all alone he stepped toward the towering structure built into the middle of the wall and reaching almost to the ceiling. There he stood for a while with his hands folded and his eyes closed. Then he climbed the steps until he reached the top and partly disappeared into what looked like a big barrel to Fransje.

Although Fransje knew nothing about church offices, he understood that this had to be the minister. His impressive appearance accorded wholly with the reverent tone that Fransje detected whenever a preacher was mentioned. He studied the uplifted face very intently and decided that he did not like the man. He couldn't have said why not, but the minister had immediately fallen on the side of the line where all Fransje's antipathies were located.

The minister opened his mouth and announced a Psalm, which he proceeded to read in a deep plaintive voice. Then a deafening noise broke out behind and around Fransje as the congregation, led by the *voorzinger*, began to sing. Kees and the boys on the other side sang along in loud voices, and Father's gruff voice also reached Fransje's ears. Now the preacher read a chapter from the Bible and then led the congregation in a long, wailing prayer. Fransje made no effort to follow the words, because the tone was tiresome and many of the words unfamiliar and thus meaningless to him. His interest began to flag, and suddenly he felt that he had been in this church before.

Before the preacher began his sermon, the babies were to be baptized. Fransje found this out when they were carried in through the same door by which the minister had entered the church. His interest rekindled, and he followed the subsequent events with wonderment.

First the preacher read a long piece out of a black book. Something seemed to be amiss, for the preacher asked the mother and father of one of the children to stand up, and he gave them a long, impassioned talking-to. Fransje didn't know what it was about, but he sensed anger in the preacher's voice, and the bowed heads of the two young parents confirmed his suspicion.

Now the other two parents had to stand up too and answer some questions posed by the preacher. Then he descended from his high throne and sprinkled water on the heads of the little children who were held by their mothers. One of the babies broke out into a plaintive cry. Fransje could see why. He wouldn't like it either if someone poured cold water into his eyes. Again the people sang, and the babies were carried out of church. The preacher once more ascended the pulpit and again led the congregation in prayer.

For quite a while Fransje heard nothing at all of the sermon, until all at once he caught the phrase "Christmas tree." The pastor was preaching on the words of Isaiah 11:1, "And there shall come forth a rod out of the stem of Jesse, and a Branch shall grow out of his roots."

Under the general title, A Significant Promise, he divided his text into three points: first, who makes the promise; second, what the promise entails; and third, to whom the promise is made. Or to put it in other words: where the promise originates—in the stillness of eternity, which has neither beginning nor end; when the promise is fulfilled—in time; and to whom the promise applies—to the hearts of God's people chosen from eternity.

He began by resolutely flinging aside the curtain of eternity to grant the congregation a glimpse of what went on in the Counsel of Peace. From there he took his listeners into the innermost hearts of God's chosen people so that a listener could compare such a heart with his own. Naturally he was more at home in his own heart than in anyone else's, and was soon holding it up as an example and standard. He repeatedly emphasized that Christ did not come into the world for all men, and that therefore, He simply could not be offered to all men, "For, congregation, He's not someone you can take when and how you choose. He is given exclusively to those whom God has elected thereto from eternity." In order to let this truth sink in, he asked his fellow travelers to that never-ending and all-determining eternity if they knew whether their name was written in the book of the remnant of the living, and whether they had ever been filled with a holy curiosity on this point. In order to help them in their self-examination, he gave them signs by which they could know that they were not without hope: "For then you will bewail your guilt day and night and cry to God, and go bowed under the painful load of your sins. And then with Jacob, you will say, I will not let thee go, except thou bless me."

His dark eyes fell on the parents of the baptized children, and he asked if they had ever baptized their wretched seed, damned in Adam, with their tears, and if they had pleaded with God to look on them in mercy. "For if God does not prevent it, they will grow up to be nothing but kindling for the fires of hell. I know what I'm talking about, people: I have nine children of my own and I have never yet come upon any of them, sitting alone and in secret, weeping over the separation between God and his soul because his sins had been revealed to him by the Holy Spirit. By nature all they want to do is go dancing and skipping merrily down the road to hell. Oh, that God might stop them in their tracks!"

Then apparently he remembered his text again, for he dwelt on the Branch for a while. This logically led him to consider the other trees that were hewn down and also the Christmas trees "with which the frivolous Christendom of today tries to cover its spiritual nakedness." He raised his voice until the whole building reverberated with it, and with violent gestures and a hammering fist he tried to drive the words deeper into the hearts of his listeners.

Fransje, who was just about to pop one of Kee's peppermints into his mouth, looked up startled. And when he caught the phrase "Christmas tree" he was suddenly all ears. Although Reverend Steenhouwer didn't speak the local dialect, so that Fransje didn't understand many of the words, he grasped the general drift of his words all too well. And one sentence penetrated his soul like a lightning bolt: "God will burn all Christmas trees, and He will throw all those who make them and take them into their homes into the fires of hell, which will never be extinguished. For according to God's infallible Word, which alone can lead us to salvation, all those who make them shall be made alike unto them."

This argument was beyond Fransje. But he didn't need it. The violent words and gestures of the preacher were all too clear. Fransje's heart pounded in his throat, and for a moment his head seemed about to burst as the blood rushed upward. He felt the same nausea that had overcome him after the accident with the fir branch. Involuntarily, he swallowed several times until it ebbed somewhat, but he was left stiff and chilled all over, and as white as a sheet. The round peppermint dropped from between his fingers. It fell between his knees onto the bare floor and rolled a long way until it came to rest several pews away.

That actually worked to Fransje's good, because when Father looked down over his shoulder at him, displeased, this new fright momentarily distracted him from the horrible image conjured up by the preacher. He shrank down as far as possible and pressed himself tightly against Father. With frightened eyes he glowered up at the prophet of doom high in his pulpit to hear what other horrible things he had to say. But he was finished with the topic, Christmas trees. And although the application following the middle song offered some comfort to troubled souls, it did Fransje no good, for the words no longer reached him. As if in a trance, Fransje tottered out of church behind Father with only one thought—Mommy! But many people were milling about outside and the faces of most of the women were hidden by their wide lace hats, so he couldn't find her. But suddenly a hand seized his shoulder and a gentle voice above him said, "Hi, Fransje. Are you going to take my arm again?"

He looked up into Kee's friendly face. "Where is Mommy?" he asked without responding to Kee's invitation. She noticed how pale he looked. Most of the churchgoers were already on their way home, and Mother, who had let the others pass, now came toward him. Fransje ran to meet her and wildly thrust his arm under her shawl.

"How did you like it in church, and did you listen closely to the preacher?" Since it was difficult to answer a double question, and since Fransje realized that Mother intended it only as a greeting, he neglected to answer. He just thrust his hand further under her arm, more than ready to leave that awful place.

The foursome set out, and soon they caught up to an old, stooped lady, who could not walk very fast. Father and the two women greeted her, and because Father was closest as they passed her, she said to him, "Didn't the minister have a fine sermon, Marien?"

"So you enjoyed it, did you?" Father replied evasively, a disgruntled look in his eyes.

They took a different street through the village than they had earlier, and suddenly Fransje saw a Christmas tree in one of the windows. And although it wasn't a bit dark out, all the candles were burning. The curtains were open wide, and Fransje could see several happy children's faces on the other side of the window. He could also hear singing. At once the dike broke and his emotions burst out.

"Mommy!" he wailed. "Look! A Christmas tree!" He yanked his hand out from under her shawl and pointed at the window in horror. "Are . . . are all . . . all those kids going to . . . to hell? And . . . and me too?"

His high voice was filled with horror. Father and Kee also

heard his outburst. The three adults looked from him to one another in surprise. He still had an answer coming from Mother, however; she replied, "That we know nothing about, my child. Only the Lord knows. I told you that the Lord loves children very much, didn't I? And maybe He loves those children too."

"But . . . but the minister said, if . . . if you have a . . . a Christmas tree in the house, then . . . then you'll go to hell!"

Mother looked at Father as if asking for help. But then suddenly she understood the anxiety that beset his soul, and without answering his last question, she told Father and Kee about the incident of a few days ago. Father ground his teeth and a deep wrinkle appeared over his nose. Fransje feared that the postponed punishment would be administered right then and there, but something strange happened instead. Father took two long strides, stopped in front of the women and pulled Fransje from between them. He swung him up to his shoulders and pressed his prickly cheek against Fransje's. He kissed his pale face—right out in the open in the middle of the road! With a quaver in his voice, he said, "You're Daddy's big helper!" His voice was so tender that Fransje's heart melted. He breathed a deep sigh and surrendered himself to the rhythm of Father's walk. The horrible phantoms—including those of the preacher—dissolved into unreal images that could no longer touch him.

They walked on in silence until they were out of the village. Then Father's voice next to Fransje's face said, "Were you able to listen a little, Kee?" Bitterness tinged his words.

Kee sighed a few times but didn't answer right away. Then, after a while, she said, "I can't say the sermon did very much for me. But maybe that was my fault. What the preacher said was true, but it just didn't do much for me," she repeated. "I had hoped that the Lord would once more confirm what I have been given to see in the beloved Son of God during the past week. But the Lord is ever sovereign and free, isn't He?"

Another moment of silence. Then Father said, "Tell us about it, if you will." And his voice was much more gentle.

"This past week it was brought home to me what it cost the Lord Jesus to save His people: how He came into the world as an insignificant worm in order to reconcile sinners with God. It was vividly made clear to me how in Isaiah it says, 'Though your sins are like scarlet, they shall be as white as snow,' but how that is only possible through the bitter suffering and death of the beloved

Redeemer. Just think how much the Lord was willing to sacrifice just to save such miserable creatures as us from eternal death! How earnestly He admonished and called us when He said, 'How often would I have gathered your children together as a hen gathers her brood under her wings.' But then He added, 'And you would not.' We're so quick to say, I can't convert myself. And it's true: we can't. But it might well be our greatest sin that we don't *want* to be either. Don't you think so?"

Saying this, she looked at Father, and her eyes fell on the face of the child on his shoulder. Her eyes were again suffused with that calm, gentle light. And without waiting for Father's answer, she continued, "Fransje, my boy, the Lord won't throw you into hell because you wanted to make a Christmas tree. It was very naughty and foolish of you, and you almost started a fire. But if you're sorry and ask the Lord to forgive you, and to make you His child, then He puts it behind Him. People don't go to hell because they have a Christmas tree, but because they *don't* have the Lord Jesus in their hearts. And people who have the Lord Jesus in their hearts no longer need a Christmas tree. What would you rather have: A Christmas tree or the Lord Jesus?"

"The Lord Jesus," whispered Fransje hoarsely.

Father's arms were growing tired, and he put Fransje back down on the ground. Fransje again walked between Mother and Kee, and this time he squeezed Kee's thin arm just as tightly as Mother's, and his step was light.

But Father still wore an unsatisfied look. He admired the way this godly woman had answered his boy, but in so doing she had also uttered judgment on the sermon they had heard that afternoon. He wished, however, that she wouldn't beat about the bush, but speak her mind openly. What he really wanted was to hear from her lips a confirmation of what he thought in his heart. Since he still owed her a reply, he said, "Yes, and man doesn't surrender very easily, does he? But when God transforms his heart, he lays down his weapons and says with Paul, 'Lord, what wilt thou have me to do?' But such a soul is no longer boastful. And he believes that God can also convert others. For then he sees himself as the biggest sinner of all, isn't that right?"

"Yes, that's right," answered Kee. "And it would be a great blessing if he continued to think small of himself. But man is so proud by nature, isn't he? And he so often becomes a big man in his own eyes. As Peter found out, one must be converted not just once, but daily. I think the minister we heard today still has to learn that lesson."

Father glanced at her out of the corner of his eyes, which showed secret admiration for this wise woman, and he envied her spiritual maturity. His peevishness disappeared and he felt himself not much older than Fransje. Just as small and just as happy, for in this way he, too, had received a blessing this Christmas day, even if not from the sermon.

But Kee wasn't finished yet. She made another observation: "When God converts someone, He accepts such a sinner as His child. If only we could always remain children; but we so quickly become grown-up in our own eyes. And yet the Lord Jesus says very plainly, 'Except you become as little children, you shall not enter into the kingdom of heaven.' If only we could believe God as wholeheartedly as a little child!"

Unconsciously she squeezed Fransje's hand more tightly to her side, and he stole a look up at her. But because he had understood little or nothing of the conversation, he took it as a special sign of affection and thrust his hand even farther under her shawl.

When they arrived home, Mother asked Kee to stay for supper. Although there would be no church tonight, they could still eat early so that she could be home before dark. But Kee said she had to be on her way because Reverend Steenhouwer would be preaching in her own church tonight, and if she left now, she could just make it. Nevertheless, Mother insisted that she first have a cup of tea or coffee. "I won't hear of it," said Mother. "You'd faint, walking such a long way without anything in your stomach."

The water in the kettle was still warm, so she brought it to a rapid boil on the fire. Quickly she buttered a few pieces of rusk and put them on Kee's saucer beside her teacup.

After drinking her tea, Kee immediately stood up and shook hands with everyone. She began with Father and ended with Fransje. Again she hugged his head against her black apron, and stroked his hair. "Goodbye, my boy," she said. "Seek the Lord early, for those that seek Him early shall surely find Him. That also goes for little boys . . . and you too!"

After she had left, suddenly the house was very quiet; her absence left a painful vacuum in their midst.

Just as Kee reached the road, a carriage came clattering along. It was the Moerland's hackney coach, taking Reverend Steenhouwer to Kapelle. Father was the first to see it, and flinging the curtains aside, he waved to Moerland in the driver's seat. The man spotted the movement and reined in the horse. Then Father pointed to Kee and from her to the coach. Moerland grasped Father's meaning. He bent down to the small window behind him, opened it, and talked to the minister inside. At last he jumped down from the box and called to Kee, who had already passed the carriage. She walked back and climbed in through the door which Moerland held open for her. Father waved once more in greeting and thanks, and then said, "If the minister is a good listener, maybe he'll pick up something for tonight's sermon."

They decided to wait with supper until the usual time. While they were still talking it over, the back door opened and feet clattered in the entry. A man's voice shouted, "Hello!" and everyone recognized it as Uncle Johannes's. He stepped into the living room, followed by Mother's youngest sister, Aunt Ma, who was carrying a sleeping child under her shawl. This was an unexpected pleasure, one that largely made up for Kee's departure. At once there was a lively murmur of voices, and the child, sleeping through it all, was safely tucked away behind the doors of Maria's closet bed, with one door left slightly ajar to let in fresh air.

The light was beginning to fade. Maria, who had been in the back room singing, returned to the living room humming to herself. Uncle Johannes was a choir leader and had an excellent voice himself. He proposed that they all do a little singing. Father immediately agreed. He couldn't carry a tune himself, but he loved to listen. He suggested that they sing the Song of Zechariah. Together they sang with enthusiasm:

> Blest be the God of Israel,
> The Lord who visited His own;
> Who by His gracious providence
> Redemption unto us made known.
> Within His servant David's tent
> Has He to us, His people, sent
> A horn of full salvation;
> E'en as He spoke by holy men of old,
> Who unto Israel foretold

How He to them
His mercy would unfold.

Fransje had climbed onto Maria's lap and let himself drift on the undulating sound of her pure voice. He didn't try to sing along, but when all the others had taken turns suggesting a song, he asked them to sing "Silent Night, Holy Night."

Although this was not a Psalm and so was never sung in their church, Father was not so narrow-minded that he could not appreciate its beauty and soundness. After "Silent Night," Maria launched into "Hark the Herald Angels Sing," followed by "While Shepherds Watched Their Flocks by Night," "O Come, O Come, Emmanuel," and other Christmas songs. The house was now completely dark, but Fransje, who usually hated the dark, was enjoying this to the full. As they finished the last song, the clock struck six.

Mother said, "Let's hurry up and light the lamp. Time for supper."

One of the leaves of the extension table was pulled out and everyone sat down to a long, sociable meal. So Fransje's first Christmas—at least, the first he was aware of—had turned out to be a happy one after all.

4

Because Fransje seldom climbed into the attic during the day, he had never noticed the pig bladder that had been hanging from a nail on the whitewashed chimney since last fall. The few times when he had been with Mother as she made beds upstairs in the morning, or when he'd been allowed to play upstairs with Wantje on a rainy day with the trapdoor carefully shut behind them, he had always stayed close to the little window. During the day the corners of the attic were shrouded in a mysterious, eerie darkness, and even his little bed was nothing like the familiar island of warm safety that it was at night when the darkness had swallowed up all nooks and crannies, narrowing his world to the protection of his bed covers and canopy.

Kees came home from school two days before New Year's carrying a handful of long, smooth reed stalks which he had cut out of a ditch on the way home. He placed them on the living room table, and before Fransje could ask what he was going to do with them, he dashed into the back room, took down the ladder and flew upstairs two rungs at a time. A moment later he returned to the living room with the parchment-like bladder, which had lost much of the air with which it had been inflated, and its elasticity as well. Now it crackled at a touch. Fransje's face was one big question mark. He was at a loss for words to ask all the questions that bubbled up in him. But at last he cried in a high voice, "What's that thing for, Kees? What are you going to do with it?"

Adopting a knowledgeable pose, Kees explained, "It's a pig bladder I got from the butcher's. And Father's going to make a rumblepot with it."

That explanation, told Fransje very little, because he hadn't the faintest idea what a rumblepot was. So he asked impatiently, "What *is* a rumblepot? What do you do with it?"

"A rumblepot is a thing that you rumble with."

Exasperated by Kees's short, vague answers, Fransje cried demandingly, "Mommy, make him tell me! What's a rumblepot for?"

Wantje jumped at the opportunity to display her superior knowledge. In a condescending tone she explained, "Look, Fransje, this bladder comes from inside a pig, and we let it dry on the chimney upstairs. Father's going to cut a piece off it and fasten one of those reeds to it, and then he'll tie it over a jam or coffee can, and then it's a rumblepot. You spit in your hand and then slide your hand up and down along the reed, and then it rumbles like a rumblepot—oompa, oompa, oompa. And you sing along with it."

Holding her left arm against her chest and clutching an imaginary rumblepot in her hand, Wantje slid her right hand up and down along an imaginary reed. As she did so, she chanted,

> I've been everywhere
> with my rumblepot;
> haven't a penny
> and my shoes are shot.
> My stomach's rumblin';
> it'll rumble till dawn.
> Toss me a penny
> and I'll go on.
> Pennies on the planks;
> many thanks.
> They're music to my ear;
> and I wish you a Happy New Year.

Fransje stared at her open-mouthed. Although he now had a vague picture of a rumblepot, new questions kept popping up inside him. A rumblepot might be a fascinating musical instrument and it looked like lots of fun, but what was it *for*?

Wantje, however, had not yet finished her explanation. After her noisy demonstration she caught her breath and continued, "Tomorrow will be Old Year's. That's the last day of the year. Then all the bigger kids go from door to door with their rumblepots, and they sing that song, and then the people come to the door and give them money."

Fransje stared at her in growing amazement. He looked at the dried pig bladder in Kees's hands and at the brown reeds on the table. A powerful desire rose up in him, a desire like one he had experienced not very long ago. His mind probed for ways and means, like a small stream of water that sought its way around numerous obstacles to reach its goal.

"Can Father make more than one rumblepot from that bladder?" he asked with ulterior motives.

"Oh, sure! There's enough here for three or maybe four of them," Kees informed him.

"Can he make one for me too?" he asked covetously. Again he turned to Mother. "Hey, Mommy, I get one too, don't I?"

"Oh, maybe. Ask your father."

From the tone of Mother's reply, Fransje gathered that there was a pretty good chance that soon he would have one of those wonderful things too. He sensed that he was one step nearer his goal. But something unpleasant stuck in his mind. Wantje had stressed that only the big kids went from door to door with a rumblepot. Now he asked himself if that included only those who were of school age. This time, in order to establish his status, he didn't address Mother as Mommy: "Mother, if Father makes me a rumblepot, may I go along from door to door too tomorrow?"

"We'll see, Fransje. You're still very young, and it would make you very tired. Besides, maybe it will be much too cold out for you tomorrow."

Convinced that even a Siberian freeze wouldn't harm him tomorrow, Fransje enlisted all his powers of persuasion to move Mother to commit herself. But she would only say, "We'll see what your father says." He finally realized that he wouldn't hurdle this obstacle until after supper. He hoped he would still have the courage then to approach Father with his request. To be sure he asked Mother's help, "Mommy, will you ask him for me?"

For the third time Wantje interrupted the conversation. "You don't even know the song," she said. "But never mind, I'll teach you."

Again she put her hands in the right position and ordered Fransje to follow her example. Then in a loud voice she chanted,
I've been everywhere
with my rumblepot . . . .
and Fransje followed her lead. But since the most important element in the action was missing, he had trouble making the proper movements with his hands and arms. A demanding teacher, Wantje wasn't satisfied until he followed her example very precisely. When she had gone through the whole verse once, she began all over again, and soon Fransje could chant a couple of lines by himself. He let her repeat the song to him until he knew the whole thing. Secretly he hoped that this would provide one more reason why his parents should give him permission to go out rumbling with the others tomorrow.

As soon as Father had pronounced the amen at the end of the closing prayer, Kees dashed to the back room to fetch the potato can and the potato pail. The pail, half-filled with water, he plunked down beside Father, and the pan he carried with him to Maria's closet bed. He threw open the doors, jerked aside the board that covered the shallow potato cellar under the bed, and dropped on his stomach in front of the hole. With both hands he shoveled the pan full of round Zeeland blues, hurtled the board back in place, slammed the doors shut, and thumped down the panful of potatoes on the table right in front of Father.

Wantje was hurrying to get the dishes cleared away. While Maria poured boiling water from the kettle over a piece of Sunlight soap, Wantje quickly wet the dishtowel and began washing the cleared section of the table.

Fransje had taken advantage of the general bustle to lay hands on the bladder. Clutching it to his stomach, he squeezed it in and out to hear the crackling of the dry skin.

In the meantime, Father had begun to peel the potatoes. As he finished each one, it dropped into the pail beside him with a little splash. He was sitting relaxed in his big chair with the potato pan on his lap, his pipe in his mouth, and his hat on his head. He was talking about the work he had done on the farm that day. A cozy hum filled the house. Mother walked back and forth to the cupboard, putting away the dishes that Maria had washed and Wantje had dried. Arjaan and Eine were reading books that they had borrowed from the library in town, and Bram was getting ready to go out.

In contrast to the relaxed atmosphere that pervaded the house, the hearts of the three youngest members of the family were gripped with suspense. None of them had openly brought the subject of the rumblepots to Father's attention, so he pretended to be completely unaware of what was on their minds. But the three children saw mischievous laughter in his downcast eyes. When the dishes were all put away and the floor was swept and Mother and Maria sat down to do some knitting, Kees gathered his courage and stood next to Father. He said, "Father, when you're finished with the potatoes pretty soon, will you please make me a rumblepot?"

Fransje held the bladder very still and tensely watched Father's face. Father finished peeling the potato in his hand, and then he replied, "I think I can do that. Did you get some reeds?" In answer Kees rushed to the back room and returned with the reeds and several jam jars in his arms.

Fransje stood very close to Father, gathering all his courage to ask his question. When he began, he made his question two-pronged, hurriedly asking, "Father, would you please make me one too, and can I go along with the other kids tomorrow too?" Though surprised at his own audacity, he was glad he had said it. In awful suspense, he awaited Father's decision. Mother and Maria involuntarily stopped knitting and also looked at Father.

Father replied, "Of course I'll make you a rumblepot. But I think you'd get tired if you went with the other kids, going from house to house all that way."

Fransje could hardly believe his ears. Father hadn't come right out and said no. Whether he would get permission now depended on what he himself would say. Vehemently he shook his head and assured Father that he wouldn't get the least bit tired. He could walk fast and far, and he already knew the song. Just listen: he held his hands in the prescribed position and began singing. But in his eagerness and anxiety to win his case, he fell victim to a typically human failing, and transposed consonants so that the first line came out:

I've been everywhere
with my pumblerot . . . .

This was as far as he got, for a roar of laughter exploded around him. Even Father couldn't help bursting into laughter, although he felt sorry for the flustered, red-faced little boy standing beside him. Fransje, however, had no idea why they were laughing so hard and decided they must be laughing at him—something he couldn't stand. He feared that now all his chances had been ruined. But bright little Wantje helped him out of his daze by telling him, "You said pumblerot and you're supposed to say rumblepot."

The humorous slip had, however, tipped the scale in his favor, for when Father recovered from his fit of laughter, he said, "If it's nice weather tomorrow and if you promise to be a big boy, then you can go along with the other kids."

Fransje's mood suddenly did a complete turnabout. Elated, he danced around the house, joyfully tossing the pig bladder up against the ceiling.

The next morning the children were up before sunrise. Father and the older boys hadn't even left for work yet; they were still sitting at the breakfast table. They looked up with irritation at Kees and Fransje when they came into the room making too much noise. Wantje, who had been awake for some time, now came tumbling out of the closet bed, and all three hurried to the mantel where their rumblepots had been waiting for them all night.

"Why don't you kids go back to bed for awhile," grumbled Bram, his eyes still swollen with sleep. "I wish I could stay in bed a little longer. I know where I'd be right now!"

But instead of sending them back to bed, Father just gave them a warning: "Don't you start raising a ruckus with those things, you hear! Your mother's still sleeping."

Mother, however, was just emerging from her closet bed, wearing a small nightcap; her dark hair spilled from beneath it in a long curl that reached halfway down her back. She was not wearing a nightgown like Maria, but a black skirt and jacket. "Good morning," she said. Fransje ran toward her with his rumblepot in his outstretched hands. But Mother didn't pick him up. First she knelt in front of the chair, folded her hands and bowed her head. Pale bare feet protruded from beneath her long skirt. The room was very quiet. All that could be heard was the water kettle singing softly on the stove and the assertive tick-tock of the clock.

Having finished breakfast, Father and the older boys prayed silently, finishing at the same time as Mother. Father put on his hat and stood up. He looked at Fransje and said, "I think it's going to be nice weather today. So be a big boy and say thank you when the people give you something. Do you know your song? And do you know how to work that rumblepot?"

Fransje nodded his head confidently to Father's multiple question. But he knew an even more convincing answer. Spitting copiously into his right hand, he managed to coax some sound from the rumblepot, but had problems with the rhythm; his frail oompahs didn't coincide with the words of his song. Wantje felt she should point this out to him at once. Slowly and painstakingly she showed him how. "Now everybody at the same time," suggested Eine, and the room was filled with a deafening clamor. When the song was finished, Father and the older boys went out. Meanwhile Mother had dressed herself, and Maria, too, had gotten up. Only Arjaan was still asleep in the attic.

"Okay, kids, go wash yourselves. Fransje, you too. You can't eat breakfast with such dirty hands. See how filthy they are!"

Fransje looked at his hands and had to admit that Mother was right. The reed had worked the spit into the creases of his skin, turning it an unappetizing white. Fransje forced himself to accept this as part of the great adventure which the day had in store for him.

At last nine o'clock came. Although the children had been ready for several hours, Mother had strictly forbidden them to go out any earlier. "Of course not," she had said. "Some people are still in bed!"

But now at last the time had come. The children dressed warmly, putting one mitten on their left hand and one in their pocket, which also contained a small, empty can with a slot in the lid for coins. Just as they were putting on their wooden shoes at the back door, Siene and Marien's three children arrived, similarly equipped. Pier was with them too. After greeting each other noisily, they decided to go out as a group. Since they wouldn't rumble at their own homes, they agreed to begin with Wullemiene. They heard voices and footsteps beside the house, however, and the next moment Neeltje and her older sister appeared, also carrying rumblepots. Without asking, they joined the others too, so a group of eight approached Wullemiene's door. A choir of eight voices rang out above the dull rumble of the rumblepots. None of them noticed that they were being less than truthful in the first line of their song. Those were the words, and they were merely acting out an age-old custom which permitted children to beg money from door to door on the last day of the year.

Wullemiene's door remained closed until the children came to the last line of their song. Then her cranky face appeared as the door opened a crack. Instinctively the children braced themselves for the shock of cold water. But when the door opened a little farther, they saw that instead of a pail of water, she held a jar of rock candy. Her old fingers fumbled in the jar and she handed a rock candy to each of the children except Pier and Fransje. Demonstratively she slammed the lid on the jar saying to Pier, "You're not getting any candy from me. You're a bully and bullies don't deserve candy."

Pier turned bright red, horribly embarrassed in front of the other children, who were all younger than he. But he was afraid to talk back to her. Fransje, who didn't like Pier, took secret, nasty delight at the other's discomfort. Wullemiene was holding one more candy in her hand and he surmised that it was meant for him. But before she gave it to him, she groped about in the pocket under her apron. She fished something out of it and asked Fransje, "Where's your pennybank?"

Nervously Fransje pulled the tin can out of his pocket along with his black mitten, which fell between his wooden shoes. He held up the can, more to show it to her than to receive the unexpected gift. Wullemiene put the coin in the slot herself, and the children were just able to see that it was a nickel. Then the door closed again. For a moment the children didn't move, as they digested their first, rather strange encounter. Pier was the first to find his voice. He sneered, "What do I care about that old witch's sticky old candy. At home I can have all the candies I want."

No one replied to his words, because they were only too aware of the double insult dealt him. They knew Pier as a domineering windbag and were not at all sorry to see him humiliated.

They moved on to Tona's house, where they expected to get another piece of rock candy—a burnt one, no doubt. But they were completely mistaken. For some reason, Tona was in an exceptionally good mood, and as soon as they began their song the door opened and there she stood looking down on the small group with a wide smile on her large, flabby face. When the song was finished, she waddled back into the house and returned with a basketful of yellow apples. She let each of the children pick one out for himself, and then her hand plunged beneath her apron too. She kept dipping into her handful of coins, giving each of the children two pennies. As she did so, she murmured words of endearment which the children only half-understood. They were too busy eyeing her precious gifts to pay much attention to her words. Nevertheless, they were all willing to put Tona on their list of favorites for now.

Since the next house was Siene and Marien's, they now walked to the road in order to reach the two houses on Neeltje's side of the fence. At each place they collected one penny each. From there they decided to go to the railroad station neighborhood. It included many houses, so they expected to make a good haul. But just as they were leaving, Neeltje's door opened and her mother appeared in the doorway. She beckoned them and called, "Aren't you going to sing for us? Come on! Let's hear what you can do."

Although it was contrary to the decision they had just made, the children were only too eager to make an exception. Neeltje's older sisters also came to the door to view the performance. When the song was finished, Neeltje's mother gave each of them two cents, including her own girls. The group was beginning to feel that business would be good.

Fransje was deeply enjoying this adventurous game that allowed you to collect pennies so easily from other people. The thought flashed through his mind that sometimes you unfairly formed a wrong idea of people, for Neeltje's mother was actually not such a bad lady. But one of the older girls quickly shattered this reassessment by saying, "Ah, Fransje Weststrate! Are you out rumblin' too? Did you collect a lot of money already? Then you can buy Neeltje a new tea set for the one you busted."

Fransje's wide-eyed stare was filled first with surprise and then with anxiety. His cheeks became bright red, and he looked at Kees and Wantje in despair. Suddenly he felt very small and miserable, and a hot flame of hate flared up inside him. Those mean, treacherous liars! All he had broken was the little teapot—not the whole set. And not on purpose. Besides, Neeltje had said that she had gotten a new teapot long ago and that her mother was no longer angry at him. He had even played in Neeltje's house after the accident, although not with the tea set. "Those rotten girls!" he ranted within himself.

Fortunately Neeltje's mother came to his help, admonishing her daughter, "You girls shut up about that! That's over and done with!" To Fransje she said, "You just keep your money, Fransje. We don't need your measly pennies."

The latter was intended as a jab and Fransje didn't miss it. Nevertheless, he was grateful for her support. At least now he was openly and formally absolved.

The children learned a lot about people as they went from door to door. Where they expected to get a good haul, often they got little or nothing, and the homes from which they expected little sometimes surprised them with their generosity, although they seldom netted more than a nickle each. Some doors remained shut even when the older children were convinced someone was home.

At one place an old man living alone invited them into the back room. He was Catholic and his walls were covered with brightly colored pictures of saints with pale, pious faces. Over the mantel hung a large crucifix, which Fransje ogled with big eyes. The streams of blood painted on Jesus' hands and side sent a cold chill down his back. He heard nothing of what the old recluse said in his cracked dialect, and he resolved to tell Mother what he had seen here. Many questions arose in him which he wanted to ask her.

But it was time for them to be on their way. The children had long finished their song and now they were unconsciously watching the old man's hands. With gnarled, trembling fingers, he fished a half penny from a greasy little money pouch and handed it to Pier. "Here," said the man, "make sure you divide that fairly amongst all of you."

The children said nothing until they were safely behind the house and out of earshot. Pier protested the loudest. "That greedy old papist! How can you divide a half penny among eight people! That old buzzard can go hang!"

Although Fransje shared Pier's feelings to some extent, his crude words made him cringe. As far as he was concerned, Pier could keep the half penny. He only wished the jerk were not with them. Sure enough, Pier dropped the coin in his own can, and took malicious delight in the fact that he had a half penny more than the others, except Fransje.

At the baker's house they got no money, but the baker's wife gave each of them a bag of broken cookies. Shortly they were having great fun comparing the delicacies in their respective bags.

After canvassing the entire railroad station neighborhood, they stopped to deliberate where they should try their luck next. A short distance beyond the railroad tracks was another cluster of homes, but they saw other rumblers who seemed to have come from there. They agreed that this would decrease their chances for a good take. Moreover, they had to keep an eye on the time.

They could turn down another road and try their luck at the farmhouses in the polder. From there they could follow the dike which was bordered by several small farm-laborers' homes and then return home by another road which intersected theirs just beyond Kees de Visser's house.

Fransje's legs were growing very tired, but he bravely marched along with the others. They were a little disappointed by the farmers' houses because they had to walk quite some distance for the thirteen cents that the route yielded each of them. Kees, however, comforted himself and the others by reminding them that they had in any case collected over one guilder each.

They decided to make one last stop at Kees de Visser's and then head for home, for it had to be close to noon. Pier, who had made his rumblepot himself and had been bragging about it at first, quickly tried to stretch the limp parchment (which had come loose for the third time) tight over the coffee can, but he couldn't. He tried to force one of his sisters to give her rumblepot to him, thereby precipitating a loud, tearful outburst. He threatened to give her a clout in the ear if she didn't shut up, and the poor child reluctantly gave in.

Fransje's blood boiled. He'd love to give Pier a punch on his nasty nose. He wished Kees would do it for him, but Kees kept out of it. If they had been going anywhere else but to Kees de Visser's, Fransje would have given his own rumblepot to the poor little girl, but now he just couldn't.

They crossed the little bridge, the older boys first, but Fransje right behind them because he felt that he had special rights here. He cast a quick glance at the spot where Kees de Visser had broken off the branch for him a little over a week ago. Although he determinedly kept the concept, Christmas tree, out of his mind, he couldn't resist peering at the stately fir trees.

A moment later the children were standing in a circle around the scrubbed blue stoop. They wouldn't have thought of stepping on the clean stoop with their dirty wooden shoes. So they gave their last serenade before a closed door.

Shortly, however, the familiar, glossy, green door opened and one of the girls answered with a friendly smile. Her eyes traveled over the faces, and when she discovered Fransje, she nodded at him and gave him a special smile. That made Fransje blush, but he only sang harder to hide his embarrassment. He sang extra hard—except, that is, when he came to the lines,

Toss me a penny
and I'll go on.

Fransje had been thinking that it wasn't really very polite to demand money from other people. But because it was in the song, he had been singing along with the others despite his reservations. With these people, however, he was determined to be on his best behavior. So when he came to the two offending lines, he was suddenly overcome by a coughing spell and couldn't go on until they came to the words, "Many thanks." In this way, he did not violate his sense of right.

The girl disappeared into the hall, to return with her father and mother and sister behind her.

"Let's hear you sing again," Kees de Visser said jovially. "I was in the living room, so I didn't hear you very well."

Once more the children spit in their hands, and once more they raised their lament about how long they had been abroad with their rumblepots, this time telling the truth. At the offending lines, Fransje found it necessary to wipe his nose on his sleeve. And then he finished the song.

The woman dug into the pocket underneath her apron and brought out a handful of nickels. Smiling, she gave each of the children one of the square coins, deliberately making Fransje wait till last. Suddenly her hand was empty.

"Isn't that awful!" she said in mock dismay. "All my nickels are gone." She paused to observe the effect of these words on Fransje. Then she continued, addressing her husband, "I don't suppose you have any nickels in your pocket, do you? All I have left is a quarter, and if you don't have a nickel, I'll have to give Fransje my quarter."

Kees understood what his wife was up to, and without feeling in his pockets, he said, "No, Mum, I haven't a nickel to my name either." Then the woman put the shiny quarter in Fransje's wet hand, and he stammered, "Thank you, Mrs. Kees de Visser."

The other children said thank you one more time and the tired little troop began to leave.

"Fransje, when are you going to visit us again?" asked one of the girls. "You come soon, you hear!" Fransje was only too eager to give his word, responding more with his eyes than with his incoherent words. Bashfully, he quickly ran after the others.

Coming home, although he was on his last legs, Fransje ran past Kees and Wantje into the house. Father and the two older boys were home and dinner was on the table. They had apparently said grace already, for they were all eating.

"Mom! Dad!" cried Fransje. "Look at all the money I got. And Mrs. Kees de Visser gave me a cotternickle!" He shook the can of money under Mother's nose. Everyone looked at the excited little boy. His cheeks were cold and red from the frigid air, and his nose was running.

"Welcome back, Fransje," said Mother, as she wiped his nose with her gray hanky. "So, did you collect a lot of money? How about it: did you get very tired?"

Father said, "Well, how's my big helper? Did you have fun? And did you go a long ways?" Usually he tolerated no latecomers at the table, but this time he overlooked it.

Meanwhile, Wantje and Kees had also come in and were just as noisy as Fransje. But Mother said, "You can tell us all about it later, but now go wash your hands and sit down to eat. Come on, Maria, you take Fransje into the back and give his hands a good washing."

But first Fransje once more wanted to tell them about the cotternickel he got from Mrs. Kees de Visser. No one seemed to know what he was talking about except Wantje. She said, "You silly, that's no cotternickel. That's a quarter." And to the others, "He was the only one who got a quarter from that old lady!" Jealousy soured her voice. Mother admonished her: "What's this? That's no way to talk about that lady!" But the others had burst into laughter at Fransje's selfmade name for the unfamiliar coin.

After dinner the children emptied their cans onto the table. Kees and Wantje counted their own money. Bram helped Fransje put his pennies in piles of five. Kees, who was the first one finished, cried, "I've got one guilder and three cents!"

For some reason Wantje had two cents less than Kees, and Bram announced that Fransje had one guilder and twenty cents. Kees tried to figure out how much he and Wantje should have, because he knew Fransje received twenty-five cents more than they did. But that didn't jibe with either his or Wantje's total, so he gave up.

"Mommy, can I put all those pennies in my piggy bank?" asked Fransje.

But Mother replied, "You can each take a nickel to buy something at the store. And, Fransje, you can put the quarter into your piggy bank. But the rest of the money we'll put together and Maria will go to the store to buy flour and yeast and oil and raisins. Then we'll make *oliebollen*."

"Oh boy! Oh boy!" shouted Kees and Wantje. But Fransje wasn't as elated. He had been imagining the joy of dropping all those coins one by one through the slot in his piggy bank, and Mother's proposal drastically reduced the game to a single motion. But then he pictured the fun and festivities that went with the traditional *oliebollen* and he, too, said, "Oh boy! Maria, can I go with you to the store?"

Maria said it was all right, but Mother protested, "The poor boy is so tired already! He's better off taking a little nap." Fransje objected strenuously and Mother understood that he wouldn't settle down until he had spent his nickel on sweets.

Fransje spent a long time hovering over the pots and pans as Mother and Maria prepared the dough, but the long preparations made him impatient. When Mother told him that before the *oliebollen* would be done, the dough had to rise a couple of hours, he lay down behind the stove with his head on his arms. He noticed nothing when Maria picked him up and put him in her bed, where he slept until the *oliebollen* were done.

It was now very quiet in the house. Fransje was sitting on the bench behind the table scribbling on his slate. Mother sat in her chair reading a sermon by a trusted old author. The cat lay under the stove sleeping. Only the ticking of the clock on the wall and the scratch of Fransje's slate pencil broke the peaceful silence.

The others were all in church, including Wantje, although Mother had advised her to stay home because she too had spent an exhausting day. But Wantje had whined until she was allowed to go along. She had been motivated not by a longing for the courts of the Lord and for a sermon read by one of the elders but by a no less powerful desire to sit beside Maria in church.

Suddenly the flame in the big hanging lamp began to smoke, and Mother had to turn the wick down a little. Fransje was tired of the slate. He had been trying to draw a rumblepot, without much success. Meanwhile his mind had been reviewing the events of the day, and all at once he asked, "Mommy, may I look at the Bible picture book?"

Mother rose and took it from the cabinet for him. He immediately began turning the pages purposefully. He remembered seeing a picture somewhere of Jesus on the cross. But he couldn't find it without Mother's help. When she found it for him, he studied it for a long time. In this picture, however, there were three crosses, and Jesus, hanging on the middle one, didn't look nearly as horrifying as the crucifix he had seen in the old hermit's place. The picture wasn't colored, and furthermore, everything was drawn on such a small scale that the sensational details didn't stand out. Nevertheless, his heart filled with compassion, especially as he looked into the faces of the grieving women in the foreground. Mother had told him about the crucifixion before, but Fransje couldn't remember the story very well.

"Mommy," he said, "this morning we were in an old man's house and he had a big thing on the chimney just like in this picture." He pushed the book across the table to Mother and pointed to the middle cross.

"Oh, that man must have been Catholic," speculated Mother.

"Yes, Pier said he was a greedy old papist."

"Hush!" admonished Mother. "You mayn't say such things."

"Why did that man have that thing on the wall?"

"Oh, all Roman Catholics have statues and pictures of the Lord Jesus and His mother and of other good people who lived long ago on their walls."

"Why? And why don't we have any?"

Mother answered only the second question. She said, "The Lord told us not to make images, because He knows that if we start making images, pretty soon we'll be worshiping them. And He doesn't want that. We're only supposed to worship the Lord, like we do."

Fransje was satisfied, and he straightway decided that Roman Catholics were flagrantly disobedient and therefore on their way to hell. But as he recalled the vivid image, a cold chill went down his back. He asked, "Why is He hanging on that cross?"

Mother looked up at him, detecting an interest beyond the usual curiosity of children his age. She pushed her book aside and, folding her hands before her on the table, she began to tell, as clearly as she could, the story of Christ's suffering and death.

Fransje didn't interrupt even once and asked no more questions. But watching his face, Mother read constantly new emotions there.

Deliberately avoiding all details beyond his comprehension, in simple words she painted the greatest tragedy that ever happened, there on the hill of Golgotha. She told of the spikes and spite, the mockery and malice, the love and suffering. And through it all the big blue eyes of her child were fixed on her in growing fascination. However, she was surprised to see that even during the most awful moments he showed little emotion. But she sensed that this wasn't because it didn't captivate him, for he was hanging on her every word. Nor was it because he didn't understand parts of it, for a barely perceptible flickering of his eyes showed that he had grasped the images.

Mother also told him about the two murderers who were crucified with Christ and about the one who repented and turned to Christ for forgiveness at the eleventh hour. For a moment Fransje's eyes left hers to glance at the picture in front of him, but then he again stared at her with undiminished attention.

Mother continued: "The one bad man was very sorry that he had been so wicked all his life. He turned his head to Jesus and said, 'Lord, I'm awful sorry. When You go to heaven by and by, You won't forget me, will You?' And then the Lord Jesus also turned His head and looked at the poor man who had done so much evil and who was also dying. And He saw that the man was really sorry, so He said, 'Yes, soon you'll be with Me in Paradise.' That's another name for heaven."

Mother intended to add a short application to her story, but now it was she who looked at Fransje wide-eyed. She saw his eyes brimming with tears; they slowly ran down his cheeks and spilled onto his shirt, leaving dark, gradually expanding blots. He made no attempt to hold back the tears or to wipe them away. Mother saw that his eyes were still fixed on her through the haze of tears, as if he was waiting for more.

She concluded her story with the words, "All people have been bad, very bad, just like that bad man. But if we are really sorry, just like that bad man, and ask the Lord to forgive us, then He washes away all our sins. And then, in spite of everything, He lets us come into heaven with Him, just like that man. So you should pray every day to ask the Lord if you can be His child. Because then someday you, too, can go to heaven to be with Him, just like the bad man."

Fransje's cup, however, was already running over. A sob escaped from his heaving chest and he desperately held out both arms to Mother. "Mommy!" he wailed. "Will you pray for me? Will you?"

Mother sprang from her chair and lifted the sobbing child from behind the table. Now tears coursed down her own cheeks too and they mingled with his. She hugged his head against her heart and with her free hand she kept stroking his hair. Gently she rocked him back and forth until his wild sobs began to subside. Then she wiped his face with her gray hanky and blew her own nose. She whispered endearments to him and finally she said, "You know what? I have a wonderful idea. Pretty soon, when Father and the other kids come home, we'll make some hot chocolate and then we'll all have another *oliebol*. And you may stay up a little later tonight because it's New Year's Eve."

She set him down on the floor and put the picture Bible back in its place on top of the linen closet.

A little later the other children came home. Mother asked them which elder had read the sermon and what text it had been based on. She asked Wantje what Psalms they had sung, but she could remember only two of them, so Kees and Arjaan had to help her out. "Were there a lot of people in church?" she asked Maria.

Then the door opened again and male voices rumbled in the back room. Fransje recognized one of them as Father's, but the other he didn't know at first, although it sounded familiar. Then suddenly it came to him: that was Verplanke's voice. He was the first to step into the room, followed by Father. Mr. Verplanke had beat Father home, but he had waited for him behind the house.

As was the custom, Verplanke shook hands with everyone. He began with Mother and ended with Fransje, who confided that he had gone out with his rumblepot today. "So!" said Verplanke, sounding impressed. "You're sure growing up in a hurry! And did you collect lots of money?"

"Mm-hmm. Lots and lots! And Mommy made *oliebollen* with it."

Verplanke laughed at the image Fransje's words evoked. His eyes disappeared in a mass of wrinkles and Fransje thought what a friendly man Mr. Verplanke was. He asked, "Do you still have your rumblepot? Then you'll have to play for me, and Wantje too." Fransje ran to the back room to fetch the already discarded instruments and returned triumphantly with them to the living room. Kees made no move to get his. Once more the two youngest children performed their song.

Verplanke dug his wallet from his pocket and gave each of them one guilder. Neither one had expected such a belated prize, and Kees was inwardly berating himself for his stupidity. This time they were allowed to put the money in their piggy banks.

In the meantime, Mother had put some milk on the stove, telling Maria to mix and dissolve the cocoa and the sugar.

A feeling of good fellowship settled on the room. Father and Verplanke were talking about the sermon they had just heard, while Mother listened attentively. Fransje was struck by the fact that Verplanke was talking much more than usual, and by the happy look on his face. The other children felt quietly compelled to listen to him too.

Father didn't say very much. Now and then he asked a question meant to keep Verplanke talking rather than to interrupt him. Father also looked happy, as did Mother. What Verplanke was saying seemed to please everyone.

Fransje did not understand that Verplanke had obtained a special blessing from the church service tonight. He was still so affected by it that he laughed and wept by turns. The text of the sermon that had been read was, "My times are in thy hand." This had been remarkable because one morning during the past week Verplanke had woke up with that text on his mind. The words had moved his heart so deeply and had filled him with such inexpressible comfort that he had dissolved in tears.

This wasn't the beginning of the story, however. For weeks, yes months, he had lived under a dark cloud and in inner turmoil about the state of his soul before eternity. He could certainly not deny that there had been times in his life when the Lord had dealt with him. But despite these spiritual experiences, he had nevertheless come to see very clearly that he could not build on them for eternity, nor could he meet God with them.

Though deeply troubled and fearful, he had been unable to talk to anyone. Not to his wife and children who didn't belong to his church, didn't understand his beliefs and would have nothing to do with them. Not to Marien, because he had thought that Marien had never experienced such a thing and would therefore not be able to understand or give him support either. So he had gone his way alone without seeing any light, lamenting to God night and day. Then slowly his life had changed as God led him step by step into the redemptive suffering of the Lord Jesus. He was taught to see that this alone could be the ground of our salvation. True, he didn't feel confident enough to say that the precious Lord Jesus was now his Savior, because, well, that was no small thing; nevertheless, his heart continually went out to Him, and he was forced to say, "O, dearest Jesus, look down on me in mercy!"

It would certainly be a divine miracle if he were made part of that number. Nevertheless some hope had been planted in his heart—a hope which he fervently hoped and prayed would not be disappointed.

Thereafter death did not stalk his footsteps as closely as before, and this past week his soul had been deeply touched by those Bible words. And tonight, miraculously, the sermon had been about those same words—a sermon which had been written more than two hundred years ago by a faithful minister of the Lord who had been singing before God's throne all these years.

Father had been listening attentively, his heart quickened by the emotional account of this fellow pilgrim on the road to Zion. Now and then Mother had quietly blown her nose and wiped her eyes. Nowadays she heard this kind of talk so seldom, and although she was very happy over Verplanke's spiritual progress, she wished the Lord would also lead her a little farther.

Father, who was a little more experienced in such matters, asked Verplanke a question which, although it sounded cold, did not issue out of suspicion or envy: "So you're still building on your latest experiences?"

Verplanke's eyes filled with tears and immediately Father was sorry he had spoken. The man replied, "No, I hope not. I rely on the dear Redeemer to take my part, for He can be the only ground for my salvation. But I am nevertheless happy for what I have been allowed to see and experience this past week. For although I know these things well enough with my mind, it must also become true in one's heart. Isn't that so?"

Father agreed wholeheartedly. The room was filled not only with a sense of intimacy but also with the joy of the communion of the saints, although the members of that communion would have vied with one another in denying their right to lay claim to the title of saint.

Maria had been keeping watch over the pan of milk on the stove. As soon as it started boiling, she poured in the dissolved chocolate. She let the brown liquid come to a boil once more and then moved the pan from the stovetop to the rear, on the flat pipe. Mother said, "Fransje, you may fetch the bowl of *oliebollen* now."

Fransje ran to the pantry and returned with the bowlful of *oliebollen*. He had eaten so many of them this afternoon that he wasn't really very hungry, but they looked so good he couldn't resist taking another one. With a big ladle Maria scooped out a cup of hot chocolate for everyone. The sweet aroma pervaded the room.

"Come, pull up a chair," Mother invited Verplanke. They all sat around the table in a cozy circle. "Don't drink it right away, kids," warned Mother. "It's very hot."

Fransje blew over the edge of his mug. A thin film had formed on the surface of his hot chocolate. Every time he blew, numerous tiny wrinkles appeared, like the wrinkles around Verplanke's eyes. Without lifting his head he glanced up to assess his comparison. Verplanke's eyes met his and smiled at him, complete with wrinkles. Fransje shyly smiled back. He was very attracted to the friendly man.

Because this wasn't a regular meal, Father didn't open with prayer. But when all had eaten their fill and Verplanke had adamantly refused Mother's urgings to take another *oliebol*—the bowl wasn't empty yet—Father proposed to read a chapter from the Bible. This time Fransje was allowed to get the Bible, and Father read Psalm 90 because he thought it a fitting passage with which to end the year.

During the Bible reading tears kept running down Verplanke's face. But Fransje didn't feel uncomfortable, for he sensed that those weren't sad tears. Verplanke had never struck him as a worrier.

Maria suggested that they sing, "Hours and days and years and ages," and although it was not a Psalm, Father and Verplanke raised no objections. Verplanke sang along loudly and enthusiastically.

Then Father asked Verplanke to pray for a blessing. Fransje, who had been expecting this, folded his hands. But Verplanke balked, insisting that Father do it this time. Father, however, wouldn't hear of it, and then Verplanke acquiesced. Occasionally his voice trembled with emotion. Although his prayer used many cliché terms and stereotyped expressions current in their church circles, it also expressed heartfelt emotions which were obvious even to the children.

After the prayer Verplanke immediately stood up to go home. Although Mother protested, "My, my, what a rush!" he wouldn't let himself be persuaded to stay any longer. He said goodnight by shaking hands with everyone once again. As was the custom, Fransje again came last, and before Verplanke could make a wisecrack, Fransje said, "Next time I get chickies, I'll give you one too—the biggest one I've got."

Verplanke laughed. "You're a good boy, Fransje," he said. "Thank you." Then he left.

"Now to bed, children!" said Mother. "And hurry! It's almost ten o'clock."

The next day a warm aura of fellowship lingered in the house. The children had wished one another and their parents, one at a time, a blessed New Year—except Fransje, who didn't yet know the traditional words. But because he kept hearing them repeated again and again, impatiently he asked Wantje, "What is that little verse?"

"Oh, silly, that's no verse. That's wishing everybody a happy New Year."

"But what are you supposed to say?"

Wantje was more than willing to initiate him into the mysteries of the grown-up world, and explained, "First you shake hands and then you say, 'I wish you much happiness and blessing in the New Year. May all your needs be supplied, both spiritually and physically!' "

She had him repeat every phrase three times until he knew the entire greeting. Triumphantly he marched up to Mother to demonstrate his latest accomplishment. He shook her hand and recited his little verse. Mother said, "My, but you're sure getting to be a big boy! Did you know that pretty soon you'll be four years old? Today it's the first day of January and at the end of this month you'll be four, God willing."

Fransje looked up at her with shining eyes. "How many more nights is that?" he wanted to know.

"Oh, a whole bunch," answered Mother. "Thirty more. But they'll be past before you know it."

Fransje skipped back and forth through the living room. Soon he'd be four years old and that meant he was almost grown up. "Can I go to school pretty soon then too?" he asked.

But Mother told him that he would have to wait another whole year and then another half year. "First Christmas and New Year will have to come again and one more birthday. And then when May comes around again, then you may go to school too."

That sounded like an awfully long time to Fransje. But he comforted himself with the thought that, in any case, soon he'd be one big step closer to his goal. For when you're four years old, you're almost grown up!

All morning neighbors and friends were in and out of the house. The coffee pot stood ready on the stove. Every time it was empty, Maria made another pot. On the table was a box of *speculaas* cookies from which Mother offered every well-wisher two cookies. Although Fransje had already had two, he was begging for another one. Mother told him that then he wouldn't have room for potatoes later—which hardly struck him as a disaster. When he kept begging, she finally gave him the pieces of a broken cookie, but her eyes made it clear that now his measure was full.

An acquaintance from the railroad station neighborhood arrived to tell them that last night his wife had given birth to a well-formed baby girl. "That certainly was a beautiful New Year's present!" someone remarked.

Fransje, kneeling in front of the window, saw the mailman coming around the house on his bike. A moment later the latch of the back door was lifted and a voice shouted, "Mailman!"

Maria hurried to the back door to take the mail. She returned with a handful of picture postcards, a few plain postcards and a couple of letters. Quickly she scanned the return addresses and, blushing, she swiftly concealed two cards between her *doek* and *beuk.* The letters she handed to Father. She read aloud the names of the people who had sent the postcards. Then she read in surprise, "From Mr. and Mrs. C. de Visser and Maatje and Leentje. Who in the world is that? This can't be for us. The mailman must have delivered it to the wrong address."

But then, checking the address she read: "To Master Fransje Weststrate, c/o Mr. Marinus Weststrate. Main street." She looked at Fransje in surprise as she said, "This one's for you, Fransje. There's something written on it. Listen . . . ."

But Fransje, who had been bobbing up and down in his eagerness to get a closer look at the brightly colored postcards, cried shrilly, "It's for me! It's for me! Let me see it, Maria!" He jumped from the bench and yanked the card from her hand. Wide-eyed he gazed at the glossy picture. It was a winter landscape with a blood-red sunset and gilt-edged clouds over a winding stream bordered by snow-covered fir trees. In the foreground stood a deer, its head held high with a splendid set of antlers. On his soft brown fur lay gilt-colored flakes of snow.

Fransje was elated. None of the other children had been privileged to receive a card in the mail. He became so boisterous that Father glanced up in irritation from the letters he was opening. They were from his brothers who were policemen up north, and he was eager to find out how they were doing.

But first Mother had to look at Fransje's beautiful card. When she had sufficiently admired it, Fransje let the other children look at it, but he didn't let it out of his hands. As a result, Wantje, who was terribly jealous, would hardly deign to look at it. Maria told him, "Fransje, there's something written on the back and you haven't even heard what it says yet. Here, give it to me and I'll read it to you."

Reluctantly Fransje surrendered the card. Maria read, "Dear Fransje. We wish you a happy New Year. When are you coming to see us again? We bought this card especially for you because there are such beautiful Christmas trees in the picture. How do you like them? Best wishes from all of us. From Mr. and Mrs. C. de Visser, Maatje and Leentje."

Mother had been listening attentively, once again flattered by the interest those people showed in her child. But Fransje cried, "I was there only yesterday! They must have seen me when I was there with my rumblepot!"

"Yes, but they sent the card the day before yesterday," Maria explained to him. Fransje found that hard to understand. Nevertheless, he was very happy with the card. He asked Mother and Father if he could put it up on the mantel so that everyone could see it. Although he probably didn't comprehend the meaning of New Year, so far it had been a joyous day for him.

Now Father was going to read the letters and the other postcards to the family. After he had discovered the reason for Fransje's noisy elation, he had waited patiently. After clearing his throat, he began, "Dear Brother, Sister-in-Law, and Children. This is to let you know—"

Outside, the handlebars of a bicycle scraped the wall and hurried footsteps sounded beside the house. The door was thrown open and a voice shouted, "Hello, anybody home?"

Father stopped reading, and Mother cried, "Come on in!"

A young man entered whom the older ones recognized as one of Verplanke's sons. He looked disturbed. He shook hands with no one, asked after no one's health, and wished no Happy New Years. Mother offered him a chair, but he didn't sit down. Going straight to the point, he blurted, "I came to tell you that my father passed away last night." His voice caught in his throat. Helplessly he looked from Father to Mother.

A lightning bolt out of a blue sky wouldn't have had such a devastating effect as this Job's tiding. Even Father was at a loss for words to respond to the news.

"But my dear boy!" cried Mother in a strange voice. "What happened? He was here last night, and he was so . . . so . . . ." She wanted to say, "full of life," but caught herself because of the words' ambiguity, which would certainly have hurt the young man.

The latter replied, "Mother found him dead in bed early this morning. The doctor said it was a stroke."

They still could not digest the news. Mother once again offered him a chair, saying, "Please sit down." But the boy remained standing, his hand resting on the back of the chair. He looked at Father and said, "Mother wants to know if you'll be a pallbearer at the funeral. As you know, we have no next door neighbors, and you were good friends to my father, and you belong to his church, so . . . ."

The last statement stung Father for a moment because it underlined the spiritual dividedness of the family, but at the same time he remembered Verplanke as he had been in their midst last night. His heart overflowed and in a voice laden with emotion, he said, "Your father is in heaven. And he was much closer than we could have foreseen last night. Yes, of course I want to be one of his pallbearers. When is the funeral?"

"Of course Father's in heaven. But he could have made it much easier on himself if he had believed it sooner."

Father looked at the young man. Momentarily he felt the urge to defend his old friend and to set the boy straight. But he thought better of it. He saw that the son's grief was honest, and that he was in no mood to listen to or absorb a theological explanation.

Fransje sat huddled on the bench. At first he hadn't understood the words, "passed away." But in a shocked voice Wantje, sitting beside him, had whispered in his ear that Verplanke was dead. His first thought had been, "That can't be! Verplanke can't be dead!" But the leaden atmosphere in the room, which had crushed the light-hearted gaiety of the morning, as well as the dismayed faces around him, showed all too clearly that it was true.

Fransje could not accept it. Was Verplanke going to be put in the cemetery? And was he never again coming for coffee after church? Only last night the man had given him a guilder. In his mind he saw the shiny coin in front of him. Inexplicably he also saw the murderer on the cross turning his head to Jesus. And the murderer suddenly had Verplanke's face and it was full of smile-wrinkles because Jesus had told him, "Soon you will be with Me in Paradise."

Then, with a thump, Fransje's head dropped to his arms on the table and his body shook with violent sobs. The Verplanke boy looked at the child in surprise, and when he saw that the child was weeping for his father, tears sprang to his own eyes. In a rush, he said, "Well, I better be going. I have to see some other people too."

This time he shook hands with everyone except Fransje who was still lying forward on the table with his head on his arms. He rumpled Fransje's unruly hair and left.

The letters were lying on the table unread. Turning, Maria took the two cards sent to her by secret admirers from between her clothing and surreptitiously slipped them into her pocket.

It was dinnertime. Mother had prepared a delicious meal—a roast of large rabbit, slaughtered by Father only last night—and the whole family had been looking forward to this moment. But now that the moment had arrived, no one was hungry anymore, and all of them sat at the table glumly staring into their plates, their appetites gone.

When it came time to read the Bible, Father departed from his usual procedure: he didn't pick up where he had left off yesterday, but turned to Psalm 31. When he came to the words, "Oh how great is thy goodness which thou hast laid up for them that fear thee," he couldn't go on. His voice failed him and tears set the words before him awash in an undulating sea. He pushed the Bible to Maria, who finished the Psalm. He could not say the closing prayer either. He asked Bram to pray the customary prayer. The day which had begun so beautifully had taken a sudden tragic turn.

Three days later there was another snowfall. With the carefree nature typical of children, Fransje had quickly recovered from the blow of Verplanke's sudden death. He was playing with the neighborhood children, making a snowman. It was about ten o'clock in the morning and in the distance he saw Father coming. He ran to meet him and asked him why he was home so early. Father told him that Verplanke would be buried this afternoon and that he was going to help carry the coffin.

Fransje walked with Father into the house, although he found it very uncongenial and a little eerie, for the curtains had been taken down and the shutters were partly closed. Although Verplanke had been no kin to them, immediately after his son's visit, Father had decided that after supper they would go into mourning. Father felt that Verplanke had been a brother, albeit in the spiritual sense. Then shouldn't they mourn because he had been taken from them? Especially in view of the fact that he hadn't found much love and understanding at home.

At first Fransje had found it very interesting. But it wasn't long before the somber atmosphere had begun to weigh heavily on him, so during the day he spent most of his time outdoors.

Mother poured Father a cup of coffee and cut several slices of bread, for the funeral started at twelve o'clock and he wouldn't be home for lunch. Then Father shaved himself. In order to see in the gloomy house, he set the little mirror that usually hung beside the window on the windowsill. He shoved the table away from the window and sat down on the bench. Fransje always watched very attentively when Father shaved himself, but he carefully kept his distance from the long, curved blade and from the piece of newspaper on which Father wiped the big wads of lather. Once Fransje had stuck his finger into the soft white foam, but upon discovering the smear of dark bristles inside, he had been so repulsed that he had almost vomited.

After shaving, Father put on his Sunday suit and shoes. Mother stood on her tiptoes to brush off his back and shoulders with the clothes brush.

"All right," said Father. "I'd better get going. Be seeing you."

Fransje walked along with Father a little ways. Halfway between home and the railroad station neighborhood Father sent him back, telling him that in an hour or so they would be passing the house. Fransje understood that "they" referred to the funeral procession. He was very curious about the funeral procession, because he had but a vague picture of it, formed primarily from Wantje's descriptions.

He no longer felt like playing with the neighbor children, so he wandered into the half-dark living room. But he couldn't see well enough to play there. He didn't really feel like it either. He considered asking Mother for the Bible picture book, but in this poor light he couldn't have seen the pictures very well anyway. He felt restless and spooked.

"Mommy, when are they coming?"

"Oh, they won't be here for another half hour. Why don't you go outside and play in the snow a little while."

Fransje didn't reply. Then he asked, "Are they going to put Mr. Verplanke in the grave now?"

"Yes, he is going to be buried this morning."

"But I thought you said he was in heaven?"

Understanding his puzzlement, Mother explained, "Inside every person lives a soul. When someone dies, his soul leaves his body. His body stays behind and this is what is put into the cemetery, into the grave. When Mr. Verplanke died, his soul went straight to heaven. What they are burying today is only his body."

Fransje was silent for a while. But soon his questions continued: "But how can he see in heaven without any eyes? When are the angels coming to get his body?"

Mother thought a moment. She was surprised by all those questions. None of the other children had ever asked such questions, and certainly not at his age. She wasn't quite sure how to explain everything. But she tried to answer his last question first. It was no pleasant task; she herself shuddered at the thought of the worms and corruption eating at the body. But she might not distort the truth. She went on to explain how in the last days all God's children will rise from the grave to be clothed with new bodies. Fransje was greatly relieved to hear this, but he was still puzzled about the disembodied soul in heaven. Mother tried to explain, but his face showed that her efforts were only partially successful. She just wasn't able to explain these mysteries. So she told him, without very much conviction, that he would understand it later when he was grown up.

"Why don't you go out and see if the procession is coming," she suggested. She knew it was still too early, but she wanted to put an end to the fruitless discussion.

Through the crack between the shutters she saw him out at the road a moment later, staring in the direction of the station. The other children were still playing in the snow. Fransje sauntered toward them but kept his hands in his pockets and did not join in.

Mother worried about him. A nameless, formless uneasiness gnawed at her. Having borne seven children, she knew they all had unique characters and dispositions. But in some respects this child was very different from the others. "Maybe the Lord has something special in mind for him," she suddenly thought.

A secret joy overcame her as she let her mind run on, and she saw him called to the ministry. But then she scolded herself for daring to entertain such lofty ambitions, and softly she sang,

> Unto me, O Lord Jehovah,
> Show Thy ways and teach Thou me,
> So that by Thy Spirit guided
> Clearly I Thy paths may see.

Fransje came back into the house to ask how long it would be. Mother told him they would be here any minute.

"Are you going outside to watch too?" he asked.

"No, I'm staying in the house. I'll look through the shutters."

Fransje was disappointed that Mother wasn't coming out with him. He would feel much safer with Mother at his side. But Mother told him that it wasn't proper for grown-ups to stand outside to watch a funeral procession go by. Again he walked to the road, and this time he saw something black moving in the distance. Immediately he ran back to tell Mother. Then he was off again.

At first he stood in the middle of the road, but the closer the procession came, the farther he retreated to the side. Finally he was standing pressed into the hedge along the front yard.

The procession was very near now. Fransje stared openmouthed. In front walked a man dressed in black and wearing a stovepipe hat. Then came two horses with black cloths draped over their backs, almost touching the ground. Tall black plumes swayed back and forth with the horses' heads. Behind them rolled a shiny black carriage which had a top, but no sides. From the canopy hung heavy black curtains tied back in sweeping folds to the corner posts of the carriage.

On each side of the carriage, walking with long, slow strides and slightly bowed heads, were three men. Suddenly Fransje recognized Father, who was the tallest. Luckily he was walking on Fransje's side of the road. For a moment Father lifted his head and gave him an almost imperceptible nod. Looking between the men, Fransje saw the long, rectangular shape of the coffin, but it, too, was covered by a black cloth. Under it lay Mr. Verplanke—Mr. Verplanke with the wrinkles of laughter around his eyes.

A long column of men followed the carriage. Some of them were dressed in black and others wore black armbands. Fransje recognized one of them as the son who had come to tell them the news of his father's death.

The carriage rolled by almost soundlessly. More vivid than the black carriage against the white snow was the impression that this scene made on Fransje's mind. He stared after it until he could see nothing but a black, bobbing cluster in the vicinity of Kees de Visser's house. Then he decided to go in. But suddenly his ear caught the faint sound of tolling bells. He knew that the sound was spilling from the Gothic tower of the old church in the village. He stopped and listened to it. The distant, melancholy pealing seemed to pluck at his heart so that he didn't know whether to laugh or cry. He turned around and slowly strolled into the house to Mother.

5

After a few days the snow had disappeared. At night the temperature fell below freezing, but the days were beautifully sunny. The roads dried and the children could play outdoors. To Fransje's delight, the shutters were open again. Although he spent the greater part of the day outside, when he did pop inside for a moment, the airy brightness in the living room pleased him.

The rumblepots had been discarded as the bladders began to deteriorate; they had been tossed on the manure pile behind the empty vegetable garden. But the unused reeds gave Kees the idea to make them into arrows. A long, supple willow branch became a strong bow, and he whittled arrowheads from pieces of elder wood.

Fransje had watched Kees's activities with great interest. After Kees had taken a couple of shots, Fransje asked him if he, too, could try it once. Knowing that Fransje was too small to manipulate the bow, Kees patiently handed him the bow and an arrow and showed him how to hold them. But the bow was much too long and awkward for Fransje, and his arms were much too short. Nor could he perform the three necessary movements at the same time. When he drew back the string, he held the arrow with his right hand, and when he released it, he forgot to let go of the middle of the arrow with his left hand. Disappointed, he gave up, and asked Kees if he would make him a little bow. But Kees said that to make a little bow you needed a short stick, and a short stick wouldn't bend. He had a good idea, however: Fransje could fetch the arrows after Kees shot them.

Fransje did this three times and then he saw through the arrangement. Gasping for breath, he sullenly told Kees to go and fetch his own arrows. He walked to Neeltje's house and asked her to come out and play with him.

Kees took his bow and arrows to the road. He shot them one after the other to see how far they would go, using the trees along the road as a measure. When he had shot the last arrow, however, he had to go and pick them up himself. That had been such a nice job for that lazy little Fransje. He decided it would be better to shoot at a target; then he wouldn't have to walk as far. With a piece of chalk that he had rescued from the wastepaper basket at school, he drew a circle on a large tree trunk and tried to hit it from a specified distance.

A thrush flew up from the steep bank of the ditch and landed a little farther away. Unthinkingly Kees aimed at it with his bow and arrow. But at once he saw Father's stern eyes before him, and quickly he lowered his arm. Father had emphatically hammered it into his and Arjaan's heads never to shoot at one another or at other children, or at birds. He was a passionate bird-lover; even the ordinary, insignificant sparrow had a place in his heart because it also had a place in God's Word. Although Father was nowhere to be seen at the moment, Kees bowed to his authority.

Fransje's thoughts seldom returned to Verplanke's death. When it did occasionally enter his mind, he instinctively refused to dwell on it. Like the hearts of all children—and of most adults too—his heart was drawn to happiness and light. He didn't think of his birthday very often either. A month encompassed so many days that their number was beyond his comprehension. He drifted along unfettered on the stream of time like a little boat.

The New Year's card which he had received from the De Vissers still stood on the mantel. When his eyes fell on it one afternoon, he suddenly remembered that they had asked him to visit them again sometime. At once he felt the urge to go. He climbed up on a chair and took down the card. Holding it under Mother's nose, he asked, "Would you tell me what it says on this card once more?"

Mother read it to him. Then he asked, "Mom, is it all right if I go and visit them a little while?" Mother thought it over for a moment, trying to produce a proper reason to give to his visit. Then she said, "I think so. You can go and thank them for the beautiful card."

Fransje was up in the clouds. At once he grabbed his coat and hat and allowed Mother to help him dress. He put his card in his coat pocket and gave Mother a loud farewell kiss.

"Stay on the shoulder of the road, and be polite to the De Vissers," Mother admonished him. Fransje eagerly gave her his word and disappeared. On the road he turned around once more to see if Mother was watching. He waved to her and then vanished from view. A little later she walked to the road to see whether he had arrived yet. She was just in time to see him walking across the little bridge.

In response to his bashful, "Anybody home!" one of the girls let him in with a friendly smile. She said, "Ah, Fransje! Did you come to pay us another visit? How nice! Come on in!"

He followed her to the large family room, where Mrs. de Visser and the other girl were sitting at the table sewing. All three were wearing their big hats. Kees de Visser sat at the other side of the table writing in a big book. Fransje went down the row shaking hands. But when Mrs. de Visser pulled him toward her and lowered her head to him, he took this as an invitation for a kiss, and blushing, he gave her one on the cheek. She seemed to like it, for she laughed and gave him two in return, one on each cheek. But then one of the girls objected, "That's not fair, Fransje. All we got was a handshake. Aren't we going to get a kiss too?"

Fransje was beginning to enjoy this. He went to them and gave both of them a noisy kiss on their soft cheeks.

"And what about me?" asked Kees, trying to sound slighted. But Fransje made no move to correct his oversight. He suspected that Mr. de Visser's cheek might be just as prickly as Father's and that perhaps his breath also smelled of chewing tobacco. "I don't blame you, Fransje," laughed De Visser. "Big boys don't kiss each other, do they?" These words flattered Fransje, and his liking for the man grew.

"I came to thank you for the nice card," said Fransje. "I still have it, see?" He carefully drew the card from his coat pocket and showed it to the foursome.

"Good boy!" said the girl who had let him in, smiling. "But you're not going to leave right away, are you? Here, let me take your coat and hat." She did so and hung his clothes on a chair in the corner of the room.

"Shall we have a nice cup of hot chocolate?" asked the other girl, standing up to get the necessary ingredients. Fransje nodded bashfully. Mrs. de Visser inquired about his mother and father and the other children. He felt quite at home here, in such a congenial atmosphere. He sat on a chair behind the table close to the big windows, and to please them he took a long look at his card. Meanwhile, however, he was pondering a problem. From having the card read to him he knew that the girls were called Maatje and Leentje, but which was which? Just then one of the girls said, "Leentje, why don't you show Fransje that big book with all the Bible pictures?"

Fransje had just enough time to ascertain which one was Leentje—the other one was thus Maatje. Her proposal was such a delightful surprise to him that his eyes sparkled with joy.

Very carefully he turned the pages of the big book until he came to the first picture. A number of brightly colored animals were gathered, calm and unconcerned, about two unclothed people, partially concealed behind some very beautiful flowers and happily surveying the activity around them.

Fransje knew that they were Adam and Eve in Paradise. A few pages farther he saw two rock piles. From one a thin plume of smoke rose straight to heaven, while from the other a dark, billowing cloud sank to the ground. Beside it stood a man angrily looking down on another man who lay at his feet. Those were Cain and Abel, Fransje knew. He said nothing but gave each picture a long and thoughtful look. For some pictures he did not yet know the story, but he didn't ask anyone to explain.

Maatje brought him a cup of chocolate and Leentje let him pick out a cookie from a tin that was almost full. Fransje had just turned to the picture of Jacob's dream. Leentje glanced at the book and asked him, "You know who that is, Fransje?"

"That's Jacob," replied Fransje. "He was bad. He lied to his father and then he ran away and then he dreamed about a ladder full of angels."

He related the story almost word for word as Mother had told it, and Leentje stared at him open-mouthed. The others were listening as well, no less surprised at his knowledge. Putting down the cookie tin, Leentje went to stand right beside Fransje. She turned a few pages and asked him about the next picture. Again he related a detailed story. This one was about Joseph who was thrown into a pit by his brothers. Then the girl turned over a large number of pages and pointed to a picture of the crucifixion. Again Fransje told the whole story, dwelling especially on the conversation between the one murderer and Jesus. As he did so, he once more saw the wrinkles of laughter around Verplanke's eyes, although neither of the murderers looked like him. The darning of the two other women lay forgotten in their laps. Kees de Visser's pen had for some time been arrested in the middle of a word. Then Mrs. de Visser asked, "How old are you, Fransje?"

"I'm almost four years old," Fransje replied proudly. "Mother said my birthday comes on the last day of this month."

"You better drink your hot chocolate now," advised Maatje. Leisurely they all emptied their cups. Fransje was careful not to slurp, for Mother had taught him that slurping was very rude. Blissfully he nibbled at his delicious cookie.

Suddenly a shrill ringing erupted from a corner of the room near the hall. It frightened Fransje; he thought an alarm clock was running off somewhere. But De Visser stood up to take a black object from a small cabinet, and he held it against his ear. He talked into another black thing attached to the cabinet. Fransje didn't know what to think. He looked at the mother and the girls with large, wondering eyes. They couldn't help laughing at his puzzled expression, but they remained silent and gave him no explanation. De Visser stopped talking and hung the black object back in its place.

"Why did you talk to that thing?" Fransje asked him. They all laughed.

De Visser said, "This is a telephone, Fransje. A man in town talked to me through it."

This was totally beyond Fransje's comprehension, and he asked himself whether De Visser wasn't teasing him. But out of politeness he said nothing further.

Then De Visser remarked that he had to go to town a minute to run an errand. In the hall he quietly told Leentje to keep Fransje busy until he returned. He would call from the post office and then they had to let Fransje talk to him. He took his bike from the shed and pedaled away.

Fransje had spent time enough with the big picture book. From a closet in the corner near the window, Leentje fetched a coloring book and a box of crayons. "Here," she suggested, "why don't you color for a while?"

Fransje eyed these treasures eagerly. He paged through the book awhile and then turned back to the first page. On it was a picture of a large rooster, a few chickens, and several chicks, which strongly reminded him of his candy flock. But these all had empty bodies which had to be filled with colors. He became so engrossed in his coloring that when the phone rang, it frightened him again, and he yelped, "There it goes again!"

The women laughed. Leentje, who had taken the black object from the hook, said hello and then called Fransje to the phone. "Here," she told him. "It's my dad. He wants to talk to you."

She held the instrument against his ear and lifted him up so that his mouth was close to the mouthpiece. A voice crackled in his ear, "Hello there, Fransje! Do you know who this is?" Though Fransje understood the words, he did not recognize the voice, and so he didn't know what to say. He shook his head slightly. "I'm Kees de Visser," the voice crackled again. "And who did you say you were?" This time he had to say something and he answered, nonplussed, "Fransje Weststrate."

"And whose boy are you?"

"My mother and father's."

"See? I told you we could talk over a telephone."

This time Fransje nodded without speaking.

"I'll be back shortly. Bye, Fransje. See you in a few minutes."

"Bye," Fransje responded faintly. Leentje lowered him to the floor and hung up. "My, but you're a big boy!" she praised him. "You can already talk over a telephone!" Fransje blushed. What would they say at home!

Shortly thereafter the door opened, but it wasn't Kees de Visser who entered. It was a man and a woman and a little boy about Fransje's age. The three visitors shook hands with the women, and the man said to Fransje, "So, my little friend. And whose little boy are you?"

The man, it seemed, was Mrs. de Visser's brother. Therefore the little boy called her Aunt Janna; from this, and from the beautiful clothes the visitors were wearing, Fransje concluded that they were rich and important people. In Fransje's circles she would simply have been called Auntie.

The little boy walked over to Fransje to see what he was doing.

"What's your name?" he asked straightforwardly.

"Fransje. And yours?"

"My name's Jan Blok. What's your last name?"

Fransje told him his last name. Soon they were good friends. Jan Blok told Fransje that he lived on a farm on the other side of the train tracks. Fransje should come over to play with him sometime, he said. He interrupted his mother, who was deep in conversation with the other women, to ask her, "Mother, can Fransje come and play with me on the farm sometime?"

"Sure, he can come this spring, when the weather gets a little warmer. Now it's still much too muddy around the farm."

Jan was obviously no stranger in this house. He took Fransje into the corner to the same closet the coloring book had come from, and he dragged out all kinds of playthings with which he appeared to be familiar. He told Fransje that these were his toys whenever he visited Aunt Janna's. Soon the two boys were so busy playing that neither of them noticed Kees de Visser enter the room. But he cried, "Fransje, how did you like talking over the telephone?" Then Fransje told Jan that he had talked to his uncle over the telephone. This, however, was nothing special to Jan, who had often talked over the phone.

Fransje was a true product of his environment. He considered it a matter of course that Jan had much nicer clothes than he, because Jan's parents were obviously rich. Thus, there was no question whatsoever of jealousy. There was one piece of clothing, however, that Jan wore which caused Fransje to sin against the tenth commandment. That was his pants. It wasn't because the material was of so much better quality than Fransje's threadbare corduroy pants, nor because of the much lighter color of the soft woolen fabric, but it was because of the *kind* of pants Jan was wearing. They were pants with real suspenders—elastic suspenders with bright red and blue stripes. Fransje's older brothers all wore suspenders too, but his brothers were so much older than he, that he considered it natural. Not long ago he had been walking about in skirts. But here was a boy who wasn't even as tall as Fransje and he was already wearing suspenders. This he certainly had to tell Mother!

Jan's father and mother stood up and said it was time to go. Since they were going in the same direction as Fransje, Jan's father offered him a ride. Leentje helped Fransje into his clothes. Secretly she slipped a bag of chocolate flicks into his coat pocket. As she crouched in front of him, softly she asked him, "Are you going to give me another kiss?" Quickly he complied, at the same time looking to see if Jan was watching.

After saying goodbye, Fransje and Jan followed the latter's parents to the little bridge. At the side of the road, its reins tied to the bridge railing, stood a horse harnessed to a glossy black carriage. Fransje asked himself how he was going to get by the horse's huge head, and he wished he were already on the road. But then he saw Mr. Blok untie the reins from the iron railing and lead the horse onto the road by its harness. Next Mr. Blok opened the carriage door and helped his wife inside. Jan followed on her heels. Then Mr. Blok said to Fransje, "Okay, now it's your turn!" Only now did Fransje realize that this beautiful carriage belonged to Jan's father, and with a pounding heart he took his place on the soft upholstery patterned in pleated diamonds. He heard Mr. Blok shouting from the driver's seat, "Giddyap!" and the coach began to roll.

It was a short-lived pleasure, for a moment later they stopped and Mr. Blok once more opened the door. Fransje saw that they stood right in front of his house. The man seized him under the arms and set him down on the ground. "Bye-bye, Fransje!" he heard Jan call, and then the carriage rolled on.

Fransje sat on the bench behind the table giving an enthusiastic and exhaustive account of the afternoon's events. Meanwhile his subconscious conceived a plan, and as soon as he had finished his story, he said, "And, Mom, Jan had suspender pants like the big boys have. Can I have suspender pants, Mom? I still have that guilder in my piggybank that Mr. Verplanke gave me, and that's enough to buy suspenders, isn't it, Mom?" Mother smiled at the clever observation, but then she said, "But who's going to pay for the pants?"

Since Fransje was secretly of the opinion that that was Mother's headache, he didn't reply. He just repeated his plea with greater insistence. To lend his words force, he tried to bribe Mother. He slid the bag of chocolate flicks toward her and said, "Here, you may have these. And then I can have a suspender pants, can't I Mom?"

Mother smiled again, but she didn't take him up on the transaction. She sat and stared out into space for a few moments. The boy did need a new pair of pants, and if he was so eager to have a pair of suspender pants rather than the rompers usually worn by boys his age, it made no difference to her. However, she postponed a definite decision, saying, "We'll see. Maybe for your birthday."

Fransje was convinced that his plea was as good as won. He asked how many more nights before that day would come. Mother said a whole bunch—fifteen. He sighed. Fifteen nights sounded like a very long time to him, just as far off as it had sounded two weeks ago.

A regular visitor every Saturday afternoon was La Bruyere, the village tailor, who no doubt owed his name to Huguenot ancestry. Popular usage had corrupted the name to the more easily pronounced Lebroor, which is how he was addressed. When talking *about* him, however, people often referred to him by the less complimentary title, Ragthief. Although it was not always meant to imply anything, the title did derive from gossip that he sometimes cut his material too small in order to cut costs.

The weekly visits—usually between twelve and one—did not mean that he received a new order every time. What he did receive was one guilder, which was Mother's weekly payment on the bill which she kept in the drawer of the linen closet and which La Bruyere had made out for clothes that had been doing service for some time already—work pants and Sunday suits for the older boys and a breast jacket for Maria.

La Bruyere was very hard of hearing and consequently spoke in a loud voice that dominated the room. He belonged to the same church as Fransje's parents, and loved to discuss religion and politics. This irritated Father, because he only talked externals, avoiding all spiritual conversation. Father was usually home when the man came, shaving himself at the small mirror near the window. La Bruyere had no idea that he irritated Father. No doubt this was due to the partial isolation caused by his deafness. So he chattered on undaunted.

When Mother had pushed the guilder toward him and he had dutifully noted it on the long strip of paper, she asked, "Could you make a pair of pants for Fransje? Corduroy," she quickly added before he could ask what to make it from.

"Rompers I presume?" he asked, as if that had already been established.

"No, he would like suspender pants, so why don't you make him a pair of regular shorts."

Fransje, who had been following this conversation with great interest, put his hand in his mouth to stifle a cry of joy. He was really going to get a pair of suspender pants! In his imagination he could already see himself outfitted just like Jan Blok. He was thereby making a big mistake; his comparison was much too literal. He did not suspect that in a week this mistake would cost him bitter tears.

Mr. Ragthief produced his tape measure to take Fransje's measurements. Father turned his lathered face to the tailor and called, "Make sure his pantlegs come down over the knees, eh?" Father had a strong dislike for shorts and would prefer to see all boys wearing long pants. But because that wasn't the custom, he chose this middle road, much to the chagrin of Arjaan and Kees, who had to go dressed in a cross between shorts and long pants. Although they shortened their suspenders as far as they could, the stubborn crotch prevented the pantlegs from rising above their knees. Mother was also in favor of having the knees covered, to protect the boys' stockings when they fell.

Fransje was not at all pleased by the way La Bruyere turned him around so roughly and put his hands in places that triggered Fransje's sense of shame. But if he wanted a new pair of pants, he'd just have to put up with it.

With repeated licks to a pencil stub, the tailor wrote a few figures on a smudged scrap of paper, and in a loud voice assured Fransje that he'd have his beautiful pants done next week.

"It's for my birthday," Fransje confided. He did not tell him this in order to be friendly, but merely out of relief that the man had finished fumbling about with the tape measure.

Now that Fransje's birthday was drawing closer, he began to show more interest in it. He could now count off the days on his fingers, which brought the anticipated event within the scope of his conception. Not that he harbored expectations of more presents. He considered himself greatly favored that he had received suspenders and would soon receive a pair of pants to go with them. Thinking of his birthday, however, made him stop and think about the concept, time. He was three years old now. But soon he would be four. And before he was three, he was two, and before that one, and before that . . . nothing! Then where was he before that? That was a question for Mother.

"Mom, where was I before I was a little baby?"

"Nowhere," answered Mother. But Fransje could not conceptualize that. To his mind he had always existed; he must have come from somewhere.

"Then where did I come from?" he persisted.

Having had to answer such questions before, Mother replied without hesitating, "The Lord gave you to us."

"You mean the Lord came to our house and gave me to you? Did you see the Lord? What did He say to you?"

Mother hadn't expected these questions and asked herself how she could sidestep the biological facts without doing violence to the truth. She replied that the Lord didn't come Himself to deliver babies, but that He used a doctor who did it for Him. And even if the Lord had come into the house, they wouldn't have been able to see Him, because the Lord didn't have a body like people. And the Lord didn't talk like people either. He speaks in the Bible, she said, and sometimes very quietly in people's hearts. But then you still don't hear a voice like a human voice.

This explanation, however, helped Fransje not one whit. Did the doctor have a supply of babies, and how did he know where to bring them if the Lord didn't have a voice like his? Besides, that still didn't answer the question of where the doctor got all those babies. Did God make them in heaven and did the angels bring them to the doctor? How come the doctor was so favored that he was in touch with God and angels when this was denied to everyone else? And if God made babies in heaven, then he, Fransje, had been there, something he had long suspected, although he remembered none of it.

One question piled on the next, and helpless, almost pleading, he looked at Mother. He could not even put all his questions into words, but the few that he was able to formulate made clear to Mother that she had not given him the right answer.

True, she had used almost the same answer before when the other children had been small, and then it had been usually sufficient and satisfactory. When they grew up without ever asking her any more questions in this area, it had been obvious that they had obtained further enlightenment elsewhere. It would have been best, of course, if all these things could have been discussed freely and honestly with children, but she didn't feel competent to do so. Besides, this child was still much too young. So she told him what she should have told him right away:

"No, Fransje, the Lord doesn't make babies in heaven, and He doesn't bring them to the doctor either. He gives them right to their mothers. But how He does it and how that works I can't tell you yet. You're still too young to understand that."

Fransje immediately sensed that he was standing before an awesome mystery. A great respect and deep awe silenced all further questions in him. Actually he was glad that Mother had said this because he sensed that his mind couldn't understand it all anyway. All he wanted to know was whether Wantje knew these things already, but Mother could honestly set his mind at ease. Wantje, too, knew nothing about it.

"And Kees and Arjaan?" he asked.

"I haven't told them either."

Then he asked Mother to tell him about when he was a little baby. Mother related various details from his baby years, which he enjoyed tremendously. They all seemed to be about someone else, a tiny creature he could contemplate outside of himself, while in the back of his mind was the pleasant knowledge that Mother was talking about him.

The last week before his birthday passed as usual. Every morning he said to Mother, "So many more nights," each time putting up one less finger than the day before. This, however, was more a fixed routine he had established for himself than a sign of impatience. At the same time there was the happy realization that his new pants were coming ever nearer. He had imagined the moment when he would put them on so often that sometimes he felt as if he were already wearing them.

Finally the long-awaited morning arrived, the morning of Saturday, the thirty-first of January. Instead of getting up early, however, he slept so late that Wantje could no longer contain her impatience. She crept up the ladder and tiptoed to his bed, where she poked her head under the canopy and cried, "Wake up, Fransje. It's your birthday today!"

Sleepily Fransje opened his eyes and stared into Wantje's face. He hadn't understood what she said and looked at her blankly. Then Wantje repeated the message, and suddenly Fransje was wide awake. He sat up and clambered out of bed. But then he sent Wantje downstairs, because first he had to do something at which he allowed no spectators.

In the living room he ran with outstretched arms to Mother, who scooped him up and kissed him on both cheeks.

"Congratulations, my boy," she said and kissed him again. Like their special New Year's greeting, the family also had a special birthday greeting, and Mother said it to him: "Congratulations at the increase of another year. May you live many more and one day pass on into His blessed presence."

Wantje, the only other person at home, shook Fransje's hand and recited the same greeting. Before letting go, she also gave him a kiss, and then she held her open hand under his nose. In it lay a large glass marble with a bright red, ornate center. It looked like a flame or a strange flower with a glass ball coagulated around it.

"This is for you," Wantje said triumphantly. "For your birthday."

Fransje took the marble between his thumb and forefinger and held it up in the light. His eyes drank in the gentle sparkle with deep satisfaction, and he cried, "What a bootiful marvel! Is it for me? Just me?" His difficulty with the word "beautiful" caused him to make the second error with the word "marble," an error that didn't escape alert little Wantje and spurred her to correct him. To make up for it, she said, "Yes, it's for you. I bought it just for your birthday with that nickel I saved from New Year's."

Fransje was touched by her self-denial and lack of selfishness. He walked up to her and gave her a ringing kiss.

Mother said, "After you eat your breakfast, I'll have something for you too. But first you have to finish your breakfast."

Fransje could hardly contain his amazement. All he had counted on was the new pair of pants, which would come in the afternoon, but now he had already gotten two other surprises. Quickly he ate breakfast and dressed. Then Mother took from the cabinet something light blue. She lay it down folded in front of him on the table. Fransje carefully unfolded it and cried, "Oooh! A new shirt! A new shirt! When did you buy that, Mom?"

"I didn't buy it, Fransje. Maria and I made it on the sewing machine. Now that you're going to get a new pants, you'll also need a new shirt. Right?"

Fransje hadn't the words to express his happiness and astonishment. He hadn't seen them working on the shirt at all. They must have made it when he was sleeping.

But more surprises awaited him. As he was trying on the shirt, Kees came downstairs. In his hands he carried a small bow and a bundle of short arrows. Fransje saw at a glance that they were not Kees's. Kees held the objects out to him saying, "Here, Fransje, this is for you. I found a branch I could make into a little bow after all. And I also made some arrows for you. For your birthday."

The shirt, cut amply with an eye to Fransje's growth, still hung unbuttoned and open about his body, the sleeves reaching to the middle of his hands. There he stood, the bow in one hand and the bundle of arrows in the other, staring speechlessly at his new treasures with beaming eyes. What a joyous day his birthday had become! Immediately he wanted to go outside to see if he could handle his bow. He shed his new shirt and pulled on his old one. He wanted to run right out, but Mother stopped him. "First wash your face. Did you think I was going to let you run out like that? The sand is still in your eyes."

Another surprise awaited him. He was busily playing with his bow and arrows beside the house, a determined look on his face. He'd keep trying until he had mastered the noble art. He was already four years old today—a big boy. And big boys had to be able to shoot a bow.

He was improving; the arrows went farther each time. One arrow flew all the way to the road. As he walked toward it to pick it up, the mailman rode around the back of the house on his bicycle. Parking it against the wall, he called to Fransje, "Are you Fransje Weststrate?" When Fransje nodded, he added, "Here's a card for you."

Fransje ran to the mailman and accepted the card with a trembling hand. It was a beautiful card, a picture of a boy resting his head on a white, curly-haired puppy. Underneath it were gilt letters. Into his mind flashed the thought that the De Visser family must have sent it. Mother could tell him whether he was right. He ran into the house and shouted, "Mom, look what the mailman brought me! Who sent me the pretty card!"

Mother looked on the back of the card and read, "Sender: Maria." The only other writing was their own address. She turned the card over and remarked, "My, that's a beautiful card! Aren't you the lucky one today!"

Maria, who worked in the fields during the summer, had little work during the winter, so she was happy to serve as a housemaid at the big farm a few mornings a week. Therefore she wasn't home this morning; however, knowing ahead of time that she'd be absent, last night after catechism she had bought a card in town and dropped it into the slot at the post office in the hope that Fransje would get it on his birthday.

Fransje's cup was so full that he was almost afraid it would run over. And this afternoon La Bruyere would deliver his new suspender pants!

After lunch Fransje quickly slipped into his coat and ran outside. He stood in the middle of the road and stared in the direction of town to see if he could spot a bicycle coming. It had to have a large, rectangular basket attached to the front of the handlebars, for that meant it was La Bruyere's. At that moment he was the only person in the world of interest to Fransje. For he would soon arrive with the joy to crown all Fransje's joys.

Fransje stood with his hands in the pockets of his coat. He felt the large, smooth glass marble and nervously let it roll repeatedly from his sweaty hand. Finally he thought he could discern the white speck of the tailor's basket. He stared so intently that numerous tiny, twisting speckles appeared before his eyes. It didn't help to look away, for as soon as he focused his attention back on the moving white speck, the irritating little fish swam back. Fransje would have to be patient until the bike came closer.

Yes, Fransje's eyes had not betrayed him: it was indeed the tailor. A moment later he braked right in front of Fransje. Lifting his right foot off the pedal, he stretched his leg back until his black, leather slipper found the long pin jutting from the rear axle. From it he leaped upwards and sideways to land beside the bike.

"Hello there, sonny!" he cried in a loud, nasal voice. "I've got your new pants with me." He propped his bike against the wall, opened the black canvas covering the basket, and lifted out a small bundle wrapped in a dark blue remnant. Then he tied the canvas shut again.

Fransje meanwhile had run ahead of him into the house and announced, "Here comes Lebroor with my new pants!"

The tailor was talking even before he entered the house. He tossed the blue bundle onto a chair and shook hands with everyone present. Then he made himself at home, sitting down at the table. Father was again shaving himself, and he shouted at Father's back, "Nice weather, eh Marien?" Lips contorted, Father answered without turning his head, "Yup, it's unusually nice for this time of year."

From the cabinet Mother took the long strip of paper and some money. This time she gave La Bruyere two guilders, which he obligingly noted on the paper, immediately thereafter adding the cost of Fransje's new pants.

Fransje could hardly contain his impatience. Wasn't the man ever going to unwrap the bundle?

Maria, too, arrived home. Now the entire family was in the room. Most of them ignored the prattle of the garrulous man, but that didn't seem to bother him. Arjaan and Kees were giggling conspiratorially as they whispered the word "ragthief" back and forth to each other.

Suddenly the tailor turned to Fransje and shouted, "Come here, sonny, and take off your shirt and your pants. Then we'll see if your new pants fit you."

Fransje stared at him in astonishment. He was deeply offended on two counts: first, the man had twice called him "sonny," a title which he hated because Pier was sometimes so addressed by his mother; secondly, and even worse, without batting an eye the man had asked him to take off his clothes in front of him. Just the thought of it made Fransje blush. He made no move to comply. But Mother, who considered the request quite reasonable, and who also had to observe proper manners, began to unbutton Fransje's shirt. When she felt him holding himself stiff and passively resistant, she used more force and threw him a stern look. If he wanted to get the coveted suspender pants, he'd have to abjectly surrender and bear the humiliation.

In the meantime La Bruyere had opened the blue bundle behind Fransje's back and triumphantly produced a little pile of cloth. For a moment Fransje forgot his underwear and stared at the black object in surprise. He was abruptly and utterly disillusioned; all this time he had been envisioning light colored pants just like Jan Blok had been wearing. Again he turned bright red, and instinctively retreated farther between Mother's knees. But the tailor unfolded the pants, and bending forward toward Fransje, held it open at the boy's feet. "All right, step into it!" he boomed.

Fransje looked down. A nauseating smell rose from the new cloth. But that sickness in his stomach wasn't the worst of it. What he saw in that brief moment filled him with such revulsion that suddenly his heart turned to stone. He shot another glance at the horrible sight before him. Then he turned his head and buried his face in Mother's apron. He squeezed his eyes shut so tightly he saw yellow and red spots, but it did little good, for he kept seeing the thing that had filled him with such loathing. A shudder racked his body at the thought that soon that thing would embrace him in obscene intimacy—the thing with the stiff fly from which large, glistening buttons stared at him like so many lascivious eyes; the thing with the large, bulky pockets that didn't hang down flat as in his old pants, but jutted diagonally as in the work pants of the older boys; the thing which was so stiff it could stand up by itself! Suddenly Fransje was very sure that he wouldn't wear that thing. He was physically repulsed by it, and to him it seemed a living thing bent on violating his sense of shame; it seemed possessed by an impulse to touch him in places he himself touched only when necessary. His cup of well-being, which only this morning had been at the point of overflowing, lay shattered at his feet.

A leaden stillness weighted the air around him, threatening to squash him under its weight. In the ominous stillness the ticking of the clock clanged like a hammer on an anvil. Dazed, he asked himself how long it would be before the thunderstorm broke. La Bruyere was the first to break the oppressive silence by saying, "Come on there, sonny, one foot at a time!"

Mother roughly turned Fransje around and grabbed one of his legs. She forced it in the direction of the gaping pants and protruding pockets, and said curtly, "Come, let's get those pants on."

Fransje knew that now the storm had begun and his entire being yearned for the moment when it would have spent itself. But it still loomed before him. He had no choice but to look death in the eye. Jerking his leg out of Mother's grasp, he cried in a cracked voice, "I don't want those pants. I don't want them. They make me sick! They make me sick!"

Mother tried to save the situation by once more roughly grabbing hold of his leg, but in so doing she lost the battle. Fransje suddenly became a wild animal. Shrieking, he clawed at Mother's hand with both his hands and twisted his body from side to side to escape from her grasp. His mouth foamed and he bellowed a stream of unintelligible sounds.

One more time Mother tried to salvage her honor and authority and began to give him a sound thrashing. But then Father suddenly jumped between them. He barked at Mother, "What is this anyway?" The words were actually meant for La Bruyere. Taking two long strides, he snatched the small pants out of the hands of the nonplussed tailor and flung them toward the doors of the built-in-bed. "He doesn't have to put that thing on if it upsets him so!" he added angrily.

"If that doesn't beat all!" protested Mother. "We ordered it!"

"I don't care! He's much too small to be walking around in a wooden box like that. Use your head!"

La Bruyere had no problem at all following this conversation, because it was conducted at high volume. Nervously he plopped back into his chair and soothed Mother, "It don't matter, missis. I can take them pants back. I have to make one for another little boy about the same age. It don't matter at all." He reached for the long strip of paper to scratch off the last numbers.

Arjaan and Kees, who had been watching the drama with pounding hearts and tremendous suspense, breathed a sign of relief that the storm had subsided. In nervous exuberance they put their heads together and Arjaan muttered almost out loud, "Look at that old ragthief. How can a pair of pants made for Fransje fit someone else?"

Fransje was still sobbing. He was surprised that the storm was already over, and even more so that Father had so unexpectedly taken his part. Mother had released him and made no move at all toward reconciliation. He dared not turn to Father, afraid that he would be punished for his rudeness and unmannerly behavior. Undecided and lost, he stood between Mother and La Bruyere. But then Maria took pity on him. She stepped in among the threesome, scooped Fransje up into her arms and carried him into the back room. There she gave him some water to drink and washed his face and wrists with a cold washcloth.

"Did you get my card this morning from the mailman?" she asked him. Fransje nodded emphatically while dry sobs kept welling up in his breast. Gratefully he looked at his big sister and, when he calmed down a little, he asked, "Will you get my coat and hat from the living room? And my shirt and pants," he added as he remembered that he was still in his underwear. "I'm going to play outside."

But Maria didn't do what he asked. She lifted him from the table and carried him back into the living room. There calmly and solicitously she helped him into his clothes and then loudly said to him, "Fransje, why don't you go and play outside now for a little while. It's such beautiful weather today."

Without looking at the tailor, Fransje passed behind his chair on his way to the hall. Out of the corner of his eye he saw the shapeless little pile of cloth lying on the floor in front of Maria's bed. However, he forced himself not to look at it openly. He had no desire to see the loathsome fly and the gruesome buttons and the gaping pockets ever again.

Outside he reflected on the fact that his new suspenders were now useless. He couldn't wear them with his rompers. He'd just have to wait with suspenders until he was older and Kees grew out of his partly worn-out and therefore much softer pants. Even then he would demand that Mother first give it a thorough washing so that all traces of its previous owner would be expunged before he would permit it to touch his body where he tolerated no contamination.

He was carrying his bow around his shoulder the way he had seen Kees do it and he held two arrows in his hand. But he didn't feel like shooting. Without knowing what he really intended to do, he began to walk. He purposely headed toward the village because he emphatically did not want to see the tailor again, and he knew that soon the man would continue in the other direction.

Briefly he considered going to the De Vissers, but he immediately dismissed the thought. He remembered that he had met Jan Blok there last time, and this was too vivid a reminder of what had just transpired.

Aimlessly he walked along, kicking pebbles with his wooden shoes. He kept his head down looking for new pebbles as each one landed in the canal, so he didn't see the shiny new bike coming toward him until a girl dismounted right next to him. It was Leentje de Visser. Cheerfully she greeted him, "Hi there, Fransje. Where are you going all by yourself?"

Surprised and glad, Fransje looked up into the friendly face above him. "Nowhere," he answered. "I'm just going for a walk. Where are you going?" He blushed after saying this, for it was a bit forward of him to quiz Leentje this way.

The girl saw by his red eyes that he had been crying, but she didn't want to hurt his feelings by mentioning it. She answered, "Oh, I'm going to see my Uncle Johannes and Aunt Lene. You remember them: Jan Blok's mother and father. Do you want to come along?"

Fransje's eyes lit up. He couldn't help looking at the carrier on the back of her bike. He didn't have to tell Leentje how much he would like to go with her. But he was afraid to say yes.

Leentje understood his hesitation. She set his mind at ease by saying, "I'll just be a little while. We'll be right back. Your mother won't be worried because we won't be gone that long."

Then Fransje looked at the bow and arrows in his hand. He didn't dare take them with him on the bike because then he wouldn't be able to hold on. But Leentje had a solution for that too. She took the bow from his shoulder and hung it on the headlamp, and the arrows she put in the brown satchel hanging from the handlebars. Holding the bike with one hand, she hoisted Fransje upon the carrier with the other. "You can hold onto my apron, under my shawl," she said, hopping onto the seat.

Never having been on a bike before, Fransje enjoyed the new experience hugely. When they passed his house, he quickly turned his head away because he didn't want them to see him. It grieved him, however, that he could not wave to Mother, and that in turn reminded him of the painful gap between them.

Leentje chatted with him over her shoulder. Several times she asked him if he was comfortable and admonished him to hold on. A little later they passed the first houses of the railroad station neighborhood, and shortly thereafter the bicycle tires were bumping over the railroad tracks. Soon Fransje saw a large barn and beside it a stately house. At the gate in the hawthorn hedge which separated the yard from the gravel road, Leentje jumped off the bike and wheeled Fransje up the walk. Then they went inside.

Jan gave Fransje an enthusiastic welcome and cried, "Did you come to play with me?" Fransje looked at Leentje and answered, "Leentje said we have to go right back." But Leentje said, "Oh, you two can play for fifteen minutes or so, I think."

Jan immediately took his friend to a corner of the large living room beside a window that looked out on the railroad tracks. From a built-in cabinet under the window Jan pulled a pile of toys. But then he gave Fransje close scrutiny and said, "You cried. I can tell by your eyes."

Fransje blushed deeply and bent low over the toys. But he did not try to deny it.

"Why did you cry?" Jan wanted to know. "Did your mother give you a spanking?"

This in any case Fransje could deny, although it had been a

close call. He took hold of a toy and suggested they play something nice.

But Jan wasn't sidetracked so easily. He persisted, "First you have to tell me why you cried." Fransje saw no way to escape his inquisitor and, stammering, he admitted, "Because I didn't want to put on the pants the tailor made for me."

That made Jan laugh. Fransje was immediately ready to take offense because he didn't realize that his condensed explanation could not possibly give Jan a clear idea of the hurt that was still so fresh in his own mind. Again tears sprang to his eyes, and sympathetically Jan asked what was wrong with the pants. Fransje was forced to tell the whole story. He told Jan that he had very much wanted a pants just like his, and that the tailor had come with a stiff, ugly thing that stank and had pockets just like those in men's work pants. He kept quiet, however, about the foremost reason for his revulsion, neglecting to mention the yawning fly. He ended his story with the words, "And they were supposed to be for my birthday!"

Jan had listened to Fransje's sad story with deep interest. Although he had never had to wear one, he could well imagine how queer it would look if he had to wear a miniature replica of his older brothers' work pants. And then on your birthday to boot! Suddenly he jumped up and ran to his mother. "Mother, it's Fransje's birthday today and he wanted a pants just like mine, and now the tailor brought him a stinky one. Mother, can Fransje have my pair, the ones that are too big for me?"

The woman looked from her son to Fransje in astonishment. She had no idea what Jan was talking about.

"And he even cried. Just look," Jan added, trying to convince his mother.

Fransje was so embarrassed he wished he could sink through the floor. He stole a glance at Leentje who was eyeing him compassionately, and once more tears sprang to his eyes. But Jan's mother still understood little of Jan's plea. She asked, "Why did his new pants smell?"

Fransje had a skilled advocate in Jan, but he wasn't in the mood to appreciate him. Jan's mother suspected that Fransje was a little spoiled at home, just like her own son, who was also the youngest. She studied him a moment. He really didn't look like a spoiled child. She was acquainted with his family and realized that there couldn't be much to spare with such a large family, especially during the winter. She knew that the farmer whom Fransje's father worked for didn't have enough work to keep the two oldest boys working full-time, and that his oldest sister also worked only about a half day a week. She was acquainted with them because they belonged to the same church as she did. And although she wasn't at all sentimental or overly pious, she told herself she ought to give those people a helping hand once in a while.

Again she looked at the little boy, who was biting his lips to keep back the tears. She felt sorry for him. She saw the strong plea in her son's face and also read a silent urging in Leentje's eyes. Without saying anything she left the room. A little later she reappeared in the doorway with something gray hanging over her arm. She called, "Fransje, will you come here a moment?"

Fransje reluctantly went to her. She shut the door behind him and took off his outer clothes. For the second time today Fransje was standing in his underwear. To his own surprise, however, this time he didn't have the humiliating feeling of being naked. Whether it was because she was dressed in *doek* and *beuk* exactly like his own mother (except that she was also wearing her large hat) or because she acted as if it was the most ordinary thing in the world to undress a little boy, Fransje could not say. The women held open the soft cloth of the pants just as La Bruyere had done earlier that afternoon. Willingly he lifted first one leg and then the other, and his sense of shame wasn't violated even when she closed his fly.

"You're quite a bit bigger than Jan," she said in surprise. "It fits you exactly." She plucked a couple of pins out of her *doek* and fastened the shorts to his undershirt.

"You may take these pants home with you. They are yours now. A birthday present. Let's go back into the living room and show Jan and Leentje how nicely they fit and how sharp you look."

Fransje felt as if he were dreaming. The unbelievable, that which he had so fervently desired but no longer expected, had suddenly become a reality!

Elated Jan leaped and danced around Fransje. "Look, Fransje, now you have pants just like mine!" he shouted three times in a row. Leentje looked on with a quiet smile. "Now you'll look nice when you go to church tomorrow," she said happily. She was reminded of the Bible stories he had related to her when looking at the pictures in the big book.

Fransje was at a loss for words to express his happiness.

"But now it's time for us to get back," said Leentje. "Fransje's parents don't even know he's here."

Jan protested, saying that they had hardly had time to play. But his mother said that Fransje would have to come back some other time.

Fransje was lying in his little bed in the attic. The lamp had not yet been taken away, for the other boys were not yet in bed. He was mulling over the day's events. Now he was a big boy. He was already four years old. And he had a beautiful pair of suspender pants—one that raised no aversion in him whatsoever. And tomorrow he would wear them to church, with his new suspenders and the new shirt that Mother and Maria had made for him.

He had told Mother that he was sorry for carrying on the way he had. Mother had run her fingers through his hair, saying that he should also ask the Lord for forgiveness.

Fransje's hands were folded across his stomach under the blankets. He thought he actually should get on his knees to talk to the Lord, but he was too tired and it was too cold in the attic. He'd do it this way. He began by telling the Lord how happy he was with his new pants. And with his new suspenders. And with Maria's beautiful card. And with his bow and arrows. And with his marvelous marble. And with . . . and with . . . and . . . .

6

The first two weeks of February brought such unusually mild weather that it seemed spring had already arrived. Even at night the temperature didn't drop below freezing, and during the day the sun traced its brilliant course across an almost cloudless sky. The banks of the small canals, until recently dormant under a layer of last year's yellow, frozen grass, were slowly and tentatively turning green as new, tender grass boldly shot up between the dead tufts. Here and there the first daisies lifted their pleated red-rimmed, dazzling white hats to the life-giving light. In the flower garden in front of the house the hibernating wallflowers had stretched themselves, forming within their hearts small bundles of buds, which seemed about to burst into the velvety brown and bronze flowers which would fill the yard with their ravishing fragrance.

These signs of renewed life had prompted Kees and Arjaan to put their little corner in the front garden in order. They had dug up a box full of grass clumps which became a narrow green border to mark their domain. Inside it they had planted several clusters of daisies. Fransje had given them plenty of help, running inside to Mother afterwards to ask her if he, too, could have a spot in the garden. But because the whole garden had already been parceled out—even the older boys and Maria each had their own plot—Mother told him to wait until they had all come home. Then he could ask them if he could have some of their territory.

The farmers were also thinking of plowing and harrowing, and sent their regular hands to check the farm machinery and put it in working order. Father had firm plans to start work on the vegetable garden in the back yard Saturday afternoon. He hoped, when he got the chance, to also open the smaller of the two dirt covered mounds of potatoes in order to get the seed potatoes ready.

Yes, spring must be near, for one evening Kees came home with two sticklebacks which he had caught in one of the small ditches that emptied into the draught ditch that flowed past their house on the other side of the road. Fransje stood wide-eyed admiring the little fish as they frantically nibbled at the bottom of the jam jar with their pointed little snouts as if looking for a way to escape. One of the fish was pale red along his gills and the front of its belly. Fransje thought it must have bled, but Kees told him that it was a male stickleback and that the other one, which was almost completely silver, was a female stickleback.

Fransje was busy pondering how best to phrase his question so that Kees would give him one of those cute little fish, preferably the red-breasted one. But then, suspecting that his chances were rather slim anyway, he asked bluntly, "Kees, can I have one of those little fish?" As he had feared, however, Kees said, "I've got only two of them. First I have to catch a whole bunch more, and when I have enough of them, then I'll give you a couple."

From the way Kees said this, Fransje gathered that "enough" in this case meant so many that Kees's jar (his former rumblepot) looked more like a jar of canned herring than like a miniature aquarium. So he cried impatiently, "But that will take a long time! I'll go and catch one myself tomorrow!"

Mother, who had just come walking into the back room to fill her kettle, heard Fransje's last words. She saw the two boys looking in the jar on the sill of the semicircular window and immediately she understood what Fransje was talking about. Shocked, she asserted, "Not on your life! You're way too small to go catching little fish. I'll not hear of it. If you fall into the water and drown, then what? Then we'll no longer have a Fransje."

Fransje didn't reply. For an instant he saw himself lying on the bottom of the deep ditch in the cold water, and involuntarily he shuddered. But at least he could go see if he could spot any little fish swimming in the ditch. And if one should swim close to shore . . . .

The next morning as soon as he was outside he shoved his feet into his wooden shoes and headed for the rabbit hutches behind the vegetable garden. That's where he had thrown the jar from his discarded rumblepot when he'd been able to think of no further use for it. He had to hunt awhile until he saw part of it protruding from the manure underneath the hutch. Seizing it gingerly between thumb and forefinger, he pulled it out. He gagged at the fetid, brown muck clinging to the outside and partially filling the inside of the jar. Carefully he rubbed most of the muck off in the grass. But even then he held it at arms length.

His conscience nagged him, but he tried to quiet it by promising that he was only going to see if he could spot any sticklebacks in the big ditch. Then he advised himself to wash the jar first, just in case. He couldn't very well do that in the back room, however, for the jar was much too filthy. And he figured he had better stay out of Mother's sight.

He kept his eyes fixed on the back door. Unfortunately it opened at just that moment. Mother emerged to empty a pail of water into the slophole. Quick, the jar! All Fransje could do was hide it under his shirt. Calmly he strolled toward her.

"Hi, Mom!" he called sweetly.

"Hi, Fransje. What are you doing?"

"Nothing. I'm just playing."

Mother saw the bulge on his stomach and also noted his strange behavior, and immediately she guessed what was in his mind. Though strongly tempted to teach him a good lesson, she caught herself. If she questioned him now, he could lie his way out of it, and that would hurt her and also weaken her words. No, she would let him go his way for awhile and see what was really on his mind. So she only asked, "Are you going to be a good boy?"

Relieved, Fransje eagerly gave his promise—almost too eagerly. Mother stepped back into the house. She stood beside the stove with an oblique view out the window at what would happen outside. Fransje was already in the middle of the road. He cast a stealthy look at the window, and then he headed toward the village. Mother now moved closer to the window. She covered her golden headpieces with her hands to keep them from glistening and exposing her if he looked back again. He did, indeed, stop once more, turn, and cast one last glance at the window. Then he angled across the road until he reached the edge of the ditch. Quickly he looked both ways and then sat down on the bank, his legs stretched down toward the water.

It was high time for Mother to follow. When she arrived on the road, he had disappeared from sight. She hurried to the edge of the ditch and saw him some distance away, sitting on his haunches at a projection in the bank right above the gleaming surface of the water. With his left hand he hung onto a clump of brown grass, while he splashed in the water with his right hand, holding something that flashed in the sun—the jar.

She forced back a cry. Already she was berating herself for letting him go this far, but now she had to do something, and fast! In her stocking feet she ran down the tar road until she thought she was parallel to the spot where he was concealed. A quick prayer that God would spare him flashed through her mind. The ditch was deep, and the water had a powerful current, for it drained off excess water from the Hontenisse Polder to the sea. Therefore the people in the area called it the Waterway. She suppressed her voice, calling as if from far away, "Fransjeee!"

The splashing stopped a moment, but then it resumed. It pained her to think that he was lying once more—by pretending that he hadn't heard her. She called a little louder, and again the splashing stopped. This time Fransje decided to peek over the top of the bank. At once he saw Mother. He scrambled up the bank to stand disconcerted, staring at her.

Mother asked herself what she should do now. She said, "Didn't I tell you in so many words not to go fishing for sticklebacks because you're too small and might drown if you did?"

In Mother's voice Fransje heard grief at his disobedience and also deep anxiety. He looked up into her face and stammered, "But I wasn't going to catch any. I was only going to look at them."

This comical evasion threatened to undermine Mother's anger. He appeared to be fully convinced of the legitimacy of his excuse. Nevertheless, she couldn't let him off the hook so easily. Without saying another word, she stepped forward and took the jar from his hand. Beside him a large rock jutted up from the ground. Pulling Fransje aside, she let the half filled jar drop on the rock with a dull crash. Glass and water splashed against her dark blue apron and his black stockings. With long swift strides, she pulled him along to where she had left her wooden shoes and then back to the house. She still didn't say anything and left him standing in the middle of the living room. She returned to her work without another look at him. She acted as if he weren't there.

For some time Fransje stood there turning back and forth on his heels, not knowing what to do. His conscience was bothering him, and he felt tears burning behind his eyelids. When Mother stepped into the living room, he suddenly began to sob. He ran to her and threw his arms about her legs. Mother, however, made no move to take him back into her good graces. She said, "Out of my way! I have a lot of work to do!"

Then Fransje began to howl. He held her even tighter, wailing, "I'm sorry, Mommy! I won't do it again, honest! You can spank me with your slipper because I was naughty!"

Mother no longer tried to pull herself loose from his grasp. She put her hand under his chin and tilted back his head. With a deep sadness in her eyes, she looked into his, and softly she asked, "Will you really, truly never do it again?" Her eyes seemed to spring open a new source of tears; limp with grief, Fransje could only nod his head.

Father didn't get the chance to dig up his seed potatoes from their winter stash, for the wind, which had been blowing from the south for several days, suddenly swung around to the east. All night it wailed in the branches of the large elms in front of the house and stripped them of their small clusters of bronze blossoms. In the morning they lay scattered across the road and front yard like lumps of brown sugar. The attic window, facing east had been rattling for hours; it finally awakened Eine, who got up shivering and dug some rags from a basket behind the trapdoor to stuff around the window.

In the morning Fransje insisted on going out. Although Mother wrapped her black shawl over his coat and pulled his wool cap down over his ears, he didn't brave the cold for long, because the change in weather had been too great. The new grass on the edge of the ditch stood up like stiff, gray bristles. The wallflowers clinging to the wall had rolled up their top leaves and drawn up their shoulders. They stood shivering in the biting wind, which swept the elm blossoms spiraling about their feet.

Fransje decided to go back in. In the back room his eyes fell on a jar standing in front of the little half-moon window, and he saw that the white stickleback was floating on its back, its spines outspread. The red-breasted one looked bluish and opened its little mouth sporadically as it made slow, jerky swimming motions. The water was covered by a thin layer of ice. Fransje resolved to draw this to Kees's attention when he came home from school at noon.

The sun was like cold fire; although it shone all day, it could not warm the wind's frigid breath. Mother emptied a pail of dirty water into the sewer drain and spilled some of it on the cast iron drain cover. It froze into windblown ferns before her eyes. In the house the stove purred so fervently that its potbelly glowed red all day. Even so, when the door to the hall opened even for a moment, Fransje felt the cold climbing up his legs. Mother had to keep reminding the children to close the door behind them.

Two days later the frozen puddles in the fields were crowded with children on ice skates. Arjaan and Kees hardly stopped to change clothes when they came home from school. At once they were on their way again, their old strap-on skates draped about their necks. Wantje too had a pair of skates. She had no shoes—Mother wouldn't let her use her Sunday shoes for this purpose—so she walked to the ice in her wooden shoes. Once there, she pulled a pair of old socks over her stockings and cheerfully bore all pains and cramps in order to participate in the wonderful sport.

Fransje, of course, had no skates, but he begged to go along anyway. After bearing much whining, Mother finally gave in. She charged the boys to see to it that Fransje was not left standing on the side freezing.

When Wantje took a brutal fall on her posterior and stumbled to the side to catch her breath, Fransje begged to try the skates on his stocking feet too. Arjaan helped him and pulled him around the edge of the large puddle. But to hold up his little brother as well as himself put too great a strain on his sense of balance and soon they fell on top of each other. Fortunately Arjaan managed to cushion Fransje's fall with his own body, and he didn't get hurt. But Arjaan grimaced painfully as he caught the point of Fransje's skate in his stomach. They tried once more, but Fransje could not hold his ankles straight; they kept twisting painfully. When at last one skate ended up on the side of his foot, a disappointed Fransje concluded that skating was even less fun than trying to walk with snow caked to the bottom of your wooden shoes. He couldn't understand how the big kids could move so fast on those rebellious things, even playing tag on them. He was secretly pleased to see, however, that there wasn't a single boy his age among them. There were a few boys present about as big as he was, but one of them stood crying, blowing in his hands and calling his big brother. At least Fransje wasn't doing that.

In the Hontenisse Polder was what once had been an estuary: after the land had been drained more than one hundred years ago, it had remained like an arrested river or an elongated lake. It stretched from one inner dike to the other, broken only by a dam where the railroad crossed it.

After three days, even the middle of this channel was frozen, and daredevils had ventured several meters onto the ice until a frightful crackling had sent them scurrying back. On Saturday two men were out marking the dangerous middle section with poles. If the cold weather held, on Monday they would lay out an oval skating rink several kilometers in circumference.

Bram and Eine had also dug up their skates, and in his after-supper prayer Father asked the Lord to keep them from recklessness. He didn't tell them that there had already been skaters on Hontenisse Pond Friday. He had seen them because the farm where he worked bordered the pond. Besides, most of the skaters, rather than make the long detour along the dike, cut through the driveway beside the farm and across the meadow behind it. The older boys knew this too, but out of respect for Father's authority, they did not mention it either.

When Father stepped out Saturday night just before retiring, he was struck by how unusually dark it was: the stars, which had been glittering in the sky like cold diamonds all week, were nowhere to be seen. The wind had changed direction and sighed plaintively in the hawthorn hedge and in the apple trees beyond. "We're in for some rough weather," he told Mother when he came back in. "I think there's a snowstorm brewing."

The next morning he found his prediction borne out, but much more dramatically than he could have expected. When he pulled the back door open, a wall of snow higher than his knees confronted him. The bathroom, which jutted out at right angles to the back room, seemed afloat like a specter in a bluish white world, and the low rectangular hedge extending from it like a reaching arm, dissolved into the gray darkness. The hedge looked half its usual height and sported a snow blanket half a meter high, which was barely visible against the latticework of branches behind it.

As his eyes adjusted to the darkness, Father noticed with surprise the size of the snowflakes dropping noiselessly like wads of cotton. He had never seen anything like this before. He stood motionlessly watching it for some time, reminded of the text: "He giveth snow like wool."

However, he had been on his way to feed the rabbits. He put on his wooden shoes, which he left on a clean burlap sack beside the door overnight, and took a big step over the snow piled in the doorway. His notion that he would find solid footing beyond it proved ill-founded; when he shifted his weight to his leading leg, he pitched forward full-length into the woolen mass. His pipe flew from his mouth, and then the cold, wet snow closed over him. He scrambled back to his feet and beat the snow from his clothes. He had lost one of his wooden shoes. First he had to find it and his pipe. He groped in the snow, finding his wooden shoe at once; but the pipe was another matter. "Never mind," he thought. "It will show up when I shovel the walk pretty soon." But the shovel was in the shed behind the vegetable garden. He considered putting off feeding the rabbits until it grew lighter outside, but his feet were wet already anyway and he had to clear a path, so he might as well wade through the deep snow now.

A short while later he had cleared a square in front of the door and from there he shoveled a canal around the house to the road. When he reached the road, he was completely out of breath. Realizing that they could hardly go to church in all this snow, he was deeply disappointed, for he always eagerly anticipated Sunday, even though an elder usually read the sermon. He waded through the front yard and opened the shutters. His hat and shoulders were already white with snow. After brushing himself off once more, he stepped back into the house.

Mother had gotten up in the meantime and was just about to rouse the boys since Father had stayed out so long. But he told her that she could let the children sleep in this morning because they couldn't go to church anyway.

During breakfast Fransje asked how the birds were going to find something to eat with so much snow on the ground. Father was just about to say that they could take care of themselves, glancing outside for proof, when he became aware that he hadn't heard a sparrow chirping all morning. Then he realized that all the sparrows must have been buried alive underneath the rooftiles where they nested during the night. Fransje asked why the sparrows hadn't flown away when it began to snow, to which Father replied that they had been sleeping all night and only realized what was happening when it was too late and could no longer get out through the heavy layer of snow. Fransje thought that was terrible. "Aren't there any sparrows left in the whole world?" he asked. Father comforted him by assuring him that there were lots of sparrows out in the country, where they nested in hayracks and under the eaves of barns and sheds. When the snow was gone, they would come to the house looking for bread crumbs.

Fransje gazed out the window at the layer of snow in the yard and on the road. The front hedge had disappeared, transformed into a white dike in a white sea. Even the smallest branches of the elms in front of the house wore a thick layer of white wool. The barns in the fields seemed to have sunk into the ground, for only the tarred walls were visible. The white roofs above had merged into the general grayness of the surrounding winter landscape. Suddenly Fransje heard the startled cry of a thrush as in a flutter of wings it vainly tried to find a foothold on the snow-covered hedge.

"Hey, there's a bird!" Fransje cried joyfully. "Mom, can I give him a piece of bread?" Father told him to throw it behind the house on the sidewalk; otherwise it would sink away in the snow and still wouldn't do the birds any good.

Not a single person passed on his way to church. Mother doubted there would be very many people in church today, except those who lived nearby. Although the family couldn't go to church, that didn't mean they wouldn't observe the sabbath. When the table had been cleared, Father took an old, hefty book from the linen closet and paged around in it for awhile. The paper was brown and spotty as if someone had spattered coffee on it, and the print was very fine and close. Occasionally dark pictures appeared which Fransje couldn't make sense of, for they consisted of curlicues and leaves around the head of some man or of some strange creature.

Father seemed to have found a passage he considered appropriate, for he cleared his throat and told the boys, who were reading books, "Okay, boys, close your books and pay attention. Fransje, are you going to sit still?" Then he began to read.

It was a sermon by Bernard Smytegelt, "in his lifetyme faythfull Servaunt of the Gospell at Middleburgh," on the text "He will be our guide even unto death" (Psalm XLVIII: 15). Somewhat into the sermon, Father read:

> Attend closely a moment. To guide unto Death hath a threefold Sense. First, saith God, I will lead thee unto Death, that is, I will lead thee till thy Deathbed. Second, on thy Deathbed I will be thy Guide in thy struggle with Death. And third, when thou hast suffered Death, I will guide thee through and beyond Death. Is this not sufficient? I tell thee, unto Death, in Death, and when thou hath passed away, after Death, I shall be thy Guide . . . . When I send thee into that fryghtfull Valleye, saith God, I will be with thee; there no one shall have accesse to thy Herte but I; thou shalt have no other thoughtes but of the Grace of God in Christe.

None of the other children thought this style strange, for they had heard it since they were toddlers. Of all the sermons they heard read in church, they liked Smytegelt's the best, because his were simple, clear, and above all, short.

To Fransje it was a sacred language somehow related to the Lord. To sit still all that time, however, was quite a trial for him. Now and then out of the corners of his eyes he peeked outside to see if any more birds were coming out. He kept hearing the words "death" and "dying," however, and was reminded of Verplanke. He tried to imagine his final moments and what it must be like to suddenly cease living. In his imagination he stood at Verplanke's bed waiting for him to pass from life into death. But then suddenly Fransje himself lay in the bed and Verplanke stood beside it looking at him. Fransje shuddered. He wished it weren't Sunday today, and he could go outside and play in the snowdrifts.

Father hadn't begun the sermon with a prayer, nor did he end with a prayer. He felt it his duty to read a sermon, but he didn't play church. If he had been an elder, he might have behaved differently, but he refused to arrogate any rights or duties to himself not given him by God.

Since it snowed all day, Father read two more sermons: a sermon on the Heidelberg Catechism and a regular one in the evening. He ended the Sunday with his customary long prayer.

Toward evening the wind shifted to the northeast, and for the second time Father predicted bad weather. The wind began to moan around the house and whistled through the bolt hole in the window frame. Mother stuffed a rag into it and Father hung his hat over it. Eine made sure the attic window was battened down before he crawled into bed, because he didn't want to get out again in the middle of the night.

Fransje slept all night oblivious to the roaring wind which had become a storm. When he arrived downstairs the next morning, he was planning to go out and play in the deep snow right after breakfast. But a big surprise awaited him. The wind had torn the thick blanket of snow into long shreds which it had scattered willy-nilly across the road like white dunes. In some places the road surface was completely bare, while a little farther down the road the snow was piled in huge mounds with sharp spines. All the trees had lost their beautiful white fur. Fransje was struck by how strange it looked outdoors. In sudden surprise he cried, "Look, Mom, the ditch is gone! Look!"

Sure enough, the deep, wide channel was completely covered. It seemed to Fransje that he could walk right out into the fields beyond. Delighted, he cried, "Mom, now we can walk right into the fields! See? That's what I'm going to do pretty soon."

Those words gave Mother a terrible fright. In a voice shrill with consternation, she warned him, "Fransje, my boy, don't you dare try it—ever! You hear! You can't walk over the ditch on the snow. You'll fall through the snow into the water underneath, and then you'll be buried alive just like the sparrows under the roof-tiles!"

Now it was his turn to look frightened. It all looked so safe and solid, he wanted to try it anyway, just a little ways, step by step. His mind was already working out a plan. But then all at once he remembered his fishing expedition, and this time he told satan to get behind him.

The storm had helped those working on the ice on Hontenisse Pond because at least now they didn't have to clear the snow from the entire surface. They didn't have to do anything at all on one side of the long oval, but on the other side they had to shovel away quite a few of the snow dunes which had been thrown long and far across the ice. Groups of people were already out on the wind-cleared half on Monday afternoon enjoying themselves. The ice was strong enough now, and every young person who didn't have a job was out on the skating rink.

One of Mother's distant cousins who lived in the railroad station neighborhood and who was something of a petty entrepreneur, loaded a pile of boards and studs and pieces of canvas onto his wagon and drove it to Hontenisse Pond. Not far from the ice he constructed a large booth. On his next trip he took a large, rusty stove, a long tabletop, a few wooden horses and benches, and his restaurant was finished. In town he had heard that plans had already been drawn up for an ice festival. That usually meant lots of spending money in everyone's pockets, and he rubbed his hands together in anticipation, anticipating its transfer from their pockets to his.

Arjaan and Kees were also excited about the coming ice festival. On the school grounds they heard much talk about different aspects of the festivities. Every afternoon the principal dismissed school an hour early, and then the ice was crowded with school children. Since Father had given the children permission to go skating on the pond, Fransje was left home all by himself for the entire day. He would have loved to go along with the other boys, but Mother said it was much too far and much too cold. But two days later she unexpectedly relented.

Mother's cousin was so busy he couldn't keep up by himself. His pregnant wife was due anytime, so she couldn't help him. He had his eye on someone else, however. If he could get her to help him, then he'd be well set up. One evening he dropped in on Father and Mother to ask if Maria could come and give him a hand. Father had to think it over first. It was, to be sure, somewhat unusual, but on the other hand, it was honest work, and he could think of no religious objections. Finally he said, "If Maria wants to, I won't stop her."

Maria was slightly hesitant about having to meet and talk to so many strange and familiar faces, but the job also attracted her. So they came to the agreement that Maria would serve as a waitress in the booth every afternoon. When Fransje whined to go along with Arjaan, Kees and Wantje the following afternoon, Mother gave in. If he became cold he could join Maria in the booth for a little while to warm up. But she added a warning, "Don't stand by the booth begging, you hear! Because that looks awful."

Arjaan suggested taking the sled. With plenty of snow along

the road, they'd be able to walk faster. Besides, then there'd be no danger he'd have to carry Fransje on his shoulders, should he grow tired.

Of course, they took the shortest route to the rink—along the farm where Father worked. Fransje vaguely remembered having been there before, and involuntarily he looked at the watering hole where the horses drank during the summer to see if the geese were still there. The waterhole was, of course, frozen, but the geese had kept one spot open. As the children passed by, the lethargic birds scolded them, honking noisily.

At the sight of the happy throngs on the ice, the children could hardly wait. Quickly they strapped on their skates and were ready to go. But Fransje cried, "I want to come too! Arjaan, take me with you!" Feeling sorry for him, Arjaan said, "Sit down on the sled and I'll give you a ride around the rink."

Tying the long rope around his own waist, he told Fransje to hold on tightly. Soon they were flying across the ice, and Fransje felt the cold wind whistling along his ears. Every now and then the sled fishtailed to the left or to the right and he had to fight to stay aboard. But he enjoyed the wild, dangerous ride tremendously. Before he realized it, they had circled the entire rink. Arjaan pivoted on his skates and grated to a halt. He swung Fransje around a few times until his momentum was also broken. Then they were standing before the booth where Maria was serving several customers. She served large cups full of steaming chocolate milk with flat cake squares called *janhagel* and syrup-glazed rolls called *jikkemiene*.

Mother had told Fransje not to beg, but he couldn't help it that his mouth was watering. "Hi, Maria!" he shouted excitedly, but he was disappointed by the lack of warmth in her reception. She greeted him, but as if he were a stranger, and then she went on with her work. There was a little room on the bench. Fransje sat down with his back to the table so as not to see the delicacies, for penniless as he was, they were inaccessible to him anyway. But a little later the customers left, and for a while no one else came. Arjaan was still off skating.

"Here, Fransje," Maria's friendly voice said behind him. Quickly he turned toward her and saw in front of him a steaming cup of hot chocolate with a glistening roll beside it.

"Drink it down quick and eat your roll," she urged him. She had put the money for it in the cigar box, paid for with the small tips she had already received this afternoon, but if some acquaintance should see him, perhaps they would jump to the conclusion that she was being generous with someone else's goods. The milk was so hot, however, that Fransje had to blow on it energetically before he dared drink it. Finally the cup was empty and the roll gone.

"Why don't you go ride your sled awhile now," advised Maria. "But make sure you don't get in the way of the skaters. Play in the snow at the side of the rink."

Fransje would rather have stayed with Maria a little longer, but suddenly a group of noisy young men came bursting in, grabbing for the bench to slow themselves. Laughing and panting, they collapsed on it. "Hey, Maria, how about some hot chocolate!" they shouted. "*Janhagel* and *jikkemiene!*" One of them sang, "Ma-ri-a! Ma-ri-a! Hot chocolate, *janhagel* and *jikkemeine*, Ma-ri-a!"

Frightened, Fransje sprang from the bench and cleared out with his sled. He shuffled back to the ice, where he looked for Arjaan or Kees. But there were so many people milling about on the ice, he couldn't possibly pick them out. He couldn't catch a glimpse of Wantje either.

The ice was far too dangerous and far too slippery for little boys, so he waded through the snow at the edges. Around the bend was more snow, but shallower and smoother. Dragging the sled behind him, he headed toward the field of snow. It was quite an expanse, stretching all the way to the railroad grade. There the pond wasn't as wide but ran to a blunt point, bordered on both sides by tall, brown reeds. A path had been trampled in the snow from the skating rink to the railroad grade. Occasionally someone with skates hanging about his neck walked down the path, climbed the grade and disappeared in the direction of the railroad station about one kilometer down the tracks. Fransje wanted to go over there and take a look. The sled slid much easier here.

At the railroad grade, Fransje saw that the tall reeds were topped by large, woolly plumes. To take a closer look, he left the sled behind him beside the path and carefully approached the wall of reeds. Near the reeds all the snow had been blown away. The ice was very slippery here, and he had trouble keeping his footing. Never before had he seen such tall reeds. They were about three times his own height, much taller than the reeds in the waterway in front of his house. Carefully he bent down one of the long stalks and tried to break off the large plume. But that wasn't easy. The flexible stalk bent easily enough, but the tough fibers wouldn't break.

The sight of those beautiful plumes right above his head drove him almost wild with desire. He must have; he would have this plume, and not just this one, but many more. Mother would be so pleased! Then she could put them on the mantel or on the linen closet in a vase. In his mind he could already see them standing there. He already felt the pride that would well up in him whenever anyone asked where Mother had found those beautiful plumes and she told them that Fransje had picked them for her. He twisted and tugged until one of the tough fibers broke just underneath a stubborn knot. That gave him an idea. He took hold of the stalk with both hands just below and above the knot, and with a hard wrench, he snapped it in two. There, that was one! He bent down one stalk after another, not stopping until he had such a big bouquet of plumes he could hardly hold them. All this had taken him a long time, however, and suddenly he thought that the time must be getting on.

The setting sun had set the whole sky afire. In the west hung low undulating clouds which the sun had conjured into splendid hues—blood-red and orange and purple and gold. Where the clouds were thin the sky shone through, the color of green apples. Fransje had never before seen anything so beautiful. The clouds reminded him of Maria's hair when she combed it out and let it spill down her back, gleaming in small waves like the coruscating clouds.

The thought of Maria suddenly spurred him on. He slipped and slid back to his sled, and with the plumes in one hand and the rope in the other he followed the snow path back to the booth. Maria told him to go find the others right away because it was time to go home. He hurried to the bend of the skating rink in the hope that one of them would spot him. When neither Wantje nor the boys appeared, he decided to follow the edge of the long rink to look for them. Now and then skaters passed him, but there weren't as many as there had been in the afternoon. No matter how much he looked and searched, however, he saw no trace of the other children.

He didn't know how long he had been walking, but suddenly he noticed that he had come to the end of the long pond at the foot of the dike. And he still hadn't found the others. The clouds had lost all their splendid colors and now looked like dark smudges above the horizon, fleetingly touched by red and green. He had no choice but to circle back along the other side of the oval rink. His legs were tired from slogging through the snow, and his hands and arms were stiff from pulling the sled and clutching the plumes.

In the east a half moon rose over the distant roofs of the farm where Father worked. It was growing dark already, but so gradually that Fransje didn't notice. The white snow contrasted sharply with the dark ice. Nevertheless his heart was seized by a great uneasiness. At this rate they were all sure to get home late.

Wearily he trudged on. His eyes ached from looking. He considered calling Kees and Arjaan but immediately rejected the idea. That would frighten him, and he wasn't frightened yet. Just uneasy.

Very few skaters passed him any more. Only a few passionate lovers of the noble sport were still out practicing their step-over turns. The ice sweepers were also gone. Fransje decided to go back to the booth and to Maria: she could take him home.

Finally he reached the booth. There his little world crumbled; everyone had vanished. The benches had been pushed behind the table and in one corner stood a pile of boxes and baskets waiting for the owner to come and pick them up. The dark rectangular interior gaped at him, mysterious and threatening. For the first time Fransje was really frightened. Worst of all was the knowledge that Maria and the others had gone home without him. His heart hammered in his throat and his eyes burned with tears that crowded forward. He realized, however, that crying wouldn't do him any good. Not here, where there was no one to hear or help him. He thought of Mother and of the safe, cozy living room. He had to get home! He had to get away from this desolate, winter wilderness, this cold, forbidding place.

He thought of the way back, past the farm to the lonely road that led to the railroad station neighborhood where it intersected the long road that ran by their house. His legs were almost giving out. But he had to go on. Then suddenly he remembered the geese. He could almost see them coming out of the darkness and hear them coming after him, scolding. He felt their sharp beaks snapping at his britches to drag him back to the waterhole. He broke out in a cold sweat, knowing all at once that he could not go home that way. But to go home along the pond to the dike was also out of the question. For then he had to make the long detour over the dike—the dike with its three rows of trees and dangers lurking behind every tree, waiting to leap out at him.

A decision had been made, deep in his subconscious. He was already walking before he was aware of it. He was going home along the railroad tracks, just as he had seen others doing a few hours earlier. Fortunately he didn't know that this was forbidden, and that the local policeman had intercepted some of the trespassers at the station and had written them tickets. He only knew he had to get home and that he was going along the railroad tracks.

He was already on the slippery pond and saw the white bank of the railroad grade ahead of him. But suddenly he tripped over a bump in the ice. He flailed wildly with his arms to catch his balance, but his tired legs refused to cooperate, and with a smack he fell backward full length. Violently his head hit the steel-hard ice. His sled shot into the reeds, and his plumes fluttered into the sky like a flock of gray pigeons, scattering in all directions. Dazed he lay still, staring up at the little stars dancing behind his eyelids. A dull pain flowed hotly down his neck and shoulders and down his back until it met the pain radiating from his posterior. Yet he didn't cry. A vague feeling of pity arose in him as if for someone else who needed his help. Dizzily he lurched to his feet. He raked the plumes together with a few sweeps of his arm and arranged the stalks. Where was his sled? He had to have his sled! The sled! Finally he spotted it. It had shot far into the reeds near the mouth of the channel that drained Hontenisse Pond. Fransje didn't know that this same waterway ran past his house and far beyond the village to the sea dike. Nor did he know that the ice was very thin here, due to the constant movement of water flowing out of Hontenisse Pond and the narrow channel at ebb tide. It had not frozen until the low temperatures of a few days ago. Scattered here and there between the reeds were sections of white ice suspended about ten centimeters above the new, dark ice underneath. They hung there marking the previous water level.

Fransje went after his sled. Suddenly he heard a frightful cracking sound, but he didn't realize the danger he was in. Right after his fall God had sent an invisible angel with orders to lead him home safely. At home no one was worried yet because the children had just finished saying that Fransje was coming home with Maria.

He grabbed the sled-rope and with the ice cracking alarmingly under his feet, he turned back to the snow path. This was easy to find, for the half moon reflecting on the snow provided plenty of light. He had but to follow in the footsteps of his predecessors. With sore limbs and leaden legs he struggled up the grade until he reached the rough gravel path beside the rails. Luckily the trampled snow had leveled it somewhat. Wearily Fransje plodded on in the direction of the station.

Halfway there, he heard a rumbling noise that grew louder and louder as it seemed to come closer and closer. He turned his head in the direction of the sound and suddenly saw a shadowy monster with two blazing eyes thundering straight toward him. It was the five-fifteen express which passed through the station without stopping on its way to Rotterdam. Fransje froze in his tracks, not knowing what to do. The next instant the monster was passing right by him, shaking the earth with its mighty momentum. It tore the wind to shreds, alternately sucking him in and pushing him away. The angel, however, put an invisible hand on the boy's head and pushed him down on his knees in the snow, his face in the wildly fluttering reed plumes. At the same time he sent the policeman home by making him think there were no more trespassers coming down the tracks anyway. A little while later Fransje was again staggering on.

Just as he was finally trudging around the house, there came Father, with long, hurried strides. As soon as he realized that the small figure was his lost lamb, he took two leaping steps, swept the boy off the ground and pressed him to his heart. One of the plumes snapped and fell into the snow. Father could not speak. His chest heaving, he ran to the back door, the sled bouncing along behind him, tugging at Fransje's stiffened fingers. Fransje let go of the rope and suddenly there was warmth and light, and the faces of Mother and the others all turned toward him. Bram and Eine were getting dressed to go out to look for him too. But he was back already! He was back! Kees and Arjaan were sitting behind the table with bowed heads, and Wantje had been crying.

Fransje's outing had become an adventure that none of them would easily forget. The plumes were now standing in a large, white pitcher on top of the linen closet.

The eagerly anticipated festival did not materialize. Every time a day was designated, a thaw set in and the ice became unsafe.

Every time it seemed that winter was going to end just as abruptly as it had come. But then it began to freeze again and the game started all over once more.

Although he couldn't skate himself, Father didn't object to the children skating, but he did see the hand of God in the continual disruption of the ice festival, because he was convinced that such things encouraged sin and excess and lust. In order to make up for the children's disappointment, the principal gave them a whole afternoon off.

Fransje, however, was not at all eager to go to Hontenisse Pond again. He went one more time with Maria, just to please her, and because she had promised very emphatically that if he wanted he could stay with her in the booth all afternoon. He didn't suspect that Maria was so eager to take him because she wanted to make up for her thoughtlessness of the last time. He would much rather have remained at home where the older boys had built a snow house for the smaller children. When it wasn't too cold, this was where he spent the greater part of the day with Neeltje and Siene and Marien's girls.

Meanwhile, March had arrived and still the polder looked like a polar landscape. It seemed as if it had always looked like this and always would. Fortunately all the children remained healthy—thanks to fresh air and exercise and their robust appetites. The road was clear, but on both sides of it were high dikes of snow as if walls had been constructed along the roadsides. Around all the houses ran trenches—deep interconnecting channels between high, white walls. They looked a little like archeological excavations, the unearthed prehistoric foundations gleaming in the sun. The children thought it wonderful, for it inspired them with numerous ideas for new games.

A fantastic scene during the day, at night it became a fairytale world. A full moon stood high overhead smiling down on this unreal world as if reminded of its own bleak lunar landscapes. It lured the young people outdoors, and even married couples and little children ventured outside after supper to wander through the trenches or to watch a snowball fight. Usually it wasn't long before the grown-ups also joined in.

One evening as usual Bram and Eine had gone to visit friends in the station neighborhood. There, too, the young people had been infected by the general boisterousness; laughing and roughhousing they ended up at Moerland barn. The big doors were standing open, and one of the boys saw a buggy standing inside. It didn't belong to Moerland, but to Willam van Houten, who, like Mother's cousin, was something of a horse trader. Because he didn't have a barn himself, he stalled both his horse and buggy at Moerland's.

One of the Van Houten boys was also with the group. He was a little slow-witted, and although he couldn't claim any of the boys as friends, they let him tag along like an overgrown puppy. Though he wasn't bright enough to participate, he took great delight in the wild antics of the others. He confined himself to pounding his knees in laughter. Suddenly one of the boys said, "Hey, I've got an idea. Let's take Van Houten's buggy out for a ride!" The idea met with immediate approval from the others. "That's okay, isn't it, Bert?" one of them asked the dull-witted fellow. "Sure," he said. "I think so. As long as you don't bust nothing." The others put his mind at ease. "Are you crazy?" they asked superfluously. "Of course we're not going to bust anything!"

As if at a prearranged signal, they all ran into the barn and in a flash they had hauled the buggy out onto the road. A short way down the road they passed a few girls about Maria's age. One of the boys invited them aboard for a ride, and to loud laughter the girls climbed into the buggy. They galloped on in the direction of the village. Four boys were pulling the two-wheeled carriage by the shafts and two others were pushing it. Bert van Houten ran along behind laughing and pounding his knees.

One of the girls was a friend of Maria's, and when they reached the Weststrate house, she asked the fellows to stop a moment. She hopped off the buggy and ran around the back of the house to ask Maria to come out and join the fun. Maria first asked Mother's permission, which she gave only hesitantly. But Fransje was also in the room. Kees and Arjaan were off playing outside and Wantje had fallen asleep. She was so tired from skating that she had crawled into bed right after supper. Father was visiting Uncle Johannes.

"Maria, can I come too? Mommy, can I go with her?" Mother was about to say no, but Maria was one step ahead of her and said, "Come on, Mom, let him ride along. What harm can it do? We'll be back in a jiffy." Apparently she was still doing penance to Fransje. He was already putting on his coat. Mother said, "But be careful! Don't pull any crazy stunts." The latter was also meant for Maria.

Fransje was up in the clouds. He sat between Maria and her girlfriend. His high little voice rang out above the witticisms and chatter of the teenagers. Soon they were passing Kees de Visser's house and a little later they were in the village. In no time the buggy was surrounded by singing and jostling boys and girls. Together they pulled the chaise from one street to another. Fransje felt like a king surveying his willing subjects.

As soon as the boys from the station neighborhood saw their chance, they freed themselves from the mob of villagers to pull the buggy back, for they were afraid it wouldn't survive the rough treatment. Among the last group of houses, however, was a small store, which was still lit up. One of the boys shouted to the girls, "I think we deserve a treat for the nice ride we gave you!"

"All right!" replied Maria's girlfriend. "I have some money with me."

"Me too," added Maria, and the other girl also had money with her. Parking the chaise along the road, they all trooped into the little store. At once it was so crowded that Fransje had to be set on the counter so that he wouldn't be stepped on. A little old woman asked them, "What would you like?"

The boys asked for macaroons, and the girls also treated them to pieces of chocolate. The old woman gave Fransje a hard candy for free.

"But now we better go home!" cried Maria. "Fransje should be in bed already."

When the group stopped in front of the house, Maria wanted to take Fransje inside with her. But he begged to go along with Bram and Eine to bring back the buggy. Bram said to Maria, "Oh, let him come with us. We'll be right back anyway."

The boys first brought the other two girls to their destinations and then took the buggy back to Moerland's barn. They had all enjoyed themselves tremendously, including Bert and Fransje. Their fun, however, did not come to a happy ending. For as they turned onto Moerland's yard, they saw someone standing there waiting for them. It was Van Houten. He ran forward and stopped them. Waving his fists over his head and swearing furiously, he hollered, "Who gave you guys permission to take my buggy from the barn and run it into the ground? You'll have to pay for it; you better count on it! I'm reporting you all to the police. I know every one of you: you two boys belong to Marien Weststrate, you two to Flup Soenke, and you . . . ." He was breathless with rage and excitement. When he caught his breath, he again started to swear.

But then Bram interrupted him: "We didn't run your stinking old buggy into the ground! Besides, your own son was with us and he said it was okay. And if you report us to the police, we'll tell him how you swore at us. Then we'll see who gets a bigger fine—you or us. We've got six witnesses."

This short, convincing speech momentarily left the angry man at a loss. He lowered his arms and stood there stuttering at them, his jaw falling slack. Then he spotted Bert who had been hiding in the background behind one of the big wheels of the chaise. He leaped at his son like an angry tiger and hauled him from his hiding place. Again he let fly a stream of awful curses. Then he gave Bert such a hard slap in the face that the boy reeled back yelping like a dog. That made his father even angrier. Again he attacked him, beating him to the ground with both hands. He hammered him with his fists and kicked him with his wooden shoes wherever he could—against the head, on the back, between the legs, and in the stomach. Bert bellowed like a dying animal, but his father's mad ranting drowned out his loudest screams. The boys had never heard such terrible blasphemy before and had never seen a defenseless human being so cruelly abused. They stood by speechless, as if nailed to the spot.

Fransje, who had first shrunk back behind Bram's legs in fear, was now standing in front of him seething with indignation. He too stood petrified, watching the gruesome spectacle. Each time the berserk little man let loose with another stream of curses, he felt his neckhairs rise. He was surprised that Bram or one of the other boys didn't put a stop to it, for they could easily master the small man. They, however, stood by watching the one-sided battle as if they had lost their wits.

Another volley of curses rent the air, and the man once more moved in on his son. This was more than Fransje could take. He felt his legs propelling him forward. They carried him close to the wildly flailing arms and legs. He grabbed Van Houten's coat and tried to pull him away from Bert. The man reluctantly looked back, and then stared down into the pale, angry face of the little boy behind him. He opened his mouth to spew out more oaths, but Fransje beat him to it. In a high voice he cried, "You bully!

You mean old bully! You swore! You're gonna go straight to hell 'cause the Lord heard you swear. And He also seen you kicking Bert near to death. You bully! You mean old bully and swearer!"

Fransje's heart was hammering in his throat. He was still holding on to Van Houten's coattail, braced to hold the man back if he tried to attack Bert again.

The older boys looked on the strange drama wide-eyed. Bram and Eine were ready to jump forward if the man lifted one finger against their little brother. Bert was still lying on the ground, but as soon as he heard Fransje's high, angry voice and no longer felt any blows, he had stopped bawling. Now he lay moaning softly, and his head was bleeding.

Then something strange happened. The angry man let his upraised fists drop limply to his sides. Then he clamped his hands to his face. His shoulders jerked and suddenly a wail like that of a small child broke from his lips. He turned on his heel, crying, "Push that buggy into the barn and get home—all of you! You too, Bert!"

Still sobbing he walked away, faster and faster, until he was running, and disappeared behind the barn.

Groaning, Bert got up and limped down the road. The boys looked at each other. Silently they put the chaise back in its place. Then they closed the barn doors. Without saying a word, they too headed down the road. Fransje walked between Bram and Eine. When the group separated, one of the other boys said, "I don't think we have to worry about him going to the police."

Eine took hold of Fransje and swung him up onto his shoulders. He said, "Hold on tight to my hair. That's it: give it a good pull. I need it."

Bram looked up into the pale little face that was now above his, and he said, "You know what, Fransje? You're bigger and braver than all those big boys and me and Eine put together."

Fransje took this to refer to his high perch on Eine's shoulders. But the tone in which Bram said it made him very proud and happy.

7

A prevailing southwest wind had finally routed the harsh winter, and again spring rallied to reclaim its vacated territory. The snowbanks along the road were shrinking so fast you could see them recede. Here and there the farmland poked its back and elbows through its tattered white winterwear. The ice in the drainage ditches was still covered by a dirty coat of slushy snow, which was settling more every day. Brown tufts of grass on the banks cropped up through the snow like dry ragmops. A silent, invisible force moved through the polder like a quickening breath, whispering, "Winter is gone, the season of song is at hand."

The thrushes which had been hopping about in the snow huddled against the cold like rolled-up, brown socks, now smoothed their feathers against their gaunt bodies and tried to still their burning hunger by looking for worms and insects under the clumps of grass along the ditches.

Fransje watched in amazement when they disappeared completely under the dead grass. Had he not seen them disappear, nothing but the tiny pieces of straw and dirt flying up from the roadside would have betrayed the fact that they were there. The sight of the disappearing birds awakened a primitive instinct in him that bound him directly to the half-naked savages dressed in animal skins who centuries ago had haunted the marshes which were now part of the flooded area around the island. He had felt this impulse before the hard winter began, when he had wanted so badly to go catching sticklebacks. This time, however, the impulse was much stronger. It was something completely new to him, something that made his heart beat faster and his blood pulse in his temples. He would have liked to dash at the bird, but that mysterious instinct also warned him to proceed calmly. Thoughts stampeded through his mind like wild horses. But his will firmly and resolutely reined them in and forced them into orderly ranks. He wanted to catch one of those birds, and he knew how to go about it.

He waited until he saw one come swooping down. His eyes sharply etched in his mind the spot where the thrush had landed. Motionless, barely breathing, he remained rooted where he was until the bird disappeared into the grass. Luckily it was on his side of the ditch and not far down the bank. He didn't even have to crawl down the slope, although it wouldn't have been dangerous because the ice under the snow was still strong. But now it would be even easier. Now he did not need to violate his conscience.

Slowly and silently he stole to the place he had measured out with his eyes and etched into his memory. He was almost there now, about a half meter from the bank. First he forced his racing heart to slow. He bent forward over the edge of the ditch. A cry of joy almost escaped him, for he saw the tip of the thrush's tail protruding from a clump of grass. Had the bird not been making little jerking movements, he wouldn't have spotted it, because its color blended so well into the immediate surroundings. Everything now hinged on Fransje's next move. Carefully he removed his cap and sank noiselessly to his knees. Then he lay down on his stomach in the snow, his head just above the bank of the waterway. Trembling, he raised his right hand. Then he lunged forward. His hand closed around the body of the unsuspecting bird.

The thrush uttered a startled metallic cry and buried its wirelike little claws in Fransje's wrist. But Fransje wouldn't let go, no matter how much the bird hurt him. With a flourish he brought the little creature up close to his face. He admired the bright little eyes, the elegant little head, the strong bill, and the blushing breast. Immediately Fransje fell in love with the little creature. With difficulty he scrambled to his feet, as he got a better grip on his precious catch with both hands. He had to show it to Mother.

Mother was only mildly impressed by his catch. She asked, "What are you going to do with the poor little thing? Why don't you let it go?"

Fransje put up a strong protest, not just because his hunter's pride was threatened, but because he no longer wanted to part with the dear little creature. He called on all his powers of persuasion to change Mother's mind. At last she said, "We'll see what your father says when he gets home."

Meanwhile Fransje's brain had been working feverishly. The steps he would have to take unfolded before his mind's eye one by one, in logical sequence. "Mom, will you set up the ladder for me?"

"What do you want in the attic?"

"There's an old birdcage behind the trapdoor. I can put my bird in there until Father comes home."

The birdcage belonged to Father; long ago he had kept finches in it. It was now stored behind the trapdoor along with a number of other seldom-used objects. To this idea, too, Mother raised objections, for Father couldn't abide having the children play with his personal possessions. At the same time, she realized that Fransje couldn't very well keep the bird in his hands until the evening. She lifted the ladder from its pin and set it against the wall. Then she climbed into the attic herself and returned a moment later with the little cage. Nervously Fransje slipped his proud prize in through the little door. At first the thrush fluttered frantically against the bars. Then it sat down on the cage floor, its tail feathers and wings spread out and its little breast heaving.

"He needs something to eat!" cried Fransje. "He's hungry." He ran to the pantry for a crust of bread. Breaking it into little pieces, he pushed it between the bars. "And thirsty!" he added. He pulled the little glass fountain with its blue top out from between the bars and filled it with water.

The frightened thrush, however, neither ate nor drank. Fransje was offended at its refusal of his gracious gifts. Mother soothed him by telling him that the bird would probably eat later when it had caught its breath and got over its fright. She advised him to leave the bird alone for awhile. So Fransje followed her into the living room. Every two minutes, however, he returned to the back room to check on his bird. Once he saw the thrush shake out its feathers. But otherwise it quietly sat in a corner of the floor of the cage and not on one of the perches, as Fransje would have preferred. Nevertheless, he was thankful that the bird was no longer fluttering wildly as it had at first.

Father's reaction was much more favorable than Fransje had expected. Apparently he saw his own love for birds reflected in his youngest offspring. But he was very doubtful whether the little creature would become acclimated to its small prison. The biggest problem would be supplying the bird with the right food. In any case, he allowed Fransje to keep his prize. He said that as soon as the ground became a little softer Fransje should go out looking for worms.

For fourteen days the thrush endured its small world. Then it died, apparently having pined away for the freedom of wide open spaces. One morning Fransje found it lying dead on its back in the bottom of the cage. Its tiny feet were drawn up into its belly like rusty little fists. Fransje could hardly eat breakfast, for he kept seeing its little eyes, covered by thin membranes like drawn shutters. Deep in his heart he blamed the bird for having abandoned him. After all, he had looked after it so well. In his confused mind questions popped up like mushrooms. Chewing slowly on a piece of bread, he asked, "Mommy, is the bird in heaven now?"

"No, Fransje. Birds don't go to heaven."

"You mean he's in hell!" he cried, shocked.

"No, birds don't go to heaven or hell."

"Then where is he? When Mr. Verplanke died, he went to heaven, didn't he?"

"Remember I told you that human beings have souls?" replied Mother. "Mr. Verplanke's soul went to heaven. But animals and birds don't have souls. That's why they can't talk like we can."

Fransje, however, found this hard to swallow. During the past two weeks he had begun to view the graceful, lively little creature as a person; now he couldn't believe that it had suddenly passed away into nothingness. He could easily believe that the cat had no soul, or if it did that it would go to hell; it had eyed his bird so wickedly that hell would serve the cat right. But his beautiful bird with the reddish-brown speckled breast, which even had wings to fly about in heaven . . . ! Anyway, Fransje would bury it. He would make a little grave for it, just like for a human being. Maybe Mother was wrong . . . .

Just as Mother unraveled Wantje's bungled knitting and reset it, so April restored the ruined beginnings of spring prematurely begun by February. Little by little the old elms began to weave a fragile veil of new greenery about themselves. The wallflowers once again picked themselves up, and as if to make up for lost time, they broke open their alabaster vials to let their lovely fragrance flow over the yard. Even the daisies which Fransje had helped to plant had survived the hard winter, thanks to the warm snow blanket. Pertly, like kittens, they thrust up their little heads to watch the sun float across the sky. The winter wheat in the polder also owed its survival to the snow. It rippled with a soft sheen in the wind and the sun.

The land was suddenly bustling with activity. Massive brown and gray Belgian horses, nodding their heads, drew long dark lines across the dry farmland. It was time to plant potatoes as well as other summer crops. Bram and Eine were again working regularly. Maria, too, had to help plant potatoes. Soon the sugar beets would come up, and shortly thereafter they would have to be thinned. After that there would be plenty of work until the sugar beets would have to be harvested—far into the fall, when often a thin film of ice would coat their fleshy leaves early in the morning. Mother began to breathe easier, for with this extra income she'd gradually be able to make a dent in the long list of credit she had run up.

Fransje was also busy. He, too, had a piece of ground in the front yard. He did not get it from the older boys, although he had asked them. They had been unwilling to part with any of theirs. So Mother had given him the long, narrow strip along the wall under the front window. It was only as wide as a rake, but its length made up for the lack of width. The location had one big drawback, however: every morning Fransje found the middle part trampled by whoever had closed the shutters the night before, or perhaps by Father, who opened them in the morning.

Fransje had planted daisies in it. But they required a lot of work. Kees had told him that the oftener you transplant them, the prettier they became. Eventually you'd not only get double blossoms, but they'd even turn all red just as the edges were now. Then they had been upgraded into chrysanthemums. Already on the same strip of ground were a bunch of German irises, called scissors-and-knives in that area. Along with the strip of ground, these, too, now rightfully belonged to Fransje. If a humble flower like a daisy could be upgraded by transplanting, just imagine what beautiful flowers scissors-and-knives would produce if Fransje transplanted them often enough! He had dug up the fleshy bulbs with their long wormlike roots at least five times. And he took it very ill of the plant that it didn't show its appreciation but was instead drooping limply to the ground.

Busily working in his garden with Neeltje, he cupped his hands around his mouth and shouted through the open window, "Mommy, come on out and see my garden!"

No answer came from Mother, who seemed not to have heard him. Neeltje, however, gave him an answer he hadn't counted on, and which hurt him more than a slap in the face. "Nyaaa! Mama's boy!" she jeered. "You called your mother Mommy, just like a baby."

Fransje stared at her, speechless. She had struck his most tender spot, or rather, his two most tender spots. First of all, she had demoted him to the small-fry, while he very badly wanted to be seen as a big boy; and in the second place, she struck at his love for his mother, because the name Mommy represented everything she meant to him.

He stood and thought how he in turn could strike back at Neeltje so it would do the most hurt. He could hit her in the face, being stronger than she was, but that would only show that he was a little boy and would only prove her right.

Neeltje stood there looking at him tauntingly. He threw down the old spoon with the broken handle that he had been digging with, and snapped, "Get out of our yard! I'm not playing with you anymore!"

Neeltje didn't hesitate even for a moment. She skipped out of the yard to the road. There she stopped, singing derisively, "Nyaaa! Mama's boy! Mama's boy! Fransje is a baby! He still calls his mother Mommy. Nyaaa! Mama's boy!"

That was more than Fransje could take. His face red with fury, he stooped and grabbed a big dirt clod. Fortunately he missed Neeltje with it, who ran off with a taunting laugh. Deeply humiliated, he ran into the house. Mother saw that something was wrong and asked, "Have you been picking a fight with Neeltje again?"

With this she unintentionally dealt him another slap in the face, because the fight had been for her honor. The worst of it was that he didn't have the words to explain or to defend himself.

So he changed the subject and asked, "Can I look in the picture book a little while ?"

Mother gave it to him and went on with her housework. This time Fransje began from the back. One of the pictures was of a terrible fire with leaping flames and billowing columns of smoke. Yet in the middle of it was a space in which two large groups of people stood. Separated from one another, both groups were looking toward the center where someone sat on a huge, raised chair. He seemed to be saying something to the people. There were also vague outlines of hovering figures with wings, apparently angels.

He had seen the picture before, but because it was so complicated, he had never before taken a close look at it. This time it arrested his attention, and because he couldn't make any sense of it, he had to quiz Mother. Luckily it was just coffee time, and after Mother had settled into her chair, he asked, "Mother, what are all those people doing there, and why is it . . . why is there fire all around these people?"

Mother was somewhat surprised that he addressed her as Mother, and she smiled at the altered sentence structure: apparently he couldn't remember the verb "to burn." She looked at the picture and read the caption. Then she told him it was a picture of the last judgment. One day the end of the world would come, when the whole world would be purified by fire. First the Lord would open all the graves and everyone would get back his body, and then everyone would have to appear before God's throne to give an account of his life and to be judged.

As simply and clearly as she could, she described the apocalyptic scenes of the last day and explained that this meant the coming of eternity for all people. She herself did not have a very clear notion of all these events herself; as she was explaining, hundreds of questions arose in her own heart and mind, but in childlike faith she let them rest. She didn't realize that her simple description evoked very vivid, sharply etched images in Fransje's mind. This time, too, he didn't interrupt her and posed no further questions. He took one more close look at the picture and then closed the book. "I'm going outside again," he said unenthusiastically.

He sauntered out to his little garden and picked up the spoon. But he didn't feel like doing any more gardening. Morosely he wandered across the road and sat down in the hollow between two exposed roots of a large elm. Absentmindedly he poked at the ground between his legs with the end of the spoon. With short bursts of speed, a beetle dashed between the blades of grass and the pebbles. It must see them as towering trees and mountains, thought Fransje. Fransje ran the spoon over the tiny insect. The legs thrashed a moment. Then it lay still.

It's dead, thought Fransje. But the little beetle wouldn't go to heaven or hell. For it, dead was dead because it had no soul. But people did have souls. Fransje too had a soul. And when he was put in the grave his body would have to wait there until the last day. Then eternity would come. How many nights was that—eternity? Mother said that eternity would never, never, never end, so it made no sense to count it in terms of so many nights. He was four years old, and Kees had told him that that was more than a thousand days. So it must be more than a thousand nights too. But in eternity even a thousand years was just a drop in the sea.

He tried to imagine an endless period of time. His finite mind, however, kept thinking an end point, a point of rest; yet the relentless idea swept him on. His mind was like a thrush bobbing over the landscape looking for a place to land. He wanted a bird's-eye view of eternity. In his imagination he conceived an immeasurably long period of time, and aloud he said to himself, "One hundred thousand years." But after one hundred thousand years would follow more time. One hundred hundred hundred thousand thousand hundred thousand. The spoon slipped from his fingers. His eyes stared sightless out over the sunny spring farmland.

Suddenly a new idea entered his reeling mind. What if he himself were sent to hell? The idea of eternity now took on a completely different visage—a horrible visage. In hell there were no angels with white wings and people with wrinkles of laughter about their eyes. In hell there was no singing, but only weeping and wailing because of the fire that never, never dies. In hell there was only cursing and complaining. That's where the devil was, Mother had once told him; the devil who took out his evil whims on you.

A cold sweat broke out on Fransje. Hell. What if he were sent there? He wasn't so wicked as to pray to images, like the Roman Catholics. But he wasn't very good either. Just a little while ago he had thrown a clod of dirt at Neeltje. And sometimes he quarreled and fought with Wantje and Kees. And often he was disobedient to Mother. Not to Father: Fransje was much too afraid of him. But to Mother and Maria . . . .

Hell. An eternity. One hundred hundred hundred thousand thousand thousand . . . . First in the dark grave for who knows how long. Then before God's throne. And then . . . . A cold chill passed over him.

He didn't want to go to hell. He couldn't go to hell! One of Siene and Marien's girls, who sometimes talked about such things too, said that if you quickly said a prayer at the last minute, you'd be let into heaven. Fransje could say "O great and beneficient God" and his morning prayer by heart already. Yes, that was what he'd do. When he came before that big throne, he'd quickly fall down on his knees and say his prayers.

The devil was working on Fransje again. He was pushing Fransje's thoughts down the dark, twisting corridors of despair. Fransje did not know that he was at that very moment getting a foretaste of the terrors of hell, for this terror was without the flames, which to his mind were a necessary part of hell. Yes, the devil goaded him farther and farther until he was backed into a corner of the darkest corridor.

What if God didn't give him a chance to quickly say his prayers? Or what if the Lord couldn't see or hear him because of the crowd before His throne? Then even this last remedy would do him no good. He'd be mercilessly tossed out into hell.

But he couldn't go to hell! He didn't want to go to hell! He didn't want to suffer the awful pangs and pains of hell as eternity rolled endlessly on and on. Hundred thousand hun . . . .

A bizarre plan took shape in his tortured heart and mind. He pictured his last moments with only the worst to look forward to. He forced himself to take full cognizance of what would happen and what he had to do in that last moment. When he was dying, he'd ask Mother . . . to take the paring knife . . . and stick it into him after he was dead, just as she stuck a pin into cloth. Then he'd have the knife with him when he arrived in . . . hell. And when the pain of the fire began, then with cold deliberation he'd . . . he'd do something much more painful than fire. He'd . . . he'd . . . take the knife and . . . deliberately cut himself into pieces. Just as Father cut a dead rabbit into pieces. And then he'd be dead—dead once and for all. And then hell couldn't harm him anymore.

Fransje heaved a tremendous sigh. He had been staring into the distance with wide-open eyes for so long, seeing nothing but the horrible scenes of his imagination, that his eyes burned. Those thoughts had been planted in Fransje's mind by the devil, who didn't consider it beneath his dignity to drive a child into a tight corner with such illogical reasonings. The father of lies from the beginning, he had achieved his purpose. Now he could leave Fransje to his fate, for he had just made a covenant with death and an agreement with hell.

Swing high, swing low,
Flowers in the meadow,
Flowers blooming on the dike;
Whoops! Fransje tumbles off the dike.

"Now you'd better walk again for a while," said Arjaan. He and Kees had been carrying Fransje between them on their clasped hands as they chanted the little nonsense song. They still had a long way to go, however, and Arjaan suspected that he'd have to carry Fransje later. They were on their way to the sea dike. Pier was also with them.

Each of the three older boys carried a pail which they were going to fill with lamb's ears, an edible, wild plant that grew on the clay banks below the sea dikes. According to the almanac, high tide would arrive at nine o'clock tonight, so now, shortly after school was out, it had to be low tide. The family had eaten almost all the vegetables Mother had canned for the winter, and they were all tired of salted green beans, sauerkraut, turnips, and winter carrots. Fresh, tender lamb's ears would provide a welcome change. At least, that is what Siene and Mother had shouted to one another from their respective back yards earlier that afternoon. Immediately they had agreed to send the boys to gather a pailful after school. The days were growing longer and they could be back with it just in time for supper.

When Mother gave Arjaan and Kees the errand, Fransje begged to go along too. Mother and Kees, for quite different reasons, weren't very enthusiastic about the idea. But Arjaan, who felt sorry for Fransje, put in a good word for him and promised to take care of him. He promised to keep a close eye on him to see that he didn't fall in one of the runnels left by high tide. Fransje promised Mother that he would be a good boy and not cry or beg Arjaan to carry him, because then he wouldn't be allowed to go along ever again.

But now Arjaan and Kees had already spoiled him by swinging him on their hands. Fransje, however, was smart enough not to protest when they tired of it. They were still much too close to home. He was in high spirits, walking on clouds because they were going to the seashore. As far as he could remember, he had never been there before. He wished that Pier wasn't going along, but since Pier had more right to be going than Fransje himself, he'd just have to put up with him.

The weather was beautiful. The new vegetation had spread a soft green veil over the fields, which had been bare a short while before. The long rows of elms along the road and on the dikes in the distance were wearing fuzzy green caps. In the grass on the banks of the ditches and in the pastures thousands of dandelions with blazing hearts reflected the golden light of the sun, looking like tiny suns themselves. Now and then a mare accompanied by a prancing foal·came to the fence to stare in curiosity at the happily chattering group of boys. Fransje was very pleased by this attention. But Pier yelled loudly, throwing his empty pail across the road to frighten the animals. Her tail held high and farting loudly with the sudden movement, the mare ran off. The foal ran after her with comical stiff-legged little hops, much to Pier's delight.

It was a long way to the sea dike. Fransje kept dropping behind and then he had to run to catch up. That made one of his stockings sag and then he had to stop to pull it up again. The boys were walking much too fast for his liking. But he didn't complain. He was ready to make even greater sacrifices if necessary for the privilege of going along.

By way of the old inner dike they finally reached the much higher sea dike to which it was connected. Suddenly Fransje was standing before a high cement wall on top of the dike. The wall stretched endlessly in both directions. Pier was already standing on top of it, wildly waving his pail. Kees tossed his pail over the top and also hoisted himself on the wall. Fransje looked up at Arjaan. "Come here, Fransje," he said. He put down his pail and grunted as he lifted Fransje up. But he didn't allow him to stand on the wall. "Sit there and don't move until I get to the other side," he warned.

Fransje looked around and was overcome by sudden dizziness. Over Arjaan's head he saw the green fields lying far below the dike. The dike thrust steeply up from the fields to where Fransje had been set on the wall. Out of the corner of his eye he saw the glaring expanse of bare mud flats at the foot of the dike, stretching endlessly to the hazy horizon. The sun traced a bright stripe across the water of the distant channel. A few ships were slowly drawn along as if on the ends of long, thin lines of smoke.

With trembling hands Fransje clung to the rough edge of the wall. He was glad when Arjaan seized him again from the other side. Now he, too, dared to stand up with Arjaan's help. Once more Fransje glanced down into the polder. Arjaan pointed out their house, a small gray-brown smudge under a lumpy hedge. The hedge was formed by the two rows of elms that undulated toward the village on the right and the station neighborhood on the left.

Arjaan noticed how tightly Fransje's hand gripped his. He said, "Now you better come down off the wall Fransje. We have to go and pick lamb's ears."

Where the sea dike curved, a large whimsically sectioned triangle of sallow green grass had been formed. This ground was about a meter and a half higher than the smooth clay beach beyond. The line that separated the two areas was very irregular, and even on the mud flats there were some small green islands.

Gray runnels snaked across the large grassy plateau to the mud flats beyond. This strange landscape impressed Fransje deeply. He descended the concrete steps of the reinforced side of the dike and squeezed between a long row of poles. In front of them lay a sloping road of uneven bluish-black basalt blocks that fit together like cells in a honeycomb. Fransje bent to pick up a couple of dark brown "clappers" (kelp air bladders) from the dry seaweed. He asked Arjaan what they were. Along with the seaweed, large wads of hay and straw were wrapped around the poles. This debris had been left behind by high tide and had laid out all afternoon drying in the sun.

Pier and Kees were already well into the grassy triangle. One after the other, they jumped the slick-edged little runnels. Arjaan again had to urge Fransje to hurry. They had to get their pails filled with lamb's ears. After a short search they found a place where the tender leaves had not yet been harvested. There were always a few unemployed men around who came with huge sacks to harvest the leaves to sell from door to door.

Fransje stuck close to Arjaan as he had promised. On this

strange terrain, he felt none too sure of himself. A little farther on, Pier and Kees had found a good spot and were now bent low, cutting industriously. Arjaan was not far from one of the narrow, deep runnels. Fransje couldn't resist a cautious peek over the edge. On the bottom a narrow stream of water gurgled over sand and shells. It seemed to be calling to the distant sea, "Wait for me! I want to come too!" A few air bubbles danced gaily on the surface, bobbing along like tiny glass boats. Fransje wanted to see where they would go. Along the runnel the ground was relatively level and dry. He followed its windings until he stood on a jutting piece of land and could go no farther. Suddenly he saw before him the picture of Moses on Mount Nebo; Moses had also stood on such a high outcropping of land.

Behind him he heard Arjaan calling. His faint, distant voice ordered him to come back at once. Fransje obeyed, but as he was following the runnel back upstream, he heard an even fainter voice calling. It was Pier, who stood far away hollering and waving his arms. Fransje couldn't hear what he was shouting, but he saw Kees running toward him. He asked Arjaan whether they weren't going to see what was going on too. Arjaan was also curious. Leaving the pail so they'd be able to find their good spot back, they hurried toward the other two boys. Arjaan had to help Fransje jump across several runnels.

Pier had made a great find. Excitedly he told how suddenly a duck had flown up out of the grass. Had he been a little faster, he could have caught it with his bare hands. But anyway he had the two eggs that had been in the nest. Triumphantly he held them up, one in each hand. Wasn't he lucky!

Fransje admired the shiny, greenish-white eggs, wishing he were as lucky as Pier. He'd look around for eggs too. Pier put the eggs in a little hollow between the lamb's ears in his pail.

But Arjaan said, "You don't even know if they're any good. Maybe they're already bloody inside."

Pier hadn't thought of that. He took them from the pail and ran with them to a nearby runnel. "They sink like a rock!" he cried joyfully.

Arjaan returned to his pail. Mother had told them to try to be back before supper. They couldn't afford to waste any more time.

Fransje wanted to go hunting for duck eggs, but Arjaan warned him not to stray too far away. Zealously Fransje searched the thickest clumps of the tallest grass. Although he saw many ideal spots to build a nest, apparently the ducks had seen it differently, for his hunting expedition was fruitless.

The other boys had better success. After about an hour their pails were almost full. Before they left they went to look at the large runnel that cut the grassy plateau farther on, and which made a sharp turn seaward near the corner of the dike. "Maybe there will be little flounders in it," suggested Pier. He spun out a long story about the dozens of flounders he had caught there last year. Arjaan and Kees let him talk, knowing that he was a braggart, and that if lying were fatal, he'd have been dead long ago.

When they came to the dike, Pier suddenly had a terrific idea. You know what they could do? They could build a fire with all that dry junk and bake the eggs in it. They would taste darn good. To convince the others, he told them he'd give them each half an egg.

Arjaan raised objections. Kees was already half persuaded, but he pointed out that they had no matches. Pier responded with a sly grin and dug a box of the illicit objects from his pocket. Fransje noticed that Pier had pockets just like those La Bruyere had made in the pants meant for him, and his aversion to Pier deepened. But to build a fire and have baked eggs—why, that sounded like a terrific idea to him!

Pier was already gathering dry straw. Kees helped him. Arjaan climbed to the cement wall and looked to make sure no one was coming. When he returned, a sinuous, blue column of smoke was already coiling up from the pile of straw. The eggs were lying on top. In the heart of the pile, the fire began to snap and crackle. A small, yellow tongue shot up, licking hungrily at the straws. Soon Pier and Kees were dancing around an aggressive little fire.

Fransje shrank close to Arjaan. He was a little frightened, but he also thought it splendid. Dangerous, but splendid! He had started a fire once himself and had not forgotten that terror. Pier came carrying another armload of debris, such a huge load that he dropped bunches of it along the way. The ravenous fire growled out a thank you to Pier. In one big gulp the fiery red mouth swallowed the whole armload. The sparks flew about the boys' ears. Now it was a real bonfire!

The fire was insatiable. It swallowed everything in reach, in cluding the small bunches that Pier had carelessly dropped along the way. At first, however, the boys didn't notice. They noticed nothing until they saw that one of the poles close to the fire was also aflame. That could be dangerous; it ought to be put out. But the heat of the fire forced them to keep their distance. They couldn't reach the short pole. Laughter died on their lips. On the other side, too, the fire was spreading along the ribbon of dried flotsam that they hadn't yet picked up. Two, no three other poles were smoldering. Suddenly flames curled upward along their bare torsos and shortly they were blazing torches.

Arjaan was the first to realize what peril they were in. Frantically his eyes scanned the dike first one way and then the other to see if he could find a stick in the washed-up debris. There were plenty of short chunks of driftwood and weathered blocks of wood but nothing that resembled a stick. He ripped off his coat, rolled it up, and furiously beat at the outermost ranks of the advancing flames. He shouted to Pier and Kees to help him. Briefly they seemed to gain the upper hand, but as soon as they attacked a new front, the previous place burst back into flame. A long row of poles were now ablaze. Even the grass, withered by the heat, began to burn. The fiery tide also began to spread sideways and swept up the dike to the cement steps.

If only they had water! The water in the runnels was too far away. Before they could get a pail of water, the fire would have spread over the whole dike. Frantic, the boys ran around in circles. Their faces looked like masks—sweaty and smudged with smoke. Suddenly Arjaan remembered that there was water in the ditch on the other side of the dike. He dumped the lamb's ears on a heap at the base of the cement wall and hurled his pail over it. It rolled down the steep bank, and soon he was tumbling after it. He yelled to Kees and Pier to do likewise. But Pier was busy scooping handfuls of mud. The fire laughed at the small lumps of clay. Roaring, it rolled past them, spreading farther and farther like hot red lava.

At first Fransje watched in mute terror. From the beginning he had been afraid. But as long as the boys had still been having fun, he had felt quite safe in their exuberant, carefree self-confidence. To him they represented a world more daring, more dangerous than his own. Being so much bigger and older than he, surely they knew how far they could go.

But when the laughter had died on their faces, giving way to anxiety and later to undisguised fear, his frail support had crumbled. Screaming he had grabbed Arjaan. But Arjaan had roughly shoved him aside, shouting at him to get out of the way. All his security shattered, Fransje had thrown himself in the grass away from the fire and was now lying there bawling.

When he saw Arjaan jumping over the wall, he thought he was making a run for it, leaving him behind. So the cause was hopeless! Scrambling up, he ran to the wall, but he couldn't even see over it, much less climb it. He pounded against the rough moss-covered wall with his fists, screaming, "Arjaan! Arjaan!"

Suddenly a horrible thought leaped into his mind. This was what Mother had told him about not long ago. This was the beginning of the great fire of the last days. Soon the whole dike would be on fire and it would form a flaming wall—cutting off their way home. And the fire would reach out farther and farther until it turned the whole world into a huge, seething sea of flames.

His terrified heart screamed, Mommy! "Mommy!" bellowed his parched mouth. "Mommy! Mommy!" Soon his throat was so swollen and his vocal cords so strained that they could only produce hoarse, intermittent croaks.

Suddenly Arjaan's smudged, panting face appeared above him. "Fransje," he shouted, "stop your screaming!" But this only aggravated things. Fransje held up his arms to Arjaan, and when Arjaan jumped down beside him, he nearly pulled his clothes from his body. Arjaan, however, tore himself out of Fransje's grasp and dashed toward the fire with his half-filled pail. There was a whoosh and a loud hiss followed by a few small clouds of steam. And that was all. Untamed, the roaring arms of flame flailed drunkenly about.

Arjaan looked at it despairingly. Kees and Pier came up beside him. Where the fire had started was now a black, bare spot with little plumes of smoke rising from it. There the fire had consumed everything. The bare spot, however, was but a small island surrounded by a high wall of leaping flames which forged farther and farther outward. The boys had no weapons in this one-sided battle.

Suddenly, in the distance Kees saw someone coming. He was carrying something that looked like a stick. Or was it a rifle? He was also carrying something over his shoulder—a sack or some such thing. Someone coming to harvest lamb's ears? Or the game warden? Or the police? Kees grabbed Arjaan and Pier by the arms and pointed. Arjaan thought it was the game warden. When Pier heard these words, he whirled to make a run for it. But Arjaan was one step ahead of him. He dived for Pier's pail and scattered the lamb's ears over the concrete lining of the dike. "You're staying here!" he panted. "You're the one who started it, and you're staying here until the fire is out!"

The man came closer. He wasn't the game warden or the police. Nor was he looking for lamb's ears; he seemed to be a beachcomber from another village. He saw the boys' precarious situation. Without a word, he emptied his sack. He tossed it to Arjaan and said curtly, "Wet that in the ditch on the other side of the dike." And to Kees and Pier, "Get your pails!" He himself grabbed Arjaan's pail and hurried toward the sludge below the basalt blocks. Three wide sweeping scoops and the pails were full. He carried two of them himself and with a jerk of his head he signaled the two boys to follow him with the other one. Downwind from the fire he plopped gobs of mud at its leading edge and he did the same on the other side. Taking the dripping sack from Arjaan's hands, he smothered the fire on the outermost poles. Then he fetched more mud. He didn't stop until the whole fire was surrounded by a steaming, thick ring of mud. The flames were no match for this energetic, well-planned attack. Soon it was smoldering feebly behind the wall of steaming mud. Once more Arjaan was sent to wet the sack. With it the unknown rescuer beat out the last flames.

All this time the man hadn't said a word. Calmly he put his things back into his sack. He slung his sack over his shoulder to continue on his way. But before his sweating body stepped into motion, he said gruffly, "Now I suppose you guys are going to start another fire tomorrow." The boys said nothing. They only shook their heads. Then the man left.

Fransje had seen little or nothing of all this. He had thrown himself down in the grass some distance away, where he lay limp as a wet paper sack, his head on his arms. He had no more tears to cry or voice to bawl with, and his mind was numb. His whole body was trembling and violent sobs racked him from head to foot. Had the world perished yet? And had he been left behind all alone? And Mommy, was she . . . ?

Then he heard the rustle of footsteps in the grass behind him. Two strong hands set him on his feet. When he opened his eyes,

Arjaan was kneeling in front of him, and wiped his swollen face with his red hanky. "Let's go, Fransje." His voice was filled with tenderness and compassion. "We're going home. See, the fire's out!"

With burning eyes Fransje looked around him. There was the long bank of the dike with the high cement wall. There were the broad mud flats. And yonder stood Pier and Kees. But the flames were no longer leaping about like screeching devils. The way home to Mother was no longer blocked. Joy welled up inside him bringing new tears to his eyes.

"O God!" he sighed hoarsely. Though it almost sounded like profanity, Arjaan knew Fransje wasn't swearing. He took his little brother by the hand and led him back to the scattered lamb's ears. The boys rinsed their pails in the ditch. The lamb's ears were probably dirty, but they'd just have to sort them and take out all the grass and straw when they got home. Half-burnt poles protruded from the dike like rotten teeth in a grotesquely misshapen mouth.

Arjaan was dead tired. But Fransje couldn't go another step; his legs felt like rubber. Arjaan gave the two pailfuls of lamb's ears to Kees to carry and took Fransje on his back.

Already the sun hung low over a distant farm. What time was it? They had better hurry or else they would be raked over the coals when they got home. This thought gave rise to another worry. Arjaan put Fransje down for a moment. He looked him straight in the eye and said, "Listen, Fransje. Don't tell anyone at home about the fire. Okay!" Arjaan needed a lot of tact to express his feelings so that they would be properly received. On the one hand, his words should convey an implied threat, and on the other, an urgent plea and friendly agreement.

Kees had also stopped. He put down both pails and dug into his pocket. He fished out several pieces of chalk that he had rescued when he emptied the wastepaper basket at school, and he held them under Fransje's nose in a blatant attempt at bribery. "Look, Fransje," he said. "You can have these. But then you have to promise you won't say anything about the fire when we get home."

Fransje readily promised with a series of little nods. Once more he clambered up on Arjaan's stooped back. They were all vastly relieved that the horrible adventure was over. Relief made them boisterous. Pier was again the loudest. "Too bad about those eggs, eh?" he said. "I wonder what happened to them? But that was some fire, wasn't it? I bet we could have put it out without that guy's help." The others didn't reply.

The light was beginning to fade when they came home. The boys removed their own and Fransje's coats in the back room, because the strong smoke smell would certainly have given them away. They washed themselves with special care and with plenty of soap to cover the smell. Arjaan washed Fransje's face and hands, and whispering, once again bound him to his promise to say nothing about the fire. Then, the oldest in the lead, they marched into the living room. "Hi, Mom, Dad, kids!" they said one after the other.

Father gave them a stern look. He was just getting ready to read the Bible. So they were late for supper. Did they have a good excuse?

Yes, most of the lamb's ears had already been cut, so it took them a long time to fill their pails. A credible story. If they were telling the truth, it was certainly a valid excuse.

But Maria, who had gone to the back room to fetch something or other, came back into the living room and remarked, "Something sure smells awful in the back room. As if something burnt. Mother, did you burn the dishrag when you took the pan off the stove?"

No, Mother hadn't burned the dishrag. She hadn't even used the stove in the back room. Fransje saw a chance to help shelter the boys from suspicion. He'd help them out of the fire. He cried, "Arjaan and Kees didn't make a fire at the dike! Honest!"

The two boys shrank down at their places behind the table. Luckily their blushing faces were hidden in the dusk. But Father needed no further proof to confirm his suspicions. In a stern voice, he asked, "Well, what's the story? Is that why you were late?"

"Yes, Dad," said the two bowed heads.

"Then you know what's next. Say grace, eat, close, and straight to bed!"

Father was definitely angry. None of the children could remember ever being spanked by him; nor had he ever sent them to bed without supper, because that had too often happened to him when he was a child. His words, thrust home by his penetrating blue eyes, could cope without such drastic measures.

That night Fransje had a strange but wonderful dream.

All alone, he is playing beside the road. Suddenly a stranger stands next to him. Without a word, he takes Fransje's hand. Although Fransje has never before seen the man, he feels neither fearful nor shy. As he glances up into the man's serene face, peace and contentment flood his heart. At ease, he unconditionally yields himself to the stranger.

Together they stroll toward the village. Tall elms line both sides of the road, straight and still like candles. Not a leaf stirs under the soft gray sky. The earth exhales peace into the mild air. No one else is to be seen on the road, and they stroll on unhurriedly. Fransje doesn't even think to look back at the window. Neither Mother nor any of the others even enter his mind.

There is something strange about the road, however. Where Kees de Visser's house should be, there is no house. And where the village should begin, there are no houses either. But strangest of all, Fransje does not expect to see any. Houses and people simply do not enter his mind. Everything is exactly as it should be; and everything is good.

The road climbs imperceptibly upwards between the trees, until they drop out of sight. But it stretches on, straight and smooth, always rising, and on either side of it, rising with it, are hedges of gray-white clouds, which make Fransje feel protected. They look just like the long hawthorn hedges in spring, unclipped, as seen from a distance, but without thorns and leaves. Their fluffy, gray-white color is unbroken by the gleam of bright colors or sunlight. The light that envelopes them is the light of a peaceful summer evening.

An inexpressible quiet joy pervades Fransje's heart. But not surprise. Everything is new and strange; yet he feels as if he has returned to a familiar place from which he has been absent for a long time but for which he has been longing all the while with a great, silent yearning, at last now fully satisfied.

Now and then the stranger bends over him. As Fransje looks up into his eyes, his heart floods with new, inexpressible joy and love. Not a single question arises in him, for he knows everything directly. And he knows that this quiet road leads to heaven, although not a word has been spoken.

Higher and higher the road rises, slowly but steadily. But this isn't the tar road that runs past their house to the village. This road is as smooth as glass, but not hard or slippery like ice. Nor is it black, but rather, the same color as the cloud hedge beside it. He walks on soft gray cloud.

A wondrous relation exists between Fransje and the stranger, though not a word passes between them. Now and then they briefly look at each other, and then they know all. At the meeting of their eyes, a stream of thought flows from heart to heart, and also a renewed stream of love. About them drift the fragrances of wallflowers and sweet williams and roses and violets. And the air is bright with the distant sound of blackbirds, although there isn't a bird in sight.

The stranger vaguely reminds Fransje of all those whom he loves. He resembles Mother and Bram and Maria and Kee of Kapelle and Leentje de Visser and Verplanke. And yet he is wholly himself. Fransje loves him like he has never loved anyone else. His heart melts like wax within him.

Fransje is aware that he is no longer wearing wooden shoes. He is barefoot, and the road of gray-white clouds feels soft underfoot. His sweater, shirt, and pants have vanished too. Instead, a long, shimmering white robe hangs in pleats from his shoulders to his toes. He doesn't find this strange or surprising; it only heightens his sense of peace and joy and love.

Far in the distance, at the end of the rising road is a gate. Both doors are standing wide open, and white light pours out between them. Although the gate is still far away, Fransje can clearly see someone standing in the midst of the light. He can even make out his face. Fransje knows who it is. It is the Lord. The Lord is waiting for him.

Then, for the first time, fear steals into his heart. It does not replace his former peaceful happiness, but it does precipitate a conflict within him. Suddenly the fear is winning. He grips the hand of his companion more tightly, and lifting his head toward him, he seeks his eyes. Then the first word breaks from his lips, and it echoes like a cry for help: "Jesus!" he cries.

He awoke with a start. It was dark around him. He groped about with his hands and felt the covers. But still he did not realize that he was in bed. Vaguely he was conscious of an immense emptiness and homesickness in his soul.

He told no one about his remarkable dream, not even Mother. Unconsciously he felt that to put it into words would tarnish it.

But he did reflect on it often, every time he once more tasted the nameless yearning in his soul.

Thereafter the horrible specter of hell lost much of its power.

8

How unspeakably lovely the world was! Fransje, at least, didn't have the words to express his wonder. He could only open himself to the beauty of the world and let it sink into him; for it was too overpowering for his frail selfhood.

Quite naturally he didn't compare the present scene to its appearance a month before, when the hawthorn hedge, now a green wall between him and the orchard, had formed a high white barricade along an equally white trench. Not that he had forgotten it, but to him that seemed years, even ages ago. He had now entered a completely new time in his life, and he found himself in an entirely new world despite the familiar surroundings. Nor did this summer lushness remind him of the ethereal beauty he had known in his dream.

Fransje sighed, gazing up into the high, deep blue sky. Across it floated a few sluggish, snow-white clouds. He inhaled the sweet breath of the blooming orchard; around him twittered an exuberant jubilation of birds. He stood motionless in the middle of this miracle called summer. In one hand he held an old, cracked saucer half-filled with small glossy leaves which he had picked from the hawthorn hedge. He was pretending that he was preparing a bowl of salad, a game that he and the neighborhood children had often played during the last two weeks. But this morning he didn't need their company. Besides, he hadn't yet seen or heard any of the other children.

He stood there chewing slowly until he became aware of a bitter taste in his mouth. It came from the wad of hawthorn that had been chewed into a green pulp. He bent forward and spit the soupy mass on the ground. Now he was just like Father, who chewed tobacco. But when Father spit, it was brown and smelly.

Suddenly he was startled out of his reverie by a loud bird crying three quick cuckoo's and then hissing as if it, too, were clearing its throat to spit. Fransje looked up and saw the big bird fluttering awkwardly between the high tops of the pear trees. For a moment it tried to find a perch on one of the small top branches but then it tumbled on disappearing behind the trees. Fransje just caught a glimpse of a small bird pursuing it with jerky, bobbing movements before it, too, disappeared. The hurried cuckooing continued, but farther away toward the rear of the orchard. Wantje had taught Fransje a little verse which suddenly ran through his mind:

> Birds all lay their eggs in May,
> except the godwit and the cuckoo bird;
> they have found a better way.

And he knew something else. Arjaan had talked about the cuckoo bird during suppertime a few days ago. Fransje had been ready to dismiss the story in disbelief, but Father had confirmed it, and he should know—he knew a great deal about many kinds of birds. That nasty, lazy cuckoo simply refused to build a nest or to hatch its own eggs like any decent mother bird. It just laid its egg on the ground, took it in its beak, and then carried it to the nest of some little finch who then hatched it for the cuckoo. And the baby cuckoo was just as nasty as its mother, for it hogged all the food that its foster parents hauled to the nest so that it grew much faster than the baby finches. With such an oversized bully in it, the nest soon became too small, and then one by one the nasty intruder cold-bloodedly pushed all the other little birds out of the nest until it was the only one left. And those other poor little birds all died, of course.

Ever since he had learned this, Franje had hated cuckoos. He regretted having to hate them, for he admired their call. But now they reminded him of Neeltje's mother. You couldn't trust her nice words either. And he didn't like Wantje's little verse anymore either, because it began nicely about birds and then in the same breath mentioned godwits and cuckoos. Why couldn't they lay their eggs in May like any other decent bird? Fransje wasn't surprised at the cuckoo. He suspected that it had something to do with his other dirty tricks. But then Fransje asked himself what was wrong with the godwit. He didn't know what it looked like, but its strange name and unusual laying habits seemed to bode no good.

Fransje did love birds. He knew that the little verse was right, saying they all laid eggs in May except those two oddballs. He knew the location of many nests. But all except two were under the roof tiles, and since he couldn't reach them, they really didn't count. But he did know approximately where they were located because he saw the industrious sparrows flying back and forth every day carrying long strands of straw. They weren't too fussy about their nests; in several places the straw dangled out of the opening onto the roof tiles. There was also a starling nest right beside the chimney. It was the noisiest nest of all. As soon as Fransje woke up in the morning he heard the piercing, hungry cries of the baby birds right above his bed. He could tell exactly when their parents were feeding them, for then a storm of chirping and screeching broke out, which slowly subsided after the parents had left to look for more worms.

The two other nests, however, attracted his special love and attention because they were in the hawthorn hedge in the back yard near the rabbit cages. One of them was a black thrush nest, and he was the only one who knew about it. First there had been four brown-speckled pale green eggs in it. But they had become four dark, downy fluffs with large round heads. As soon as they heard any rustling, they stuck their heads out above the sides of the nest, and then their heads were four large square holes—hungry mouths screaming for more worms. Their mouths were outlined in yellow, as if they had eaten a sandwich and the butter had stuck to their mouths. Fransje had accidentally discovered the nest as he poked around the rabbit cages, suddenly scaring the nesting thrush which flew up with loud squawks of alarm. Standing on an overturned pail and parting the branches a little, Fransje could look into the nest. Sometimes he was tempted to take one of the downy creatures from the nest and hold it against his cheek, but he had found that he could not reach them. The nest was too far in the dense, prickly branches. Moreover, he didn't wish to disturb their peace and safety, for in each of the four baby birds he saw something of himself, and in the nest he saw his own little bed.

Actually he had almost persuaded himself that this was the nest of his dead thrush, even though the dark-colored parents bore little resemblance to it. Only their song resembled that of his thrush, though these black thrushes sang even more beautifully.

Fransje also knew where to find the enclosed nest of a chiffchaff: high in the mushroom of hawthorn Father had created by constant pruning. Its large green head sat on a skinny neck—a thick branch that stuck straight up out of the hedge. Fransje hadn't discovered this nest himself. Eine had pointed it out to him. His other brothers and sisters knew about it too. From the way the parents kept flying back and forth, Fransje inferred there were baby birds inside. These parents were even smaller than the baby thrushes. How many babies there were he had no idea. He would like to peek through the little hole in the side of the cute little nest. It looked even more like his bed than the other, because it had a canopy. At night he sometimes pretended his bed was the chiffchaff nest and that he was just as small as one of the baby birds. This gave him a wonderful sense of safety and brotherhood.

He had told none of the neighborhood children that he knew there were two nests in the hedge because he was afraid that eventually Pier would find out. And Fransje was sure that the big bully would disturb the nests.

Fransje sighed again. He had been standing there musing for so long that he hadn't noticed that the saucer in his hand had gradually tipped further and further, spilling the little green leaves on the ground. But that didn't matter. The game was beginning to bore him anyway. Now he would search the branches of the hedge for June bugs. Kees had told him that there was nothing those beetles liked better than hawthorn leaves.

Kees had a June bug in a jar on the windowsill in the back room. He had put hawthorn leaves in the jar and the June bug was eating them. Fransje would love to have a couple of them too. If they liked hawthorn leaves so well, they must have discovered the hedge, and then chances were some of them were hiding there until dark. Kees had told him that June bugs only fly after dark and that they spend the day sleeping in some hiding place. But Kees had caught his along the big dike when he went hunting June bugs at night with some friends. Pier had even caught two.

After school he tied a piece of thread on one of their numerous legs and then he whirled the beetle around until it spread its wings and started flying. Kees didn't do that, and if Fransje found one, he wouldn't do it either, because Father had strictly forbidden it. You may not torture animals. You may kill rats and mice and flies and mosquitoes, but quickly, so they don't suffer. Torturing animals is a sin. The Lord doesn't like it. But killing harmful animals quickly is no sin. This raised questions in Fransje's mind. If you may kill them off, why did the Lord take the trouble to make them?

Sitting on his haunches, he carefully turned over the leaves of the nearest branches, devoting special attention to the clusters of buds forming here and there. But his efforts went unrewarded. He thought it stupid of those June bugs not to come into the hedge, where there was plenty of food. However, Kees had promised that sometime when he went to the big dike again he'd take Fransje along. If the weather was good and the wind wasn't too strong, maybe they'd go tonight. There couldn't be any wind, for if there were, June bugs didn't fly.

Just as he was about to pick up his saucer to bring it back to the house, Fransje heard the clip-clop of horses' hooves on the tar road. In itself this wasn't strange, but then a familiar male voice shouted, "Whoa!" and the horse stopped. Fransje looked up. It was Father; he was just tying the reins to the tree in front of the house.

That was strange. Father was a laborer, not a groom, and laborers usually didn't drive horses. Fransje ran forward and shouted, "Father, what are you doing with the horses?"

"Hello there, my big helper!" answered Father with a hint of a coming surprise in his voice. "I took the horses to the blacksmith and now I'm taking them back to the farm."

"Why did *you* have to take those horses to the blacksmith?" Fransje wanted to know.

The alert question made Father smile. He explained that the groom was sick and that the boss had asked him to take the horses to the blacksmith.

One of the horses was wearing a harness, but the other only a bit and bridle. For this too Fransje wanted an explanation. Father told him that the harness had been repaired and now the horse was carrying it back to the farm. Both horses had needed new shoes, too.

"I have a good idea," said Father. "First I'm going into the house for lunch and then I have to go back to the farm. But I really could use a man to help me bring back these horses. Do you know anyone who can help me?"

Fransje beamed. Hardly believing it, he looked from Father to the horses and then back again to Father. Laughter danced in Father's eyes as he continued, "If you can help me, you'll have to drive the horse with the harness, and I the other one. But then you'll have to sit on his back, of course, and I'm not sure you know how." He deliberately avoided the word *dare*, putting it on the level of know-how. Fransje recklessly threw himself into the psychological trap; in answer he dashed to the back door, kicked off his wooden shoes, and ran into the house shouting loudly. Mother had already seen Father and the horses and understood what was going on, which was a good thing, for she couldn't possibly have made any sense out of Fransje's excited story.

Father came into the room wearing his work shoes. But he was careful of Mother's mats, taking long, huge steps to his chair. He opened his lunchbag, held his hat in front of his face for a moment, and began to eat. He offered Fransje part of one of his sandwiches, and although Fransje wasn't at all hungry and even had to overcome a certain aversion to the contents of Father's lunch, he nevertheless proudly accepted it. After all, now he was a groom too, so he had to eat during the lunch break.

Mother also sat down to relax at the table, joining Father in a cup of coffee. To heighten the festive mood, Mother poured Fransje a large glassful of milk.

Father was talking about his trip into town and told them that he had met someone at the blacksmith who had two young pigs, one of which he wanted to sell. He had asked Father if he needed a pig. Father's tone suggested that he was considering it. And Mother's question—what was he asking for it?—indicated that the idea appealed to her too. Father still had some old boards lying beside the rabbit cages; he could build a fence around the slophole with them. And he could fix up the old shed a little so it could serve as a temporary pigpen. Then they'd have to get rid of the rabbits. Now that the older children were bringing in a little money maybe they could make a go of it. And if everything went well, then next winter they'd have a nice bit of meat, bacon, and some lard. This summer the younger kids could gather a fair amount of peas and barley and oats, and dig up potatoes this fall, and collect sugarbeets that fell off the wagons as they bumped along. It would all help a great deal.

Fransje was so excited at the imminent prospect of sitting on a horse, that he paid little attention to what Father and Mother were discussing. He sat sideways on the bench in front of the window so that he could keep an eye on the horses. They stood quietly, their heads hanging as they dozed. Now and then they nodded violently and shook their heads hard to keep the flies away.

Father stood up. "Well, see you at noon," he said to Mother. And to Fransje, "Shall we get going and see if we can bring those horses back to the stable, my big helper?"

He didn't have to ask Fransje twice. Fransje grabbed his cap and dashed outside ahead of Father. "Bye, Mother!" he shouted as an afterthought. It was phrased deliberately, for big boys who could ride horses no longer called their mothers Mommy.

Father lifted him high in the air and set him behind the horse's huge head. "Hold on tight to the rings of the harness," he warned Fransje. Fransje nodded. His face was bright red, but not from fear. He was surprised at how tremendously large horses really were, seen up close. He felt as if he were straddling the top of the dike—not a green dike with a cement wall on top, but a smooth, brown, living dike which just fit comfortably under the arch of his legs. Nevertheless, the height did make him a little dizzy, so he took an even tighter grip on the harness. He cast a sidelong glance at the window. Yes, the curtain had been pushed aside and Mother nodded her encouragement. He did not, however, dare to put up a hand to wave and was content to throw her a quick nod.

Meanwhile Father had jumped upon the other horse, and after once more warning Fransje to hold on tight and not to let go, he steered the horses to the middle of the road. Hot prickles ran up and down Fransje's back and his hands went clammy with sweat, but he didn't notice. Beneath him he heard the dull thud of the huge hooves, and he felt the rocking of the magnificent back. That word magnificent, though unknown to him, described the sum total of all that swept over him, culminating in a deep and quiet pride. Now he also dared to look around him. His eyes searched for Neeltje or the other neighborhood children. This event would raise him meters above his playmates, even above Pier; Fransje doubted very much whether Pier had ever ridden a horse.

Father held the reins of Fransje's horse in his right hand and steered his own with his left. Both animals were so easy-going that he didn't fear an accident. Leaving their own row of houses behind, they approached the railroad station neighborhood. But before they reached it, they turned left and passed the familiar barn housing Van Houten's chaise. The incident with the chaise, however, did not enter Fransje's mind. In the distance he could see the farm where Father worked. He knew the way there himself, for he had been there before. He asked himself if the geese were still there. But with Father beside him, and sitting high on the horse's back, he need not be afraid of them.

Beginning to feel a lot braver on his high, rocking mountain, he asked his horse's name. Then he said, "Giddyap, Sarah!" which was completely unnecessary, since Sarah didn't pay the slightest attention. She only turned her sensitive ears to the rear for a moment. Otherwise she calmly plodded on, nodding her head. Fransje became talkative, chattering rapidly about everything he saw, and more. Now and again Father good-naturedly grunted something in return. Fransje wanted to know if Father knew where there were bird's nests out in the fields, and if he knew one with a cuckoo's egg in it. Father did know where there was such a nest, and he told Fransje that after they had put the horses in the meadow, Fransje could come with him out into the fields. Then he'd point it out to him so he could see it. Fransje cried that then he'd bust the egg of that dirty cuckoo bird. But Father told him he could not do that. He said that the cuckoo didn't know any better and that the Lord had created them that way. If need be, Fransje was ready to excuse the cuckoo on the basis of Father's authority, but then it was the Lord's fault . . . . Fortunately Father explained a little more, saying that everything the Lord has made is good, and that since animals can't think like people, they can't sin. And that even if Fransje threw the cuckoo's egg out of the nest, the birds that had built it would leave it anyway, and their eggs still wouldn't hatch. Finally Fransje began to understand vaguely that this was God's way of maintaining a certain balance in nature, which in some way unknown to Fransje was necessary and good. With this, Father prevented the devil from steering Fransje's thoughts in a dangerous direction.

When they stopped behind the large barn, Father lifted him from his high seat. Then he pulled the harness over Sarah's ears and nose and let the horse find her way to the meadow by herself, followed closely by Father's horse, Prince. Stiffly Fransje stretched his cramped legs. His underpants stuck to his seat, wet with sweat. But no matter; it had been splendid. Now he was certainly grown up! He could already ride a horse. And as if reading his thoughts, Father said, "You're quite the helper already! You can already handle a horse!"

As they had passed the large barn, Fransje had looked at the water hole. It was almost completely surrounded by waving green reeds, except where the horses always went to drink. A few geese were peacefully sunning themselves or preening their feathers. They hardly looked at the two riders, and didn't scold at them at all. Fransje wanted to go back for a closer look at the big birds, but Father hadn't the time for such a detour. He had to get back to the field to weed sugar beets, where Bram and Eine had been busy all morning. Father had contracted to do the field for a specific amount, that is, he had to maintain the field until the beets were harvested and delivered in the fall. Now it depended on him and the boys whether they made any extra money on it; the harder they worked, the greater the chance of earning extra income. Maybe Father could make enough to build a new pigpen before winter.

The beet field lay next to Hontenisse Pond and could be reached by crossing the pasture where the two horses were now grazing peacefully. Father took such long strides that Fransje had to trot to keep up. As they crossed the pasture Fransje saw all kinds of flowers that he wanted to pick, but Father said there were lots more along the beet field. He could pick those.

Bram and Eine looked up in surprise when they saw their little brother coming with Father. They asked him if he had come to help. But Fransje proudly told them that he had ridden on Sarah's back. Then Eine said the same thing Father had said at the barn: "You're getting to be a big helper! You can already ride horseback!"

Fransje walked beside the weeding men until he was bored. Then he wandered to the end of the field to the long pond. Father called after him to stay away from the water, and Fransje assured him with a wave of his arm.

Beside the beet field ran a deep furrow, partially overgrown by short reeds and tall weeds. On the pond side it formed a low dike gently sloping toward the water. A broad strip of tall, tender grass grew here, and closer to the water's edge waved the young reeds, rustling softly. The longest stalks had already formed new heads, but they didn't look the least like the fuzzy tassels standing in the pitcher at home. These were purple-brown in color and did not stand erect, but drooped in graceful arches. Fransje wanted to go nearer to examine them, but he remembered Father's command and his own promise. However, he did venture a little farther into the grass. Suddenly he discovered a whole patch of sky-blue flowers, a thousand of them he thought, and they all had bright yellow-orange hearts. He sat on his haunches and energetically began to pick. He'd take them home for Mother.

Just as he stood up, he heard Father's voice insistently calling his name. Perhaps he was afraid that Fransje was too near the water. Fransje had to show his find to Father and the boys. Carefully he clambered over the low ridge and crossed the beet field, taking care not to step on the young beets, for Father wouldn't like that at all, and the farmer even less.

From far off he could already see that a visitor had arrived during his absence. It wasn't another farmhand because he wasn't holding a hoe. Since Fransje didn't know the stranger, he approached hesitantly. In order to establish his presence, he said to Bram, "Look at the pretty flowers I found!"

Without stopping his weeding, Bram said, "Those are forget-me-nots. I bet you picked them for Mother, eh?" Fransje nodded. Then Father said, "Hey there, Fransje, say hello to the boss."

So this strange man was the farmer for whom Father and the boys worked. Bashfully Fransje complied with Father's request and said, "Hello boss." The farmer answered, "So, my boy, did you come to help your father and brothers with the weeding?" This made Fransje even more bashful, and he asked himself whether the boss really expected him to work. He blushed and glanced up into the farmer's mischievous face. Then he blurted, "There's no hoe for me!"

When the farmer laughed, Fransje knew that it had only been a joke. To demonstrate his good will, he showed his forget-me-nots to the farmer. But the latter misunderstood and thought Fransje was offering them to him. He said, "Why, thank you. My wife will appreciate them. She loves flowers. I'll tell you what: why don't you give them to her yourself pretty soon. But first I have to check whether there are any eels in my traps. Maybe you can give me a hand with that."

Fransje looked at the man blankly because the word eels was

completely unfamiliar to him. Eine helped him out of his befuddlement by telling him that the boss had set fishtraps in Hontenisse Pond and went out in his flat-bottomed scow every now and then to empty them. "And you can help him, Fransje."

Meanwhile the farmer had exchanged a few words with Father, and when Fransje looked at him questioningly, Father said, "Go ahead, Fransje. But be very careful and sit still in the boat, and listen good to the boss. When we go home in a little while, we'll come past the farmhouse and pick you up."

Fransje could hardly believe his good fortune. All kinds of unexpected surprises were being sprung on him this morning. He'd have plenty to tell the neighborhood kids tonight! At the moment, however, he didn't know what he was going to tell them, except about riding the horse, because he had no idea what this new adventure would mean. But he didn't have to wait long, for the farmer said, "Well, Fransje, shall we go take a look?"

Fransje followed on his heels like a puppy. First the farmer walked to the end of the beet field, where it met the pasture. Then he turned left and followed the barbed-wire fence to Hontenisse Pond. The scow was tied to the last fencepost, which stood in the water. It looked like a large, rectangular box with a wide board nailed across each end. Fransje guessed that those were the seats. In the bottom of the scow he saw a couple of boxes, a pail and a few other tools. Lying across one of the seats and protruding far beyond the end of the boat was a long, thin pole. The farmer leaned forward and pulled the boat toward him. No grass and reeds grew here; the soft gray clay was trampled by thousands of hoofprints. No doubt Sarah and Prince came here to drink.

"Over here," he heard the farmer saying. The man picked him up and lifted him into the boat. "Hold on tight to the bench and sit still. And above all, don't stand up!"

Fransje nodded and shook his head in answer, sorry that he couldn't be himself with the farmer and that he was too shy to speak, or to even find words for his feelings. And he was glad that the man said no more than absolutely necessary. His face, however, looked quite friendly and soon Fransje felt more at ease. For the time being he put the bunch of forget-me-nots on the bottom of the boat under his seat.

The farmer picked up the long pole, and slowly and steadily he began to push the scow away from shore. Soon they were in the middle of Hontenisse Pond. Although Fransje held on so tightly that his knuckles were white, he didn't feel the least bit afraid. His tense posture reflected his unconscious attempt to control all the new sensations bombarding him—he lacked the words, even in his mind, to express them. Ahead of him lay a long, smooth stretch of water that reflected deep blue sky and the snowy white clouds. Far to the right a green wall of reeds undulated to the distant dike with its rows of tall elms and in the other direction to the railroad dam. Suddenly Fransje recalled his horrible adventure on the skating pond last winter. He wasn't frightened, but he thought how strange it was that this beautiful spot could have looked so threatening then. Now the peaceful scene reminded him of Paradise, although he couldn't have said why. There was still danger round about. The glassy surface of the water looked as if you could walk on it, but Fransje knew better. Only Jesus could walk on the water, and Peter once.

The air was alive with the jubilant song of skylarks. From somewhere between the reeds came the piercing cries of a coot. A little farther on a mother duck chugged across the water like a tugboat, pulling a long row of baby ducks behind her. Fransje sighed. If the Lord Jesus were with them now, he'd ask Him if they could go for a walk across the water together.

The farmer leisurely poled the scow along. Here his long pole barely reached the bottom. Every time he pulled it up a cloud of black mud and silver bubbles boiled to the surface. After glancing at Fransje several times, the farmer concluded that the boy would give him no trouble. Although he didn't say a word, he was obviously enjoying himself and soaking it all in. He noted the unusually serious expression on his face, one that didn't seem to fit his age, and he asked himself what was going on in that young head. But he didn't disturb him with unnecessary chatter. The little fellow seemed well able to entertain himself.

The scow was approaching an indentation in the reeds along the opposite shore. Several poles rose out of the water with ropes that disappeared beneath the surface. The farmer pushed the scow against the reeds, and behind Fransje's back he jammed the long pole into the bottom of the pond. "Make sure you sit still, Fransje," he said. Then he untied the ropes and slowly, gradually pulled some brown netting out of the water. Fransje's eyes stood wide open. This must be one of the fish traps that Eine had mentioned. The brown netting narrowed into a long sleeve in which round hoops were fixed at regular intervals, each one a little smaller than the one before.

Suddenly Fransje squealed and shouted, "A snake, a snake!"

After the long silence the farmer was startled by the unexpected cry, but then he laughed. Reassuringly he said, "No, Fransje, that's no snake. It's an eel. There will probably be more in the trap. Wait and see."

Again and again Fransje saw something long and thin writhing wildly, slithering through an opening and disappearing in the water as it slipped into the next, narrower section of the trap. The farmer had to push the scow a little closer to be able to unfasten the rope from the top of the farthest pole. Then he hauled the whole trap into the boat.

Now Fransje could study the wriggling mass first-hand. The eels looked even more like snakes than they had from a distance. He was afraid of the creatures; at the same time he was attracted to them as if mesmerized. His primitive instincts were so aroused that he had to restrain himself from jumping up off his seat to subdue the squirming, tangled mass. But they were the farmer's eels; besides, how would he do it? A cold sweat of excitement and fear broke out on him.

The farmer opened the end of the trap and the whole mass cascaded into a box. But the eels didn't like that a bit. Coiling and lunging, they leaped against the walls of their dry prison. Fransje feared they were about to escape; already he could see the biggest one coming for him. But the farmer seemed unconcerned. Leisurely he reset the long trap. Since none of the eels succeeded in getting out of the box, Fransje asked if he could look at them from nearby. That was all right with the farmer and taking his hand, he led him closer. Fransje knelt down beside the box.

"Snakes," he thought, "dangerous, twisting snakes just like in the picture in the story Bible." But they weren't snakes. They were eels, and eels were a kind of fish that people fried and ate. Did they taste good? The only fish they ate at home were smoked herring, and they looked much different, stiff as a board. And sometimes they ate dried cod, which was even stiffer and had to be soaked in water overnight.

Before Fransje could react, one of the biggest eels succeeded in slipping over the edge of the box. Instinctively he tried to grab it to toss it back into its prison. For an instant he felt something cold and slippery in his hands, and then the eel was slithering underneath his seat.

The farmer had been secretly keeping an eye on him. Fransje's stunned look made him laugh. He explained that you couldn't hold eels in your bare hands. They were much too slippery and quick. First you had to wet your hands and rub them in sand or coaldust. Then those slippery creatures couldn't escape.

After emptying traps in two other locations, the farmer docked the boat at its former spot. He had made a good catch. He estimated that there were ten or twelve kilos of eel in his fishnet sack.

Fransje hadn't forgotten to take his bunch of forget-me-nots from under his seat. He regretted not being able to take them home to Mother, but the boat ride was worth the sacrifice. The flowers looked a little limp, but if the lady put them in water right away they should revive.

The farmer looked at his watch. It was twenty-five to twelve. They had plenty of time to show their prizes to his wife before Father and the boys came to pick up Fransje.

The large farmhouse stood east of the huge barn. Between them lay a stretch of grass with a bare circle in the middle where the horses that powered the mill had worn a path. A gravel path ran from the back door of the house to the door in the middle of the high barn front. Along the rear of the house stood a row of linden trees, pruned and clipped to form a high hedge, a hedge on thick stilts. Under the trees groups of chickens snuggled in the sand.

Just as they reached the gate, the farmer remembered that he had to first get something from the barn. So he said to Fransje, "You go ahead into the house. I'll join you in a minute."

Fransje did as he was told. He didn't know the farmer's wife, but usually he was less bashful toward women than men. Undaunted, he followed the gravel path along the linden trees and started toward the back door, of which only the bottom half was closed.

Why didn't Fransje remember that Father and Maria sometimes talked about Norma, the bulldog? Was it because he had never seen the dog? Even this past winter when he had passed the house on his way to the pond, he had never seen the bulldog, because it had been deliberately locked in the barn.

Whatever the reason, Fransje's head was so full of horses and forget-me-nots and eels and all the wonderful adventures of this morning that there was no room for thoughts of a dog. Nor could he know that this one hated children, because it wasn't used to them. Fransje already had his hand on the cold, iron ring of the latch; as he called "Hello!" in his reedy little voice, he gently pushed open the bottom of the Dutch door.

Whether he had been at that moment asking himself if the farmer's wife had a friendly face and if she would be happy with the flowers he couldn't say afterward. However, it hadn't been the lady who appeared, but some indescribable monster, whose short, speckled hair stood threateningly on end as it leaped at him with a hoarse, suppressed growl. Fransje had just caught a glimpse of that large, gruesome head with its pushed-in face and bright red, dripping jaws. But he knew for sure that the big head had slammed into him and that the jaws had clamped onto his thigh. Then there had been a burning pain, a loud scream, and a flood of tears, that was still ebbing in dry sobs. Now the terrible monster with the demonic head was locked up somewhere behind one of the many doors that opened into the cool hallway.

Fransje's pants were torn. A square piece of fabric hung from his pants like an open trapdoor, exposing his bare leg. The leg was bleeding from a twin row of small wounds inflicted by the creature's teeth. The farmer's wife raised the torn pantleg and washed off the blood with a cold washcloth. Then she rubbed a little salve on the wound and wrapped a long, narrow strip of cloth around Fransje's leg. At the same time she nervously tried to soothe him with her words, which fell like healing oil on his distraught soul.

Incredibly Fransje still held the bouquet of forget-me-nots in his hand. The lady asked him if he had picked them for his mother. He shook his head. "They're for you," he said in a quavering voice. The farmer, who was standing right beside his wife, explained that Fransje had picked them for her and that he had also given him a hand emptying his eel traps.

"Then you have earned something!" she cried, feigning astonishment. "Come," she said to her husband, "fetch a bag from the drawer and give Fransje a big batch of eels to take home with him." She herself made a familiar plunge of the hand underneath her apron and dug a quarter from her pocket. "This is for the beautiful flowers you picked for me!"

Actually, she thought, she ought to sew his pants, but his father would be here soon, so she hadn't time. She pulled a few pins from her *doek* and pinned the torn patch back in place. "You'll have to ask your mother or Maria to fix it for you, my big boy." Being called a big boy comforted him more than the quarter and the eels. "Well," she said, "your father should be here any time. Let's go see if he's coming yet." She took him by the hand, carrying a bright linen bag in the other. Dark spots stained the outside of the bag and occasionally someone seemed to elbow it from the inside. Those creatures were still alive!

As they came to the gate, Father and the boys appeared from behind the barn. The farmer came out to stand beside Fransje and his wife, and all three waited for Father to arrive. Then the farmer and his wife took turns relating what had happened and expressing their regret. Father felt sorry for his little boy, who had been so eager this morning, but he realized that it had been an accident, and was no one's fault. Eine took the bag of eels and Bram lifted Fransje onto his shoulders.

"Well, have a good dinner," Father told the farmer and his wife. "Bye, Fransje!" the lady called after him. "Will you bring me flowers again sometime? Then we'll make sure Norma can't get you." Fransje nodded half-heartedly. The salve had eased the sharp pain, and now that he was sitting safely on Bram's shoulders, the whole incident no longer seemed quite so terrible. He began to tell about his adventure on the pond. He said that he should be grown up pretty soon because he could already ride a horse and help empty eel traps. Although he hardly prized the traumatic ending of the otherwise perfect morning, nevertheless being bitten by a big dog did give him a vague sense of pride. He couldn't understand, however, why the farmer and his wife would want to have such a mean, horrible monster around the house. And had it ever bitten Father or the boys? "No," said Father, "because Norma knows us. The dog is only mean to people it doesn't know and to kids because it isn't used to them. Norma is a watchdog and has to protect the boss and his wife and keep thieves away from the farm."

Fransje thought the dog well-suited for the job. He could understand why no thief would dare enter the yard after dark. But why did they want a dog that was so frightfully ugly? Weren't there much nicer looking dogs that could guard the farm just as well and that didn't lie in wait for innocent children? It would be a long time before he ever went to that door again.

Now he suddenly remembered that Father hadn't shown him the cuckoo's egg. There had been no time. What a disappointment! Fransje asked if he could come back to the field this afternoon, but Father thought it would be better for him to wait until next week. The egg had been in the nest only two days and it took about three weeks to hatch.

Fransje's eyes fell on the bag of eels which was now completely wet on the outside. He asked Eine whether those creatures were dead yet. No, they were very tough, Eine told him; they lived even after they had been gutted and cut into pieces and were baking in the pan. Fransje wasn't ready to believe that. Into his mind flashed the horrible vision when he had resolved to cut himself to pieces should he end up in hell. A cold shiver went down his back and instinctively he clutched Bram's neck more tightly. Forcefully he pushed the picture out of his mind.

How unutterably beautiful the world was!

Fransje felt as if he hadn't time enough to absorb it all, or as if for some reason he had arrived too late and had to make up for lost time.

He was walking beside Mother on the big dike on the far side of the farm where Father worked. They were on their way to Aunt Jane's, Father's sister, who lived in one of the corners of the Hontenisse Polder. Mother went there for a visit once a year. Father would also come later, straight from work. They'd stay for supper and then go home together.

Fransje had only a vague picture of Aunt Jane and her big family. They lived so far away, closer to the next village than to Fransje's. Therefore although the polder belonged with Fransje's village, they also went to church there. They came to Fransje's church only when there was a preacher.

Aunt Jane's family was even larger than theirs. When Fransje asked if there would be any kids his age to play with, Mother answered that the youngest child was older than Fransje, and that was a girl. Next a boy who was a couple of years older than the girl, so he'd probably be in school. However, since it was such a long walk, school would probably be out by the time they arrived.

In the meantime, Fransje had plenty to occupy his attention.

Like an excited puppy he constantly raced ahead and back and up and down the gentle outer slope of the dike. Then he would come to Mother to show her one of his finds, or to ask her to explain something. Mother told him not to dash around so, or soon he'd be dead-tired, and they still had a long way to go. But he assured her that he wasn't tired at all. Just look how fast he could run. Away he flew again around a tree to the ditch at the bottom of the dike.

The grass here wasn't very long because apparently cows were pastured on the dike. Fransje hadn't seen any cows yet, only what they had left behind. He told himself to watch out that he didn't step in one of those greenish brown cakes during his ramblings. He was looking for treasures—flowers, June bugs, and bird nests. There weren't many flowers here; the cows had seen to that, sparing only the purple thistle flowers which they wouldn't touch. But Fransje wouldn't have anything to do with them either. Those nasty things had prickles sharp as needles. The occasional hawthorn bush standing here and there between the tall elms yielded nothing but scratches on his hands. No matter; he had two June bugs at home—one that he had caught himself a few days before and one that Kees had given him from his surplus. They were a pair. The wings of the female were much lighter than those of the male, as if they were sprinkled with flour, so the children called the female a miller and the darker male, a baker. Not finding any bird nests was no surprise to him. No doubt the birds were afraid of those big, clumsy cows which trampled their nests underfoot.

Now Mother and Fransje were almost directly opposite the farm where Father and the boys were working. The gray-red ridge of the barn roof peaked above the leafy island of the orchard. The roof of the house was barely visible behind a gigantic tree on this side of the island. This tree rose far above the others. Fransje wanted to know what kind of tree it was. If it were an apple or a pear tree, wouldn't that make a lot of fruit! But Mother told him that it was a walnut tree. Since Fransje didn't know what walnuts were, he lost interest.

He scanned the fields to see if he could spot Father and the boys. But they were nowhere to be seen. He assumed that they were working on the other side of the barn. And he thought it was probably a good thing the farm was getting farther and farther away, as the dike angled toward another dike, intersecting it in the distance. Norma couldn't possibly see him here. Fransje wondered where the monster was hiding right now. It was probably lurking in some dark corner watching for a little kid to come on the yard so that it could bite him just as it had bitten Fransje.

As his eyes swept the wide fields, they caught the distant glitter of sunlight on the water of Hontenisse Pond. Vivid memories of his wonderful boat ride with the farmer and of the writhing eels prompted him to race toward it. He stumbled down the steep side of the dike, crawled under a barbed wire fence on his stomach, and dashed down a beaten wagon track at the foot of the dike. Mother anxiously shouted after him not to go too close to the water. He followed the deep waterway until it disappeared into the mouth of the pond on the other side. Farther on, several coots were cruising in and out of the reeds along the shore. Again the center of Hontenisse Pond held a piece of blue sky in its bosom.

Mother had told him not to go near the water, but the temptation was strong. How he would love to once again glide across that silver surface in the farmer's boat! But no matter how the water drew and beckoned, he was imprisoned on shore. Did eels come close to land? He peered hard into the water at his feet, but his eyes found nothing but the distorted reflection of a little boy standing on his head on a floor as deep as the sky. In the slow ripples of the gently rocking water, he looked as if he were trying to fly. A strange thought welled up in him. What if the sky were down instead of up; then he could let himself fall and he would drop right into heaven. Then he could also find out what that mysterious, smooth, blue roof called the sky looked like close-up. Wouldn't there have to be a trapdoor for him to go through? If the Lord knew that he were lying outside flat on his stomach waiting to get in, He certainly wouldn't send him away now that nothing separated him from heaven but a thin glass floor?

Fransje was so absorbed in his reverie that he didn't hear Mother call his name twice. This was hardly strange, for in the background of his musing had been a constant clamor which he had suppressed from his consciousness as he tried to penetrate the floor of his heavenly abyss. But now Mother's voice was calling him insistently; hearing a note of anxiety, he turned with a sudden jerk. High above him on the dike he saw her beloved shape. The dappled shadows of the leaves dallied across her snow white hat and soft face. The sun struck a blazing shaft of yellow light from one of her golden headpieces. Fransje still made no move to go to her. But Mother knew what to do. She said, "Fransje, did you see all those bird nests over there? I know where there are lots of bird nests."

"Where?" Fransje wanted to know.

"Come up here and I'll show you."

In a few seconds he was standing beside her; then she pointed to the tops of the trees in the near distance. Only now did the strange clamor penetrate his consciousness. He stared wide-eyed at the strange spectacle in the distance. There was a steady beating of wings as large gray-blue birds flew busily from one tree to another and from one branch to another. There was also something strange about the trees. They were completely bare and the branches looked as if they had been whitewashed—not neatly like Mother did it, but sloppily as if the whitewash had been thrown on by handfuls. One tree looked as if a whole pailful of whitewash had been poured down along its trunk.

Fransje wanted to walk over at once to take a closer look, but Mother prevented him. "You better not stand too close," she said, "because then you'll get just as dirty as those trees." Fransje didn't understand what Mother meant and tried to slip out of her grasp, but she held him tightly by the shoulder and guided him down the gentle slope to the very bottom of the dike. There they slowly continued on their way, until they were directly opposite the colony.

"What are those big birds called?"

"Those are herons," answered Mother. "They come here every year to build their nests and have their young."

Fransje wanted to ask so many questions that he didn't know where to begin. How he'd love to take a peek into those large, crude nests. If only he dared and were able! But it was out of the question. His eyes traveled up the straight trunks rising from the dike like pillars. Even the ladder at home would be much too short. But supposing he had a ladder that was long enough, he still wouldn't dare venture between those huge, beating wings and the hoarse shrieks.

Why were all those birds crowded so close together, and why didn't they build their nests under the shelter of leaves? Their eggs and their babies were unprotected from the rain. Those crude, sloppy nests bore no resemblance to the solid, well-crafted nest of the chiffchaff, or to his own bed.

Mother said, "Come, we must move on." But Fransje was not yet ready to leave this strange place. He held his head locked back to miss nothing of the activities of the heron colony. He pulled on Mother's hand wanting to go back to the top of the dike to get a closer look at the strange trees. But again she said, "You don't want to get dirty like these trees, do you?" Fransje still didn't know what she meant, but then he saw a long, white jet plummeting earthward. Then he understood. So that was what all the whitewash on the trees was! Those filthy birds! Yes, but they were also magnificent, and so large! What tremendous wings they had! They'd be fit for an angel, except they were blue instead of white.

But Fransje was still puzzling over the problem of wet eggs and wet baby birds. Mother told him that herons were really water birds; although they couldn't swim they lived near and in the water. That was why they had picked this spot close to Hontenisse Pond, where they could find plenty of food—eels and frogs and other kinds of water animals. Their feathers were made so that the water couldn't soak through them. The rain ran off the herons just like it did off the roof of the big barn where Father worked.

Yes, the world was beautiful and full of mysteries. But also full of cruelty and danger. The farmer caught eels and ate them, and the herons caught and ate eels too. Moreover, the trees in which the herons were nesting were dying—those beautiful, noble trees on which God had worked so long to make them tall.

"Can you eat herons?" he asked, following up his own train of thought. That made Mother laugh. "I don't think so; at least, I've never heard of anybody doing it."

But were there animals that caught and ate herons? Yes, when Mother was a girl, she had heard her father say that there were otters in Hontenisse Pond and they managed to jump a heron once in a while.

That frightened Fransje. Now Mother had to describe an otter and tell him whether they attacked people too. And whether there were other animals that in turn ate otters.

No, most wild animals were afraid of people and hid from them. (Oh, so that was why Fransje hadn't seen any otters when he was in the boat.) Mother doubted that there were animals that ate otters. There were people, however, like the game warden and perhaps the farmer too, who set traps to catch otters because their pelts were worth a lot of money.

Fransje sighed. Although the world was beautiful and life full of surprises, an invisible power roamed through it trying to snatch everything into death with its grasping claws. And although most animals were afraid of people—except Norma—even people could not in the end escape those grasping claws. Just take Verplanke for instance.

Fransje had been walking silently behind Mother for some time. They had already passed the intersecting dike. Even the cows placidly lying in a corner chewing their cud couldn't arouse Fransje's hunger to know, nor could the comical turnstile that admitted them to the next section of dike. Mother suspected that he was brooding about something again. So she said, "Look over there, Fransje! See those nice flowers?"

Here there were no trees along the dike. But the grass on both sides of the narrow path on the crest was so long that Fransje could barely see over it. And because the path was so narrow, they had to walk single file. Mother stopped and let him pass. Then she pointed to a field white with daisies. At once he dived into the waving sea of green and waded into the middle of the daisy field. This magnificent sight erased all somber thoughts from his mind. Myriads of white faces with blazing yellow hearts seemed to be cheering inaudibly, their silent chorus mingling with the jubilant song of the invisible larks high in the blue sky. He knelt down in their midst, spread his arms wide, and gathered an armful of blossoms to himself. He pushed his head into their teeming whiteness and with an exhilerated heart inhaled the pungent, invigorating fragrance.

"Mother!" he cried exultantly. "Look at all the beautiful flowers! (He no longer said *bootiful*, because Wantje had patiently but firmly helped him through that briar patch of vowels.) I'm gonna pick them all, and when we go home pretty soon I'll take them all home with me!"

Mother smiled. She had succeeded in her purpose, and she waited indulgently to give him an opportunity to pick an armful of the stately flowers.

Aunt Jane seemed to be a cheerful, friendly woman. She was glad to see Mother and wasted no time in setting a pot of tea. She patted Fransje on the head and told him how much he had suddenly grown up, which pleased him greatly. And to prove to her that her observation was well-founded, he confided that he could already ride a horse and that he had already been in a boat. In reply Aunt Jane held out the candy jar to him, from which he swiftly and skillfully extracted the biggest piece. Then with the ease of a mother of a large family she led him to the corner of the room where the toys were piled. Soon he was so engrossed in them that the animated chatter of the diligently knitting women faded to a cozy background for his playworld.

A little later the room was suddenly filled with the four young voices of Fransje's cousins—two girls and two boys. First they shook hands with Mother, and with the same ease displayed by their mother they joined Fransje. He didn't really know any of them, but in a short time they were just as familiar to him as Wantje and Kees and Arjaan.

Aunt Jane coaxed all of them outside with a piece of rock candy. "Play outside now for a little while. It's such beautiful weather."

Aunt Jane's house was very unusual. Not only did it stand alone, without any neighbors, but it was also built, not beside or on the dike, but into it. All windows and doors were located either in the lower sides or in the rear of the house, that is, in the side facing away from the road on top of the dike, thus what would logically be the front of the house was really the rear. Inside, nothing betrayed its unusual location. A long, semi-dark hallway separated the spacious living room from a smaller room that served as kitchen. In the part that disappeared into the dike were the built-in beds, two in one room and a third in the kitchen. The hallway also ran into the dike, but where the front door should have been there was a large storage room. Above was an ordinary attic like the one in Fransje's house, only much larger. But when you got outside you could climb right onto the roof because the bottom row of roof tiles was about a foot above the top of the dike. Fransje could hardly resist the temptation to try, but he was held back by good manners and caution. However, he asked his youngest male cousin, who was three years older than he, whether there were any sparrow's nests under the tiles, to which he replied, "I don't know. Probably. But if we touch the roof tiles, we get whacked by Father, because he doesn't want any broken." That warning was sufficient for Fransje, and he resolved not to lay so much as a finger on the tiles.

One of the cousins suggested they play hide-and-seek. She recited a counting-out rhyme to determine who was "it," but Fransje was counted out on the first round. The oldest cousin finally ended up being "it." He said he'd count to a hundred while the others found a hiding place.

Then Fransje spotted something else that was unusual. Along the vegetable garden lay a pond—once a creek that had emptied into the Scheldt River. But this one wasn't nearly as wide and long as Hontenisse Pond. Astonished, Fransje asked if this was part of Hontenisse Pond, and learned that it was called Mill Pond. Then he wanted to know if there were eels in it and if they had a boat to catch them in. And had they ever seen otters swimming in the pond and did any herons live nearby?

To all these questions he got negative answers. They had seen herons standing in the water fishing for food, but they didn't live around here. The only animals around here were coots and sometimes wild ducks and once in a while a muskrat or something like that.

"What about our goat?" said the youngest cousin, a little girl, in wounded tones.

"Do you have a goat?" Fransje asked with keen interest. "Where is it?"

"Come on, we'll show you," the others said. They descended the dike, first passing the chicken coop and then the pigpen, until they were in the vegetable garden. Carefully they walked the narrow path between the plant beds until they reached the grassy bank along the pond. This looked a lot like the spot near Hontenisse Pond where Fransje had picked the forget-me-nots. His eyes scouted around to see if he could spot any here.

"Our goat is so tame we can ride it, just like a horse," he heard one of his cousins say. Fransje pricked up his ears, and a hopeful light shone in his eyes.

Not far away stood the goat, which had seen them coming and, lifting its head high, it bleated questioningly. The oldest boy ran ahead, untied her and climbed on her back. Steering the animal by the horns, he goaded the laboring beast toward the others.

Fransje couldn't believe his eyes. With some aversion he eyed the large, rubbery udder with its two long, uneven teats flopping around between the thin legs. A goat surely wasn't as graceful as a horse. The goat was so much smaller than Sarah that Fransje couldn't help imagining himself much bigger now than when he had sat on Sarah's back.

The other boy wanted a turn too. Since he was quite a bit lighter than his brother, the goat went considerably faster. The boy steered the animal almost to the reeds and then came back.

"Would you dare do that, Fransje?" asked Antje, his youngest cousin, thereby influencing and determining his answer. Had she asked him if he'd like to try it, he probably would have thought it over first, and then he could have said no without losing face. Now his self-respect forced him to exclaim loudly, "Of course!" With this he surrendered his freedom of choice; from that moment he was but a pawn of circumstance. Before he fully realized what was happening, his two cousins had lifted him onto the goat's narrow back. Instinctively his hands fastened on the rough, ribbed horns. But the goat didn't budge. Whether she smelled that he was a stranger or sensed that he was inexperienced no one knew. Fransje made a fruitless attempt to regain the initiative and save his pride by shouting in a high voice, "Giddyap, goat!" But the animal only shook its head as if to say, "Not me! You carry yourself."

One of the boys knew a better way to get the goat moving. He gave her a hard, unexpected slap on the flank and shouted, "Giddyap, girl! Go!" That helped. The goat sprang forward and sprinted toward the reeds in the deepest part of the pond. Fransje almost lost his balance but managed to tighten his grip on the horns just in time. Eyes wide with horror, he saw the wall of reeds rushing closer, strangely able to make out even the dark water between the thin stalks. He fully expected the stupid animal to fling itself into the middle of the pond. But then Fransje's body got another tremendous shock as the goat suddenly pivoted and, head lowered, darted in another direction like a raging tornado—without Fransje. His hands still clenched, he arched through the wildly thrashing reeds to land with a splash in the dark water.

For a moment darkness and silence surrounded him, except for a penetrating whistle and a soft bubbling in his ears. Then for a split second he felt an irrational desire to go to sleep, to forget all the traumatic events of the last few seconds—or were they ages?—like a bad dream. But his first breath—which inhaled not air, but water—brought him back to reality in terror. Flailing wildly with his arms until his fingers fastened on the tough roots of the reeds, he desperately jerked himself up as if tearing himself from the deadly embrace of a huge, black monster. He broke to the sur-. face. Air bubbles burst in his ears, water poured from his nose, but he saw light, he was breathing air. Then he felt a strong hand seize him and drag him onto the grass—back into the sunlight, back into life.

The children on shore first stood staring pale-faced and wide-eyed at this unexpected drama. Everything had gone so fast that they, too, had barely had time to follow the rapid course of events. But then their eyes fell on the comical sight of Fransje with his muddy face, the duckweed plastered in his hair, and his wet clothes clinging to him like wallpaper. That sight shattered the taboo that had bound them at first. A roar of laughter burst from their wide open mouths. They slapped their thighs in unrestrained glee; they held their stomachs and almost doubled up; they sobbed and sputtered and gasped. And all because of Fransje, Fransje who had just returned to life. Once again his heart began to pound. His face turned white under its muddy mask. He glanced about for his cap, but it must have been on the bottom of the pond. He didn't care. He darted a look of hatred at the laughter-contorted group of children. Then he said something he had never said before: "Drop dead!"

Then he ran away to Mother. The water squished between his toes. His feet made slurping sounds in his wooden shoes. He wasn't even surprised that he hadn't lost them in the water. What would Mother say? "How often haven't I told you not to play near the water?" But it wasn't his fault. It was . . . yes, whose fault was it? The other kids? But they hadn't known the goat would buck him off either. He was very angry at all four of them for laughing at him, but it wasn't really their fault. It must be the goat's, he decided. It was the fault of that crazy beast which he'd begun to view as something like a horse. "Stupidstupidstupid goat!" he hissed through his clenched jaws, accentuating every word with a dull crack of his angrily slip-slopping wooden shoes. Never, never again did he want to lay eyes on a goat! Never in a hundred years!

Whether it was because of anger or a chill he didn't know, but his teeth were chattering. And he asked himself what he was going to do. What he'd like to do was run straight home without stopping, but he didn't know the way by himself. Besides, he'd have to face Mother sooner or later. Better sooner. He resolved one thing—that he wouldn't cry, no matter what happened. What would he tell Mother, and Aunt Jane?

That problem, however, was solved by one of the boys who had trotted after him and who arrived at the door at the same time he did. Fransje was still so angry at him—at all four of them—that he hardly looked at him. The boy ran into the house, where he excitedly related what had happened. Fransje couldn't understand what he was saying, nor what the women replied. But he didn't have long to wait, for Mother and Aunt Jane were already standing in the doorway. There was anger and disgust on Mother's face and Aunt Jane exclaimed, "Ohmygoodness whatonearth!"

With one hand she grabbed the moprag lying outside beside the door while she wrapped her other red arm around his bedraggled little body and lifted him up. Without another word, she carried him into the kitchen where she set him down on top of the moprag. Unceremoniously she began to undo and strip off his wet clothes, until he stood stark naked before her.

In the meantime Mother had gotten a washcloth with which she belabored his face and hands. Every time she started to scold him, Aunt Jane interrupted her by talking about something else. At the same time she dried Fransje's body with a blue checkered towel. She was far from gentle so that soon his skin glowed pink. It actually hurt him, but he didn't want to cry because he realized that she wasn't doing it out of anger.

Getting dressed again, however, was a wholly different matter. And although Fransje had dreaded undressing the most, he couldn't help asking what his replacement clothes would look like.

Aunt Jane quickly put an end to his uncertainty. She took a pile of clothes out of a drawer of a chest in the corner near the window and knelt in front of him. As she pulled an undershirt over his head, she ordered her own children, who were standing in the hall looking on tittering, to shut the door.

The undershirt was quite long, but Fransje forced himself to be content with it. Meanwhile he examined the other pieces of clothing with a critical eye. When Aunt Jane next snatched the indispensable jersey from the little pile, she accidentally tipped it over, enabling Fransje to verify in a glance that the pants were a pair of patched suspender pants. In itself this was hardly peculiar, but that one glance confirmed his fearful premonition: it had pockets just like the thing La Bruyere had once made for him. His body grew rigid so that Aunt Jane had to say, "Come on, put your arms through the sleeves."

Mother was perspiring. She feared that this would lead to a scene, and she didn't know how to handle the situation to avert it. Gesturing nervously and in a quasi-cheerful voice, she began to assure him that he would be able to take the clothes off as soon as he got home. So he only had to keep them on for a little while. And she had a wonderful idea! Tomorrow he could wear his Sunday pants until his everyday one had been washed. But then he'd have to promise to take good care of it so nothing happened to it.

Her words had only a negative effect. They merely speeded up the development of the drama that she feared and was desperately trying to head off. Fransje tenaciously clung to his resolve not to cry, but it cost him such superhuman effort that his words sounded like an outburst when he cried obstinately, "I don't want those pants on! I don't want them on!"

Aunt Jane tugged the jersey down and picked up the underpants. That was too much for Fransje. At once he saw that they were much too long; moreover, they were the kind that filled him with revulsion. The oversized fly was lined with three huge, yellowed, bone buttons which had stained the surrounding fabric with brown rust spots. Fransje was determined that neither this gruesome thing nor the bulky suspender pants would touch his body. This time he'd probably end up getting a sound thrashing, but he was ready to suffer this if need be. He felt as if he were about to fall into a dark waterhole for the second time. Aunt Jane hesitantly held the underpants in her hands and looked questioningly from Fransje to her sister-in-law. She suspected that as a latecomer he had been thoroughly spoiled and thought that if only she had him under her wing for a couple of weeks she'd have him cured of that in a hurry. Half apologetically she said, "I haven't got much else. You have to remember that Willem is three or four years older than him."

Fransje latched onto the words in one last effort. He cried, "Those pants are way too big for me and I don't have suspenders!"

This objection was not without weight, and both women suspected that even their ever-present pins wouldn't be able to make him presentable.

"It's too bad Antje isn't a boy," sighed Mother. "Then there'd be no problem."

Aunt Jane's face lit up. Hopefully she suggested, "We could put her clothes on him. It hasn't been that long since he wore skirts."

Fransje stared at her in astonishment. Back into skirts? He, who was already old enough to ride a horse and help catch eels? His face turned bright red in embarrassment and humiliation. What evil powers had conspired to put before him such an awful choice? Why couldn't he keep on his own clothes and play with the other kids? But his own clothes were wet and muddy. And he couldn't walk home dressed like this. At least Antje's clothes didn't have any obscene, staring eyes made of yellow buttons nor any gaping flies. They just had tiny black hooks and eyes that were almost invisible. He knew exactly what they looked like. Wantje's clothes were identical, and on rainy days when the two of them had to stay indoors they had sometimes swapped clothes just for fun.

He relinquished his rigid posture and with a slight shrug he yielded. Soon he was transformed into a little farm girl, except with clipped hair. He was even wearing a white cotton underpants with two "trapdoors," held up by laces tied to his waist. But it wasn't visible anyway. His short puffy sleeves reached just over his shoulders.

The skirt sported countless small pleats and black and white stripes; the pleats were very carefully sewn to display alternately a series of white and then a series of black stripes. The skirt was part of the Zeeland costume and was a miniature version of the much longer skirt worn by the older women. Although under his breath Fransje mumbled, "I don't care!" he knew only too well that he would have to brave another barrage of mocking laughter from the other kids, and again when the older ones and Father arrived.

Through the peaceful stillness of the evening strolled a tall man, a much shorter woman and a small boy. They were Father and Mother and Fransje, although from a distance Fransje now looked like a little girl. He was tired out from the long, eventful day. Soon he would ask Father to carry him, but not yet. He wanted to show that he was a big boy, notwithstanding the skirts and the humiliation he had undergone today.

For a while they followed the same dike that Mother and Fransje had traveled earlier that afternoon, but by and by they descended from the dike and turned down a road that led between the fields. Now and then Father and Mother commented on the crops growing in the polder. Everything was doing well. The sugar beets were already so tall that the glistening leaves of one row touched those of the next, covering the paths between. The early potatoes were already flowering. The flax should begin to flower too pretty soon. And the wheat was standing straight and proud with firm green heads.

A late thrush sat on a fence post singing its evening prayer. When the threesome came too close, it quickly said amen and dropped off the pole; it swooped low between the banks of the ditch until it disappeared. A light haze wove a filmy blanket over the fields as if to protect them from the chill of the summer night.

Suddenly Fransje and his parents stood before the miracle of a white poppy field in blossom. It looked as though summer had forgotten to clear away a huge rectangle of snow. Fransje uttered a cry of rapture. He had never seen anything so exquisite. The sea of white flowers reminded him of the middle section of the church when all the women were wearing their large lace hats.

He asked if he could pick a bouquet of those beautiful flowers and then he suddenly realized that he had forgotten his bouquet of daisies. But Father told him that the petals would fall off if he picked them. Besides, the farmer who had planted the poppies didn't want people picking them. Although it was with reluctance, Fransje respected the property rights of the rich farmer.

He asked Father to lift him up so that he could get a better view of the white sea, and when Father complied, he immediately made himself so comfortable that Father guessed his underlying reason. So he put Fransje on his shoulders and held one foot and one hand in each of his own large hands.

Fransje wanted to know what the farmer was going to do with all those flowers. Nothing. They'll become large seed pods full of poppy seed. What is poppy seed? Something people make oil from. No, not kerosene. A thick, greasy oil. What do they use it for?

Fransje had many more questions: about a few late birds hurrying to their nests or to cover, about the first stars winking in the sky, about the frogs bellowing their evening concert along the ditches and creeks, about all kinds of things. But Fransje didn't hear Father's answer to his last question, for the peaceful evening had also gathered him under the shelter of its wings.

9

Although it was midsummer and the sun shone until late in the evening, the days seemed much too short not just for the farmers and the farmhands, but also for Fransje. His world expanded farther every day, and every time he thought he had penetrated deeper into the mysteries of life, he discovered new wonders. And he did not give up until they, too, yielded their secrets. His actual horizons had not broadened appreciably, for in his explorations he seldom got any farther than Jan Blok's farm or sometimes the low dike where Arjaan herded cows after school for a dairy farmer across the tracks. Now and again he also visited the De Visser family where he was always a welcome guest. But he usually saved these visits for rainy days when he couldn't play outside and got bored at home.

Once he accompanied his brothers to the sea dike, but not for lamb's ears. The plants were much too large and tough, now that they were blooming with large purple combs. The boys went looking for snails. Because the others all loved them, Fransje forced himself to like them too, although it required some effort for him to chew them. Although prying the snails undamaged from their gray stone houses was an art and a pleasant diversion, Fransje was repulsed by the soft, curled end that always more or less crunched between his teeth as if there were sand in it. This time the boys were careful not to make any fires!

Actually Fransje had never been any farther from home than Aunt Jane's house in the Hontenisse Polder. He sometimes recalled the visit, but he refused to relive in his mind the episode with the goat, for it undermined his self-respect. To the neighbor children he sometimes bragged about being able to ride a horse, but wisely held back the fact that he hadn't been able to apply the noble art to a goat. Fortunately it had been dark when he had come home dressed in Antje's clothes. He told Jan Blok about riding Sarah only once, and then only to inform him, since Jan had often ridden horseback.

But his imagination was not at all confined to the relatively small boundaries of his world. The stories that Father and the older boys and Maria brought home from work, and those that Arjaan and Kees and Wantje brought home from school, so stimulated his imagination that the horizons of his world constantly moved outward. And then, of course, there was the old, familiar Bible storybook, which subtly enlarged his spiritual world and deepened his spiritual life.

In this domain he had discovered a power intent on destroying man, not physically first of all, like the breath of death that touched all life, but eternally. This power was the devil, the sadistic ruler of the kingdom of darkness. However, Fransje didn't picture it as a dark place, but as a flaming abyss. One night he had even dreamt that he went to hell. Cold shivers still ran down his back whenever he recalled it. It had been a terrible dream, in every respect the direct opposite of the other dream in which he had slowly strolled to heaven on the hand of that great, indescribably precious Friend and Confidant.

That awful dream had been no slow stroll into ever greater peace and joy but a frantic succession of increasingly horrible images. The most horrifying moment was when the devil with his own hands dragged him to a blazing, flaming pit. And the devil had Norma's grinning face with the terrifying difference that his open jaws were blazing as fiercely as the pit. But a torment far exceeding all these came when Fransje, his eyes huge with terror, spotted among the hazy group of onlookers one person who was laughing uproariously at him. This tore his heart to shreds, for that person was none other than—Mother!

Fransje still remembered that he had awakened with a hoarse scream, sitting upright in bed stiff with fear. He had hoped that one of the boys would wake up and come to reassure him. But they snored on without a care. A little later there was some thumping in the back room and soon he heard footsteps on the ladder. He was already sure that it was Mother, personally coming to be the opposite of what she had been in his dream. It wasn't Mother, however, but Maria who had been wakened by his cry of fear. He could dimly make out her features in the dusky night which never became completely dark during the summer. Whispering, Maria bent over him and gently laid him down and tucked him in. As she did so, the end of her long braid swept his cheek, and the soft caress swept away much of his frantic fear.

All of the following week, however, he held it against Mother, for he couldn't entirely erase the horrible image from his memory. Finally he couldn't bear it any longer, and without telling her about the dream, he asked her, "Mom, if you was in heaven and I had to go to hell, would you feel sorry for me?"

Before giving him an answer, Mother tried to discern what was behind the strange question. This child's recurrent concern with hell puzzled her, and she asked herself if it was something she had said. But she could honestly say that the word was seldom mentioned in her family; neither she nor Father had ever threatened any of the children with it, as was sometimes so quickly done in some families. Thus she found it strange that he brought up the subject again. Somewhat evasively she said, "Good grief, child, what gives you that idea?"

Since too much was at stake for him to let himself be put off like that, he persisted. Then Mother told him that if she died before him and were admitted into heaven, her happiness would be perfect, so it followed that she wouldn't know he wasn't there if he weren't let in. But even if she did know, she wouldn't be able to grieve for him, for there is no sadness in heaven.

But this answer did more to confirm his awful dream than to assure him that under such frightful circumstances he could count on her compassion. He didn't even follow up with a second question. Seeing by his face that there was more behind the question than he had let on, Mother went to him and took him in her arms and said, "If I get to heaven first, I'll wait for you until you come too. And if you love the Lord very much and keep asking Him for a new heart, even after I'm gone, then the Lord will give you one, sure as can be. And then He'll let you into heaven with Him. Won't we be happy then! Then we'll sing at the top of our voices along with the angels and all the other grown-ups and children that are there."

Without knowing it, simply by her positive approach Mother had assuaged his anxiety. Nevertheless, he could not entirely ban the awful dream from his memory.

Yes, the farmers were busy, and so was Father. Because he contracted for most of his work, every summer he dropped his regular work for three or four weeks to mow the hay dikes for dairy farmers who vied for his superior skills weeks ahead of time. Bram and Eine then tried to keep up the fieldwork by themselves until the mowing was done. During this time Father worked twice as hard as usual and much harder than was wise because he didn't want to disappoint any of the small farmers and because mowing brought him exceptionally high wages. He left the house before sunrise and didn't return until long after supper. Then he was exhausted and drenched with sweat, and as soon as he had eaten he vanished behind the doors of the closet-bed. Fransje would have liked to go along with him for a day, but Father told him he'd be terribly bored spending a whole day so far away from home. Father did not say that he himself would be too tired to carry an equally tired Fransje home on his shoulders.

Sometimes Father came home with his lunchbag full of partridge eggs, which he had uncovered when he mowed down the tall grass in large swaths. He gave them to Wantje and Fransje; they would blow them out and eventually string the empty shells together like beads. He did feel sorry for the birds, but he said that the birds would abandon them anyway now that their nests were exposed. If the eggs had not yet begun to brood, Mother caught the contents in a glass, beat them with milk and sugar and then gave it to Father to drink. He needed it because he was as skinny as a rail. Looking anxious, Mother said she would rather do with a couple of guilders less than see him work himself into the ground. But Father laughed at this, elaborating in his mind his precious dream of building a fine, new pigpen this fall with the money that he was secretly hoarding even after handing over a much larger weekly salary on Saturday than usual. The money was stashed in a secret place in the attic, and no one else in the family knew about it.

A little while ago Fransje, too, had earned some money. It was during gooseberry season; suddenly all the neighbors had been allowed into the orchard to pick berries for its owner, Mr. Van Boven. He also owned the building where Fransje lived and which his parents and the other neighbors rented for one guilder a week. Although everyone addressed him as Mr. Van Boven, behind his back they called him The Jew. Whether he owed this name to his appearance—he was short, had a hooked nose, and wore a black cap pasted down on his white mane—or to certain practices was hard to say; apparently both played a role. In any case, Fransje picked berries for him. And every time he filled his pail, he brought it to the apple shed in the rear of the orchard. There Van Boven weighed them and immediately paid him in cash. The older kids told each other that The Jew cheated the younger kids by pretending the berries weighed less than they really did, but Fransje thought it was wonderful that the man paid him every time he brought him another pailful. Moreover, he thought it splendid that he could walk around in the orchard as if it belonged to him and that he could view the house from this new vantage point. Now their house looked as if it stood in the orchard partially concealed between the trees. He also found three bird nests, one of them right in the bush he was picking. All the nests were empty, of course; the baby birds had long since flown.

Fransje remembered the nasty thorns with mixed feelings, however, for they had considerably diminished the joy of earning money. One thorn had burrowed under his thumbnail, where it had broken off and festered for days. He could still see the red lines of the scratches the bushes had left on his hands and arms. He would much rather have helped pick the red and black currants, but the neighborhood children told him that The Jew didn't want any little kids picking them because they squashed the berries; he didn't want any "wet" pickers.

Fransje's two youngest brothers and Wantje were already talking about summer vacation. They said they'd be happy when they didn't have to see that crummy school for three weeks, but there was little conviction behind the boys' words. Arjaan knew that then he'd have to herd cows all day, and although it wasn't hard work, it left him no time for daring adventures with his more privileged friends. And Father had already impressed on Kees how much his help would be appreciated in the fields. For although he contracted for most of the work, this did not mean that he merely kept the outer rows of the field looking good. On the contrary, he was known as one of the most conscientious workers in the district, so he had a reputation to uphold. And that required everyone's cooperation. Father didn't hesitate to put even Mother to work when it was unusually busy, to the great displeasure of Bram and Maria, who felt that Mother had more than enough to do at home.

Vacation time was also an exceptionally good time for gleaning. Now that they had a pig, they could reduce the cost of feed markedly by gleaning peas and barley and wheat during and after the harvest of these crops.

Kees hoped he'd have one free Saturday, for he and his friend Jan, a baker's son from the railroad station neighborhood, had conceived a splendid plan. Once during a geography lesson their teacher had described a flooded tract of land that had once been part of their island and was now located somewhere outside the dike of their own polder. He had told them that the land came to the surface at low tide and was then accessible on foot and claimed that you could see traces of the people who had inhabited the island centuries ago. Never before had Kees listened so carefully to a lesson. But he hadn't completely believed his teacher, for he had never heard anyone in his own village mention this flooded land. And after all, the teacher was a stranger here, not from Zeeland. But when Kees inquired about it at home, Father not only confirmed the story but even elaborated on it, because as a young man he had often worked on the dikes and had helped construct and sink breakwaters offshore. Then Kees found out precisely where the flooded land was located: beyond the Hontenisse Polder, even farther away than Aunt Jane's house. That was when the plan had been born to go there with Jan on the first available Saturday that low tide came at a convenient hour.

Kees, however, had made one mistake: in his enthusiasm he had told Fransje all kinds of stories about the adventurous journey. This was very natural, of course, for what fills the heart spills over from the mouth (he did wisely refrain from telling any of his plans to Father and Mother) but he didn't immediately realize that Fransje's deepest instincts were easily aroused. Even at the first story Fransje had almost shouted, "Kees, can I come along too?"

Of course he couldn't go along; it was much too far and dangerous. He was way too small and Jan wouldn't want any little kids trailing along. But if Kees and Jan found something, they would take it home for him.

Despite all his big-boy talk, even then Kees had realized that he should have kept his big mouth shut about his splendid plans, for Fransje would keep at him until he got his way. Kees carefully prepared his friend by telling him that if he could get away at all they might have to go as a threesome instead of a twosome.

The closer the appointed Saturday loomed, the less Kees let on about the big plans brewing in his mind. If necessary, he was reconciled to the idea of taking Fransje along, but one word from Father could scrap the whole venture. Now everything hinged on Father not finding some job for him to do in the fields. Kees made an arrangement with Jan that if he didn't have to work he'd come and pick him up at seven o'clock Saturday morning. Kees planned every detail. After supper he'd quickly slip away and stay away from Father as much as he could. He'd go to bed earlier than usual to avoid arousing suspicion. And for the rest he'd just hope that if Father had something planned for him, he'd simply forget to tell him because he didn't see him.

But with one sentence Fransje wiped the entire fabric of carefully wrought calculations out of Kees's hands like a flimsy spider web: during supper he said very matter-of-factly, "Tomorrow I'm going to the sea dike with Kees and Jan."

Kees felt as if the ground were sinking under him. His heart began to pound, and after shooting a murderous glance at Fransje, he hid his flushed face over his food.

For a moment there was a stillness in which the ticking of the clock sounded like hammer blows in Kees's ears. Then came the rumble of Father's voice as he said in a calm, ordinary tone of voice, "Be sure you don't pull any crazy stunts and don't get too near the water. And above all don't start any fires!"

Although Fransje had let the cat out of the bag, instinct told him he'd better not say more. He simply promised to take Father's warning to heart. Kees breathed a deep sigh. He suddenly became very talkative, but wisely he said nothing about his adventurous scheme. He just promised to take good care of Fransje and first to faithfully do his work at home. After the great relief at not having to work in the fields tomorrow, it was worth it.

After supper Kees ran to the station neighborhood to tell Jan the good news. He breathed easier now that he was freed from the frail web of calculations, except for a couple of preparations he could easily take care of tomorrow morning after Father had safely departed to the fields.

As soon as Kees heard Father saying, "Well, goodbye!" and heard his footsteps fading out behind the house, he got up. For a moment he considered sneaking downstairs unnoticed and leaving without Fransje. But his conscience told him to pray first, so he dropped to his knees and mumbled,

O glorious and abiding Light,
O Sunlight to our fading sight,
O Maker of the earth and sea,
With all our hearts we thank Thee.
Another night have we been blessed
By Thy gracious peace and rest;
Send to us Thy angel band
To keep us out of Satan's hand.
Amen.

True, the well-worn words spilled from his lips like potatoes out of a sack as he repeated for the umpteenth time the sentences Mother had taught him even before he could pronounce them; nevertheless, the very act and posture of praying awoke a voice in him that said he might not pull such a dirty trick on Fransje. After all, thanks to his little brother he had gotten an official leave of absence. He tiptoed to the little bed by the chimney and peeked under the canopy. There two large, bright eyes calmly stared up at him, and a wide-eyed voice said, "Is it time to go, Kees?"

Kees nodded. "Yes, but be quiet. Take it easy and don't make any noise." He sighed, wondering how big a headache Fransje would be today. But he made no attempt to change his little brother's mind. A current of compassion stirred in his heart as he looked down at the little character who put such great trust in him and looked up to him so much. He flipped back the thin blanket and helped Fransje out of bed. Fransje, too, dropped to his knees and without stumbling, said the same morning prayer that his brother had whispered a moment before—except that Fransje prayed out loud.

Repeatedly Fransje had to suppress his urge to talk. That wasn't easy, for he was very excited in anticipation of their long, adventurous journey. But he was quite aware that by talking too much he might give Mother second thoughts and perhaps jeopardize their going.

The older boys and Maria had already left. Only Wantje was still asleep. Mother was quietly having breakfast alone. She looked a little startled to see the two boys up so early. Feeling obliged to give her some explanation, Kees told her about the geography lesson. And anticipating her, he promised to be very careful and take good care of Fransje. To be on the safe side, however, he did not tell her that they might not be home until suppertime because they had a long way to go. Maybe they'd even find silver or gold coins, he suggested, blatantly trying to buy Mother over. It wasn't dangerous in the least because the ancient town site was far from the channel and high tide didn't arrive until five this afternoon.

Mother said little. She prepared a few sandwiches and wrapped them in a paper bag. She had never seen the flooded tract of land herself, but she had often heard her father talking about it. She knew it wasn't dangerous, or at least not if the boys didn't pull any crazy stunts. "No fires, eh?" she said as an extension of her own thoughts.

A flow of chatter now erupted from both boys, for Mother's indirect assent had removed the last obstacle.

Jan was already waiting for them, and when he saw them coming in the distance, he came running to meet them. Like Kees, he was carrying a shovel. The threesome turned down the familiar road leading past the farm where Father and the two oldest boys were working. Coming to the dike, at Kees's suggestion they skirted it along the far side because Father might be working somewhere where he could otherwise see them. You could never know: Father might have changed his mind. They didn't reappear until they neared the heron colony.

Jan and Kees couldn't resist trying to climb one of the bare trees. But they were forced to give up. The trees had long ago died under the abuse of their noisy inhabitants. Bark hung in long, loose strips along the trunk and kept breaking and falling off, taking the boys with them. Moreover, the herons had raised an alarm and were flying back and forth screeching wildly.

When they went on, they didn't take the dike leading to Aunt Jane's house, but turned left and followed the one that led to the distant, treeless sea dike. There they turned right. According to the directions they had gleaned, they would have to walk another half hour before they reached the flooded land which was supposed to be located somewhere on the monotonous gray, alluvial mud flats. It was obvious that high tide had been not so long ago. The row of short poles along the bottom of the dike, with their inevitable crowns of seaweed and other washed up debris, were still wet. Small puddles of water still glistened here and there on the hollowed surfaces of the uneven basalt blocks. Whenever the boys clattered across the hard boulders in their wooden shoes, they heard little crabs scurrying away. But they couldn't see them, because the creatures were hidden deep between the narrow gaps and seams of the huge blocks.

Fransje, who had become quite tired already, although manfully concealing it, seemed to catch his second wind. For there were all kinds of treasures to be found in the seaweeds which the tide had washed ashore. Who knows, suggested Kees, maybe they'd find a bottle with a note in it from a shipwrecked sailor on a deserted island. If not, there were always dead seagulls, or beautiful bamboo sticks, or boxes of rotting oranges, or large pieces of driftwood, and much more.

After scavenging around like this for about an hour, they reached a point in the sea dike where it jogged sharply to the left. They pulled off their stockings and stuffed them into their pockets. That way they didn't have to worry about having them stolen or losing them. Their wooden shoes could always be dried in the sun.

Fransje enjoyed sliding over the slippery clay barefoot in his wooden shoes. He deliberately sought out the shallow puddles, splashing the water up his legs. He wanted to know what all these little piles of clay were that looked just like clusters of worms. They weren't worms, Kees told him, but they had been made by worms. They lived deep in the clay and gorged themselves with mud because there were little bits of food in it and then they spit it out—"Only out the other end," he added with a little snicker. "Just look," he said. With his shovel he dug a deep hole in a spot where there was a big pile of "worm-spit" and soon he unearthed a long purple-red, ringed worm. Yes, Fransje was convinced that this was going to be a very adventurous journey. Eagerly he asked himself what they would find soon on the flooded land itself.

The mysterious spot so blended with the mud flats that the boys had to search some time before they finally found it. They wouldn't have known that they were walking on it if they hadn't suddenly come upon a diseased yellow tree trunk standing alone in an expanse of clay.

So there must have been land here at one time. Once this had been a tree with branches and leaves like the trees in front of their house. Birds had sat in it and maybe even built nests in it. Fransje studied the bleak plain with a new eye. In the distance stretched the green line of the sea dike, clusters of dark treetops rising above it here and there. A little farther to the left a tall tower pointed its blunt finger into the sky. But it wasn't the tower of their own village. Fransje tugged at Kees's sleeve and pointed to it.

"Oh, that must be Kapelle," replied Kees without interest. "Look how close to Kapelle we are," he said to Jan. They hadn't noticed it earlier because they had been walking along the foot of the sea dike.

"Maybe somebody buried money under that tree," speculated Jan. Immediately he started to dig in the clay and Kees hastily followed his example. Then they discovered the second sign that they had indeed found the flooded land. Under a thin layer of alluvial clay their shovels hit a hard, tough layer of dark soil which had the same composition as the unplowed, wet clay of the polder during the fall. They could hardly get their shovels into it. No matter how hard they stomped on their shovels, their efforts were in vain. The sweat began to bead on their faces and soon they had had enough.

A little farther the ground was littered with pieces of pottery; there the original ground wasn't even covered by alluvial clay. Nor was the ground smooth, but lumpy and rough, and if possible even tougher than around the tree stump. So the boys abandoned the idea of doing some digging. They couldn't even penetrate shovel-deep into the strange surface.

Fransje squatted among the potsherds. One of them caught his eye because of its color. It too was half buried; just a small, wavy edge stuck out of the ground and it was lodged tight. Fransje dug around it with his finger, but he couldn't get it loose. It posed a challenge that Fransje found hard to resist. He scratched around the potsherd with all his fingers, but it was like digging in a mass of hardened rubber. If only he had an old spoon or a shovel like Kees and Jan. "Come on, Kees," he called over his shoulder. "Bring your shovel over here."

The boys came to him. Surely they could unearth that thing. Carefully Kees broke up the tough soil with his old pocket knife and then scraped it away from the mysterious artifact. Apparently it was still intact, for what had first looked like a mere fragment continued to curve and still wasn't completely uncovered. Fransje kept wanting to put his fingers in the hole to speed up the work, but Kees asked him if he wanted to lose a finger. At last Kees's knife slipped under the artifact; he had reached the other end. With his shovel he pried up the dull brown object, and there before their feet lay an almost undamaged stone mug or vase. Fransje dove forward and picked it up with both hands. "I found it!" he cried, jubilant and proud. "It's mine!"

Yes, the other boys conceded it was his. They jealously examined the strange little vase. It had one handle and the thin layer of glaze was still fairly shiny. The wavy edge was the base; from there it flared into a round little body toward a perfectly circular opening. It must have been a drinking cup. Fransje asked himself if long ago perhaps a little boy like himself had drunk from it. It reminded him of dear, familiar things, like his little bed and the candy chickens from long ago. He'd take it home and put it on the mantel. Then he could look at it every day as much as he liked.

Jan and Kees were now avidly searching through the potsherds. They must be getting "warm" here, for it would be strange if Fransje's cup were the only intact object among all these pieces. But no matter how much they poked and scratched and dug, they found nothing but fragments of broken pottery. Meanwhile Fransje had gingerly cleaned out the inside of his cup in a pool of seawater and now carefully carried it around, his finger hooked through the little handle.

A little farther on they spotted another peculiarity in the land, as if someone had been plowing there. They hadn't seen it earlier because the ground sloped and it had been hidden from their sight by the ridge above the slope. Quickly they ran toward it. Fransje was soon left far behind because he didn't dare run too fast with his little cup. Then he noticed something strange in the way the boys were standing: they looked so dumbfounded and confused that Fransje's curiosity was aroused. He quickened his pace until he was beside them. He stepped forward to see what they were staring at so strangely.

To his consternation, in and beyond the obviously disturbed

ground he saw a ghastly profusion of bluish black bones scattered about. He probably wouldn't have known the jagged things sticking out in all directions were bones if there hadn't also been mixed among them a number of unmistakable, grinning skulls, which he recognized from pictures in the Bible storybook. The scene was made even more gruesome by the unearthly, blue-black color of the skulls which made the yellow teeth seem to flash. Fransje, who had climbed onto a mound of the upturned earth, quickly stepped down again. Overcome by a strong feeling of impropriety, he clung to Kees like a frightened puppy.

Jan concluded that this must have been the cemetery, and that over the course of the years the sea must have discolored the bones. But that didn't explain the obscene chaos that existed here, obviously of quite recent date.

The boys didn't know that only a few weeks before several professors and students from the University of Leyden had been digging here in search of complete skeletons of various sizes of both sexes and that either they hadn't taken the trouble to decently rebury the rest or had been prevented by high tide.

With his shovel Kees tried to pick up a bone sticking out of the tough ground near his wooden shoe and fling it away. When he accidentally scraped it with the sharp end of the shovel, he heard the same sound as when a moment ago he had bumped the shovel against the pieces of pottery. This was the first time Kees had seen human skeletons, and they looked much different than he had pictured them. He had always imagined they would look just like the animal bones he had often seen: white and with the hardness of wood instead of black and hard as stone like these bones. For a moment he hoped that maybe they had made a mistake, that maybe this spooky spectacle wasn't real but a mirage, and soon they'd be having a good laugh about it.

Kees squatted down to take a closer look at the strange object and again hit it with his shovel. Again it rang like steel on stone. Then he gathered enough courage to scratch it with his fingernail; it felt just like scraping his fingernail over a potsherd. Now he picked up the long bone and banged it against another one lying nearby. This time it sounded like stone on stone. Although that didn't solve the mystery, now he no longer felt as if he were handling human bones—human, even if dead for hundreds of years. The fact that they were warm from the sun and not cold helped too. Daringly he stepped into the middle of the excavation among the litter of bones. They were of all shapes and sizes, with parts of skulls scattered here and there. He actually picked up one of the grinning heads and peered inside through the eye sockets.

Not wanting to be outdone by his friend, Jan followed Kees's example. At first their voices betrayed uneasiness at this strange experience, but because they wanted to show each other that they weren't at all frightened, they grew more and more loud and daring. They took a skull in each hand and knocked them together, allowing the sound to convince them that these were just two rocks.

Fransje looked on with horror. He wanted to protest, but didn't really know why. In vain he searched for words to make his brother and his brother's friend desist from what seemed horribly sacrilegious, but he didn't know if it actually was, nor how to put it to them. His heart pounded in his throat and his dry lips whispered incoherent words. His eyes flew to the little mug hanging from his trembling hand. He half expected it to have turned into a grinning skull too. He heaved a sigh of relief when he saw that it was still the same lightly glazed, precious object. Nevertheless, he held it a little farther away from himself.

The two boys became more and more audacious. First they tried to break the skulls by dropping them on top of each other, and when that didn't succeed, they hurled them against each other as hard as they could. Then they discovered that these gruesome objects were made of no ordinary stone, for they couldn't break them. They did knock out a few teeth, which got lost among the large clods of clay.

Fransje was seized by a new fit of nausea. Suddenly his body contracted around a stabbing pain in his side and he vomited. But Kees and Jan didn't notice. Now they were actually playing marbles with the skulls. Straightening up and wiping from his eyes the tears that had followed his vomiting, Fransje shuddered at what he saw.

It was too much for him. Suddenly the flooded land seemed like an endless graveyard full of graves that could open at any moment to swallow him. He uttered a loud cry and began to run toward the sea dike, skidding on the slippery clay which coated the strange ground a little farther on, swinging his arms wildly to keep his balance. But he didn't slacken his speed and he never looked back.

So engrossed were the other two boys in their wild game that at first they noticed nothing, but when the flailing figure caught their eyes, they were brought back to reality. "Fransjeee!" shouted Kees, but his fleeing brother didn't stop or look back. Fransje couldn't hear him because of the slopping of his wooden shoes. Now it was Kees's turn to become frightened, for to his consternation he saw that Fransje was running in the opposite direction from which they had come; he was running toward the place where earlier that morning Kees had seen the glitter of a large runnel from the dike. Kees grabbed his shovel and raced after him, repeatedly calling his name. Jan followed his example. Finally the voices penetrated to Fransje's ears. When he saw the boys coming after him, he stopped and waited.

Kees had meant to give him a good bawling out, but he was checked by the ghastly pallor of his little brother's face, and for the second time that day the look in Fransje's face pricked his conscience. At the same time it confronted him with the problem of how to keep Fransje from giving a detailed account at home of his behavior on the flooded land. He tried to divert Fransje's attention to his little mug and built him up indirectly by saying to Jan, "Boy, that Fransje is lucky! He found himself a beautiful cup and we didn't find nothing!"

Jan caught on and added more of the same. But he had a more direct method. With his free hand he dug into his pocket under his stocking and came up with a quarter. "You know what?" he said. "Since we're so close to Kapelle, why don't we go into town and buy something? Maybe we'll see an ice cream cart. Then we can each have an ice cream cone. Or else we can buy a chocolate bar or something in a store."

They were all glad to substitute this attractive prospect for their morbid thoughts of the burial ground; suddenly the dike was green again and snow-white clouds were sailing across a cheerful blue sky. Fransje took one last glance back at the somber territory ruled by death. But it had already dissolved into the gray plain of the alluvial beach, barely distinguishable from the hazy horizon. He'd be happy when he was back on firm ground where grass and flowers grew and where butterflies and bees fluttered and buzzed around you. His face slowly regained its normal color, and he, too, made a few remarks. But he carefully avoided every subject related to the flooded land. He didn't even respond to their praise of his find.

Having come to the dike, the boys washed their muddy legs and wooden shoes in a pool of sea water between the basalt blocks and then set their shoes in the sun to dry. A little later Fransje climbed the dike to take a look at the village. Not far away he saw a trail running down the dike which became a narrow, winding road that led to the village. He wondered how they'd find their way home afterward. He wasn't looking forward to the long walk at all, for suddenly he felt extremely tired. He let his gaze travel across the countryside, deliberately avoiding the place where the sunken land should be. Then he heard Kees calling him. Kees asked him if he wanted a sandwich. He went back down, although he was really more thirsty than hungry.

Mother had given them six sandwiches, so there were two for each of them, because Jan hadn't thought to bring any. Food tasted good to them, but eating the dry bread made Fransje even thirstier. With difficulty he swallowed down one sandwich. Then he asked, "Are we going home pretty soon?"

Yes, it was high time they were starting out. What time was it? Their wooden shoes were still a little wet, but their stockings would take care of that.

In the village they looked for something resembling an ice cream cart, but their efforts went unrewarded. Finally Jan asked a group of young children if they knew a place in the village that sold ice cream. But the little ones just stared at him stupidly, not seeming to know what he was talking about. So the boys slowly sauntered through the village until they finally spotted a small candy store. There they bought a couple of chocolate bars.

Under normal circumstances this was a rare treat for Fransje, but this time he wished they had bought something else because the chocolate formed a thick clot of saliva in his mouth which he could hardly swallow. He asked if they couldn't find a drink of water somewhere. Jan said, "Pretty soon, Fransje. When we've gone a little farther. We have to hurry."

Soon the village lay behind them. They were again surrounded by flat fields readying themselves for the harvest. The distant dikes reminded them how far they had to go before they were back in familiar surroundings. Fortunately Kees and Jan seemed to know the way, for in a little while they turned down a side road leading past a short row of houses, the last in the area. Once more Fransje said that he was terribly thirsty, and Kees promised him that they'd stop at one of the houses to ask for a drink of water.

When they came a little closer to the houses, they saw in front of the largest one, the one in the center, a horse hitched to a three-wheeled cart. The large, fox-colored horse was tied to the gatepost as was common. A man came around the house carrying a heavy sack on his shoulders. A woman watched him as he dropped it into the cart, her arms akimbo. The boys were still too far away to make out their faces and saw the scene only as a chance to ask someone for a drink of water.

But Fransje suddenly had a strange sensation. He couldn't make out the faces either, but the posture of the woman suddenly—he didn't know why—caused immense gladness to well up in him. Not because her clothing reminded him of his mother; most women wore the same costume here. But she suddenly evoked the sweet joy of the beautiful dream he had had long ago.

The man went to the back of the house again, apparently to fetch another sack. But the woman slowly strolled past the horse, and after petting its head positioned herself as if to await the three boys. And then suddenly Fransje knew who she was even though he still couldn't see her features very well. Something in her pose, or perhaps a mysterious affinity told him that it was Kee—Kee of Kapelle. What surprised him was not that she was standing there before him, but that he hadn't even thought of her this morning when the others had told him that the village behind the dike was Kapelle.

Leaving the two boys behind, he ran to Kee. The woman was already holding out her arms to receive him. "Hello, Fransje, my boy!" she cried. "Where did you come from, and where have you been, so far from home?"

Fransje held up the little mug and said, "To the flooded land with Kees and Jan."

"And does your mother know you're so far from home?"

Fransje nodded.

"Come along into the house and I'll get you each a glass of milk and a piece of honeycake."

She waited for Jan and Kees, whom she invited into the house with a friendly smile and gesture, and she followed them to the back of the house carrying Fransje on her arm.

"Lukas, look who has come to visit us. This is Fransje Weststrate and his brother and friend." Then she put Fransje down and descended the stairs into the cellar. Soon she was back carrying a large, white pitcher. From a cupboard she took a large honeycake and three glasses, which she poured brimful of milk, saying, "Well, boys, drink up. You must be thirsty after walking all that way."

Jan and Kees were quite bashful, but not Fransje. Drinking greedily he gulped down the cool drink.

Lukas had a deep, gruff voice but a friendly face. He said, "You fellows are in luck. I was just getting ready to take a few sacks of wheat to the mill at Valckenisse. I've been trying to get away all week. If you boys want, you may ride along that far."

There was no mill in Kapelle, so he had to get his grain milled in the village between Kapelle and their own village. The boys beamed. What a stroke of luck! That would save them an hour of walking in the hot sun.

Kee drew Lukas's attention to Fransje's little mug. To Fransje she said, "Maybe long ago a little boy like yourself drank from it."

Fransje nodded. This had entered his mind too. And maybe some of those bones had belonged to that other Fransje. Kee seemed to be reading his thoughts, for she continued, "He died long ago. But if he loved the Lord, then his soul is in heaven now. And in the last day the Lord will make a new body out of his bones which are buried somewhere out there. And He'll do that for us too, if we love Him and are His children."

None of the boys replied. Jan and Kees were blushing as they asked themselves if perhaps they had been playing with the little boy's bones. To Fransje, however, Kee's gentle voice and prophetic words cast a wholly different light on the gruesome burial ground behind the dike.

Lukas told them it was time to go. Kee rose and once more went to the cupboard. This time she returned with a basket of early apples, and giving each of them two, she said to Kees, "Will you tell your mother and father that I hope to stop in tomorrow? You're having a preacher tomorrow, aren't you?"

Yes, that was true. Fransje had heard it mentioned at home, but it had completely slipped his mind.

"Yes, I love to listen to Reverend Kok," Kee continued. "So if it's good weather, I hope to be at your house tomorrow, God willing."

When they came outside, Lukas set Fransje on the grain sacks in the middle of the wagon, while the other two boys sat on the back with their legs dangling over the end. Kee watched the departing group until they disappeared in the distance, where the road passed through a gap in the dike. Then she put up her hand for the last time to wave goodbye.

Slowly she walked to the back of the house. She was vaguely aware of a deep feeling of tenderness and longing. As she took hold of the doorknob to the back door, the words of a Psalm spoke insistently within her:

> Jehovah's truth will stand forever,
> His covenant-bonds He will not sever,
> The word of grace which He commands
> To thousand generations stands;
> The covenant made in days of old
> With Abraham He doth uphold.

As one practiced in godliness she knew that the Lord wished to tell her something by this, but she wasn't sure what. Perhaps it was related to tomorrow's worship service, which would be led by one of His faithful servants and which she had heard would include the celebration of the Lord's Supper. It might also be related to her love for the little boy who had dropped in on her so unexpectedly. She wasn't sure, so childlike she asked, "Lord, what do You mean? What do You want to tell me?" Then forcefully these words came to her: "My soul desired the firstripe fruit."

She knew that this was the answer to her whispered question, and that it had to be related to the child who had stirred up such tender feelings within her. But this hardly meant that she now suddenly saw and discerned the matter clearly or immediately understood God's message. But one thing she did accept: that God had something special in store for this child. And she believed his name was written in the book of life and of the Lamb. With tears welling up in her eyes, she whispered, "Oh, dear Lord. You have not yet abandoned or forgotten Your church; You still remember Your covenant and confirm the promises of Your Word."

She sat down at the table and opened the Bible. Did the Lord have something great in mind for the child? Was He preparing him like young Samuel of long ago? She wasn't sure where the text that had come to her a minute ago was to be found, but her own comparison made her suspect it must be in connection with that prophet. For a time she paged through the chapters of Samuel and Kings, but she couldn't find the words anywhere. Finally she gave up. She would just have to wait in patient trust to see how the Lord would fulfill the words. Like Mary, she hid them in her heart, knowing from experience that in His time God would shed further light on them.

Fransje was busy lining up the chairs for the customary prayer before going to church when Kee's white cap came floating along the green hedge toward the back of the house. The whole family had been watching for her, because Father expected her to be here this morning if she knew that they were celebrating the Lord's Supper.

Quietly she came into the house, shook hands with everyone, and calmly waited by one of the chairs until the others began kneeling before them.

After prayers, at Mother's insistence Kee had a cup of tea and a biscuit. "It's going to be a hot day," she said, for the third time wiping the perspiration from her face with a white handkerchief with a border of black polkadots. Yes, said Father, he thought so too. They might be in for a thunderstorm this afternoon.

Kee gave Fransje a paper bag of peppermints, with the usual admonition to share them nicely with the other kids. Then it was time to leave, for the first churchgoers were already passing the window. Mother had to warn Fransje, who was still toying with the peppermints, to hurry up. So he forgot to take a drink of water, which he had been planning to do all morning because he was so thirsty probably because of the salty piece of spiced cheese he had eaten at breakfast. He ran after Father and the two women until he caught up with them. He put one of the peppermints in his mouth so he wouldn't feel so thirsty. This, however, hindered rather than helped, for soon his mouth was full of thick saliva just like yesterday with the chocolate bar. That was stupid of him not to take a quick drink! Now he'd have to wait until they got back home after church, for Father wouldn't be a bit pleased if Fransje asked for a drink somewhere along the way.

Father, Mother, and Kee were talking about spiritual matters as they walked along. Did Kee know the Lord's Supper was going to be celebrated this morning? Yes, she had heard about it, but because she hadn't really been sure, she hadn't been able to prepare herself properly. (Or was her experience of yesterday afternoon the Lord's way of preparing her? She was inwardly amazed but said nothing about it.) Nevertheless, it didn't escape Father that, as they said in their circles, she was spiritually attuned, as was shown by the enviable tenderness that infused her words.

Inside the church Fransje's eyes were immediately drawn to a table covered by an immaculate white cloth set up in the space between the pulpit and the reader's lectern. On the table were several objects, but he couldn't see them because they were also covered by white cloths which someone must have neatly ironed, for the sharp creases were clearly visible.

Since Fransje had never seen the Lord's Supper celebrated before, at once a whole series of questions arose in him. He couldn't pose them here, however, for Father would tolerate no talking in church, not even whispering. That's why Fransje no longer sat between Kees and Father, but along the aisle on the other side of Father.

A little later the door to the consistory room opened and the elders and deacons marched in, led by the minister. Fransje was immediately impressed by the man's appearance. He was tall and thin, and he looked very old to Fransje. Most striking were his gentle features and the snow-white hair that framed his forehead and temples. From his corner Fransje quietly and reverently observed him, knowing immediately that he liked the stranger very much.

After the opening songs and prayer, the preacher introduced his sermon which was based on Revelation 22:17: "And the Spirit and the bride say, Come. And let him that is athirst come. And whosoever will, let him take the water of life freely."

Fransje looked up in surprise when he heard these words, and suddenly he was again painfully aware of his thirst. Although it was the second time that these words had been read this morning, this was the first time Fransje heard them, the first time the chapter had been read by the reader and the familiar drone of his voice had passed over him like a moaning wind. Because the minister read the words dramatically and with special emphasis, Fransje was forced to listen. And because they vividly reminded him of his thirst, he waited in suspense to hear what the minister would say. So the first sentence struck him like a bolt of lightning, for the preacher didn't mince any words, but asked directly, "Are there people here who are thirsty, spiritually thirsty? Then this morning they can quench that thirst, for in His incomprehensible love and mercy the Lord has provided us not just water, but wine—bread and wine. And now He invites all those who are truly hungry and thirsty to come and eat and drink.

"Those who thirst—for it is primarily to these that the text is addressed—can come and quench their thirst at the Fountain of good, the Well of living water, which points to the precious Son of God, who Himself cried on the cross, I thirst! so that God's beloved children would never have to perish with thirst.

"Perhaps there are those who thirst, but who do not consider themselves worthy to sit at the King's table. Or who are besieged by doubts that theirs is a true, genuine spiritual thirst. Or those who can't believe that this invitation is for them. Perhaps there are those souls who are seeking for greater certainty and sigh with longing, but who cannot believe that their names are written in the book of life of the Lamb. These are souls troubled by the doctrine of predestination; they can't believe that God has chosen them from eternity. But let such souls give the words of our text another close reading and they will see that there isn't a word about predestination in it. Not because there is no such thing, for if there weren't, not a single soul would ever have come to the Lord or ever will come. But God the Holy Spirit chose these words in order not to scare off any of the sighers and the seekers. It simply says, And whosoever will, let him take! Of course that doesn't imply an Arminian free will. Far from it! But it implies a will that is wrought and molded by God Himself; this can be recognized as a constant yearning, a constant longing and waiting for God. Whoever longs for God in this way, often in secret and without anyone else's knowledge, crying day and night, "Oh that Thou wouldst rend the heavens asunder; that Thou wouldst come down!" wills in the sense of our text, for that is a will put in man's heart by God Himself.

"So if there are such souls present this morning, then Reverend Kok tells them in God's name that there is a place for them here, that they may come forward to taste and see that the Lord is good for man who in himself is wicked and has spoiled everything and is no longer worthy of the Lord's trouble . . . ."

Reverend Kok didn't realize, no more than did Fransje, that what he had just proclaimed was diametrically opposed to what Reverend Steenhouwer had proclaimed here about eight months ago. Much of what the preacher said was beyond Fransje's comprehension and his attention kept straying elsewhere. But again and again his look was drawn to those friendly eyes, the gentle gestures, and the impressive figure standing there proclaiming the Word of God so calmly and assuredly. Fransje was glad to be able to watch him peacefully from his corner in the pew. Although he wasn't conscious of it, the heavenly words also helped quench his spiritual thirst because his love for the man flowed from his love for God.

Yes, but his bodily thirst wasn't diminished; on the contrary, it grew sharper with every mention of the words *thirst* and *water*. He had tried to satisfy it by taking another of Kee's peppermints, but once more he had ended up with a mouthful of thick saliva and such a cloyingly sweet taste that he carefully took the candy out of his mouth and dropped it on the floor in a corner near the bench.

His situation confused him, for on the one hand he wished church were over so that he could go home for a drink of water, and on the other hand he wished he could sit here all day in the presence of this sweet messenger of peace.

Someone else had also fallen under the spell of the comforting words—Mother. She almost drank them from the preacher's lips. Her heart was like wax in her bosom, and for some time she had been silently weeping into her white handkerchief, weeping in longing for God and Christ Jesus. A little later when the minister descended from his elevated pulpit and issued the invitation to come to the table of the Lord, it was as if an invisible hand lifted her from her seat and led her forward. For the first time in her life she too proclaimed the Lord's death till He come—for the first time in her life because never before had she felt free to do so.

But the service was not yet that far. The minister had not yet finished his last point and was still preparing the congregation for the climax. Even now he didn't resort to wild gestures or dramatic arm-waving. And not once did he pound his fist on the Bible. But in his holy zeal and quiet struggle against a fatalistic passivity ingrained in the Zeelanders' character, he used a visual demonstration. With his right hand he took the glass of water from under the lectern and held it down over the edge of the pulpit as if offering it to the congregation.

Then he continued, "It is as if God were saying, Is there anyone here who is thirsty? Then let him come, for here's water for you. Is there anyone here who believes that I'll give him water for nothing, then come and drink your fill and I'll quench your thirst." Then he paused to let his words sink into the hearts of the people before him, still holding out the glass.

Yes, there was someone who was thirsty and who believed the

preacher's words and who was willing to accept the invitation. It was Fransje. Before Father realized what was happening or could grab him, Fransje was on his way toward the glass of water, the unexpected answer to his screaming thirst. He pattered forward to the Lord's table, and being very careful not to touch the white tablecloth, he stepped toward the pulpit. There he stopped and reached up.

An almost tangible hush filled the church. Not a foot shuffled and not a cough sounded. You could have heard a pin drop. Father made a move to fetch his little sermon-disrupter back, but he immediately changed his mind, realizing that he would only create a bigger disturbance. Tensely he awaited the outcome of the little drama.

The minister saw Fransje coming and at once grasped the situation. His voice laden with emotion, he said, "Wait a second, my boy, I'll be right down." He opened the door in the side of the pulpit, descended the steps, and approached Fransje with the glass. But he didn't hand it to him. He put his left hand behind Fransje's head and with the other hand brought the glass to Fransje's lips. And Fransje drank, and drank, and drank. He drank until the last drop trickled down his throat. The water was lukewarm, but at least it quenched the fire that had been eating at him all morning. As he drank he looked up into the friendly face high above him. When the glass was empty, he wanted to go back to his seat, but the preacher stopped him. He placed his hand on Fransje's head and in a voice trembling with emotion, he said to the congregation, which had been breathlessly following this drama: "Dear congregation, I couldn't find a better application of what I have been telling you than what you have just seen. Although this child does not yet understand the spiritual implications of my words, in childlike faith he has done what God asks of His children, namely, that they listen to His invitation and put as much trust in His words as this child did in mine. For we must all become like little children—like this child. If not, we shall in no wise enter the Kingdom of heaven."

Then Fransje was allowed to return to his seat. The preacher said that there was no need to continue the sermon, for they had already heard—and seen—the application. He went on to read the liturgical form for the Lord's Supper and then invited the people to come to the table. Although he abhorred whispering in church, this time Father himself was guilty of it in order to impress on Fransje that he must stay in his seat when Father went forward, because the Lord's Supper wasn't for children.

Before Fransje left for the afternoon service—he insisted on going because he wanted to be near the preacher—he made sure he wouldn't be plagued by thirst again. He drank so much water that he risked having to disturb the service by leaving church to answer another urgent need. Fortunately he soon fell asleep and didn't wake up until it was time to go home. As soon as they were out of town, however, he darted behind a tree and relieved himself of his painful excess.

Although Mother preferred to leave him home with one of the older children, Fransje also begged to go along to the evening service, purely out of adulation for the preacher, whose hand he could still feel on his head. He had never been to church three times in one day, and in this terrible heat it wouldn't be easy for him to sit still so long.

The weather had become almost unbearably humid. All day hazy, ominous thunderclouds had been shuffling across the horizon. The church was crowded, partly because of the many visitors from neighboring villages, especially young people who were taking the opportunity to join a cooling bike ride with the discharge of their Sunday duties. Chairs had to be put in the aisles and around the pulpit to provide seats for everyone.

This time, too, Fransje didn't hear a word that the reader droned from Ezekiel 37. But when the minister announced his text, Fransje's attention was caught for the second time today, and suddenly in his thoughts he was back on the flooded land. The text told about a valley of dry bones which at God's command and at the prophet's word came alive again.

In a fitting afterword to this morning's communion service, the preacher applied the episode to the condition of the human soul: through His longsuffering grace God made dead souls live. But it all went over Fransje's head. The preacher could not know that there were two exceptions to his assumption that there was no one in the congregation who had ever at one time seen as many human bones as the prophet saw in his vision. Therefore he dwelt on it, describing all too clearly and vividly the forbidding, macabre valley full of glistening bones. Nor could he know that mentally Fransje was constantly correcting him by painting the bones a bluish black as if they had been dipped in ink.

He listened in suspense to find out what happened to the bones, secretly hoping that this would also apply to the other bones out there on the mud flats. He was listening so attentively that he didn't even notice the church growing strangely dark, nor did he hear the distant rumble of thunder.

Then something extraordinary happened.

When the preacher made Ezekiel cry, "Live!"—making his voice ring through the church just for that moment—a purple flash shot past the windows, immediately followed by a deafening thunderclap that made the earth creak and tremble. The thunderclap was immediately repeated, echoing and re-echoing in the dense ceiling of clouds until it gradually faded away like the bellow of a fleeing beast. Most people flinched at the violent explosion and cast anxious glances at the windows, for the transom windows at the top were standing wide open. But Fransje, who had been completely unaware of the coming thunderstorm, almost fell out of his seat in fright, latching onto Father's pantleg with both hands just in time.

The preacher stopped a moment and also cast a glance at the windows. But they had already been transformed into glass washboards as the water gushed over them, distorting the scene outside beyond recognition. The custodian hastily stood up and nervously began yanking at the ropes of the transom windows in his vicinity. The men sitting closest to the other windows followed his example, and then there was only the muffled sound of the pouring rain.

During this delay the Lord had an opportunity to gather the dry bones, bind them together with sinew and muscle, cover them with flesh and stretch a healthy new skin over them. This was how the preacher pictured the resurrected valley to the congregation. The gruesome litter of black bones had vanished from Fransje's imagination, although in his mind they did keep trying to reappear from behind the skin and flesh, because he knew they were still there.

But now the minister transported him to the last day when all human skeletons would be dressed in new bodies and awakened to new life. And, oh, what glorious bodies those would be for God's dear people and children! Not a spot or wrinkle would they have, and those bright, radiant eyes would never shed another tear. No one would ever say, I feel sick. And just as Fransje was asking himself if all those people would be walking around naked before

God, the preacher dressed them from head to foot in, naturally, the long, white robes of salvation—the same as those worn by the angels in Fransje's Bible storybook—and he also put palms of victory in their hands and golden crowns on their heads. Then there would be feasting in heaven—the marriage feast of Jesus and His bride. New wine would be served so that no one would ever complain of thirst. And there would be no more death.

Riding on the preacher's words, the Spirit entered Fransje's heart. Fransje saw the doors of eternity standing open. And when in holy curiosity he stole a peek inside, such an indescribable longing arose in his soul, such a breathless desire to be among that saved number, that he wished he could go there this very minute. For the first time in his short life his abiding desire to grow up fast had to yield to this new, irresistible, all overpowering desire.

Outdoors the newly washed and refreshed world was bathed in the golden light of the setting evening sun.

10

As he gleaned, Fransje reflected that his desire to grow up fast was just like the ripening of the grain. Perhaps all the ears of grain that he was gathering and put in his sack whenever he had a handful, had also wanted to grow up fast. It had happened very slowly, almost unnoticeably. He could still remember how at first this field of stubble had been just like a large carpet with very short hair. Then the hair slowly began to grow until it formed heads. But after that it took a long time before the long, waving stalks lost their bright green color and slowly began to pale. At last the whole polder had been one golden yellow quilt from which the sweating workers with their razor-sharp sickles had cut off larger and larger pieces. Long rows of shocks still stood in the fields like soldiers on parade, but not for long, because the wagons were noisily bouncing back and forth, and one by one the shocks were being broken down and stacked onto the wagons like so many separate sheaves. After that the high wagonloads swayed across the fields toward the large barns where the hay was either driven inside and stacked up in the large lofts beside the threshing floor or brought somewhere behind the barn and laid in large top-shaped clamps. And this was all done with great care, as if each sheaf was a building block which had to be put in exactly the right place.

One of Fransje's greatest joys was to be allowed to ride along on top of the loaded wagons. It was just like floating along in a tall ship. He felt scared, but safe; the whole load wobbled and swayed as the horses pulled it across the uneven terrain, and yet the top-heavy loads never tipped. For the farmhands knew exactly how to tie the ropes onto the wagonrack so that the hundreds of sheaves stayed neatly bunched.

Fransje hadn't been sent out to glean by his parents; he had wanted to come himself, for it showed that he was grown-up. Besides, Siene and Marien's girls did it too, and they were no bigger than he. Moreover, he liked the work, at least for a while. When he got tired of it, he just quit and went home to show Mother how much he had gleaned. He had his own gleaning sack of which he was very proud. Actually it was an old sack of Maria's which she used to wear under her apron. It had two straps which tied around the waist; when it was full, it looked like the milkbag of a goat but without teats.

Yes, growing up was also a very slow process. If you tried to stand by and watch it, focusing your attention on it, it escaped you and slipped between your fingers like an eel or the smoke from Father's pipe. The next moment it surprised you: you could already do this and you had already experienced that, just like the older boys—riding on a wagonload of wheat, for example, and climbing down the rack without the help of the farmhand. Since the horses all reminded him of Sarah, he was not scared of them at all.

Growing up fast actually involved doing the things the older boys could already do and experiencing the things that they had experienced. If you successfully passed through such experiences, you could properly count yourself part of their class and social group, even if you still had not caught up to them in size and age. Afterwards you could also brag about such things to the other kids, like Neeltje and Jan Blok. Of course, there were things you couldn't brag about, like the adventure with Aunt Jane's goat, because that would only undermine their respect for you. And there were also things older boys prided themselves on that only filled him with disgust when he thought of them. If they were a necessary part of growing-up, then he, Fransje, would just as soon not grow up.

Again the memory of two incidents assaulted his mind so that, stricken, he stopped, still bent over as if gleaning. Wantje and a few other kids were gleaning a little farther on. He was alone between two rows of shocks. At the moment there wasn't even a wagon in the vicinity.

The memory of the two incidents continued their assault unabated, and he wasn't able to repel either one of them. The first memory took him back several weeks to the adjacent field, which was now plowed and reseeded. Thin shoots of winter wheat were already beginning to trace faint lines from one end of the field to the other.

That field had been the first one on which he had gleaned—peas for the pig. It was nice work that he liked to do. Pier and his sisters were there too, as well as Wantje. It was Saturday afternoon, hot, brooding weather. Suddenly the sky became very dark and there was rumbling in the distance. Frightened, the girls headed for home. Fransje, however, had resolved first to fill his gleaning sack to surprise everyone at home and show them how big he was; as a result, his retreat was cut off by a fierce downpour.

Pier had also stayed, because he was a greedy pig, according to Kees and Arjaan. All Fransje could do was to seek shelter behind one of the tall racks draped with pea vines. Pier did the same behind the next rack, but when he saw Fransje, he came dashing to join him. Soon the rain seemed to be coming from all sides and they were getting wet anyway. But Pier knew what to do. They could crawl underneath the mound of pea vines, for it was hollow, and if you were small enough you could even stand up inside.

The rain could not penetrate the thick walls of their cozy hideout. Although Fransje wasn't pleased with Pier's company at first, eventually he found the mound quite homey. But then came the horrible experience. Just the memory of it still brought the blood rushing to his face. That awful Pier had told him all kinds of confusing things that Fransje didn't understand at all. Certain allusions, however, were only all too clear and called up images in Fransje's mind that nauseated him.

But that wasn't the worst of it. After Pier had talked to him very chummily and intimately for some time, he asked him to do something that Fransje didn't understand at first, and that he indignantly refused when he did. In the semi-darkness of the small space he saw that Pier had shed some of his clothes and was standing half naked before him. When Fransje tried to squirm out through a space under the rack, Pier pulled him back and, swearing and threatening to thrash him, forced Fransje to touch him and hold something in his hand. Fransje felt as if a black curtain had descended before his eyes, and his mouth tasted as if he had taken cod liver oil.

Then suddenly a crackling thunderbolt exploded and from far away an anxious voice called Fransje's name. Pier stopped bothering him and quickly straightened his clothes. But before they left their hiding place, he swore that he'd kill Fransje if he ever squealed on him.

Pier didn't have to worry, for Fransje would never mention it to anyone—not out of fear of Pier's threat, but because the mere thought of the horrible adventure revolted him. Did Kees and Arjaan do things like that too? Was that part of growing up? One thing he knew for certain: even if it was part of growing up (which he found hard to believe), he would never have anything to do with it. Then he would sooner die as a little boy.

This last thought reminded him of his second troubling memory—the memory of that powerful, mysterious longing which Reverend Kok had awakened in him Sunday evening and which conflicted with his longing to grow up. To make a choice between them was very hard for Fransje, and it sometimes precipitated such a struggle within him that he hardly knew where to turn. He would still like to grow up fast, the sooner the better in fact, although he refused to contaminate himself with the filthy things that seemed to go with it. But sometimes the vivid memory of the pea field episode so overpowered him that he was forced to conclude that he couldn't grow up without being tainted: then, albeit driven by necessity and against his natural desires, he fearfully chose the only other way out.

The sight of the emptying fields made Fransje melancholy. Even the potato fields, which would soon be harvested too, had lost their bright green color; all that remained above ground were pale, shriveled stems and sickly yellow leaves. The only crop that was still a fresh green was the sugar beets, but for some reason they could not lift Fransje's spirit. Those large, fleshy leaves seemed to have nothing in common with the gaily rustling leaves of the elms in front of their house. In fact, these too were beginning to turn yellow, and when Fransje pointed this out to Mother one day, she said, "It will soon be fall. In a little while all the leaves will fall from the trees and then winter will come again.

Then maybe we'll have some snow and you can go sledding again."

But that prospect didn't appeal to him in the least. He wasn't at all ready to put away the profusion of summer treasures and experiences he had gathered. Fortunately that wasn't necessary yet, for unexpectedly Jan Blok's father came by at his son's request to pick Fransje up. He was just on his way back from town, and Fransje happened to be home.

The orchard behind the Blok barn had become a magic forest. The sunlight playing between the branches fell in thousands of strips, some narrow and some wide, casting an almost unearthly light on the ripening pears and apples as they pulled the branches low to the ground. Fransje hadn't known there were so many kinds of apples and pears in the world. But they all seemed to be present in this magic forest. He quickly learned to identify the most delicious varieties. He ate so much fruit that he had to go "out back" several times that day. But that didn't matter; there were so many sheltered spots here that such natural duties meant but a brief interruption of their play.

Sometimes the boys pretended they were bandits or explorers and other times that they were tigers or gorillas. Gorillas didn't live on the ground, but in the trees. The low, sturdy apple trees didn't object to being climbed by two little boys. Meanwhile Fransje kept a sharp lookout for birds' nests, because this looked like an ideal place.

In a corner of the orchard which was surrounded on three sides by a high hawthorn hedge was a pile of large, dead branches pruned from the trees, another of the plentiful elements for adventurous games in this orchard. The woodpile could suddenly be a raft, or perhaps even Noah's ark. Just as they were about to climb on it, they saw a long, slender animal slip under the bottom branches. It wasn't a rat, for Fransje knew what they looked like; he had seen them often enough around the pigpen. He knew that most animals were afraid of people, even of little boys like himself and Jan, so he wasn't frightened. Yet they were somewhat intimidated, and when they had climbed to the top of the mountain, they made extra noise, wildly jumping up and down to remind the unknown denizen that he should be afraid of them.

To his delight Fransje discovered that there were still late flowers blooming in the tall grass of the orchard—purple and yellow flowers whose names he didn't know. And the hawthorn hedge, too, looked as if it were blooming again, not white flowers this time, but red ones. They weren't flowers, however, but red berries which had grown where the flowers had fallen off. From nearby they looked just like the beads in Mother's and Maria's necklaces. The boys couldn't resist tasting them. They didn't taste bad, but they couldn't compare to the juicy pears and apples which were also free for the taking. So they decided to make another round through the orchard to see if they could locate all their favorite trees.

On the way home Fransje became aware of a dull stomach ache, which bothered him quite often of late. This time, however, it was sharper than usual and he regretted having eaten so much fruit, for that must be what was causing it. Mother always said you got stomach aches from eating unripe fruit. He was sure he hadn't eaten any unripe pears or apples, but he must have had too much of a good thing, and that probably gave you a stomach ache too.

He wondered if Adam and Eve had gotten a stomach ache too after eating of the forbidden fruit. He'd like to know what kind of fruit it was. In his mind he suddenly saw Paradise before him in the enchanting dress of autumn. But there must have been more animals in Paradise than in Jan's orchard, and then you didn't have to be afraid of them or run away from them.

Arriving home, he complained to Mother about his stomach ache. But she immediately guessed its cause, and comforted him with the assurance that he would feel better tomorrow. He had trouble forcing down one slice of bread, the minimum demanded by Father, who wouldn't tolerate anyone at the table who refused to eat. Fransje's stomach ache wasn't a valid excuse, since it was caused by eating too much fruit, and fruit was mostly water, which was no substitute for solid food.

After two days the pain had disappeared. Now and then he still had a strange, unpleasant sensation, but he had grown so used to it that he hardly noticed it anymore. The family was not very sympathetically inclined, and if you complained too easily you were called a sissy. He decided that next time he visited Jan Blok, he wouldn't eat as many pears and apples as last time.

Thinking about the orchard suddenly reminded him of the De Visser family, probably because they, too, had an orchard. He hadn't been there in weeks, so since he didn't feel like playing with Neeltje and Siene and Marien's girls, he decided to visit his old friends.

As usual he was received with open arms. Although he had become much more at ease and free in their midst, he never became overly bold or "snooty," as Mother called it.

Kees de Visser wasn't in the house with the women. To Fransje's question, Leentje replied, "Father is in the orchard picking apples. But you may go and call him because he's supposed to go to Bergendaal. The train will be here in an hour."

Fransje knew about Bergendaal: it was "candy city," where Maria and Bram sometimes went on certain holidays. But Kees de Visser was going there on an ordinary weekday and on the train to boot! Oh, how Fransje would love to ride on a train! That would really be something to brag about. Suppose Mr. de Visser asked him to come along!

Finding Mr. de Visser took some time because he was standing at the top of a ladder in the dense foliage of a tall tree. If a couple of apples hadn't fallen down and he hadn't heard some rustling, he wouldn't have found him at all.

The man was happy to see Fransje. He carefully descended the ladder with a basket full of shiny apples under one arm. Fransje helpfully picked up several large apples lying under the ladder and started to put them in Kees's basket. But Kees stopped him; he said, "Those are bruised, Fransje. We can't sell them because they'd rot in no time. But I'll tell you what," he continued, "maybe your mother would like them to make dried apples." He pointed to two empty boxes and told Fransje he could pick up all the good windfalls he could find, here and under the other trees in the row he had already picked. He could use Mr. de Visser's basket and every time it was half full he could empty it into one of the boxes. Maybe one of his big brothers or his father could come to pick them up tonight with a wheelbarrow.

That was a pleasant surprise! He went to work immediately, but then he remembered his message. Kees de Visser smiled. Yes, he was just about to go in. Wasn't Fransje coming in with him for a cup of tea?

De Visser went to the station on his bike, which he would leave there until his return that night. Spiritedly Fransje strode back into the orchard. This orchard too was entirely surrounded by a tall hawthorn hedge, and an attractive little portal of hawthorn shrubs formed an arch over the gate.

Engrossed in his work, he forgot his mild disappointment that De Visser hadn't asked him to come along. What a lot of apples the man had dropped! Some were so badly bruised their skins were broken, while others were already starting to turn brown. Those he'd leave, only putting the biggest and nicest ones into his basket.

Here, too, there were rows of berry bushes, but the berries had been picked long ago. Those that De Visser hadn't picked the birds had taken care of. He heard them singing somewhere in the branches. Suddenly a wild rabbit darted from between the berry bushes. It stopped a moment to survey its surroundings and then rapidly continued its bobbing, zig-zag flight. Farther away a strange, spotted cat was slowly creeping forward along the bottom of the hedge. Occasionally it stopped, its tail slowly switching back and forth as it peered upward, no doubt to look for birds that might be within its reach. With an ungainly flutter of wings a thrush tumbled down onto a protruding branch near Fransje; looking up at the bird, he suddenly saw before him his own thrush of several months ago. Frightened by Fransje's sudden movement, it uttered a few shrill cries and flew away. Now for the first time Fransje suddenly saw the large owl which had been staring at him for some time with its large, blank eyes. When their eyes met, it also took flight, flying so silently that it almost seemed a fleeing spirit.

Fransje, who had been standing motionless for a long time, had to shift his foot a bit. As he did so, a large, green frog leaped high out of the grass. The only creature that paid Fransje no attention was a large cross-spider, which calmly went on weaving its half-finished web.

Fransje felt as if he were in Paradise, for it too had contained many kinds of animals. Except there had been many more and also large ones, and they hadn't been afraid of Adam and hadn't run away. They had come to him instead so he could pet them. Why didn't these animals understand that Fransje wouldn't hurt them either but only pet them or talk quietly to them? They must not trust him. Well, it wasn't any wonder. Nasty kids like Pier were always looking for ways to hurt animals, by throwing rocks at them or shooting at them with bow and arrow. Now, of course, the animals no longer trusted any kids, not even those who loved animals.

The thought of Pier would inevitably have reminded him of the ugly incident under the pea field had his attention not suddenly been diverted by a very peculiar tableau a short distance farther into the orchard. Sunlight everywhere fell through the gradually dying foliage in narrow beams. But several trees away from him there was a large gap in the leaf cover, where a dead tree had undoubtedly been removed. Into the gap poured a wide beam of unbroken sunlight that magically burnished the yellow leaves of the berry bushes with gold.

Like all children Fransje had an inborn tendency to let his imagination run free and create something familiar from the oddest shapes, such as cloud formations. But this time his imagination was not projecting shapes according to its whim, but the shapes compelled his imagination to see something that hadn't been in his mind at all. The tableau struck him as unmistakable. A rather large bush taller than the others caught most of the sunlight, so that its leaves, stirring gently in the soft breath of the wind, contrasted sharply with the dark tree trunk behind it.

"Jesus!" flashed through his mind: the light and shadow looked just like Jesus as He was pictured in Leentje's big picture book. Look, He had long, deep blond hair, a smiling radiant face which moved as if He were speaking, and His outstretched arms were clothed in long, loose sleeves. Then Fransje's imagination took over. Soon the smaller shrubs were multitudes of people listening to Jesus. Now he could clearly discern men and women and even little children. Look, two of them were standing right by His knees, and He was going to pick them up and take them on His lap. Then He'd lay His hand on their heads and bless them.

Entranced, Fransje stood and stared. His legs wanted to carry him forward to that other-worldly tableau, but instinctively he knew that the marvelous mirage would burst like a soap bubble if he did. He realized that if he didn't want to destroy the vision, he had to stay where he was.

The apple which he had been holding in his hand had become warm. All the while he had been digging into the dry little follicle on the bottom of the apple with one bent finger, but he was unconscious of it.

"Jesus!" he whispered with dry lips. And then he was once more overcome by that strange longing—first hesitant and imperceptible but then growing stronger and more urgent. It was the same longing he had felt that Sunday evening in the church during Reverend Kok's sermon. But now it was even more intense and comprehensive for it had something visible to focus it. The longing reminded him of the stranger who had taken his hand in the beautiful dream of long ago. And of Father, who could sometimes unexpectedly be so gentle, and of Mother, and Kee of Kapelle, and Verplanke, and Jacob at the bottom of the ladder, and Moses, and the disciples, and of the multitudes of the saved in heaven. Although he had never consciously learned the Psalm, the following lines passed clearly through his mind:

> When I in righteousness at last
> Thy glorious face shall see,
> When all the weary night is past,
> And I awake with Thee
> To view the glories that abide,
> Then, then I shall be satisfied.

How long he had stood there daydreaming, he had no idea, but suddenly he was startled out of his reverie by the rustling of footsteps in the tall grass, and a clear female voice called, "Fransje, where are you?"

It was Leentje, who had come to see how Fransje was doing. When she saw him, she asked from a distance, "Did you pick up lots of apples?" Fransje looked at her, and his white face shocked Leentje. Worriedly she wondered whether he was sick, but when she asked him if he didn't feel well, he just shook his head. Then she asked him if he had tasted any of the delicious apples. No, he didn't care much for apples, he answered. Maybe he'd rather have a pear, suggested Leentje. A little later Fransje was sorry that he had said yes to that, for with a happy air of promise, she took him by the hand and led him to a different corner of the orchard, to a row of tall pear trees, striking for their exceptionally large, shiny leaves. Their green luster had not yet been withered by autumn's breath. At first Fransje thought there were no pears on the tree, but then he spotted their long, graceful shape and peculiar color. Their skins were not shiny like those of the varieties he knew, but dull and rough. Where the stem attached to the branch the fruit was very long and slender and then widened into a grayish globe.

Leentje touched a few until she found one that felt soft under her fingers. "Here, Fransje," she said, "try this one."

As his teeth sank into it, Fransje's mouth filled with delectable nectar. Never before had he tasted anything so delicious! Leentje picked another one for herself and together they relaxed and enjoyed the delicious fruit. When he finished his pear, she offered him another one, and although he had resolved not to eat any apples for fear of getting another stomach ache, he couldn't resist the temptation and eagerly accepted the extra large pear Leentje had found for him. He consoled himself with the thought that last time the stomach ache had probably not been caused by eating fruit anyway.

Leentje helped him pick up the apples and fill his box. Meanwhile she prattled on about a variety of things. She praised Fransje for being such a big boy because he worked so hard. Then she asked him what he wanted to be when he grew up. "Stableman," he said without hesitation. But when Leentje tried to discuss it further just to be friendly, he interrupted her and said, "But maybe I won't grow up."

Leentje looked at him in surprise. Again she was struck by his unusual pallor. Trying to divert him, she said, "But Fransje, all kids grow up. Just think of your brothers. I can still remember when they were as small as you."

"Yes, but all little boys don't grow up. Sometimes they die when they're still small. Look at the little boy in the Bible!"

"What little boy in the Bible?"

"Oh, that boy who went to see his father out in the field and then he got a sunstroke and a little later he died."

Leentje had no idea what story he was talking about, and for a moment she suspected that he had confused a couple of stories.

"What was the little boy's name?" she asked.

"I don't know. But it's in the picture book. Later a preach . . . a prophet came and made him alive again. He lay down right on top of the little boy, with his mouth on the boy's mouth, and then he prayed, and then the boy was alive again. I wish I had been alive then. Then if I died like that little boy, Mother could call the prophet too and then maybe he would make me alive too."

The whole conversation made Leentje very uncomfortable. Something in the child's pale face hinted that there was more behind those words than either he or she suspected. The fact that he knew so many Bible stories—apparently even more than she did—and that he pondered them deeply was very unusual in children, at least in the children she knew. But then she reminded herself that he was from a very religious family; at least his father and mother both participated in the Lord's Supper and were known as truly born-again people. They were very good people, who gave no one occasion to talk. So it was perfectly possible that they often discussed such things.

She and her parents and her sister belonged to the same church and were undoubtedly also considered good people; nevertheless, there was a difference. None of them were recognized as truly born-again people, and she feared rightly so. At least she knew that she herself was not yet truly born again. And apparently she spent less time pondering spiritual matters than this child. Could he already be born-again, as young as he was?

She crouched down in front of him and looked straight into his earnest face. Then she asked him directly, "Fransje, if you died now, do you think you would go to heaven?"

Fransje gave her a strange look. He wasn't sure what Leentje was after. And remembering the two contrasting dreams, he couldn't give an unqalified yes or no. At a loss, he shrugged his shoulders, but still under the influence of the fascinating tableau he had seen before Leentje's arrival, he volunteered, "But I'd like to sit on Jesus' lap some time . . . ."

Leentje's eyes brimmed with tears. She inclined her face to his and without asking him for a kiss she pressed one onto his pale cheek. Slowly she stood up, taking him in her arms at the same time. "You know what?" she said in a forcedly light-hearted tone. "We'll go into the house for another cookie, and then pretty soon it will be time for you to go home to your mom."

Happily fall was in no hurry; the transition to winter wasn't as abrupt as Fransje had feared. The elms in front of the house did gradually shed a few leaves, but they had been doing so for several weeks, and as far as Fransje could tell the foliage hadn't become any thinner. Only yellower. He didn't think about the coming winter. There were so many other things to look forward to. Kees had mentioned that he and Jan wanted to go back to the flooded land once more, but this time Fransje didn't respond. He had no desire to go there ever again.

But he was looking forward to the day when the pig was to be slaughtered. That would be next month. Not that he was anticipating the slaughter as such, for he had decided to stay in the house until the cruel, bloody deed was done. He had no special fondness for the large, sluggish beast with its pale eyes peering out from under big, floppy ears and its unbearable stench. The thought, however, that the butcher was going to plunge a large knife into the animal's neck and that the mysterious force called life that now enabled it to move and eat and grunt would drain out of it along with its blood until the animal lay still caused a shudder to run down his back.

He refused to dwell on this necessary step, however, and his thoughts leaped forward to the delightful moment when he would get the first piece of bacon rind from their own pig, and when the pig bladder would be blown up and hung to dry on the chimney above his bed so it could be made into rumblepots some day.

Meanwhile there were the daily joys of the seasonal games the children played, and which he wanted to learn too so that he could be big. At present the game was tops. He had practiced with extreme determination until he had finally mastered the art. But it was a dangerous game. If you were shooting arrows and you lost your arrow you could always make yourself another one. There were plenty of reeds in the ditches and also lots of elder groves in the immediate area. But if your top flipped into the ditch, you had to try to fish it out without Mother catching you. Nor should you spin your top near windows, because woe to you if it broke one of them! And if you whipped your top so far that you couldn't find it anymore, then the fun was over because you had nothing to play with. You couldn't make another one yourself. Even Father, who could do almost anything, didn't know how to make a top. And to buy a new one was out, for Mother said money didn't grow on trees.

And then suddenly that awful stomach ache was back. This time it couldn't be blamed on eating too much fruit because the apples he had picked up in De Visser's orchard had long ago been sliced and dried at the bakery. Now they were stored for the winter in a large tin standing behind the trapdoor in the attic. Not much was left of the two boxes full he had picked; the tin wasn't even half full—that was how much the apples had shrunk.

Usually Fransje didn't complain to Mother about stomach aches because she was always quick to bring out the *Haarlemmer* oil, which he disliked so strongly it almost made him vomit. He preferred to keep the stomach ache. One afternoon, however, he could hardly force any food down his throat. The steaming potatoes and the revolting odor of cooked savoy cabbage, so nauseated Fransje that he suddenly doubled up and vomited.

This ruined everyone else's appetite too, but he could hardly be blamed. Looking worried, Mother lifted him from behind the table and carried him to the back room, where she washed him. She felt his hot hands and forehead and concluded that he had a fever.

"I'd better tuck you in bed for a while," she said. "I'll put you in Maria's bed."

One of the bed's doors was left open and the curtain was pushed aside. Then Fransje could watch the others from the safety of his coach. Mother put a cold, wet cloth on his forehead and informed him that she would give him some *Haarlemmer* oil. He raised such a fierce protest, however, that Father came to his aid by saying, "Why don't you wait awhile with that; it may make him throw up again."

The stomach ache vanished just as suddenly as it had come. Actually enjoying himself in his safe nest, Fransje didn't beg to be let out to play. His feeling of contentment was probably a side-effect of the fever raging in his body. After a little while he fell asleep and he didn't see or hear Father and his brothers and sisters going out. When he woke up, he was hungry. A big surprise awaited him: Mother had steeped two rusks in a bowl of milk and sprinkled them with lots of brown sugar. His favorite treat!

After a few days he was better again. His stomach ache was completely gone and the fever had disappeared. Ascribing it to impurities in the body, Mother had insisted on giving him a few drops of *Haarlemmer* oil in a spoonful of milk at regular intervals. So now she credited the medicine, as well as God, with healing him. She could no longer keep him inside because the pleasant fall weather irresistibly drew him outdoors.

A light mist hung over the polder, evoking a feeling of safety and coziness for the world seemed small and intimate. Hundreds of small round lace curtains hung from the wet hawthorn hedge. They were spider webs. It looked as if the spiders had hung them out to dry on the hedge, for the mist had threaded thousands of tiny silver beads onto every thread. Invisible before, all the webs were now quite noticeable.

Every so often a few tired leaves floated down out of the gray ceiling searching fussily for a place on the ground to retire. The air was so still and peaceful that Fransje could almost hear them fall. His eyes wandered about the small world surrounding him. It just included the last house in their row. But beyond it was a soft gray wall of fog.

The vegetable garden beside the hedge had also changed. Everything worthwhile had been picked except a short row of brussels sprouts and some beets. The summer vegetable plants were dead and brown and half decayed. Fransje was allowed to walk right through the garden if he wanted to, and even to play and dig in it. One spot he had to stay away from, however: the corner near the slophole. There Father had dug a large rectangular hole where their potatoes would be stored during the winter. Then it would no longer be a hole, but a small dike, for the potatoes would first be piled high, then covered with straw or reeds, and last of all buried under a layer of dirt. Then the potatoes were protected from rain, frost and snow. They would be covered as warmly as Fransje in his little bed.

Father had said that he hoped to dig the potatoes up soon. He and the boys had been harvesting the farmer's potatoes for the last two weeks. And since he was already talking about doing sugar beets, they would have to hurry. Mother would again have to lend a hand. That meant Fransje would have to go along to the fields too because he couldn't very well remain home alone.

When Fransje overheard the plans, he danced about in joy. He wasn't sure exactly where their potato patch was located, but perhaps it was close to Hontenisse Pond. And perhaps the farmer would drop in on them again and take him along to help empty the eel traps. Suddenly, however, the ugly snout of that horrible monster, Norma, loomed up in his imagination. Immediately he asked if the potato field was close to the farmhouse. What a relief! It lay behind the orchard and extended halfway to the dike, far away from that frightful dog.

The next Tuesday brought the long-anticipated moment when he could turn down the familiar road to the farm.

Father and the boys had already been working hard for several hours. Mother had first had to make the beds and tidy up the house. They expected to arrive just in time for the coffee break. Mother was carrying a large, enameled coffee can full of hot coffee; for this special occasion she had added sugar as well as milk. The can was wrapped in a thick layer of cloth to keep the coffee hot. Father and the boys would love it. Here and there blue trails of smoke marked the location of burning heaps of dry potato greens. To Fransje's question whether it wasn't dangerous to start fires and whether the farmers wouldn't get angry, Mother replied that the farmers wanted it done because the piles of potato greens were too hard to plow under. Was Father going to burn the greens of their potatoes too? "Maybe. We'll see," said Mother.

Fransje stopped, staring into the distance. His eyes followed the row of elm trees on the dike to where he knew the heron nests were. He was struck by the increasing barrenness of the trees. Only the crowns were still covered by a frail yellow haze. Mother had been right about the leaves. Bram asked him what he was staring at. No, you couldn't see the herons from here, he replied. Besides, if they hadn't left already, they would be leaving pretty soon, for they spent their winter in a far-away country.

Father was very pleased with the potato crop. There were hardly any diseased potatoes, and every plant had some ten or twelve of the large purple-blue tubers as well as several planters and little ones. The latter were for the pig. The potatoes glistened with a soft sheen in the dark, loamy soil. Now and then Fransje helped Mother fill her basket, but he kept running off to look for treasure. In a bare spot where the potatoes had already been harvested, he heaped up the potato greens. Later Eine would light it. To start such a fire was all right because it didn't endanger the surroundings.

The next day passed much more slowly for Fransje than the first. The novelty was already wearing off and he sometimes became bored. But then Eine pointed out all the blackberry bushes growing in one of the shallow ditches dividing the fields. Fransje immediately raced over there. The bushes were covered with delicious berries. Each lovely, plump fruit was a heart-shaped cluster of tiny berries. What Fransje found most beautiful, however, was the gray-blue hue that was caused by a very thin film of wax on the berries. It disappeared when you touched them, and then they looked blue-black and much shinier. There were so many blackberries, he wished he had a pail for them. Since they didn't have one, he couldn't take any home. Mother told him he couldn't put them in a lunchbag because then they'd all get squashed and the juice would seep through the bag. Fransje thought it a shame that all those blackberries would go to waste, but he couldn't very well eat them all himself. However, Father said the birds liked them too, and that they would eat most of them. And the overripe blackberries that fell on the ground would be eaten by tiny insects, or they would send down roots and sprout new plants for next year. In nature very little went to waste.

Fransje was glad to surrender them to the birds and even to the insects, except to the earwigs which scared him. For the children told each other that they crawled into your ears and made you deaf because they burrowed all the way into your head. Fransje knew what the nasty creatures looked like. Each had two mean little pincers at the tail-end of its thin body with which it could pinch viciously. If you touched it with a stick, it curled its tail-end upward and the little pincers went to work.

Fransje couldn't walk far in the shallow ditch, for hundreds of spider webs barred his way. He repeatedly had to scramble in and out of the ditch. Of course, he could easily break the fragile webs by simply walking on. But he didn't want to. He didn't want to destroy those splendid works of art and make the spiders do all that work over. He knew what a long time it took, for he had often watched spiders as they spun their webs. Besides, he didn't want those sticky cobwebs all over him because they were hard to get off your clothes. He was also a little leery of those fat spiders; they could scurry over you so swiftly. When they hung there placidly in the middle of their webs, you'd think they were asleep. But touch them with a straw and they shot to some hiding place like an arrow from a bow, or they let themselves fall straight down on a silver thread that ran out of their fat bums. They were such hideous things with all those legs sticking out in all directions. They looked something like the little crabs along the beach.

Wantje told him that these were called cross-spiders, and it was a good name, for they did indeed have a grisly cross on their bulbous backs. They were also rather cruel creatures, for they lived off their prey. They didn't build those beautiful webs just for the fun of it; these were their traps by which they caught other insects. Fransje didn't particularly like flies, but if you were a fly happily zooming along in the air, it must be horrible to suddenly land in one of those webs and the next moment find yourself being tightly wrapped in hundreds of threads at once. Fransje had seen it happen often enough and sometimes he even caught flies and tossed them into one of those webs. But it always made him wonder how he'd like it if he weren't Fransje, but a fly. Brrr! But that was how it was in nature. Big animals ate little animals, and big fish ate little fish. But the big ones in turn were in danger of being devoured by even bigger ones. Mother said this was the result of sin. Not the animals' sin, for they had no souls and therefore could not sin. But the sin of Adam and Eve. When they ate from that one tree, the whole world was messed up. What had the animals who now ate other animals eaten before then? It was too bad spiders didn't like blackberries, because then they could eat their fill, and they wouldn't have to hang around waiting so long. There were lots of webs that didn't contain a single fly, so those spiders must be hungry. Flies weren't brainless either. They made sure they stayed away from those beautiful but dangerous webs.

Because the blackberries were very sweet, Fransje ate more than was good for him. The dull stomach ache returned. But he didn't let it bother him; he had it so often he was almost used to it.

It was fun to walk in the shallow ditch, because when he stood on his tiptoes he could just look over the banks and then the world appeared flat before his eyes. He could even look under the beet greens and see their swollen bellies. Each beet looked like it had an umbrella formed by its own thick leaves. Fransje imagined he was as little as a mouse so that he could walk under them. It would be like walking through a large forest.

About three o'clock the farmer came to see how they were doing. Happily he didn't have Norma with him. Fransje was glad to see him again, and secretly hoped the man would invite him along for a boat ride. But to his disappointment he didn't say a word about his eel traps. He didn't even mention their first meeting.

He had a much different surprise for Fransje. He said, "Fransje, see that tall tree in the corner of the orchard?"

Fransje nodded.

"You know what kind of tree that is?" he continued. Yes, that was some kind of nut tree, Fransje remembered from his mother's words this past summer. But he didn't remember the name of the nuts, nor did he have any idea what they looked or tasted like. The only nuts he knew were peanuts, which they sometimes got on Sunday.

"Come along with me," invited the farmer. Fransje followed him like a puppy. This orchard too was surrounded by tall bushes, but not hawthorn bushes this time. The few leaves on them looked just like those on the tall trees in front of Fransje's house. They weren't as dense as a hawthorn hedge either and didn't have any thorns. So Fransje and the farmer could easily push their way through. The farmer stooped and picked up something from between the leaves on the ground. He held his outstretched hand under Fransje's nose, showing him a large, elongated, dark brown object. It looked ugly and dirty.

"That's what's called a walnut," said the farmer. He wiped it clean on his pantleg and cracked it between his strong thumb and forefinger. "Here, taste it, and see if you like it." Fransje put half the weirdly shaped nut in his mouth and chewed. He beamed. It tasted delicious, even better than peanuts. "Well," said the farmer. "Look around. Maybe you can find more of them. You can keep all you find and take them home with you."

He didn't have to repeat himself to Fransje. Immediately Fransje began digging in the rustling leaves, eagerly keeping a sharp lookout. Soon he had a handful of nuts and stuffed them into his pants' pockets. The farmer, meanwhile, had crossed the orchard to the house. That was fine with Fransje, for now he was responsible to no one but himself. When he had gathered another handful, he reflected how much easier it would be if he had something to put the nuts in. Suddenly he remembered the lunchbag in which they had brought their sandwiches. Again he pushed his way through the tall bushes and ran back to his parents and brothers. Wantje, who would join them after school, still wasn't there.

Proudly and excitedly he showed them his treasure and hurriedly asked them for a lunchbag, for there were piles more of the nuts!

He didn't give away a single nut to his brothers because first he wanted to see how many he could gather in the bag. Away he dashed again, and possessively searched every nook and cranny for more of the lovely nuts. Soon he discovered that the round, black and green balls that didn't in the least look like nuts nevertheless contained one. He would have let them lie if he hadn't accidentally crushed one with his wooden shoe. Thinking they were green apples, he had at first disdainfully kicked them aside. His discovery helped him fill his bag almost to the top.

Perhaps it was due to excitement, but suddenly that awful stomach ache was back, and now it was worse than ever. Involuntarily he dropped to his knees, pressing the bag of nuts to the place where he felt the burning, stabbing pain. He blamed himself for having eaten too much fruit and deeply regretted that he hadn't left the blackberries for the birds. An intense wave of nausea made everything around him spin. Although his first thought was for Mother, he didn't go to her. Maybe it would pass. He swallowed frantically to keep from vomiting, remaining doubled up to ease the pain. It seemed to help, for a little later the attack subsided. With a clammy, purple-stained hand he wiped the sweat off his forehead.

The fun of gathering nuts had palled. Besides, not many could have escaped his searching eyes. Slowly he straightened up and decided to return to the unsuspecting group of potato pickers. Seeing them working so peacefully soothed him. Since the pain didn't return, his former good spirits rekindled. He began trotting back and while he was still quite far away he started shouting, "Mom, Dad, guys! Look how many nuts I found!"

Finally his voice carried to them. Not far away in the other direction Wantje was also approaching the small group. They all looked up from their work and saw the excited little figure running toward them waving the bag of nuts over his head.

It was a scene that they all would recall hundreds of times for the rest of their lives. Not deliberately and joyfully, but compelled as passive onlookers to a painful drama. This scene, which at first seemed as peaceful as the pastel-colored world of late fall around them, would etch itself into their hearts until every line became a deep, black furrow. Or were they, especially in Mother's case, red lines that continually wept blood?

With the bag of nuts over his head and a glad smile on his berry stained face, he came running toward them. But the new exclamation that his happy lips were already beginning to form was twisted into a hoarse scream unlike any he had ever uttered. His body buckled like a reed. The bag which he was still clutching tightly struck the broken earth with a dull thud. Then he was writhing on the ground like a worm. His face wasn't white, but ashen.

For an indivisible moment Mother sat staring at him as though paralyzed, both hands resting on the basket before her, which she was just about to move. Then she leaped up like a doe that knows her young one is in danger. The next moment she was kneeling over him. "Fransje! My boy!" she panted. "What's wrong?" His only answer was a heart-rending wail, until finally she made out the word "stomach."

Father knelt beside the writhing little figure too. Carefully he scooped him up in his large hands and laid him in Mother's outstretched arms. Wantje, who had just come walking up, first stood by looking stunned. Then she put her hands over her eyes, and crying in fear she buried her face in Bram's lap. Eine still held the potato he had picked up when the scene began and was digging his nails into the hard skin without feeling the pain that this caused.

Then the screaming stopped. Fransje lay limp against Mother's breast. He looked up into her eyes and smiled faintly. "Where are my walnuts?" he asked hoarsely. Father was holding the bag in his hand, although he didn't know when or why he had picked it up, and handed it to Fransje. "Here, my big helper," he said, and there was a pleading note in his voice. Then with a wide sweep of his arms and a few long strides he gathered together a pile of dry potato greens and made a bed with it. "I'd put him on here for a while," he suggested to Mother. Gently she laid him down. Fransje's teeth were chattering. Bram raced off at Mother's request to fetch a couple of empty potato sacks and their jackets. They all helped cover Fransje.

Mother asked him if he wanted a drink of water, but Fransje shook his head. He closed his eyes as if he wanted to go to sleep.

"Shouldn't I take him home?" she asked Father, who looked at his watch.

"It's much too far for you to carry him all that way. In an hour it will be lunch time. Let's wait and see for awhile. Then I or one of the boys can carry him."

The joy of the harvest had vanished. They all suddenly felt tired and decided to pick up the potatoes that were already dug up, cover them, and then go home.

Bram and Eine offered to take turns carrying Fransje, but Father merely shook his head. The boys and Wantje tried to keep a conversation going with Fransje, but he didn't feel like talking. At first a pale contrast to the berry stains, his cheeks were now bright red. Mother studied him anxiously. Tomorrow she would call the doctor; she didn't like the looks of it.

At home she put Fransje in Maria's bed and told Wantje that tonight she would have to sleep upstairs in Fransje's bed. If he had another attack, three grown-ups would be nearby. She asked him if he had been going regularly the last few days, and when in response to further probing and prompting he admitted that he sometimes skipped a few days, she suggested that *Haarlemmer* oil would help him feel better. Quickly she added, "Reverend Kok will be here this coming Sunday, you know, and then you don't want to be sick, do you? If you take your *Haarlemmer* oil like a big boy, perhaps you'll be better in no time and then you'll be able to go to church with us."

Fransje looked up in mild surprise. That was right, it had completely slipped his mind, probably because of the excitement of the potato harvest. With no less revulsion, but without protesting, he quickly swallowed down the smelly concoction. He had no appetite, however. Merely seeing the chewing faces around the table was more than he could tolerate, so he turned on his other side, facing the wall. Soon he slipped off into a light sleep.

It was a good thing Mother had kept him downstairs, for a little past midnight he had another attack that sent him crawling across the bed, screaming and vomiting violently. Maria had to get clean sheets and a clean nightgown for herself from the linen closet. Mother and Maria nervously hurried back and forth, and even Father, who was usually impossible to wake up, was pacing the room looking anxious. When the pain subsided a little, Mother took Fransje on her lap and gently rocked him back and forth, "like a little baby," thought Fransje, but he liked it anyway. Mother's long, black ponytail, which flowed out from under her nightcap and hung over her shoulder, kept tickling his cheek.

A worried, gloomy atmosphere pervaded the room, accentuated by the faint yellow glow of the nightlamp and the loud, inexorable tick-tock of the wall clock. Father and Mother said little, because they couldn't or were afraid to articulate their fears. Maria crawled back into her bed; she had to be up early this morning.

Finally Fransje went back to sleep. Although he didn't feel very hot, he was obviously running a fever, for the redness had returned to his cheeks and his arms and legs kept twitching. "You'd better stay home tomorrow," Father said quietly. "And keep Kees home from school too," he added reflectively. Mother understood and nodded. "Lord, please spare our boy," her lips mumbled silently as she tucked him in beside Maria. She lay awake for a long time in her own bed beside Father, who was snoring again. "Lord, please spare our boy," she repeated over and over.

About eight o'clock Fransje had another attack. Arjaan and Kees and Wantje were still home. "Run to the doctor!" Mother cried to Arjaan. "And ask him to come as soon as he can. And Wantje, tell Kees's teacher that he won't come to school today."

Meanwhile she tried to ease her boy's suffering. The *Haarlemmer* oil was forgotten, for she knew it couldn't touch the cause of Fransje's sickness. Fearful, unformulated premonitions flashed through her heart and mind. "O Lord, Lord, please spare our child for Jesus' sake," she moaned inwardly.

The doctor arrived at nine o'clock. Fransje must have been one of his first patients on his daily rounds through the polders. He took Fransje's pulse, looked down his throat, made him say aah, felt under his armpits, probed his sides and stomach and finally pressed a little harder on the lower right side of his belly. His question whether it hurt seemed superfluous since Fransje's contorted face left no room for doubt. He asked Mother when the pains had started and whether Fransje had complained about stomach pains before. He also inquired about his appetite, his bowel movements, and how often he had vomited.

He himself gave out very little information. Alarmed by the familiar pungent odor, he only said that under no circumstances was Fransje to have any more *Haarlemmer* oil. And Mother shouldn't try to get him to eat unless he asked for something. That afternoon one of the school-age children should stop by to pick up some medicine which he would prepare when he got back home.

"What's wrong with him, Doctor?"

"I'm not sure yet. We'll have to wait and see what develops. If it gets any worse, let me know immediately. In any case, I'll come by again tomorrow."

The doctor was one of the few people in town who owned a car. Fransje knew this, and now the car was standing in front of their house. Under less traumatic circumstances he would have been secretly proud that the doctor had come specially for him, but now the price paid for that honor was too high. Wearily he settled back into his pillows.

Mother quite quickly transgressed one of the doctor's commands by trying to get Fransje to eat something. She entertained the hope that if only he had something to eat, he'd probably feel better soon. But Fransje had no appetite whatsoever, not even for rusk soaked in milk and sprinkled with brown sugar, something he loved and something she tried to tempt him with.

About ten o'clock suddenly he felt much better. He called Mother to his bed and asked for the walnuts. Sitting up in bed, he emptied the bag on the blankets in the hollow formed by his legs. He dug into them with his fingers, enjoying the pock-pock and clackity-clack of the nuts as they tumbled against each other. A little later he asked for the little mug from the flooded land, and still later for the Bible storybook. Mother patiently catered to him, happy to see his interests returning, which gave her new hope. While she was standing on the chair to get the book down from the linen closet, he also asked her to bring down the reed plumes while she was at it. He wanted to see them from nearby once more.

They were covered with dust, so Mother first had to shake them off outside. He couldn't take them into bed with him, because then the dry stalks would break. Here, she would put them on a chair right beside the bed.

At eleven-thirty he suffered another attack, more severe and longer than any of the preceding. Exhausted and anxious about Fransje, Mother momentarily succumbed to a fit of nerves and, at her wits' end, sent Kees to town for the doctor. As soon as he was out the door, however, she had second thoughts. Now she was all alone with Fransje and perhaps Kees's help would be sorely needed at home. Frantic, she dashed to the back room for water and the bedpan, but before she could find the latter, Fransje's cries for help summoned her back. She struggled with the blankets which had tangled themselves about his writhing body, scraping her arm on the sideboard of the bed. "O Lord God!" she moaned. "Help us!" An idea dropped into her mind: she would call Wullemiene from next door. But she didn't dare run outside to the back door and leave Fransje alone. So she ran to the wall beside the chimney and thumped against it with a footstove. She didn't wait for an answer but shouted, "Wullemiene, please help! Fransje's sick!"

A little later the old woman was standing beside her. She asked no questions and said hardly a word. Walking into the back room, she turned on the faucet. Then she soaked a cloth in the cold water and laid it on Fransje's abdomen. That seemed to help, for he gradually relaxed. A little later, however, he vomited again, and the spasms of pain also returned.

Suddenly the doctor was standing beside them, seeing Fransje at his worst. Returning from his rounds, he had decided to take a quick look at the child because he was uneasy about the case. He yanked the sideboard out of its slots and threw the tangled blankets into the middle of the room. The walnuts clattered in all directions over the floor. "He didn't eat any of those, did he?" he asked sternly. "No, he just played with them." The doctor positioned Fransje to lessen the pain. Then he groped in his bag and took out a little envelope with powder in it. "Dissolve this in a little water," he ordered. Mother immediately complied and then fed the bitter drink to Fransje.

From the hall came the shuffle of feet. Father and the boys were home, and a little later the other children also arrived. The doctor beckoned Father and waved all the others into the back room. Wullemiene stayed in the room. Closing the door, he gave Mother and Father a piercing look. Then he said, "I advise you to take the boy to the hospital in Bergendaal as quickly as possible. There's a train at one-thirty. I'd take him in the car, but as you know, I have appointments in the afternoon and I can't leave my patients waiting. As soon as I get home, I'll call the hospital."

The doctor's words fell on their ears with devastating force. "O Lord God!" whispered Mother, clasping both hands to her breast. "What's wrong with him?" Father asked hoarsely.

"I think he has acute appendicitis. I hope it's not too late."

Fortunately they didn't know the meaning of the word "acute," but the effect of the message was not softened for the word "appendicitis" was ominous enough, especially since they had known people who had died from it. They stood staring as if struck dumb. Wullemiene broke the heavy silence by saying, "I'll look after the young ones when they come home from school. And I'll fix supper tonight too."

The doctor looked at Father, who nodded imperceptibly. Then the doctor left, and so did Wullemiene. "God keep you," she said.

The medicine brought Fransje some relief. He lay back, quietly watching the anxious faces. He hadn't understood the doctor's words at all and looked questioningly from one to the other. Mother wept silently into her gray handkerchief. So Father said, "Fransje, my big helper, pretty soon we're going on a train ride. Mother and me and you. We're going to the hospital in Bergendaal. They have some real smart doctors over there and they'll try to make your stomach ache go away."

He couldn't go on because he too got a lump in his throat. Dinner, which Mother had almost allowed to burn, had been rescued in the nick of time by Maria, who now set the table. But no one was hungry. Most of the food remained in the pans and plates untouched.

Father himself took up the Bible and turned to where they had left off last night. It was Isaiah 40: "Comfort ye, comfort ye my people, saith your God . . . ." That was as far as he got. They were the words that had freed him many years ago and assured him of his share in Christ and of his reconciliation with a holy and righteous God. Did the words also contain a promise for now? His voice failed him and the words swam in a sea of tears so that he could no longer read them. He slid the Bible to Maria, who finished the chapter. But before she did, Mother was also hiding her face behind her handkerchief. As verse 11 was being read, she began weeping softly: "He shall feed his flock like a shepherd: he shall gather the lambs with his arms, and carry them in his bosom . . . ." She thought of Fransje. And suddenly she heard again the words he had spoken to her months ago: "Mommy, when you go to heaven, will you take me along in your arms? And will you hold me tight so I don't fall?"

Father, who didn't want to say a form prayer now, could hardly finish his prayer. His words kept drowning in tears and catching in a swollen throat. Nevertheless, driven by deep need, he committed Fransje into the hands of the great Healer. He alone could help when Fransje sank to death's door. He alone could support and bear them up when they stood by helplessly. The children sat with folded hands before their eyes so they could at the same time wipe away their tears unnoticed.

There was no immediate answer to the prayer; at least no text or Psalm entered Father's soul with power. But peace descended into all their hearts, giving them the strength to do what had to be done at the moment and what God had laid before them.

"It's time for us to get ready," said Mother as she put her gray handkerchief away under the pillow in Father's chair.

11

On the way to the station they met few people, which was to be expected since the workers were all out in the fields and the children in school. Seeing them leaving, Wullemiene hurriedly threw open her front door and came shuffling toward them. She bent her old, wrinkled face close over Fransje's, took one of his hands and pressed a silver guilder into it. Then she kissed him on the forehead and said, "Goodbye, Fransje, my boy." And to Father and Mother she again said, "God keep you." That was all. Then she shuffled back into the house.

Playing in her front yard, Neeltje looked up puzzled as she saw the threesome going by. She asked Fransje where they were going and if he wanted to play with her. Then some of the old pride sounded in Fransje's voice as he told her that he was going to ride on the train and that he had to go to the hospital. Neeltje quickly ran inside to tell her mother. But they didn't wait.

Thanks to the medicine, Fransje was suffering no pain or discomfort, but he felt a little groggy. In one hand he tightly clutched a brown paper bag in which Mother, at his express request, had put the Bible storybook. He had also wanted to take along the bag of walnuts and the little mug, but Mother had advised against it. If he accidentally dropped all those nuts on the floor in the hospital, it might not be appreciated. And if the mug fell on the floor, it would break into a thousand pieces, and he wouldn't want that, would he? Then she had to promise to take good care of it and to save the nuts until he came back.

At the station they met Mr. van Houten. He hadn't come to take the train but to pick up a package from the same train they were taking. He asked them if they were going on a trip, although he thought it strange that Father was carrying Fransje. When Father in a few words informed him of the reason for their trip, he gave Fransje a look of compassion. As their eyes met, he suddenly remembered the incident with the chaise. Momentarily he averted his eyes; then taking a step forward, he stammered, "I haven't sworn since that night—honest! And our dear Lord will make you better soon."

Fransje didn't reply because he simply didn't know what to say. Besides, the train was coming. Its wheels ground and squealed as it came to a hissing, steaming halt. Doors opened and several travelers and the conductor calmly stepped down. Motioning with his head he directed Father to one of the open doors. Mother climbed in and found a seat in the empty compartment, followed closely by Father carrying Fransje on his arm. Gently Father put him down next to the window, while Mother anxiously asked him if he had any pain.

The conductor slammed the door and shouted something unintelligible. A piercing whistle sounded and the train slowly started moving. This was the moment Fransje had often dreamed about; it had looked so attractive and exciting to him, but now the circumstances were very different from what he had always imagined. He had the disillusioned feeling that although he was the center and cause of this strange journey, the initiative had been taken out of his hands; he was a passive observer who, without a will of his own, had to follow where circumstance led.

Father, too, was musing that man was more often carried along by life than that he lived it himself. A nameless weight pressed on his heart totally at odds with the consolation he had experienced this afternoon at the reading of Isaiah 40. God was giving him no light in this matter. They would simply have to walk in obedience and faith the path God prescribed for them. The Lord was not obliged to inform His children ahead of time what He had in mind for them. All of life was a blind trust—often shaky—that what God does is always for good.

Mother was sitting beside Fransje, opposite Father, who was riding backwards. She tried to cheer up Fransje by drawing his attention to the world outside the window. She pointed to their house—a tiny segment of a ridiculously small strip of red roof tiles partly hidden by the branches and scanty foliage of the orchard. Then she pointed out the De Visser house, also half hidden behind an orchard. The De Visser name suddenly brought Leentje before Fransje's eyes. Without any apparent transition he asked, "Mom, have you ever heard of little boys who died when they were still small?"

The question, which to Mother had no connection with the De Visser house at all, pierced her heart like a dagger. Appalled, she stared at him. Then she said evasively, "Yes, that happens sometimes. But not very often," she quickly added, more to encourage herself than him.

"Do all little kids go to heaven when they die?"

"If they love the Lord they do." Then she gave him a penetrating look. The aftereffects of his piercing question were still sending quivers through her heart, and before she could reflect on it she asked in a voice that sounded almost harsh, "Do you love the Lord?" Her dark eyes bored deep into his soul.

Fransje looked up strangely into Mother's probing eyes. Then he said simply, "Yes, I love the Lord. And I'd like to sit on His lap sometime, like the children in the Bible."

Tears sprang into Mother's eyes. Involuntarily she looked from Fransje to Father, who wrinkled his brow, swallowed several times, and then turned his moist eyes to the window.

In the distance lay their village. The towering steeple watched over it like a shepherd over the flock at his feet. This time Fransje remarked on it. Even the high roof of the church was visible. But it wasn't their church. He asked if they could see their church from here too. "Yes, if you look closely," said Mother. "See those rows of trees on this side of the village? That's the cemetery. And beside the last tree on that end you can see the much lower roof of our church."

No sooner had she spoken the last couple of sentences than she wished she could take them back. But it was too late. He asked, "Are there any little boys in that cemetery?"

Though everything inside her protested, she had to answer.

Helplessly, she said, "Yes, I think so. But let's not talk about that, all right? Do you like riding on the train?"

But Fransje did want to talk about it, though he was finished in a few sentences. He said, "If I'm buried there, I won't stay there for always, because on the last day the Lord will give us a new body, won't He Mom? And then I'll never have another stomach ache. And that Fransje on the flooded land has been waiting lots longer than me."

Abruptly Mother bent over him. Although she had no idea what the last sentence was about, the first one was clear enough. For the second time a dagger pierced her heart right beside the first wound. Without asking him to explain his last observation, she wept into her handkerchief, not the gray one this time, but a white one with a black polkadot border. And Father's burden grew heavier and heavier. Fransje asked himself if what he had said was wrong. Comfortingly he laid his head against Mother's arm and yawned. He felt sleepy.

Little more was said on the trip. Soon their island lay behind them and the train crossed the railroad dam into the province of Brabant. It stopped at several small stations before it finally reached the much larger station at Bergendaal, where they had to detrain.

Father again took Fransje into his strong arms and soon they were swallowed up by the crowd streaming toward the exit. The vaulted roof of the station distorted the melange of sounds into strange, hollow reverberations, but Fransje noticed none of it. Briefly he realized that this was "candy city," but it did not excite him. Not because he was afraid of the unknown that lay ahead, but perhaps the medicine the doctor had given him was to blame. In any case, all sensations and impressions came to him as through a fog, as if a curtain hung between him and reality.

The hospital, called the *Algemeen Burger Gasthuis* (General Civic Hospital), was a large, gray building several stories high. The main entrance stood open and they walked in. Fransje immediately smelled the pungent odor of chloroform that seemed to pervade the entire building. A woman who looked a little like a Zeeland farm girl smiled at them and asked if she could help them. Father called her "sister," which sounded strange to Fransje. Briefly Father described why they were here. The nun said, "Follow me," and led them into a waiting room. There Father had to answer several questions, giving their son's name, where and when he had been born, what their religious affiliation was, and whether Fransje had been baptized.

In a little while another nun came to take Fransje away. She had a friendly face, and he didn't even protest when she took him out of Mother's arms. She told him that pretty soon after he was in bed Mother and Father would be allowed to come and visit him, and that they would be here all afternoon and could sit with him as long as they liked.

He felt safe and at ease in her arms, chatting amiably with her. He asked her if she had a little boy at home too. "No, nuns don't have little boys," she said laughing, "except little boys who come to the hospital. So now you'll be my little boy for awhile." Fransje liked the sound of her voice and the lilting Brabant dialect.

A little later he was dressed in something that looked like a long, white nightgown and was lying in a high bed. The smell he had noticed upon his arrival was here too. Around his bed stood a screen so that it looked like he had his own little room. But when he had entered the ward, he had seen lots of other beds. His bed was in the corner near the door.

The nun did her work noiselessly. Now and then she smiled at Fransje. From its paper bag she took the Bible storybook, which he had refused to surrender to Mother, and she put it on the white night stand beside his bed without looking at it.

On the wall beside his bed upon a little shelf stood a statuette of a man wearing a brown cloak that reached to his bare feet. On his outstretched arm perched three or four tiny birds. There were more birds on his shoulders and even one on top of his bald head. Above the door hung a large crucifix, which Fransje could just see over the screen.

"Are you Catholic?" he asked with an intonation that clearly conveyed disappointment and disapproval. The nun smiled again and nodded.

"What's your name?" he continued, to change the subject.

"Maria," was the reply. "Sister Maria."

"I have a sister Maria too," he confided.

A man in a long, white coat entered his little room. He was carrying a paper that he read very closely. He knew Fransje's name without even asking, for he said, "Fransje, let me feel your stomach." He examined Fransje very carefully and asked him a few questions. He, too, pressed on Fransje's abdomen with the flat of his hand. That hurt. But speaking confidently he promised that they would soon help him get rid of that awful pain.

Suddenly Mother and Father were standing beside his bed. The nun brought a second chair and vanished noiselessly.

Mother was noticeably relieved to see him lying calmly in his clean bed and apparently content. Fransje was much more cheerful too. He asked her to find the picture of the boy who had been raised from the dead by the prophet. Mother took this as an encouraging sign. She had to tell him the story again. Then he asked, "Mom, will you ask the Lord to raise me from the dead too if I die?"

This frightened her again, but she didn't get a chance to answer. Two nuns pushed the screen aside and wheeled a sort of cart beside the bed. Sister Maria was one of them. In a whisper she told Father and Mother that Fransje would be operated on in half an hour and would be gone for some time. So if they wanted to pass the time by going into town for a cup of coffee, that was fine. Otherwise, if they preferred, they could wait in the large waiting room.

Cheerfully she said to Fransje that she was going to take him for a ride. "So climb onto the cart."

The seriousness of the moment weighed heavily on Mother and Father's hearts. Suddenly it hurt Mother to see how willingly he gave himself into the hands of strangers, looking less anxious than he had all day. Or was that a good sign? Nevertheless, two tears ran down her face onto his as she gave him a parting kiss. Although he knew Fransje usually didn't want him to, Father also kissed him; at least he had shaved before leaving home. He called Fransje his big helper.

"Are you going to pray for me?" Fransje cried as the nuns wheeled him away.

The doctor put a little mask over Fransje's nose and mouth and asked him to breathe deeply. In that one deep breath, the strange smell of the entire hospital seemed to sweep into his lungs. Far away he heard a voice telling him to take another deep breath. Dimly conscious of a sense of suffocation and of a stabbing pain in his side, Fransje tried to jerk free. Then suddenly all the trains in the whole world were thundering through his head as they converged on the same spot and crashed with a tremendous roar.

Huge iron soap bubbles popped with deafening explosions. Then everything collapsed, and with dizzying speed he plummeted into a bottomless chasm. Before he reached the end of his fall, however, he drifted into a world of absolute stillness.

Mother preferred to stay in the waiting room, but Father talked her into following the nun's advice. He had served in the army and was, therefore, not as shy and reticent as Mother. Moreover, he had more psychological insight, so he knew the diversion of going out for coffee would do her good. He deliberately made a detour of several blocks before he led her into a bright, clean café.

A talkative young woman came to take their order. She soon found out where her customers were from and what had brought them to the city. She gave them a sympathetic look. As was obvious from her glib, but well-meant advice to "say lots of prayers to our dear Lord," she was Catholic like most people in Bergendaal. She promised to light a candle for their little boy. Father didn't reply to that, but Mother shuddered at the words, which she considered blasphemous. Mother was obviously ill at ease here and with her eyes she signaled Father that she wished to leave.

Again Father took a roundabout way, approaching the hospital from the rear. They had to walk across the spacious hospital grounds to reach the front entrance. Several patients were strolling about the grounds, some accompanied by nuns. A few were on crutches, others had an arm or leg in a cast or bandages around their heads, and still others were being pushed around in wheelchairs. "Isn't there a lot of suffering in the world?" remarked Mother.

The clock in the high, cavernous waiting room slowly ticked away the seconds. Every time the door opened, they hoped someone was coming to tell them about Fransje. How often had they looked up in vain?

"What do you think of our boy's chances?" Father asked Mother straightforwardly. Mother's eyes flooded with tears. She shrugged her shoulders and whispered, "I don't know. But the Lord is almighty . . . . What do you think?" Father didn't know either. He said, "The Lord is keeping silent." By that he meant that God had not shed any light on the matter. They would have to wait patiently to see what the Lord had in store for their child and for them.

"Lord, make us submissive to Thy will," Mother prayed in her heart.

Fransje had been lying in his bed on the large ward for quite some time, but he still hadn't recovered consciousness. The nurses were watching for the first signs of nausea. When the worst of it was over, they sent a message to his parents that they could come.

Father gently pushed Mother before him until they were behind the screen. There lay their child, and he was breathing. He was alive! Thank God, he was alive. He had been returned to them. Perhaps everything was going to be all right after all. Perhaps that great load was going to be lifted from their hearts for good.

Mother bent over Fransje. Momentarily she flinched at the overpowering smell of chloroform. Then she kissed his face — that beloved face. Fransje turned away his head. He groaned and became restless. The nun who had been standing silently behind them noiselessly floated forward holding a little basin ready. She was just in time. Supporting Fransje with one hand, she gently pressed on the bandage under his gown with the other. Then she wiped his mouth and eased him back down onto the bed. Fransje opened his eyes and for a moment they rested on Mother's face. A wan smile played about his lips. He recognized her. Then he sank back into unconsciousness.

Another nun arrived and took them into the hall, where the doctor was waiting for them. He opened conversation by saying, "I'm glad that's over!" His voice imbued them with hope and confidence.

"How is he now, Doctor?"

"As well as can be expected under the circumstances. Of course, Fransje will have a rough couple of days, but you'll see how quickly he recovers after the third day. It's amazing how much children can take. Often much more than adults."

"Yes, as long as death stays away," Father replied.

"Of course, of course," conceded the doctor. "When are you planning to go home? Do you know when the trains to Zeeland run? I know that the last one leaves at eleven o'clock. You can stay with Fransje as long as you want, but there won't be much to do because he'll probably sleep most of the day."

Mother latched on to his confident tone as if to a life-buoy. Wasn't that doctor friendly? For that matter, so were the nuns.

Did they really mean it or were they just pretending in order to win souls or do good works to get to heaven?

Slowly Fransje regained consciousness. When Mother asked him if he had any pain, he shook his head. But when he tried to sit up, a grimace of pain passed over his face, and he immediately dropped back into his pillow. Mother told him not to sit up because the big cut in his stomach which the doctor had sewed shut could only heal if he lay absolutely still.

Fransje's eyes again fell on the image on the wall. "Who is that?" he asked. "Some Roman Catholic saint," said Father. "But which one I don't know." Fransje told himself that next time he saw that friendly nun Maria, he would ask her.

Finally the moment came which Mother had been dreading. Gently she informed Fransje that they would have to go home now but that he would have to stay here a few nights. His face fell. Couldn't he sleep in Maria's bed again? No, first the big cut in his stomach had to heal. He wouldn't want it to open up again while Father was carrying him, would he? That would be awful, for then he could bleed to death. Besides, the doctors and nurses had to keep an eye on him, because unlike ordinary people such as Father and Mother, they knew exactly what to do if something went wrong.

How long would he have to stay here? Weren't they coming back until they came to take him home? Father promised that Mother would come to see him tomorrow, and he would come Saturday. Maybe Maria or Bram would come and pay him a visit too. Was that okay? Yes, if that was how it had to be. But then he couldn't go to church on Sunday when Reverend Kok preached! Yes, but they couldn't do anything about that. They would let him know that Fransje was in the hospital and then he would pray for Fransje on Sunday. And they, too, would ask the Lord to make Fransje better.

Fransje had a very restless night. One nurse spent the entire night beside his bed watching over him. The doctors also kept a close eye on him. He was still running a temperature; however, this was not in itself alarming. The nurse noted a moderate discharge of pus, which could be either a good or a bad sign. It depended on how much was collecting in his abdominal cavity.

The next morning Sister Maria again entered the ward. First

she came to take a look at Fransje. She washed his face and hands, asking if he had slept well. He nodded. Though she couldn't take Mother's place, he was glad to see her. He pointed to the statuette of the saint and asked her who that was. Oh, that's St. Francis of Assissi. Who's that? Well, he was a very good man. He lived hundreds of years ago and did many good deeds. Why were all those birds sitting on his arm and shoulders and head? Oh, he loved them very much. They were his friends. He would talk and preach to them.

You mean he was a preacher? Sister Maria hesitated. She looked at him and then she said, "Yes, something like that." Then in sudden delight she added, "Did you know that you were named after him, Fransje? He was called Francis and you're called Fransje. That's the same name. Do you love birds too?"

Fransje answered with a heart-felt yes. But the skinny man in the long brown robe preached to the birds. Did he think they had souls? He eyed the figurine suspiciously. Sister Maria continued, "St. Francis also loves little boys. You should ask him to pray for you that you may get better soon."

"But I thought you said he was dead? Then he can't hear me, can he? Do you pray to him?"

Yes, admitted the nun, she did. Her order was named after him so he was her patron saint.

Fransje's look showed a mixture of amazement, disappointment, sympathy and indignation. Growing excited, he said sharply, "But you mayn't pray to dead people. The Lord don't like that one bit. And you mayn't make graven images either. The Lord don't like that either. You better ask the Lord to give you a new heart and to forgive you for praying to images. Then if you're really and truly sorry some day He'll take you into heaven with Him."

Fransje had learned Mother's lessons very well. He repeated almost word for word what she had told him several months ago, even using the words "graven images," which were barely part of his vocabulary.

Now it was Sister Maria's turn to stare in amazement. Was this little fellow an accursed little heretic, or . . . or . . . a pocket-sized saint? She had never heard anyone speak like that before, and certainly not a child. The amazement in her eyes slowly gave way to a look that Fransje had often seen in Mother's eyes when he had grieved her. He was sorry that his words had hurt her. By way of conciliation he said, "I'll pray to the Lord for you." And in a less vehement, much milder tone, he repeated, "And if you're really truly sorry, He'll make you His child and some day take you into heaven with Him."

Then the nun did something in direct violation of the rules of her order and of the hospital: she quickly bent over Fransje's bed and planted a tender kiss on his forehead. There were tears in her eyes. "And I'll pray for you," she whispered. "To our dear Lord," she added reassuringly.

Just before noon Fransje received unexpected company, a tall man wearing a long robe with a row of buttons that lined the front of the robe from his protruding Adam's apple to his feet. The eyes in his ruddy, smooth-shaved face were cold and gray. He had finished his rounds on the ward and now he stopped a moment beside Fransje's bed because it was near the exit.

"What's your name?" he asked without showing any real interest.

"Fransje. Fransje Weststrate."

"Have you been baptized?"

Fransje had never really thought about it, but he nodded.

"Where do you go to church?"

"In our village."

After a slight hesitation the strange visitor asked, "If you die, where will you go?"

"To heaven, to the Lord Jesus."

"How do you know?"

"Because I love Him. And if you love the Lord and ask Him for a new heart, then you're His child and then you can go and be with Him in heaven when you die."

"Who told you that?"

"Mo . . . the Lord Jesus said it Himself in the Bible. Just look in my book," he added, indicating with his eyes the book on the night stand.

Casting a fleeting glance at the book, the priest turned and mumbling a few unintelligible words beat a hasty retreat.

About two-thirty Mother returned. Fransje was fiercely happy to see her. And Mother was happy to see him so cheerful and well. He asked about Father and all his brothers and sisters and where she had put the walnuts.

Mother told him that this evening they would harvest their own potatoes. Father had asked her to tell him that. And next week the potatoes would be delivered to the house. Maybe then he'd be home again, and then he could see them piled in the cellar. Wouldn't that be fun?

She couldn't stay with him as long as yesterday because now she had to observe visiting hours. That was a sign that he was doing well and getting better. But she had brought him a surprise. See what she had brought: a bunch of grapes. She had bought them especially for him in a store in Bergendaal. "You've never tasted grapes before, have you? Here, put one in your mouth. But be sure to spit out the pits and skins!"

Had he eaten anything yet, and was the food good in the hospital? Were the doctors and nurses nice to him? And how was his stomach? Did it still hurt? Let Mother take a peek at it.

She lifted the blanket and peered under his gown. Fear seized her. Fear at the reddish brown tube that sprouted out of his belly to vanish into a large wad of cotton that was soaked with filthy, greenish brown mucus. Fear at the sight of the stomach itself, which was much larger than usual. Fear at the cold bag lying on his abdomen.

"It has ice in it," said Fransje, proud that he could provide such important information. Mother asked him if he truly had no more pain and if he truly felt better. Yes, he was okay. Here, have a few more grapes, she urged. But Fransje wasn't hungry.

Mother would very much like to speak with the doctor she had met yesterday, but she didn't see him. The nurses she spoke to all assured her that Fransje was doing very well under the circumstances. She must not worry because they would take good care of him.

That Saturday afternoon Mother decided to go to the hospital with Father. She wouldn't get anything done at home anyway. Her thoughts were constantly with Fransje. In the train they again had a whole compartment to themselves. The compartment was not joined to the others by a side aisle but by doors that could be closed. Involuntarily they thought of the first time they had made the trip; now their little boy's absence was a painful void. This time they weren't sitting opposite, but beside each other. Impulsively Mother put her hand in Father's large, callused hand—something married Zeeland couples seldom did.

And because it was an unusual gesture, her breast suddenly convulsed in a dry sob. Moved, Father looked at her. For the first time in his life he sensed what it must be like for a mother to see her child stalked by death. He put his other hand on top of her small hand and in a voice laden with emotion, he said, "Why don't we pray together." How long had it been since they had prayed together alone? Almost twenty years; when they had been newly married and before children had come.

Father prayed. But his prayer was different than usual. Not because he spoke in a whisper, but because he used different words, words that were not meant to be overheard. He used no ponderous clichés, nor the customary intonation. He was simply talking to the Lord. Yet, it wasn't only talk; it was also a quiet moan. He sobbed out their desperation on the bosom of Him who wants to be the Father of His people.

First they of course asked that their child, their Benjamin, might be spared. But if that wasn't in God's will? "O God, then receive him in Your arms. Receive him into the place where there is no sin and no pain and no sorrow, and where no one will ever say, I am sick! And, O Lord, then give us the strength to bear it and the grace to say, Thy will be done."

No conductor came to punch their cards, and at the stops no travelers entered to disturb their prayer. When they detrained in Bergendaal, they weren't sure they had said amen. But it didn't matter. God saw into the heart. And if ever two hearts had been laid bare before Him, it had happened in the train from Zeeland to Brabant.

To their question, "How is Fransje doing?" they received an unqualified, cheerful, "Fine!" But when Mother asked him if he was eating yet, he shook his head. He wasn't hungry. Impatiently Mother waited for an opportunity to take a quick look at his stomach. But the screen had been removed, and there were other visitors on the ward. Under these conditions, she was too bashful to look. She was sure his stomach looked even bigger than it had yesterday. She could tell without lifting the blankets.

When at last she had gathered enough courage, she quickly stole a look under the sheet. His stomach was indeed more swollen, but the bandages were dry and clean, which she took to be a good sign. This time Mother and Father were able to speak to the doctor. In his usual polite tone, he assured them that everything was going normally. Above all they must not worry themselves needlessly, for if something did happen, they would be informed immediately.

When they said goodbye, they promised Fransje that they'd be back to see him as soon as possible. But tomorrow would be Sunday. Would they say hello to Reverend Kok for him?

Father and Mother were both beginning to take heart. True, Father had not yet received a special light, and their hearts went out to God like twin streams, each in its own course. But the claustrophobic feeling in their breasts and the clutching fear in their hearts were beginning to diminish. They fastened onto the doctor's words that once Fransje made it through the third day, he was, humanly speaking, out of danger.

That evening, as was usual when a preacher came to town, Father went to a gathering at the house where the preacher was staying. When Father told them his youngest child was in the hospital, all showed genuine sympathy, including Reverend Kok. He quoted the words from Psalm 34: "Many are the afflictions of the righteous." To which Father replied, "Yes, as long as a man is able to repeat the next line too." This provided a good starting point for the evening's discussion of their spiritual lives. Although all were edified by it, including Father, he could not claim to have received more light concerning Fransje.

The next morning the whole family went to church. All felt the painful void in their midst, and even the younger children were more subdued than usual. Especially when they knelt beside the chairs for their customary pre-church prayer, Fransje's absence weighed heavily on all their hearts.

They felt better when in his prayer the preacher committed "a child in our midst who has been hospitalized" into the hands of the Great Healer and to Him who said, "Suffer the little children to come unto me, and forbid them not: for of such is the kingdom of God." Thereby he was doubtless remembering this summer's incident when the boy had become a living illustration for his sermon.

After church Mother and Father were stopped by several people, whose words of sympathy did their hearts good. Waiting in front of their own house were Kees de Visser and his family, and if some people had spoken to Mother and Father out of a sense of duty, here they could not doubt that the concern was genuine. Mother was especially struck by Leentje's attentiveness and she noticed that her eyes repeatedly filled with tears.

During the noon meal Maria introduced the topic they had all been avoiding: was anyone going to visit Fransje today?

In their circles Sunday was a holy day, devoted solely to the service of God. Because in the final analysis they were partly products of their ecclesiastical and spiritual upbringing, they skirted the danger of a legalistic, rather than an evangelical, Sunday celebration. Although Father didn't come right out and say so, they gathered that he preferred to wait until Monday. Sunday travel—unnecessary Sunday travel—was one of the worst desecrations of the Lord's Day. Unless it was absolutely necessary, they must do nothing that could be postponed to another day. And didn't the doctor say that everything was normal?

None of the others took up the subject, although Maria cast a stealthy glance at Mother. For a moment a tense silence hung in the room. Maria broke it by saying, "I wouldn't be surprised if Kee of Kapelle came today, at least if she knows we have a preacher. She had barely finished speaking when Kee's white cap and black shawl appeared in the window. Father, who was paging through a book of sermons, looked up and saw her coming around the back of the house. Moments later he saw someone else coming, not on foot, but on a bike.

"There comes Kees de Visser!" he exclaimed in surprise. He asked himself whether his appearance had anything to do with their talk after church. As Kee shook hands with everyone, Kees de Visser's voice sounded at the back door. "Come on in!" called Father.

For a moment confusion prevailed, for Mother had just begun to tell Kee about Fransje when Kees began shaking hands with them all, which seemed strange because they had seen him only this morning. Then followed a moment when no one said anything.

"Come on, take a chair," Mother invited Kees, but he replied that he'd better not. Again there was silence. This time it was broken by De Visser as he painfully cleared his throat.

"I came to bring you a message," he began. "The hospital in Bergendaal phoned. It was the director and he asked you to come to the hospital as quickly as possible." Helplessly rubbing his large hands together, he looked from Mother to Father.

His announcement fell like a terrifying thunderclap followed by a breathless silence. Mother was the first to regain her voice. With a cry like that of a wounded animal, she wailed, "Fransje!

Something's happened to Fransje!" She had jumped up from her chair, but fell back, crushed. Her eyes bored into De Visser's as she demanded, "What's wrong? What did the doctor say?"

De Visser could truthfully say that the doctor had said nothing else. Indecisively he turned, starting to leave. "May God give you strength!" he said with effort and stumbled toward the back door.

With deep compassion in her eyes Kee looked from Father to Mother. The few words she spoke fell like drops of oil upon the violent waves of emotion that surged through the room. "When does the train leave?" she asked quietly. At one-thirty Mother wanted to say, but she remembered that today was Sunday, when fewer trains ran than during the week.

"There's one at two-thirty," Maria volunteered. It was quarter to one. Mother was separated from her child by ages. "O God, have mercy!" she moaned. Then she hid her face in her gray handkerchief.

Father had closed his book. He sat and stared straight ahead, his hands supporting his head. At last he said in a quavering voice, "For the thing which I greatly feared is come upon me . . . ."

To this Kee quietly added, "Yes, those were Job's words. He also went through the valley, but the Lord had His good reasons, for the Lord blessed the end of Job more than his beginning." She added: if only they could all come to the same point as Job when, covered with dust and ashes, he debased himself before the face of God. Then the Lord would also come to work His glorious miracles among them. From the timbre of her words it was clear that she included herself among them.

Knowing that the prayer around the chairs would be too much for him, Father asked Kee to request a blessing, almost pleading with her. Without a word of protest, feigned or genuine, she folded her thin hands and pursed her black eyebrows. And heaven, which had seemed so high and distant the last few days, silently descended into their midst. Only once did her soft voice ask the Lord that if it was in His counsel would He return Fransje to his parents and to his brothers and sisters, and heal him completely. But with great intensity she begged God for support during this severe trial and suffering and for oneness with God's will.

Her prayer descended upon their seared hearts like a cool spring rain. She didn't rush, she didn't repeat herself, and her voice betrayed no unusual emotion, until she dwelt on the possibility that perhaps the Lord had decided to take Fransje from them. Then the words flowed more rapidly. If heaven had seemed to be in their midst a moment ago, now the gate stood wide open, and boldly she stepped forward before the throne of God and asked Him if in that event He would confirm His Word that He would gather the lambs—this lamb—into His arms and safely carry it into the heavenly fold.

Everyone wept silently, and after the amen Bram and Eine noisily blew their noses and left the room. A little later Bram returned with red-rimmed eyes and quietly sat down in his chair.

Father told him to take charge of the family, apparently assuming that the others were going to church. Mother told Kee that she was welcome to stay for supper after church. But Kee insisted that she would stay with friends in town.

Wantje was so upset that she was in no condition to go to church, so Father told Bram to stay home with her. Eine had disappeared. Arjaan and Kees quietly left the room, and Maria went to put on her Sunday clothes.

On the one hand, Mother was relieved that she didn't have to mix with all the people on their way to church. She couldn't bear to meet all those looks and answer all those questions. On the other hand, it was unbearable to sit here waiting for the minutes to pass while her heart was crying for her child who was in who knows what kind of distress, crying for her child who needed her.

Fransje lay still in his high bed, his eyes closed. His arms lay stretched out on the white sheet. Now and then he unconsciously drummed his fingers on his stomach, which bulged large under the sheet. He was no longer on the ward, but in a small private room. Occasionally he opened his eyes and looked at Father and Mother—first at Father and then lingeringly at Mother. Earlier he had whispered a little, but now he was too tired to talk.

When Mother thought he was sleeping, she again looked under the sheet. On his stomach lay two ice packs, but the bandages were dry. Now she knew why. The green pus was coming up through his mouth, not in sudden gushes like vomit, but slowly flowing down his cheek in a wide pulsating stream. The only sign that another wave was coming was a slight spasmodic movement in his stomach.

The nurses kept looking in on him. Whenever Mother was too slow to catch the discharge and it spilled on the pillow, they patiently brought another pillow case. Sister Maria came often. She said nothing, but an hour earlier she had conversed briefly with Father—a conversation of only a few sentences. Father had asked her what she thought of Fransje's condition. Evasively she had replied, "The Lord is Almighty." Something in her expression caused Father to blurt in agitation, "But we can't lose the boy! We love him too much!" Then Sister Maria had ended it with, "I know. I love Fr . . . my Fransje too. But I think the Lord loves him even more." Then she had hastened away. Mother had glimpsed two tears tumbling down her pale cheeks.

How do two parents watch at the bed of their dying child? On the one hand, they sit there as two people who are themselves dying—dying not once, but a thousand deaths. On the other hand, they are like two people caught in a dream, for nothing around them seems real or substantial; it cannot, it may not be real. The dimensions of the event far exceed the boundaries of their human understanding. But the unreality is also the result of the anesthetizing potion God has given them—the same potion that Christ refused when He hung on the cross.

Fransje was becoming restless. A grimace of pain passed over his face. His hands groped over the sheet. Mother held the basin ready, but nothing came. Then he opened his eyes and urgently cried, "Maria!"

Mother was frightened, partly because of the strange look in his eyes which rolled searchingly back and forth apparently without seeing anything, for his glance kept sliding past her. But especially because of the name Maria. Whom did he mean? His sister? Or perhaps Sister Maria, or—and she couldn't suppress a surge of jealousy—Mother Mary? Had they in the brief time of her absence stuffed him full of Roman idolatry?

"Maria!" came the urgent cry again with something of his old impatience.

Mother jumped up. She took his hand and said, "Fransje, my boy! Here we are—Father and I." Now his eyes rested on the face that was so dear to him. A glimmer of a smile passed over his face. Then he said a word he hadn't used for months, and it cut through her heart like a sword: "Mommy!"

However, he kept asking for Maria, until almost angrily he said, "Maria, sing me a song!"

Father was berating himself: why hadn't he allowed the children to come along, at least the older ones! His frightened forebodings told him that this was clearly the end. What a fool he was!

Although Maria had set off in the direction of church, she had not gone there. A little past De Visser's house, she had turned right toward the farm where she sometimes helped with the housecleaning. The farmer had a bicycle, and she asked if she could borrow it to go visit her little brother in the hospital because he was failing. Of course they said yes.

Eine hadn't gone to church either. He went to one of his friends to ask if he could use his father's bicycle to see his little brother in the hospital, because he was failing. Of course they said yes.

Neither one knew of the other's plans. They did tell Bram, but a half hour apart, because they did not want or dare to leave before Father and Mother had left.

Although Maria had left after Eine, she reached the hospital first, because Eine had a flat tire underway, which held him up for almost an hour. Therefore Maria didn't see him along the road either.

Panting from the long bike ride, Maria walked into the small room. One look at her little brother made her burst into tears. Mother's parched eyes again filled and Father's hunched shoulders jerked spasmodically. When Maria regained control of herself, Mother told her that Fransje had asked for her.

Although they were speaking in low voices, Fransje must have recognized Maria's voice, for again he cried, "Maria, sing for me!"

With reddened eyes and a stuffed nose, Maria bent over his face and asked him softly, "What should I sing for you, Fransje?"

He didn't answer right away, but a little later he said quite clearly, "Maria, sing Safe . . . ."

Maria stood racking her mind. She knew so many songs and liked to sing often, even songs Father didn't appreciate because they were Arminian. Safe . . . safe . . . safe . . . . Suddenly a light went on: Safe in the arms of Jesus! She had been singing it last week and he had asked her to sing it again.

First she blew her nose once more, cleared her throat, and then taking Fransje's hand in hers, in a trembling but clear voice she softly sang:

> Safe in the arms of Jesus;
> Safe on His gentle breast;

There in His tender mercy,
There shall my soul find rest.

Hear, it's the song of angels
Singing of love and peace
Ringing from heaven's portals
Over the glassy seas.

Father listened to his eldest daughter with bowed head. He admired her love and loyalty, and above all her courage.

Mother wept silently behind her white handkerchief with its border of black polkadots.

When the song was finished, Fransje opened his eyes for the last time. On his face was a radiant smile suffused with happiness and gratitude. And in an almost jubilant voice, he cried, "Yes!"

That was Fransje's last word on earth.

Eine arrived too late to see Fransje conscious. He pressed an impassioned kiss on his forehead and then sat down in a corner of the small room and wept until he was dry.

Fransje's spirit was still on this side of the Jordan, but the river he faced had nothing in common with the actual river of that name in distant Palestine. Nor did it have anything in common with the spiritualized concept of it familiar in Fransje's circles. Yet what faced him, though on his level, was certainly the river between life and death.

Fransje found himself, alone and forlorn, on the mud flats. He didn't ask why he was standing there. They weren't the mud flats near the flooded land, but where he had once gone to pick lamb's ears. The sky over the sea was growing ominously dark. A storm was brewing; he had to get to the dike fast.

Around his waist was a gleaning sack but it was tied too tightly. The strings cut painfully into his stomach and the sack dangling in front of him impeded his walking. Above and beyond the dike the sun was shining. The cement steps glared in the bright sunlight.

He was standing with his face to the dike. But behind him inky black columns of clouds were advancing and so was flood tide, not slowly and gradually as usual, but as swiftly as an attacking army. The black sky and the rolling water merged into a single, ominous threat. The water could be distinguished only by the pale streaks of tumbling whitecaps.

He hurried to the dike as fast as the constricting gleaner's sack, which almost cut off his breath, allowed him. Suddenly, to his horror, he discovered that his way was blocked by a deep, wide runnel. It almost looked as big as the shipping channel, and already the swiftly rising sea had half-filled it. Sea-waves rushed around the bends in wild eddies. He couldn't possibly get across it now. Gingerly he stepped down the slick slope to see if there was a shallow place where he could quickly cross. But the water was dark and roiled. He could not see the bottom.

Climbing back up the bank, he threw a quick glance at the threatening sky. For a moment the black clouds were torn to shreds by angry flashes of lightning, revealing the frightful momentum of the advancing clouds and waves.

Then to his horror another creature appeared between the rising sea and the runnel. With long leaps it bounded ahead of the waves, and with bulging, blood-thirsty eyes, wide, gaping jaws and a flaming, fiercely flapping tongue it headed straight toward him.

It was Norma, Norma with her demonic features. Fransje was trapped between the deep runnel and the hell-hound. If he jumped into the runnel, he would drown, and if he stayed where he was, he would be torn to shreds by the hound's flashing teeth. After that the rising tide would drag his mauled body out into the endless sea.

Again he turned his eyes up toward the dike. Behind it he now suddenly saw the steeple of their village, and then the whole village, no, an endless city. But the colors weren't those of a regular village or city. Much of the city was white as marble, and much of it glittered in the sun like gold. A huge flock of white doves playfully swooped around the steeple, no, around the numerous steeples. The dike, too, kept changing in appearance. The stairs were still there, still glistening white and yellow in the sun; however, they no longer led halfway up the dike, but to a huge gateway standing wide open. The gateway was the entrance to the city of the steeples and the streets of gold. And although a high wall surrounded the city, he could clearly see every street, and they led endlessly in every direction without ever running dead. Along each street bloomed tall white daisies with golden hearts, nodding poppies with lace caps, blood-red and white and lemon-yellow roses, deep-bronze velvet wallflowers, and multicolored sweet williams. Their sweet fragrances wafted over to him against the storm which nearly pushed him into the runnel. Between the splendid buildings stood tall, stately evergreens—so many that they seemed a rustling forest full of birds. He heard the melodies of thrushes, the jubilant songs of skylarks, and the warbling doxologies of nightingales. And he also heard the pealing of bells—of thousands of bells—not the somber bong-bong of funeral bells, but the heart-gladdening, welcoming, playful chiming of a carillon on a holiday.

But close behind him was Norma with her blazing jaws and withering breath. And at his feet the dark waters of the now brimming runnel rushed past him. Once more he cast a frightened glance at the other bank to measure the distance, and his heart sank into his shoes.

Then for the first time he saw the Man who had apparently been standing there all the time waiting for him. It was the Stranger from his dream of long ago. But now He wasn't misty and indistinct like the fluffy clouds that had been along the road then; now His features were sharp and clear and unutterably beautiful. The Man stretched out His hand as if to say, "Come! Don't be afraid to jump. I'll catch you and pull you up the bank."

Norma was right on his heels now. Another second and her teeth would tear into him like knives. He had no other choice: if he must perish, he'd perish. He closed his eyes and jumped. The dark, icy water closed over his head like a grave. It cut off his breath and pressed the last bit of air from his lungs.

Then suddenly everything changed. The outstretched hand from the other bank gripped his, and he was standing on dry ground looking up into the Man's face.

He had lost his wooden shoes in the water. The gleaning sack with the constricting strings had also been swept away, as well as all his old clothes. But he wasn't naked. He was wearing a long, spotless white robe that hung down to his bare feet. In his hand he held a green branch, and on his head he felt the gentle pressure of a golden coronet.

"Come," said the Man, taking him up in His arms. "Let's go through the gate into the city. There I'll introduce you to My Father, and to all the holy angels and all God's children, large and small, who came here before you."

When he heard these words and saw the indescribable beauty and splendor around him, Fransje's heart flooded with blessedness and love, peace and joy. And this was reflected in the expression of his stilled face.

12

Father and Mother accompanied Fransje to the bank of the dark river. There that inexorable mystery called death commanded them to stop. They did hold his hand to the very end, and Mother whispered words of love to him as if to assure him that she would never leave him, but at the same time they were slowly overcome by the certainty that the powerful cords of their love were not strong enough to keep Fransje with them.

Where do parents gain the strength not to succumb when they see the child they love, their own flesh and blood, die before their eyes? That strength is a gift from God that wells up from the unknown depths of their own hearts. That strength deadens their own pain and enables them to ease, as much as is possible, their child's suffering.

Fransje's parents didn't make an uproar and didn't go into paroxysms of grief. On the contrary, every quiet movement they made, every hushed word they spoke was consciously aimed at surrounding their lamb with the support of their love. They didn't even ask themselves if he was aware of all these things.

Passed away calmly and peacefully . . . passed away calmly and peacefully—the phrase kept running through Father's head after Fransje had expelled his last breath. And for a moment they had the illusion that he had slipped into a peaceful sleep, and that now all would be well.

Fransje did indeed pass away calmly and peacefully. He hardly stirred. For the last two hours he had stopped vomiting too. And after his "Yes!" to Maria's singing, he never spoke again. Only a few times did he open his eyes and stare around searchingly. Once his glance rested on Mother, and although his eyes no longer seemed to see anything, for a moment a glimmer of a smile seemed to glide over his face. Mother stood up and called his name several times, softly but urgently. But his eyes remained closed and she got no answer.

Then she found another outlet for her love. Looking under the sheet, she saw that Fransje's bandages were dry, but that the bed was wet. A wave of compassion surged up from her heart, bringing hot tears to her eyes. There lay Fransje, who took such pride in having left infancy far behind, like a helpless child in his own urine. One of his legs was twisted to the side a little. Gently she took it in her hands to straighten it; a sword lanced her heart, for the foot was already cold as stone and so was the other one. Then she knew that he would never return. After carefully covering him, she bent over his face and whispered, "Lord, please take him. You may have our child. And please do it quickly; we can't take it much longer. For Your name's sake."

Less than a minute after Fransje had passed away, Sister Maria was standing beside Mother. In her hand she had a large, white handkerchief wet with cologne. With it she bathed Mother's pale, tired face and also her wrists and arms. Then she took her by the hand and with a look signaled Father, Maria, and Eine to follow her. "You may see him again shortly," she said reassuringly. "But first the doctor must examine him and the sisters will lay him out."

She led them to the waiting room, where three days ago—or was it three centuries?—Father and Mother had waited out the operation. A little later she returned with five steaming cups of coffee. She sat down beside Mother and told them all to have a cup of coffee to keep them from fainting. She said this in a way that included herself. Softly she talked about Fransje, who was such a sweet boy and who loved our Lord so much.

Father, looking ten years older as he sat slumped and staring passively, suddenly looked up and said, almost sharply, "How do you know? How can you say that? After all, we're not Catholics!"

Sister Maria did not avert her eyes, but met his eyes calmly. Then she said simply, "In my Father's house are many mansions." It was Father who briefly averted his eyes, and when he looked at her again, they were filled with tears.

Sister Maria put down her own cup and held one up to Mother's trembling lips. Out of politeness Mother took a few swallows, her teeth chattering against the porcelain edge. "Come, Mother, you must drink a little. Fransje would want you to!"

A little later the hospital director approached the group. He expressed his deepest regrets and said he shared their grief, and his words sounded genuine. But he was also businesslike. Would they like the hospital to provide a casket, or would they rather take care of it themselves? If the hospital provided the casket, it would all go on the same bill. Did they want the bill sent to the deacons of their church?

Father and Mother had been to the banks of the Jordan, the river of death, and at times had felt as if they were descending into it themselves. But life was calling them back. They had to go on, whether they wanted to or not. And they had to make decisions.

The last of the doctor's questions touched a nerve in Father. Perhaps it stirred his pride, because to accept help from the poor fund was only for those in dire need. Or perhaps it was parental love. Probably it was a mixture of both. In any case, he brusquely replied, "No! Send the bill to us. And, yes, make a casket for him here—a decent, solid casket. Not the cheapest kind."

He looked up at the clock on the high wall. Almost eight o'clock. And Maria and Eine were still here. They would have to cycle home all that way in the dark. He made his third decision: they would go back by train too. They could take their bikes onto the train with them. Even if it were Sunday twice over, there could be nothing wrong with that. A train was due at eight-thirty. They had to get moving. Fransje didn't need them anymore, but the children at home did. A look of determination altered his weary features. The director noticed it. They'll pull through all right, he told himself.

Sister Maria again took Mother by the hand. She led the foursome back to Fransje's room. Mother saw at a glance that the bed had been changed. Fransje's hands were folded on the sheet across his stomach, which was no longer swollen. His face had been washed and his hair combed. His skin glowed in the pale gaslight, not just because he had been washed, but also because his face wore an expression of deep peace and unmistakable joy.

One at a time they kissed Fransje's cold forehead, Mother first and last. Silent tears coursed steadily down their cheeks. Then with heavy steps and broken hearts they left the small room which had become for them a portal to death and for Fransje a portal to heaven.

At home all the children were still up. The homecoming touched off an anguished storm of tears that penetrated to Wullemiene's bedroom. The old woman rose, got dressed and came in without announcing herself. She wasn't crying, but her wrinkles seemed etched even deeper into her face than usual.

"Didn't you have a minister at your church today? Did you let him know? Maybe he'll do the funeral."

Life goes on. Father had to make more decisions. Bram had better bring back the bicycle Eine had used. Then he could stop at the house where the minister was staying to tell him the news. And ask him if he'll please do the funeral. When? Oh, yes. In three days. That's Wednesday. But then the family from outside the province won't have enough time to come. Well, make it Thursday then.

At nine o'clock Monday morning the minister was already at the house to see the family. Father hadn't gone to work. He and Mother were home alone, sitting in semi-darkness because the shutters were almost completely closed.

When the minister stepped into the room, Father greeted him with the words, "For the thing which I greatly feared is come upon me!" "Yes," said the minister, "those were Job's words. May you also be able to say with him: The Lord has given, the Lord has taken away; blessed be the name of the Lord! Then you won't ascribe anything to the Lord that is improper. Perhaps the Lord took your little boy to save him from the evil day, for these are fearful, godless times we live in. Yes, I'll be honored to officiate at the funeral. I'm on my way to the railroad station now because I have an important meeting to attend, but I hope to be back Thursday morning." Then he prayed with the grieving parents and said goodbye.

All morning neighbors and friends came by to express their condolences. Most said little, but simply wept. One of the first to come was Leentje de Visser. She sat down beside Mother, weeping softly, which was more comfort to Mother than the most eloquent words. Yet she wanted to say something—something she had great difficulty expressing because it dealt with spiritual matters, and that didn't come easy in their circles. At last she said awkwardly, "I think Fransje is happy now. The last time he was at our place—you remember: picking apples—he told me he'd like to sit on Jesus' lap. I think he has his wish now."

Stammering and sobbing she spoke her words. At last she said, "We loved Fransje very much and we'll miss him tremendously. May I please come to the funeral? Then I can help Maria serve."

Of course she was welcome. They would appreciate it.

Near noon Kee's husband Lukas arrived on his bike from Kapelle. He had come at Kee's request to see how Fransje was doing, but the closed shutters of the last two houses told him the sad news before he came in. Father invited him and Kee to the funeral.

At a few minutes to four, just before the children came home from school, a black hearse brought Fransje's body home from Bergendaal. Looking through the crack between the shutters, Mother was the first to see the wagon coming. She uttered a smothered cry. Aunt Ma, Mother's sister, who had been keeping her company all afternoon, grabbed her arm and held her tightly. Mother collapsed against her and for a few moments she lost her self-control. Father went to the back door. There was a shuffling of feet in the back entry, and two men carried a dark brown oak box into the house. Father told them to put it down in front of the cabinet. Wait a minute; first he'd get the bench from the back room; the casket could stand on that.

Mother was still sobbing soundlessly; only the occasional jerk of her shoulders gave her away. Nevertheless, she said, "Go on, Ma, pour the gentlemen a cup of coffee. She dug into her pocket under her apron and tried to give each of the men a silver guilder. But both adamantly refused it. They hurriedly drank their coffee and left.

In the lid of the casket was a small square window, directly over Fransje's head. With the shutters closed, however, they could hardly see his face. "The night light!" cried Mother. She must see that precious face! Father fetched it and lit it. Then they all bent over the small window under which Fransje lay waiting for the last day, his face still glowing with an almost unearthly radiancy.

Wantje was afraid to go near the casket. Weeping, she buried her face in Mother's apron. Arjaan and Kees stole out of the house.

That evening at supper everyone ate very little, and Father could not finish his prayer. After supper more people stopped in. God sent them to occupy the minds of the grieving parents and siblings and to keep them from collapsing under the burden of their sorrow.

Life goes on. They couldn't spend the whole evening talking about Fransje and his illness and the suddenness of it. The visitors asked about the potato crop, described their own, and discussed the latest news from town. At times the grieving family couldn't believe that Fransje was in the casket. No, he was sleeping upstairs in his little bed. They would wake up tomorrow morning to discover that this strange, sad evening had been nothing but a horrible dream.

Life goes on. Fransje would be buried Thursday. But first came Tuesday and Wednesday. Wednesday the potatoes were to be delivered to the house. Why postpone? Life goes on, and so does the work—for the living. Father assigned Bram and Eine the job of sacking the potatoes they had left on the field in two piles. The sacks were upstairs behind the trapdoor. Take lots of them; better too many than not enough. Reeds had to be cut to cover the pile after the potatoes had been brought home. Because they had been so busy the past few days, it had not yet been done. But Father would take care of that himself.

Why did Father want to go cut reeds along Hontenisse Pond all by himself? Because he wanted, no, *needed* to be alone. For the last few days a dreadful battle had been raging in his soul, one that he had to fight to the end, alone. It was a battle between life and death and only God could determine the outcome.

Father had become entangled in the snares of unbelief, but this wasn't how he himself saw it. He called it being in the dark because God was silent. But this didn't diminish his suffering. He couldn't talk it over with the others. They were having a difficult time of it as it was. Beside the agonizing grief over his boy who had so often played about his feet like a romping puppy (for didn't every place in and around the house, as well as here at the farm, conjure up his precious image?), what was plaguing Father? It was a gnawing uncertainty over his boy's eternal destination.

He could not and would not believe that Fransje was in the place of torment, but neither did he have the glad assurance that Fransje was in the realm of eternal blessedness, because God had not given him any assurance. Why did God keep Himself hidden?

Father knew that one of the confessions stated that godly parents ought not to doubt the salvation of a child who has died in infancy. But he, as it were, wanted to hear it from the mouth of God Himself. For wasn't it true that God had but to speak and it was done, to command and it stood fast? The Lord had spoken to him directly so often by imprinting a Bible or a Psalm verse into his soul.

Yes, that was what Father was waiting for, although it did not occur to his heart or head to demand a sign from God, for he knew that God is not obligated to His children. Father was able and willing to acknowledge God's justice, but without that direct word from above, he could not taste the joy of faith. He was so entangled in his own reasonings that he didn't realize that he was nevertheless thereby imposing demands upon God.

But solitude among the tall, rustling reeds in which he had cut a long narrow passage to the water's edge did not bring the hoped-for resolution. He was working so furiously that he was panting with exhaustion, and sweat poured down his body. But his toil, in which he was unconsciously trying to decide his inward battle, did not fell a single enemy. He seized another bundle of reeds in his large left hand, swinging his sickle into it with his right, but he had taken more than he could cut at once. Despite the power he put behind the razor-sharp sickle, it stuck in the reeds, knocking him off balance so that he fell to his knees.

He started to surge up angrily. But suddenly his muscles went limp; his hands slumped down to his thighs and his head sank forward on his chest. Covering his face with his hands, he pitched forward onto the damp ground in the middle of the tall reeds. A violent sob welled up inside him, and then another and another, until at last his whole body was quivering and trembling like that of a trapped animal. Threatened by a complete breakdown, he cried, "Oh God! Oh my Lord God!"

Yes, it was God who had felled him—not violently nor in anger, but through the quiet working of His Spirit who can melt even the most embittered and hardened heart like wax, and suddenly cause the eyes of the soul to see everything in a wholly different light. He did not speak any words of blame or censure, but took His child, who had become so entangled in the web of his own thoughts, and pressed him to His breast and kissed away all those confused notions.

This snapped the fetters binding his heart and broke open the sluice gates of his soul. He wept as he hadn't wept for years until his whole heart and all his grief—over his own spiritual wandering and over Fransje's death—lay spilled out before God. He grieved because he had relied more on his earlier conversion and his assurance of salvation in Christ than on the finished *work* of Christ and His daily intercession at the right hand of the Father as our High Priest. He debased himself in dust and ashes before the face of the Lord. Dimly he remembered that Kee had said something to that effect. Had she, as one practiced in godliness, seen where he was going wrong? Suddenly he saw that, despite all his pious, proper talk, he had put demands and conditions on God, and had tried to make God conform to him instead of following Him in faith and obedience. God did not accommodate Himself to man's will, but man had to learn to shape himself to God's will. No, he did not see Fransje's death as a sign of God's punishment, but he was deeply grieved that he hadn't been able to end it with God. He may not have ascribed anything wrongful to God, but that still wasn't the same as glorifying God in his road of suffering. He was deeply aware that God was not obligated to give him a special message about the eternal destiny of his son. Finally he bowed low before God's face confessing that, even if He had eternally rejected Fransje, this would still be righteous and holy and good. Looking at himself, he asked how God could pick a perfect fruit from such a rotten tree like himself.

He was sobbing so violently that the words he uttered stuck in his throat, emerging as garbled sounds that no one could have understood. However, they weren't directed to any human being, but to Him who looked into the heart and saw and understood its deepest impulses. And as he lay there melting with shame before the face of his God and Father, a quiet melody began to whisper through his soul. It was so soft that he was unaware of it at first. But when at last he heard it, his mind sought to fit words to the melody. Something about grass and flowers . . . . But he was mixing a couple of different versions, so the sentences wouldn't take shape and the words wouldn't fall into place. But he was certain that it applied to Fransje's premature death. Then suddenly the words arranged themselves into the familiar strophes and the inner voice sang clearly:

> Like as a father looketh with compassion
> Upon his children, lo, in such a fashion
> The Lord doth look on them that fear and trust.
> He knoweth that our frame is weak and humble;
> How void of strength, how prone we are to stumble!
> And He is mindful that we are but dust.

The words struck a new spring of tears, but they were tears of love and joy, because God was telling him that although he had, in a sense, kept God at a distance, God loved him no less, indeed, that God's love for him was much greater even than his own love for Fransje. And he humbled himself more abjectly before God's face; if he could have, he would have crawled beneath the damp soil.

But God had more to say to him, for the quiet, soft voice sang on; without hesitation his memory continued:

> Jehovah's mercy floweth, like a river,
> From everlasting, and abideth ever
> On those that love and worship Him with awe.
> His righteousness shall bless the habitations
> Of children's children through the generations
> That keep His covenant and obey His law.

Then he stopped, for suddenly heaven seemed to come down and surround him and the empty brokenness of his heart. Not for a second did he doubt that the words came from God, for first of all, he clearly recognized the emotion that always filled him when God spoke to him; what was more, he hadn't heard or sung the verses in years. He doubted whether he had ever known them by heart.

His righteousness shall bless the habitations of children's children . . . . Did these words mean that therefore his Fransje . . . ? Again with a flood of tears, in stammered words and broken sentences he poured out his heart to the Lord. "Oh God, if that is true, if You want me to believe that, then Fransje was, Fransje *is* a Royal child. And then will You?—no then You *will* give him a Royal burial, as You do for all Your people!"

A Royal burial? What did Father mean? Only that many people would come, uninvited, to show their concern, and that here and there God's people would come forward and tell him something that would clearly confirm what he had just experienced.

Then he was suddenly reminded of the other burden which had been weighing heavily on him the last few days. He emphatically did not want the church to pay for the hospital. Nor for the casket. He had already decided that he would sell the pig and also their extra potatoes. The money from this, along with his secret savings for the new pigpen, would go to the hospital. Even if he had to do extra work for months, even years, he would pay the difference; it would be his love offering for his lamb. But the funeral would cost money too, and a Royal funeral would cost a royal sum, which he didn't have. This thought, however, did not descend on him like another burden. On the contrary, his eye of faith still saw around him eternity's glow from heaven's open gates. He closed his wandering prayer with the simple words, "I know You will also take care of that, dear Lord."

It was time for him to go home. He would return to finish the work this afternoon. He put on his coat and crossed the pasture toward the lane that ran past the farm. A Royal funeral—that needed the ringing of the church bells. This afternoon he would send one of the children to the custodian of the big church.

The farmer's wife was waiting for him at the spot where she had waited with Fransje this summer. When he came closer, she beckoned to him. In her hand she had a bag of eggs that she wordlessly handed to him. As she quickly wiped a few tears from her eyes with one hand, she fumbled under her apron with the other. Still unable to speak, she stuffed a folded bill into his coat pocket. Then she turned and hurriedly shuffled to the back door.

Stunned, Father stood watching her go. Fortunately he had enough presence of mind to call a thank you after her.

Halfway down the lane, he fished the bill from his pocket and secretly peeked at it to see how much it was. His heart pounded in his throat when he saw that he held twenty-five guilders in his hand.

As he was passing the bakery, Van Houten came out carrying two loaves under his arm. When he saw Father, he called, "Hey there, Marien! Wait up!" Catching up to Father, he awkwardly stood groping for words of sympathy. But halfway through, he burst into tears. Weeping, he prattled on about swearing and a warning, but because the boys had anxiously kept the story from Father, he understood nothing of what the little man was stammering. At last Van Houten said, "Here, I must give you this," thrusting a bill into Father's hand. It was wrinkled and dirty, but

Father saw at a glance that it was ten guilders. He thanked the man and, deeply moved, continued on his way.

It was indeed a Royal funeral—and for a little boy! Not that it wasn't a sad, heart-rending occasion. But it was also glorious.

Never had so many people stopped at the house as on the day of the funeral. And the cemetery looked as if half the town had turned out to observe. Even the children from Arjaan's and Kees's and Wantje's classes came, supervised by their teachers. Besides Reverend Kok, who led the service, the ministers and some of the elders from the other two local Reformed denominations were also among the onlookers. Why had they come? Perhaps to see how a minister from a small sister denomination conducted a funeral service, that is, out of curiosity. Or perhaps because God had told them to come because one of His lambs was being buried.

In breathless silence the large crowd listened to Reverend Kok's short address based on II Samuel 12:22-23: "While the child was yet alive, I fasted and wept . . . . But now he is dead, wherefore should I fast? . . . I shall go to him, but he shall not return to me." In their denomination it was not customary to eulogize the dead, nor, as it were, "to talk them into heaven." Even Reverend Kok, who was much more evangelical than most of his colleagues, didn't come right out and say that Fransje was in heaven. Besides, that would have made a strange impression on most of those present who didn't belong to his church, for they regarded that a matter of course. But his explanation of the text's setting and of the faith of the man after God's heart couldn't have been clearer, and it made a deep impression on the crowd. Among the adults, few were able to master their emotions. So Father obtained a twofold blessing.

Nevertheless, when the coffin, looking small and insignificant in the full light of day, was lowered into the grave, momentarily all his strength drained from him. If his brother had not seized and supported him, he would certainly have collapsed. During the minister's prayer he had great difficulty concentrating, because somewhere in the hedge around the cemetery the loud, shrill cry of a thrush filled him with longing for the living Fransje.

According to local custom Mother and the women with her remained at home during the funeral. To them, too, the painful reality that Fransje was now gone permanently from their midst began to sink in. But now, too, God did not permit this realization to crush Mother, using the many visitors to prevent her from yielding to her intense grief. Aunt Ma sat on her left and Kee of Kapelle on her right. There were also many other family members, such as Mother's sister-in-law from another province and Aunt Jane, nieces and nephews, neighbors, friends and acquaintances. Leentje de Visser and her mother and sister were there as neighbors. Leentje helped Maria serve. The near family were all dressed in black, giving to the dark room an even more somber appearance.

When the men came home, the living room couldn't hold everyone, so a number of people had to be accommodated in the hall and in the back room on chairs voluntarily hauled in by the neighbors.

Reverend Kok had also come. His train was not due for at least an hour. When everyone had at last found a seat, some of them on the floor, for a moment an oppressive silence hung in the room. Here and there someone spoke in a whisper, but everyone was waiting for the minister to speak.

It was not, however, the voice of the minister, but the soft voice of Kee of Kapelle that broke the silence. She asked him if the Lord had given him the right words to speak at the graveside and what the text of his funeral sermon had been. When the minister replied affirmatively to the first question and repeated the words of his text in response to the second, she asked him if the words had been given him or whether he'd had to search for them himself. Cautiously the minister admitted that the words of the text had come to him Sunday night when Bram had brought him the sad news.

"So you're quite confident the child is saved?" she asked him directly.

"Yes," answered the minister. "Although it may be a hard blow to Fransje's parents and to his brothers and sisters, and although God's ways are unfathomable, I believe the Lord took him away to save him from the evil day. The Bible says that out of the mouths of babes and sucklings He has perfected praise. And among the hosts that no one can count are young as well as old."

Kee nodded slightly as she listened to the minister, which indicated not only that she agreed with him but also that she wished to add something herself. Her face began to glow as she related how she had been powerfully gripped by the words, "My soul desired the first ripe fruit." That had been when Fransje had unexpectedly dropped in on her. She had always had the feeling that this child was something special, and then the words of Psalm 105 had come to her with power:

Jehovah's truth will stand forever,
His covenant-bonds He will not sever;
The word of grace which He commands
To thousand generations stands;
The covenant made in days of old
With Abraham He doth uphold.

Already at that time she had been led to believe that the words related to Fransje, but at first she had thought that the Lord had some great task in mind for him. After all, He had called Samuel as a young boy too. But the Psalm had been followed by the words about ripe fruit, and she hadn't known how to interpret them. When she had been here last Sunday while Fransje's parents were at the hospital, she had mulled over the words all day. That evening on her long, lonesome walk home, the Lord had revealed to her that He was going to pluck that young fruit. And, dear people, she had seen him, as it were, going in through the gates of the heavenly city. She had been so filled with holy jealousy because this boy had been freed so early from this Mesech of sin and misery that she had cried aloud atop the dike, "Lord, when will You come to free me too, for I am tired of sin and of this world!"

"But we must serve out God's council. That which has been revealed is for us and our children, but the hidden things are for the Lord our God. Nevertheless, in His unfathomable goodness, it sometimes pleases our great King to give His poor, blind people a glimpse into His inner chambers, and then He says, Shall I hide from Abraham that thing which I do?

"Yes, dear people, God has allowed me to come here to testify boldly that Fransje has entered into eternal glory and is now thrice blessed forever!"

Although Kee spoke very softly, in the breathless silence her words carried all the way to the back room. The people in the living room sat staring at the pale blotch of her face as if in a trance, and even in the semi-darkness they saw that it was transfused by an almost heavenly glow. Tears rolled continuously down her thin cheeks, but she wasn't sobbing, and her hands lay folded in her lap. Her words expressed such joy that the last sentence sounded like a cry of jubilation.

Almost no one in the company was able to contain his emotions, and when Kee fell silent most of the women and some of the men needed their handkerchiefs. Only Father's brothers, who came from another province, sat staring at their hands, their faces pale.

Now Father told of his experience in the reeds. Although his voice trembled with emotion and affection, his words, too, were vibrant with joy, for he had been privileged to see his prayer that Fransje might have a Royal burial fulfilled so soon. He became so aroused that he suddenly began to recite a hymn:

> Speed along, then, years and ages,
> With your gladness and your pain;
> E'en when deepest sorrow rages,
> Faithful will our God remain;
> Though all earthly friends forsake us,
> Guided by His loving hand
> To His heart we'll aye betake us,
> Looking toward our fatherland.

Then it was Mother's turn to speak. With a boldness most unusual for her, she said, "Then what we read from Isaiah 40 last week was a promise to us: 'He shall feed his flock like a shepherd: he shall gather the lambs with his arm, and carry them in his bosom!' Fransje is home!" she cried in a high voice. But then she was overcome with joy and grief.

Life goes on.

The pig and half of the potatoes had been sold. This income with the contents of Father's carefully garnered savings was just enough to pay the hospital costs, except for the casket. Nevertheless, that too had been paid for, and that wasn't all—so had the funeral, the grave, the ringing of the church bell, and the many extra groceries they had bought at the store.

Yes, the money Father had received from the farmer's wife and from Van Houten wasn't the only money that had come pouring into the house. Father's brothers had also dug deep, and Kee had left twenty-five guilders under her plate. De Visser, who as a neighbor acted as one of the pallbearers, also left some money, as did Jan Blok's father, and many others. Even La Bruyere sent ten guilders. There were too many to name them all. Exactly one week after the funeral the last gift came in, and when Father added up all the money and subtracted the money he owed, there was enough left for Mother to buy mourning clothes for the children. But then the money was gone; it had been just enough. So Fransje was definitely a Royal child, and the King Himself had seen to it that His little prince received a Royal burial.

But there was more.

Although the ostentation of some gravesites was an abomination in the eyes of Fransje's parents, Fransje's grave would not become an unrecognizable, overgrown mound after a few years, with nothing but a weathered marker with a number on it to mark its location. Leentje de Visser had seen to that.

One Saturday afternoon she had come to Father and Mother on her bike and politely but very insistently had asked them if she could put a small headstone on his grave. At first Mother and Father looked somewhat askance at this, and for a moment Mother asked herself whether she could go along with this "Roman Catholic custom." But Leentje looked at them so pleadingly and her eyes and words testified to such an unfeigned love for their child that they didn't have the heart to refuse. So now a headstone topped Fransje's grave with the simple inscription:

FRANSJE WESTSTRATE

Then followed the dates of his birth and death and Isaiah 40:11. If Fransje himself could have seen the two branches that framed these words, he would have been thrilled.

At the foot end of the grave Kees de Visser, unasked, had planted a small but perfectly shaped fir tree. He had gone all the way to a tree nursery in Brabant for it.

Life goes on.

Slowly but surely the days added up to weeks, and just as slowly and surely the distance between them and Fransje became greater. It seemed they missed him more; that the longing for his beloved presence grew proportionately stronger and more unbearable. Time and time again the question died on their lips. "Where's Fransje?" In her innocence, Wantje once even spoke the question aloud.

Mother had burned the plumes; she could no longer stand the

sight of them because of the painful memories they inevitably evoked in her. The little mug from the flooded land stood on the top shelf in the pantry where no one could see it. And Fransje's little bed was pushed foot-end first as far under the slope of the roof as it would go. In addition, it was covered by a large cloth made from two colorful aprons which Mother no longer wore.

Yet, every day they ran into hundreds of little things of his, which in their muteness seemed to shout, "Where's Fransje?" And didn't every spot in and around the house continually remind them of him? There were days when, as she did her housework, Mother relived those horrible final days step by step. Sometimes she almost came to the point of taking God's hands, which had after all guided the doctor's hands, within her own to direct them to a different outcome. Nevertheless, the Lord gave her invisible support and strength, for life went on, and her family demanded her attention.

There came a time when they deliberately avoided mentioning his name to avoid the painful memories. There came days that their joy at the knowledge that he was in heaven seemed no match for their grief at his absence.

Maria no longer sang, and generally speaking she was much quieter than before. The youngest children played outside as much as they could out of a natural impulse to flee the somber atmosphere in the house. The older boys, too, usually went outdoors right after supper and did not return until it was time to go to bed.

Maria borrowed two or three books from the library every week. She read them while she did her knitting. But she never burst out laughing, no matter how funny they were.

Father spent a lot of time reading his books of sermons after he had peeled potatoes.

In her snow white cap and black *doek* and *beuk*, every evening Mother darned or knitted one pair of black stockings after another. But she never read while she knitted. She sat quietly hunched over her work while her thoughts inexorably and almost continuously kept circling around one child—her Fransje.

Maria lowered her knitting needles for a moment, her eyes fixed on the page before her. Then suddenly the knitting dropped in her lap and, throwing her head forward onto the table between her arms, she burst into uncontrollable sobs.

Father and Mother looked up in shock. "Child, what's wrong?" Mother cried anxiously. "What's the matter, girl?" Father asked in turn. But Maria could not answer. Her shoulders shook violently. Mother dashed to the back room for a glass of water and a cold washcloth. "Here, honey," she said gently. "Drink a little and let me wash your face and hands."

When Maria had calmed down a little, Father again asked her, "What's the matter, girl?" In answer Maria slid the book she had been reading toward him and pointed to the middle of the page with her finger. Father held his hand at the place she had pointed out, but first looked at the title page in the front. It was *Uncle Tom's Cabin*. Under his breath he read:

> Has there ever been a child like Eva? Yes, there have been; but their names are always on gravestones, and their sweet smiles, their heavenly eyes, their singular words and ways, are among the buried treasures of yearning hearts. In how many families do you hear the legend that all the goodness and graces of the living are nothing to the peculiar charms of one who *is not!* It is as if Heaven had an especial band of angels, whose office it was to sojourn for a season here, and endear to them the wayward human heart, that they might bear it upward with them in their homeward flight.
>
> When you see that deep, spiritual light in the eye, — when the little soul reveals itself in words sweeter and wiser than the ordinary words of children, — hope not to retain that child; for the seal of heaven is on it, and the light of immortality looks out from its eyes.

Since neither Mother nor Father had ever read the book, they didn't know the story nor the context of the passage. But that wasn't necessary. The few lines described Fransje better than anything they had ever thought or said about him.

Father put the book down, stood up, and quietly walked outside. Meanwhile Maria readied herself for bed. The cry seemed to have done her good, and now she was actually humming softly to herself.

When Father returned, he once more read the passage softly to himself. "That we never saw it in our boy!" he said with a note of self-reproach in his voice.

"That we never *wanted* to see it," Mother corrected him softly.

Father looked at her, a still wonder in his eyes. Then in an attempt to master his emotions and change the topic of conversation, he said, "I think we're in for some snow pretty soon."

"Safe in the arms of Jesus, safe on His gentle breast," Maria's heart sang as she stood in front of the mirror braiding her hair.